close to home

a darlington romance

rachel spangler

Bywater
BOOKS

Ann Arbor
2017

Bywater Books

Print ISBN: 978-1-61294-081-6

Bywater Books First Edition: January 2017

Printed in the United States of America on acid-free paper.

E-Book ISBN: 978-1-61294-082-3

Cover designer: Ann McMan, TreeHouse Studio

Back cover photo credit: Will Banks

Bywater Books
PO Box 3671
Ann Arbor MI 48106-3671
www.bywaterbooks.com

This novel is a work of fiction. All characters and events
described by the author are fictitious. No resemblance
to real persons, dead or alive, is intended.

For Susie, because number ten is all your fault.

Chapter One

"Dad?" she asked, concern filling her voice.

He held a forkful of mashed potatoes as if frozen just inches from his open mouth.

"What's wrong?"

He lifted his eyes, so dark, so big. She'd both inherited and studied those eyes over the course of a lifetime with him. They could speak volumes, or withhold them. She searched for them in times of both joy and turmoil. She'd seen them glisten and glow, burn and freeze, shine and increasingly grow dim, but she'd never seen them so unfocused.

"Don't you like the roast beef?" she prodded, glancing down to her own plate to settle the discomfort she felt at the blankness of his stare. He wasn't an old man by most standards, but he'd aged more acutely lately, and not just in the gray around his temples or the added thickness of the lenses in his glasses, but also in a weakening of both his muscles and his memory. The once comfortable silences between them stretched longer and held less purpose, born more out of necessity than contentedness. She suspected that fact embarrassed them both equally, so she gave him as much time and space as she could, first at the office and now, apparently, at the dinner table as well.

She pushed a green bean around for a second or two before lifting it to her mouth. He hadn't answered her question. She glanced over at him again to see he still hadn't taken a bite. Never had been much of a talker, but he always ate. Sick, tired, saddened, overworked, he always made time for the simple pleasure of a well-cooked meal, and the one she'd prepared tonight usually qualified as a favorite.

"Dad?" she asked again softly, but stared back at her food searching for an answer there rather than in those cloudy eyes she barely recognized. It had to be the dinner. Something she'd forgotten, something she'd done wrong. Meat, potatoes, a green, the quintessential Midwestern meal trio. She had pie for dessert. Maybe she should tell him so.

"I had some peaches canned from the summer so I thought I would—" Her voice faltered at the clatter of metal against porcelain as his fork dropped.

He lifted his left hand to his forehead, but the right one hovered merely an inch or two off the table. She watched his trembling fingers as seconds ticked by. She willed him to move. Silently begged him to find the strength and prayed fervently for the smile she so rarely saw.

His left hand dropped, the gold wedding band he'd never removed hitting the edge of the table with a plink.

"Dad?" Her voice sounded so much calmer than she felt. "Should I call a doctor?"

He shook his head slowly, but when he opened his mouth nothing came out. Time ticked away in precious seconds. Fear clutched her chest, then squeezed like a vice. She swallowed the bile rising in her throat.

"I think I better call someone."

He shook his head a little more forcefully and scooted back from the table. Using his right hand on the seat of his chair, he pushed himself to standing, and her hope rose with him. He would be okay. He had to be. He was solid as an oak, with roots running every bit as deep. He would smile at her now. Maybe gently chastise her for being overly dramatic. He didn't need help. Neither did she. They were both fine. Everything was fine. He would say so now.

He turned, slowly, so slowly she held her breath. It caught, painful and sharp as she waited. Her head spun, her vision blurred, the earth rattled under her feet, but it was he who fell. The great oak toppled to the ground before her. The whole world shook, then went dark.

ॐ ॐ ॐ

2

The automatic door whooshed open behind Kelly Rolen. Seconds later, the accompanying rush of January air raced along the tile floor, the sharp smell of frost cutting through the sterile scent of antiseptic that had permeated her senses for hours. She didn't look up. She didn't have the energy to do anything other than stare at a square of baby blue linoleum flecked with indistinguishable specks of gray and brown. Her long, dark hair hung limply in the periphery of her vision, like curtains shielding her from the gaze of anyone else in the room. Not that there was anyone else there at this time of night—or morning, rather. Aside from the occasional nurse bustling through, she'd had the place to herself for hours. The doctors encouraged her to go home after midnight, saying she couldn't do any more from here, but she couldn't do anything from home, either. At least if she stayed here, she'd be quickly alerted to any changes.

Besides, hospitals made her feel safe. She'd never understood people who hated hospitals. She disdained their faulty reasoning about people dying in hospitals. People died outside of hospitals, too, and in much greater numbers. At least here there were strong, competent people who had training and procedures and answers. Maybe not all the answers, but more than any riffraff on the street could offer. She liked people who knew what they were doing. Order appealed to her, and she found confidence a comfort.

"Kel?" The intimacy in the voice made her wince.

She slowly looked up, blinking the haze from her eyes, before turning toward Beth Deveroux. "What are you doing here?" Her voice sounded harsh and full of gravel, but Beth only smiled the sweet, sympathetic smile that melted hearts all over town.

"I heard about your dad."

Kelly glanced at the clock, but didn't go any farther down the path of wondering who would've called Beth before six o'clock on a Monday morning. She knew better than anyone the rumor mill in Darlington ran twenty-four hours a day. Local farmers would've been down at the corner bakery for an hour now. She did wonder which parts of the story they had right and which parts had been embellished overnight.

"A stroke," she said flatly. "Left side of the brain. He's stable now. It's too early to tell what long-term damage to expect."

3

Beth eased into the chair beside her, the scent of her carrying a dizzying wash of memories. "When did it happen?"

"Just after dinner." She sent up another silent prayer of thanks that it had been a Sunday, that she'd been there, that there'd been time, enough time to at least buy them more.

"When was the last time you heard from the doctors?"

"About an hour ago."

"Do they check in often?"

"They did at first. CT scans, medicines, stabilizing, paperwork." She spoke in clipped phrases partially out of exhaustion and partially to control her fear. If she stuck to reciting facts, it was harder for the emotions to sneak up on her.

Beth nodded. "And now?"

"Less so. There's not as much to report."

"Do they have your cell phone number?"

"Beth, don't handle me." She'd hoped to sound firm, but only managed tired.

"I'm not handling you. Lord knows we both understand how futile that is." She sounded exasperated already, but not cold or judgmental. "You're one of the most stubbornly self-sufficient women I've ever met."

One of—not *the* most. The phrase didn't go unnoticed, even if the other name went unspoken.

"But if you're going to continue this vigil, you need to do it right. Wrecking yourself won't help your dad improve. This will be a long process."

"Do you think I don't know that?" she snapped, but even her anger sounded dull.

"You need sleep."

"I won't be able to sleep."

"Then you have to eat, because you've got to rejuvenate somehow."

"I'll get something from the cafeteria." She brushed the concerns away, again.

"What about a shower?"

"They have locker rooms here."

"Kel . . ." No one else had ever said her name quite like Beth, so gently, so lovingly frustrated. She had to set her jaw against the pressure building in her chest.

"I could make you some eggs, over easy, in bacon grease."

A smile threatened to push through her exhaustion.

"Think about it, a hot shower, comfortable clothes, hot food."

And you, she thought. Beth again—in her life, in her home, in her arms, even if just for a moment. Just a hug and nothing more. She wanted to lean into that vision, to let herself be soothed, cared for by someone who really did care.

Beth laid a hand softly on her leg. "It's time to go home."

Home.

She stared at Beth's elegant fingers against the gray of her dress slacks. So familiar, and yet glaringly different. A gold band accented with a single diamond. Any desire she'd had to crumble or crash into this woman, their past, or the comfort she may have offered evaporated at the sight of another woman's ring on the hand she ached to hold.

"Where's Rory?" The name sounded clipped, and she hated how much it still irked her to ask.

"She's at home."

Home.

Not her own. The home that offered Beth everything Kelly couldn't.

She wasn't tired anymore; her limbs clenched and twitched with restlessness. Straightening her shoulders, she shook the hair from her eyes and cleared her throat. "Actually, it's time for me to get ready for work."

"Work? You can't be serious."

She planted one hand firmly on each armrest and pushed herself to a standing position as she tried to stretch the tension out of her neck and shoulders. "It's almost tax season. Someone has to open the office."

"I wish you wouldn't."

"It's just me now." She forced the words past the knot of emotion. "I'm the only one left."

"You don't have to be. You can take in some help."

"Thank you for checking on me. I appreciate it, and I know Dad will, too. But I want to talk with the nurses one more time before I head out."

Beth stared up at her, pleading evident in her blue eyes, but her mouth remained in a grim line. Kelly waited for the argument, the press of an emotional appeal, or perhaps another attempt at reason, but none came. "Okay. You have to do this your way."

"Thank you for understanding."

"Knowing something and understanding it are two very different things." Beth stood, then kissed her on the cheek. "Please take care of yourself."

Kelly stood completely still as she walked away. It was a view she'd grown all too used to, but it never got easier to accept. Once the doors closed behind Beth, she sank back into the same chair she'd occupied for hours and stared out the large picture windows across the hall.

Early hints of orange light crept across the horizon, casting frozen fields in a warm glow, but it was a false heat. The ground lay icy, dead, unmoving. Changing the light didn't change its essence any more than sitting in the waiting room all night had changed her father's condition. And Beth's presence for a few moments hadn't changed anything about their relationship any more than their three years apart had changed the parts of Kelly that had allowed Beth to walk out the door the first time.

Chapter Two

Elliot Garza twisted to her left, then spun to the right, her neon pink tennis shoes squeaking against the shellacked wood of the gym floor as she pivoted, then pushed off. Free and on the breakaway, she timed the ball to the beat of her feet and sprinted toward the basket. One dribble, two, three, then up in one fluid motion, her hand lifted the ball easily toward the net. But just as it rolled effortlessly from the tips of her fingers, a glancing shoulder blow caught her elbow and knocked her off line. The hit wasn't hard, but it was enough. The ball clipped the corner of the backboard before veering out of bounds as she landed firmly on her feet.

"Hey, you can't foul me," she said, whirling to face her opponent. "You're a professor."

"Sure I can. You're my teaching assistant. I think it's somewhere in the contract that I get to abuse you," Rory St. James replied.

"I'm not your TA anymore."

"Right, and I'm not *your* professor anymore either, so we're even."

"Aw, is that what this is about?" She used the back of her arm to wipe the beads of sweat from her forehead. "You're going to miss me, so you hit me? I thought you'd worked through all your abandonment issues."

Rory rolled her eyes but smiled. "Well played. Take your shot."

Elliot retrieved the ball and bounced it a few times on her way to the foul line. She wanted to savor this moment. She didn't often get points for a zing when sparring with Rory St. James. Few people did. Now if she could just sink this shot, she'd also be up points-wise, another rare occurrence. Even though she had Rory matched in height and overall athleticism, she'd never been as quick on her feet, or maybe

7

she didn't quite match Rory's competitive spirit. Maybe that's why she'd been drawn to Rory from her first day at Bramble College. She liked to think Rory had seen a reflection of herself in her as well, and that's why she'd been so open and friendly. But Rory was those things and more to a lot of people.

She bounced the ball again, then shot, not even stopping to watch its arc through the net before jogging away. She knew she'd hit her mark.

"Eighteen to twenty," Rory called as she jogged the ball out past half court. "How about, if I come back and win this, you teach with me one more semester?"

Elliot considered the bet. "What do I get if I win?"

"The satisfaction of beating a queer icon."

"I love how humble you are."

"Humility is a tool of the patriarch," Rory said. "Take the bet?"

Elliot thought about it. She did like to win, and adding to the stakes only added to the enjoyment, but she didn't dare bet against Rory. She had an advanced understanding of odds and risk assessment, but Elliot also knew the spark in those famous emerald eyes always burned a little brighter when challenged. She liked to think the same would hold true for her, but she wouldn't bet on it. Maybe that was the biggest strike against her.

"No deal," she said emphatically. "I've been in school too long."

"There's no such thing as staying in school for too long," Rory argued, but she started her deliberate march toward the net. She had no trouble dribbling and talking at the same time. "I've seen plenty of the real word. I plan to stay in college for the rest of my life."

"That's why I have to go," Elliot said, watching her slow, easy dribble, timing her rhythm, waiting for her to make her break or offer any opening. "You have this place all locked up. Academia is full of amazing, engaged women. There's no shortage of radical lesbians with women's studies degrees."

Rory's eyes flicked toward the net, measuring her shot, calculating the risks and reward. "There's no such thing as too many smart women."

"Of course not, but there's no need for academia to Bogart them all when finance is still an old boys' club." She took steady, even breaths despite her rapid heartbeat. They were fully in the paint now. One bounce, two bounces, three bounces, steal.

She swatted the ball before it ever returned to Rory's hand, then took two quick steps to catch up, trapped it between both hands, turned, and in one fluid moment, took her shot. It hit squarely in the center of the backboard before clattering off both sides of the metal rim and dropping through the net.

"I'd love to stay," she said, turning to face Rory, "but I've got glass ceilings to shatter."

Rory beamed proudly at her, and no matter how many times she'd seen that smile, she'd never grown immune to its power. She walked a little taller, shoulders a little straighter, back to the bleachers, trying not to gloat or grin like an idiot as she took a swig of water from her stainless steel bottle.

Grabbing a towel, Rory mopped the sweat off her neck before shaking out her chestnut hair. She could pull off that rakish, mussed-up look. Elliott felt another stab of admiration. Her own amber locks hung nearly to her shoulders when wet, and if she tried to shake them, she'd only end up with weird wing-dings and cowlicks. "So if you really must leave the great ivory tower of academia, why not take an internship with a local CPA?"

"I couldn't get one," she admitted, hoping her annoyance wasn't too obvious. "You know what these little farm towns around here are like. They're beyond insular. Everyone's suspicious of outsiders."

"I thought you wanted to shatter ceilings. Doing audits for the college travel department is hardly a breakout."

"I agree." She blew out a frustrated breath. "But I need an internship in a related field, and that's all I could get around here. No one in Darlington even wants an intern, especially a queer one."

Rory snorted. "Being wanted and being needed are very different things. What if Beth could get you a shot with a CPA doing real taxes? You think you could handle a less-than-gregarious welcome?"

Elliot hoped her smile showed all the defiance she wanted to feel. "You can't change the world without a little pushback. I'll be sure to wear my big-girl boxers to work."

꧁ ꧁ ꧁

The sun had already set when she returned to the office, so she had no real sense of how long she'd been working. Darkness was the norm this time of year. She went to work before dawn, sat in a windowless hospital room for hours on end, and returned to work again after dusk. Even when she managed to get outside during daylight hours, a bitter gray film covered the sky and everything below. Stock photos of January in central Illinois didn't appear on postcards or travel guides. Instead, they filled depression pamphlets or news stories on Seasonal Affective Disorder.

She stared at the paperwork in front of her. The payroll reports for several local businesses provided her the only respite from the gray of her world. Numbers were black and white, literally and figuratively. They never blurred together for her. Focus was easy to come by within the even rows and clearly delineated columns. She liked the challenge, the puzzle, making order out of chaos. She liked the control. Maybe these days she even clung to it. But there were worse addictions to feed.

The back door creaked slowly open, and her shoulders slumped. The only person who used that entrance this time of night wouldn't bring order or a sense of control. She took a deep breath and removed her dark-rimmed glasses, folding them neatly before laying them on the precisely stacked pages before her. "Good evening, Beth."

"Hi, Kel." Beth stepped into the circle of light from the single overhead lamp. Her cheeks were pink from the cold, her dark curls windblown. "I brought you some pork chops for dinner."

"You didn't have to do that."

"I know." Her smile was so sweet Kelly had to set her jaw against the push of emotions.

"I'm not really hungry."

"Are you sure?" Beth set a stack of Tupperware containers on the corner of her desk, and the smell of home-cooked food filled the space between them.

The air grew thick with scents that carried memories. Her stomach growled loudly. As if the events of last weekend hadn't been hard enough, now even her own body betrayed her. "Maybe I could eat."

Beth wordlessly unpacked the food. Pork chops, scalloped potatoes, green beans. She laid out a fork and a knife, then unscrewed the cup top on a metal thermos. Each piece neater and tidier than the one before, Beth had thought of everything. She always did.

Kelly bit her lip to keep from saying something caustic. Anger was a natural defense, but she couldn't direct it at Beth. She'd already done enough of that for one lifetime.

"The tea is decaffeinated so it won't keep you up." Beth claimed the seat across the desk, bright blue eyes expectantly searching her face.

The tea was the last thing Kelly worried about keeping her awake tonight. She bowed her head to pray, both out of habit and as stalling tactic, but instead of reciting an internal Our Father or Hail Mary, her mind remained focused on Beth's presence. The smell of her shampoo mingled with the aroma of her cooking. *Please, God, give me strength.*

She lifted her head and opened her eyes to see Beth still there. For some reason it surprised her, as if the simple prayer may have caused the temptation to simply disappear. The absurdity of the thought annoyed her. "Are you going to sit there and watch me eat?"

"Actually I wanted to talk to you while you ate."

Suspicion mingled with curiosity. Beth had worked hard to remain friendly over the past two and a half years. She never forgot a birthday or let Christmas pass without a little gift. When they ran into each other in social settings, she always asked about Kelly's father, work, church. Even when Kelly tried to avoid her—or worse, push her away, which had been often in the early days—Beth refused to let her sulk or hide. Still, a prolonged conversation over dinner was more contact than they'd had since the night Beth had walked out.

"Don't wait on account of me." Beth motioned for her to eat, and the light caught the diamond on her left ring finger.

Kelly looked away and slowly cut a piece of the pork chop. "I'm not very good company."

"It's okay, I came prepared to do most of the talking."

Resigned, Kelly stabbed at the meat with her fork, then added a few green beans, hoping to swallow some of her unreasonable anger

11

with the food, but as soon as she took a bite, all the lingering resentment melted along with her resolve to stay stoic.

Holy Mother. In the long lonely nights, she'd convinced herself she'd exaggerated Beth's abilities in the kitchen—among other places—but now she realized she'd accepted false comfort. At least on this count. She tried not to go any further with that thought process and instead focused on shoveling another bite into her mouth.

"I visited your dad Sunday evening," Beth said softly.

The comment pulled her from the food stupor, but she said nothing.

"The nurse said I'd just missed you. She also said you were there for four or five hours every day."

"So much for privacy regulations."

"She didn't release any of his medical records," she said soothingly. "In fact he was sleeping, and I didn't want to wake him, so all I know about his condition is what I've heard around town."

Kelly snorted, "I can only imagine."

"He's well liked, Kelly. He's on the prayer list of every church in Darlington. People are concerned."

"People like to gossip. The story gets bigger every time it goes around."

Beth knew better than to argue that point with her. "Then why don't you tell me the truth?"

"He had a stroke," she snapped, but Beth didn't flinch. She didn't even frown.

"And?"

"And he's stable now, but he sleeps a lot." She shook her head. "Too much. He wakes up and he doesn't remember where he is right away. It's like he's all there, but not immediately. He processes everything slowly. You can see it in his eyes, but he can't . . . he doesn't, um . . . he can't really talk anymore."

Beth's smile fell into a grim white line. "At all?"

"He tries," she said, taking another bite to buy her time, but the taste had grown flat and bland now. "He slurs his words, but it's more than that. It's like he doesn't really remember them. Like he can look at a pencil, and see it, and know what it is, but when he opens his mouth he says 'cat'."

Beth reached out, sliding her hand across the desk, but Kelly pushed her chair back.

"It's just going to take time. He'll be okay."

"Of course he will, but it must be so scary and frustrating."

"Yeah." Frustrating, upsetting, infuriating—for him and for her.

"But it's too soon to know what's permanent and what's an aftereffect, or a side effect. We might not know for a year."

"A year," Beth whispered, and Kelly once again felt the weight of the timeline.

A year of worrying, of second-guessing, or imagining the worst. A year of uncertainty. Her stomach clenched, and she pushed the food away. "I really should get back to work."

"Kelly . . ."

She held up her hand. She didn't want to hear it. She didn't need Beth to tell her she couldn't keep up this pace. She didn't need someone else to reaffirm her fears or fuel the fire of her already blazing self-doubt. "I have to finish these audits before tax season starts next week."

"I arranged for you to have an intern," Beth said evenly. "She can start as early as Monday."

Kelly blinked at her a few times as the words sank in. They weren't what she'd expected, not the argument she'd prepared herself for. Beth was supposed to say, "You can't work so hard. Go easy on yourself. Give yourself time."

"It's up to you of course, but Elliot is a hard worker and smart. She's older too, more experienced, more mature. Not your average college kid."

"What?" Maybe her father wasn't the only one with delayed processing skills.

"She's in her last semester of the five-year Bachelor's/Master's accounting program at Bramble. The only thing between her and the CPA exam is an internship."

Kelly knew the program. She'd read about it in the paper. She and other local CPAs had even met with the dean to advise on the

13

practical content. The students would be better prepared to do taxes than some of the people working full time in other offices around town. Hell, she'd probably have more knowledge in some areas than Kelly had for her first few tax seasons. Why was she considering qualifications of an intern she neither asked for nor approved?

"I know, I know." Beth cut off her interruption before she had a chance to make it. "You don't need the help."

"Damn right I don't." She stood abruptly. "And what gives you the right to arrange for someone to work in my father's business?"

"Nothing's formal. It's just an idea. But it's a good one. Elliot is special. I care about her, and I care about you. You two could be a good fit for each other right now."

"I'm not a fit for anyone right now." She paced the small office space, fists clenched so tightly her fingernails cut sharply into her palms. "I can't."

"You don't have to be anything you're not. You're in control. It's your choice." Beth remained calmly seated. "Whatever you want is fine. This is about you. No, maybe not completely about you. I guess I'm doing this for me, too."

"You?"

"Yes, me. Well, us, I guess."

Her chest tightened.

"We go back a long way, Kel. I know you don't like to remember, but—"

"Beth . . ."

"We're more than how we ended." She pressed on quickly. "You were there for me when my parents died. You and your dad both. You were my best friend when I needed one."

Were. Past tense.

They'd been so young, little more than children, though it hadn't seemed that way at the time. Beth had been so fragile. Kelly had felt strong and steady by comparison. She didn't like their dynamic nearly as much with the roles reversed, but the connection was still strong enough to zap the anger clean out of her.

"You were there for me, every morning, every night. You made sure I ate and that I got the financial help I needed. You got me through work and pain and everything in between," Beth continued softly. "I know I can't do all that for you. I know you won't let me."

You could if not for the ring on your finger. "We're not nineteen anymore."

"No." Beth shook her head with a smile. "You look exhausted, and I'm going gray. We can't stay up all night anymore, and I don't know about you, but I can't eat cherry pie three meals a day, either."

She finally smiled at the memory of all the sympathy food they'd consumed sitting barefoot on Beth's front porch. They'd watched so many sunrises just to assure her she'd made it through another dark night. Even after weeks of those sugar-laced vigils, she'd never felt as tired as she did right now. How much longer could she really go on like this? And tax season hadn't even started yet.

"I know you don't want me here every night," Beth said, and Kelly crushed the desire to correct her, "but I won't leave you to face this alone. So you have two choices: Either you put up with me underfoot every minute messing up your filing system and asking too many questions about taxes and how you're feeling, or you give Elliot a shot at getting the job done right."

The choice was not as easy as Beth probably intended, not as clear as it should've been. The thought of working with her closely, regularly, held more appeal than it should, and that's ultimately why it couldn't happen. Beth had made her choice. They both had. Trying to pretend there could be anything else between them would only offer false comfort, and while right now any comfort seemed welcome, this was only a moment of weakness. She didn't need comfort. She needed logic, answers, progress.

And yes, maybe even an intern.

"Okay."

"Okay?"

"This intern, she would work for me? She'd be an employee?"

"Not exactly. She's a student. She'd have a teacher who would supervise her and give her a grade."

"But I'd pay her?"

"Yes, but minimum wage would be enough. She's mostly here for course credit. You'd report on job performance to her supervising professor by filling out a progress report mid-semester and then at the end of the internship, and show him samples of the work Elliot did. Technically, you'd be more like a guest instructor. You teach her things and give her assignments, but in the end you don't have any responsibility to grade her."

She bristled at the arrangement. "That seems unfair. The college just hires them out for low wages? Sounds like indentured servitude."

"I wouldn't go that far. She gets college credit, meets her internship requirement for licensure, and gets some hands-on experience to help her pass the CPA exam and get a paying job."

"Can I fire her?"

Beth laughed. "You haven't even met her, and already you want to fire her? Don't you think that's a little harsh?"

She smiled in spite of the gentle rebuke. Beth had a way of putting her concerns into perspective. She used to find the trait maddening, but now she added the quality to the long list of things she should've appreciated more. "I don't want to get locked into something I can't control down the road."

Beth's smile faltered for the first time all night. "I know this about you."

Her jaw twitched. She'd walked right into that, but there wasn't any use denying the truth neither of them could overcome. She wouldn't apologize for who she was. Maybe she should have three years ago, but time had passed, and if she couldn't change for Beth, she sure as hell wasn't going to do so for some intern.

"Why don't you send the intern by later this week?"

"Tomorrow?"

"No," she said reflexively. "I've got a lot of work to catch up on, so actually I hate to be bad company, but would you mind letting me get back to it?"

Beth rose gracefully. "Of course. I'll see myself out."

Kelly nodded and pretended to sort some papers. She should've thanked her for the dinner, for thinking of the intern, for caring. Instead she listened for the sound of the door latching behind her before dropping her head to the desk with a dull thud.

Chapter Three

Weather was one of the few areas where Darlington could compare to Chicago. The cold wind sweeping across the vast Midwestern plains felt bitter and biting, and probably a lot of other not-nice b-words. Bitching? No, that's what she was doing. Never much of a morning person, Elliot scowled at the elements and flipped up the collar of her chocolate-colored wool coat. If she had to trek across a frozen tundra at ass o'clock in the morning, she at least wanted to look good doing it. She loved the deep, rich color of the coat as much as she enjoyed the way it hung thickly down to her knees, a veritable comfort blanket with style. She imagined she cut a pretty imposing figure among the freshmen and farmers who were up this early, but she liked to think she'd stand out just about anywhere. Clothes helped project confidence both inwardly and outwardly so she dressed for the life she wanted, not the one she had. She pictured herself strolling down Wall Street or the National Mall in Washington, DC. Money equaled power, and the power to regulate money was supreme power.

That little pep talk gave her the fortitude necessary to cover the few blocks to Darlington's closest and only coffee shop. As soon as she opened the door, the warmth of steam mixed with the comforting aroma of freshly brewed java caused her to whimper.

"Easy there, Rockefeller," Rory said, taking her by the elbow. "Beth already ordered you a cappuccino with a double shot of espresso."

"Marry her now, or I swear by everything holy, I will." Elliot sank into a chair at the table closest to the door

Rory's laugh was rich and deep as she sat down next to her. "I'm working on it."

"Here." Beth set a steaming mug in front of her. "Nurse it. Don't chug."

Elliot mumbled some incoherent words of thanks and sipped deep enough to break the thin layer of foam.

"Better?"

"It's not what anyone would call a good cappuccino, but it's infinitely better than the alternative of doing without in these pre-dawn hours."

"You do know the sun actually rose over an hour ago, right?" Rory asked.

"Sunrise may have technically been an hour ago, but dawn is whenever I deem it appropriate to fully open my eyes, and this is definitely earlier than that."

"How do you plan to change the world from your bed?" Beth asked.

Rory and Elliot both snickered.

"Never mind. I walked right into that one. Sometimes I think you two really are the same person."

"But I'm much younger," Elliot said.

"And I'm better looking," Rory quipped.

Beth sighed. "Kelly's going to kill me."

"No." Elliot looked up at her quickly with what she hoped came across as sincerity. "I promise you I can do this. I won't let you down."

Beth's smile turned downright motherly. "I know. I wouldn't have put you in the line of fire unless I felt certain you could handle the challenge."

"But . . ." Rory drew out the word.

Elliot watched them share a wordless exchange.

"But nothing," Beth said breezily. "Both Kelly and Elliot are professionals with drive and high standards. They're going to be perfect for each other."

Rory raised her eyebrows, pursed her lips, then shrugged.

Whatever she'd planned to say clearly wasn't worth contradicting her fiancée, and since Rory wasn't generally one to hold her tongue, Elliot figured it must not have been too important.

"You ready to walk over?" Beth asked Elliot.

"Sure," she said, fast enough to hide the flutter of nervousness the question prompted. She didn't get first-day jitters, at least not as far as anyone else knew.

"All right." Rory clapped a hand on her shoulders, automatically causing her to straighten them. "Good luck, champ."

She could've sworn there was an unspoken, "You're going to need it," in her eyes, but she replied with an easy, "You don't need luck when you've got skills."

"In that case, enjoy your first step toward world domination."

"My first step ever was toward world domination."

Rory laughed outright, and Beth smiled despite her eye-roll.

"All right, all right." She took another healthy swig of her cappuccino, grimacing at the taste, or lack of taste, before swinging the door open wide. "Let's do this."

A blast of frigid air hit her square in the face as soon as the words left her mouth, but she gritted her teeth against the cold. Some people found that sort of thing invigorating, she told herself as she choked back a string of profanity.

Beth didn't seem to feel the icicles stabbing her eyes as she walked through the door Elliot held open. Her smile never faltered. Nothing about Beth ever faltered. She was every bit as impressive as Rory, but without the need to make sure anyone else noticed. Honestly, between the two of them, Elliot could never really tell which one was stronger, or maybe they magnified each other's strength. She supposed stranger things had happened. People were funny and emotions weird. She'd stopped trying to figure out how other people worked long ago. She could admire what Beth and Rory had, the same way she could admire a fine sports car without wanting to be a mechanic. They worked, and she had no desire to look under the hood to try to figure out why.

"Kelly's office is just in the opposite corner of the square." Beth pointed one glove-covered hand directly across the unofficial center of Darlington.

The town square looked like something off the front of a postcard or the opening of an old sepia-toned film. Neat sidewalks fronted tidy, brick and stucco two-story buildings. Faded awnings and empty flower boxes ringed the outer edge of the spot where two county roads converged and spun in a tight little circle of commerce, rather than the more common four-way stop. A circle inside the square, so geometric, so purposefully planned so long ago. This section of road was red brick, or at least it was red underneath the thin layer of dried salt left over from an early winter snowstorm. The middle of the circle, filled with dead grass and sparse, short trees, offered a meeting space for town cookouts and barbershop quartets during better, warmer, older days. But even now in the dead of winter, a small white gazebo stood, squat and a little too sharp-edged to be beautiful, but quaint enough to fit the center of the circle inside the square. To complete the picture of classic Midwestern Americana, a tattered, all-weather version of Old Glory snapped, high atop a tall metal flagpole.

Elliot was never sure what the image of small-town American life was supposed to inspire in a radical urban queer. Should it tap into some deep longing, or stir a desire for a quieter American dream? Or was the order and solemn dignity, holding onto its heritage amid a world gone mad, meant to remind her she didn't fit in here and might as well move along? Both possibilities seemed equally true at times, and yet on other days, both seemed laughable. She didn't yet know what kind of day this would turn into, but somewhere in this visual display of domesticity was a tax firm where she did belong, at least for the next few months. She didn't see any reason to waste time contemplating power, the past, or progress in the subzero wind chills when she could, quite literally, cut some corners in her path to get there.

"Easy enough." Elliot stepped off the sidewalk and into the old-fashioned brick street, holding up a hand as she went. A rusted old Chevy slowed to a stop, causing everyone behind it to hit their brakes.

"Elliot!" Beth scolded. "What are you doing?"

"Going to work," she said matter-of-factly as she strode confidently across the street.

"You're holding up traffic."

"No, I'm walking. You're holding up traffic." Elliot glanced down at her feet as she stepped onto the crisp frozen grass of the town green space, then pointedly back at Beth, who tiptoed apologetically across the brick road.

"Okay, okay, I see what you did there," Beth admitted as she caught up. "But you can't just step into oncoming traffic. This isn't Chicago."

"Right, this isn't Chicago, which is exactly why I *can* step into oncoming traffic, not that a few old men in pickups constitute 'traffic,' but they always stop."

"What if they don't?"

"Then I'll deal with that when I have to. Right now, I have to get to work." She bounded up the stairs across the picturesque white gazebo. "And this is the most direct route."

෴ ෴ ෴

The little bell above the door at Rolen and Rolen rang as someone entered. "I'll be right with you," Kelly called as she pushed the copy button on her Xerox machine and took a hasty swig of tepid coffee.

"It's just me," Beth said, poking her head around the wall dividing the public space of the office from the business side.

Kelly smiled in spite of her exhaustion. Sometimes an unexpected visit from Beth tapped into a reserve of something she did a better job of guarding when adequately prepared for her presence.

"Well, me and Elliot," Beth added.

Her frown was every bit as automatic and unguarded as the expression that had preceded it. "Right. The intern. That's happening today." The fact had escaped her mind, which was uncharacteristic, or rather more characteristic these days than ever before. She'd begun to forget appointments or lose track of time, which of course was why she needed an intern in the first place. No, not needed. She didn't *need* help, but she might like to have an extra set of eyes, or maybe she might enjoy having someone to boss around. "Well, go ahead and bring the intern in."

"Elliot," Beth whispered. "Her name is Elliot, not 'The Intern.'"

She rolled her eyes. "Elliot, right." What a stupid name for a girl. Why couldn't people just name their daughters something normal anymore? She grabbed the still-warm copies from the Xerox tray with one hand and her coffee with the other, taking another gulp before following Beth around the corner.

21

She nearly froze at the sight of the woman in front of her. She wasn't sure what she'd expected. She hadn't thought she'd given the idea of a college student any thought at all, but if she had pictured someone, it wouldn't have been the imposing figure before her now. For some reason when she pictured college-age girls, they were all petite and peppy and blonde, not tall and androgynous with square jaws and incandescent green eyes.

"Hello." The young woman shook a tuft of auburn hair off her forehead. "I'm Elliot Garza."

Yes, Kelly thought, in spite of her annoyance moments before. Yes, you are absolutely an Elliot. She extended her hand. "Kelly Rolen."

"It's a pleasure," Elliot said.

Pleasure? Something about the word sent a chill across her skin. She broke the contact between them before saying, "We'll see."

Elliot arched an eyebrow, and one corner of Beth's mouth quirked up as if amused.

Kelly's jaw tightened. She didn't appreciate being caught off guard, and she didn't appreciate that she'd let her surprise show even for one second. "I don't suppose you have any experience, do you?" she asked brusquely, walking behind an old metal and faux-wood desk to put some space between them.

"Actually, I do," Elliot said coolly. "I worked for a payroll and accounting services company in Chicago two summers in a row, and last year I worked in the university audits department all year."

She frowned. That was more experience than she'd expected. "So, no experience in a CPA office then?"

"No, but I've done taxes." Elliot stood up a little straighter, too straight, really.

Kelly glanced down to see she wore only flat-soled boots, and yet their eyes were level despite her own two-inch heels. "Well, I hope you're a fast learner because tax season started on Monday, and we're already behind."

"I'm fast at a lot of things." Elliot jammed her hands into the pockets of her rich, dark coat. "Just tell me what you need."

Need.

The word burned her up. She looked to Beth, filled with the

22

sudden urge to tell her this wouldn't work. It couldn't work. She didn't need help. She *couldn't* need help. Not from this walking, talking, tall drink of self-assuredness.

"I think you two are going to get along famously," Beth cut in quickly, shooting her one of those smiles that so clearly said, "Be patient."

Kelly took a deep breath in through her nose and released it quickly through her mouth, before nodding. "If you say so, I won't argue . . . yet."

"Then I'll leave you both to it. Also, there will be some paperwork to fill out for the university, but since this came together at the last minute, I'm sure they'll understand you both taking a few days to get your feet under you before we worry about formalities."

What a nice way of saying she didn't have to sign anything until she knew for sure she wouldn't kill the intern. Then Beth turned to Elliot, and laying a hand on her arm, gave it a little squeeze before saying, "You're going to do great."

"Thanks, Beth," Elliot said with such gentle sincerity that Kelly almost softened, though toward which of them she wasn't sure. Suddenly everyone seemed so much more human, so much more vulnerable. Beth had a way of highlighting those qualities, for better or worse.

But Beth was leaving. Kelly and Elliot both watched her go and waited for the door to shut completely before turning to size each other up again.

Alone now, Elliot seemed every bit as imposing as she had at first glance, though upon closer inspection she wasn't absurdly tall, maybe five-nine, but her long coat and square shoulders made her stature appear more impressive. Yeah, it had to be the coat.

"So . . ." Elliot said, tugging on the fingers of her brown suede gloves. "Where do you want me to start?"

Good question. One she didn't have the answer to. She really hadn't thought the whole intern concept through. She hadn't had the time, energy, or inclination to wonder about what parts of her father's business she felt comfortable handing over to a stranger. She should probably try to consider their situation as something other than an invasion of her personal space, but Elliot's presence still qualified as an intrusion. She'd never handled other people in her space very well, even under the best of circumstances. And having to hand over part of her father's workload to some student/employee hybrid did not qualify as the best of circumstances.

"Do you think you could figure out how to run a copy machine scanner?" she asked before she realized how condescending the question sounded.

"Yeah," Elliot drew out the word. "I've run across them a time or two."

"Okay, well, I have a stack of documents, W-2s, 1099s, and receipts that people dropped off. I'll need them all copied and both the originals and the copies put back in their files."

"Sure. Where do I start?"

Kelly walked over to a large table holding several plastic crates filled with an assortment of manila folders and white envelopes representing the early bird crowd, the secretaries and farmers' wives and people with so much time on their hands that they were able to turn in their taxes on February first. "You can start here by sorting the incoming information. Find the files for the client in the filing cabinet over there. Put the information they've dropped off in the file and organize the files in the crates in the order in which they were received. I'll file them by last name after I review them."

"What would you like me to do when I finish sorting them?"

"*If* you finish filing," Kelly let the doubt drip from her voice, "you can start scanning the documents."

"Sounds easy enough." Elliot shrugged off her coat to reveal a white dress shirt with black slacks and thin black suspenders. She looked like something off the cover of Vogue or some other trendy magazine Kelly had never read. The outfit was sleek, slimming, and entirely over the top for a tax prep intern in Darlington, Illinois. Though it did prove one thing: the coat wasn't the only thing to blame for Elliot's imposing stature.

Kelly brought two fingers to each temple and massaged them gently to temper the stress pulsing there. She refused to look down at her own drab khakis and lavender blouse. What did it matter what either of them wore to work so long as they actually did their work?

She watched Elliot only long enough to make sure she'd understood the directions, then grabbed a stack of folders on the way back to her office. She opened the first one without even looking at the name. Whoever it was needed their taxes done. They all needed their taxes done, and they would only grow more numerous and more needy for the next two and a half months.

She poured over the 1099s and expense reports for a journeyman welder, steadfastly ignoring the sound of Elliot at the scanner until the phone rang. She snatched it up on the second ring. "Rolen and Rolen, how may I help you?"

"Hello, may I speak to Kelly?"

"This is she."

"Kelly, this is June down at the hospital."

Her chest tightened painfully, but she said nothing.

"I'm calling to let you know your dad had a little seizure. He's stable, but the doctor wants to try a new treatment, and since you're his power of attorney, I need you to authorize use of a drug that's still in the clinical trial stage."

"I'm sorry, a what?" Her voice sounded strangled to her own ears and Elliot must've heard it, too, because she slapped a button and the scanner came to a sudden halt. "He what?"

"He had a seizure. It's not uncommon in the aftermath of a stroke." The woman on the phone continued. "He's okay. He's resting peacefully now, but we need your permission to—"

"I can't give my permission until I know more about the treatment. What are the side effects? What are the alternatives? Can I talk to his doctor?"

"She's with another patient right now, but I can ask her to call you back."

"No," she snapped, grabbing her keys and her pocketbook out of the top drawer of her desk. "I'm on my way. Please tell the doctor I'll be there in ten minutes." She didn't wait for a response before slamming the phone back onto the cradle and turning to Elliot. "I have to leave."

"Is everything all right?"

"That's none of your business," she snapped, the fear now too consuming for her to bother with politeness.

"Uh . . . okay. Should I stay and finish this?"

Kelly looked around quickly. There was sensitive information here, personal records, people's social security numbers. Who the hell was Elliot Garza anyway? What did she really know about her? And yet, there she was copying all those files. If she wanted to commit identity theft, she'd have ample opportunity even with Kelly in the office.

Shit.

She didn't have time for a moral quandary.

"You know what, I don't care. Stay, finish, do whatever, but lock the door if you leave." She pushed quickly past Elliot and out the door into the frigid February wind. She could only deal with one crisis at a time.

ം ം ം

What the hell was that?

Elliot stared out the door Kelly had fled through. The cold shoulder she'd gotten while working was weird enough, but the sudden departure seemed especially extreme. Based on her behavior over the last forty minutes, she could've called her new boss a drama queen or scattered, but neither felt quite accurate, as she was also pretty fierce.

The once- or twice-over Kelly had given her when they met made her feel like a military recruit doomed to never pass inspection. Those dark eyes had raked over her like she was a cross between an exotic animal and a sideshow attraction. She would've thought the woman had never see a lesbian before, but her relationship with Beth clearly went beyond a casual acquaintance, though even their connection seemed weird. Friendly but not easy, and yet, gentle. Kelly's fuse seemed pretty short, but Beth could soothe even the most frazzled nerves.

Elliot didn't have that skill, and she'd never really cared. She didn't want to appease anyone. She was glad people like Beth existed to comfort the afflicted, but she'd much rather afflict the comfortable. Not that Kelly seemed particularly comfortable. Her office was far from cushy.

Elliot took the two steps needed to move from the copy machine back to the center of the front room. A row of worn chairs faced a picture window with a view of the Darlington town square in all its American glory. Not a bad view if that's the sort of thing you liked, but she would've rather looked out on the Capitol Building or Lake Shore Drive. The rest of the decor was standard waiting room—a few magazines, a potted fern, a coffeemaker complete with mismatched mugs and powdered creamer. The back half of the space housed one impersonal desk stocked with staplers, hole punchers, and manila folders, but nothing to reveal anything about the personality of the person who worked there.

There had to be more, both to the space and the woman who ran it.

Her new friend, the scanner, was set near the entrance in a small hallway with a few internal doors on the way to a back door made of metal. That kind of door always led to alleys, in the city. She'd never thought of Darlington as having back alleys. Curiosity overtook her. She left her stack of papers to see what the seedy underside of Darlington looked like, but as she pushed the handle her phone rang, or more accurately, vibrated, sending a tingle through the smooth fabric of her pants.

She grabbed the phone and quickly glanced at the screen. A glance was all she needed to recognize the photo of a woman in an oversized sombrero holding an equally gargantuan margarita. The caller ID above the photo said Sydney Garza. She smiled. The shot was two years old and taken on a mother-daughter trip to San Juan a few years ago. Her mother hated the picture, which of course was why she'd kept it for so long.

She swiped her finger across the screen and said, "Hello, Syd."

"Hey babe," Syd said over the background noise of city traffic. "I just wanted to call and wish you good luck on your first day of work. When do you start?"

"I actually started about an hour ago."

"Oh shit. I didn't mean to call you at work. I didn't think you'd possibly accept a job that required you to be up before 10:00."

"I didn't have a lot of choice."

"Well, you shouldn't have answered your phone at the office. Those small-town business people still get kind of huffy about modern technology."

She rolled her eyes. "How many small-town business people do you know?"

"A few." She laughed lightly. "And by 'a few,' I mean I see them on TV."

"Yeah, well you may actually know more than I do. My boss was only here for a hot minute before she left in a huff."

"Who'd she leave in charge?"

"No one. I mean, me, I guess." She looked around as if someone else might be lurking in the building, despite knowing otherwise. "I'm the only one here."

"What?"

"She, this Kelly woman, got a phone call and said I could stay or go, then she ran out."

"Elliot," Syd's mom voice emerged quickly. "That's not normal. Who leaves their business in the middle of the morning with a new person on board? I think your boss is a meth head."

Elliot shook her head. "Not again."

"No, I am serious. I read a book called *Methland*. It's an epidemic in rural areas."

"I know, I know. You've told me several times." She'd also pointed out several suspected meth heads last time she'd come to visit.

"Also heroin use is on the rise all over. She probably got a call from her dealer. Or maybe she *is* a dealer. Does she have a lot of bling around the office?"

"No. My boss is not a drug kingpin. Really, if you could see her, I mean . . . she's like, squeaky clean and stoic and very waspy."

"That's the ones you have to watch out for. The media always tries to convince you it's the minorities, but that's to uphold the hegemony."

"I know, Mother."

"Don't call me that."

"Then stop being paranoid. My new boss is . . ." She couldn't think of the right word. "Odd, maybe."

"Is she homely?" Syd asked, then rushed to justify her comment against her feminist sensibilities. "Not that a woman should be judged by her looks, but meth users are usually pallid and drawn, and they have bad teeth. Does your boss have bad teeth?"

"No," she said automatically, then realized she hadn't actually seen Kelly's teeth. She hadn't smiled, not really. The corners of her mouth may have twitched up a time or two before Beth left, but most of the time her mouth formed a firm line. But still, she was definitely not homely. She had a sharp-edged kind of beauty that could take a person's breath away under the right circumstances.

"Is she underweight?"

"Well, she's pretty thin, but she's long and lanky, kind of leggy, so it's probably just her body type."

"Uh-huh," Syd said knowingly. "Does she have dark circles under her eyes?"

"Now that you mention it—"

"See? There's a pattern. What about hair loss?"

"No," she said quickly, then smiled. "She's actually got really gorgeous hair, long and thick and black as night, not a city night either. Like nights out here, vast, dark, and shimmering with starlight."

"Oh no, Elliot."

"What?"

"Don't hit on this woman." The mom voice returned.

"I didn't hit on her."

"Yet?"

"No. It's not like that. She's totally unapproachable. She's got this ice queen vibe, very severe, and she can barely look at me."

"Who wouldn't want to look at you? You're stunning."

She shook her head. "Moms always think their kids are stunning."

"Please, when have I ever done anything like other mothers?"

She had a point there, but that didn't make her right about any-thing else. "Kelly's not the least bit interested in me. She's straight as a pin in every way and not my type at all."

"She's leggy and stoic with long, dark hair you're practically writing poetry about."

"Okay, so physically she's totally my type, but that's all. She's sharp. She's scattered. She's guarded. And she's a second-generation, small-town CPA. The business is seriously called Rolen and Rolen. What do you want to bet it was supposed to be Rolen and Sons?"

"Well, that does make me feel better. If anything turns you off, it's submission to the patriarchy."

She laughed outright. From meth heads to political resistance, her conversations with Syd always ran the gamut.

"Wait, she's not a homophobe, is she?"

Elliot's chest tightened again. "I, um, well, the thought crossed my mind, but she seems to be friends with Beth. Or friendly. Sort of."

"Sort of?"

"Yeah, I don't know. The vibe was weird, but not mean." She remembered again the looks between them, guarded, almost wounded, but somehow caring. "Hard to read and harder to explain."

"Oh no, is this some love-the-sinner-hate-the-sin bullshit?" Syd's voice grew maternal once more. "I don't want you working in a place where you're not safe emotionally anymore than I'd want you to work for a meth head."

"Well, that can't be helped. I'm going to run into homophobes in my life."

"You'd run into fewer of them in a city than you would down there among the children of the corn."

Elliot shook her head. She couldn't have this conversation again. Neither of them needed that kind of doubt right now. "I can handle myself. People have been pretty good down here so far. I mean, most of the time."

"Please notice how quick you were to assure me your boss wasn't on meth and how you've yet to deny she might be a raging homophobe."

She had a point. "I don't know if she's some born-again nutcase or even a run-of-the-mill bigot, but I can deal with whatever I'll have to deal with, whenever I have to deal with it. I had a strong female role model while growing up."

"Damn, you always have an answer for everything."

"Yeah, which is why you should just stop arguing with me. That, and also I better get back to work."

"Okay." Syd sighed. "What are you even doing?"

"Scanning." Elliot's sigh echoed her mother's. "Endless amounts of scanning."

"Isn't that a little below your skillset?"

"Yeah, well she didn't exactly let me finish talking about my skillset, but I don't think it would've changed anything if she had. I get the feeling I'm going to have to prove my worth."

"Then I hope your meth head, bigoted boss is lucid enough to have her mind blown, because you're worth your weight in platinum and twice as rare."

She laughed. "That's such a mom thing to say."

"I'm hanging up now."

"Bye." Elliot pushed the end call button on her phone and slipped it back into her pocket. She glanced around the drab office once more. The place was so quiet. So sterile. So void. She didn't do well in stillness. It creeped her out. But she replayed her conversation with Syd as she resumed scanning her stack of receipts for everything from cattle vaccines to sewing bobbins. She smiled at her mother's predictions of Kelly's likely drug addiction one minute while warning her off a romantic attraction to her the next, right before jumping to conclusions about Kelly's raging homophobia. She would've worried about her mother's assumption that she could fall so easily for an anti-gay drug lord if not for the pride in her voice as she declared her worth. And Syd was right. She was a strong, driven, independent woman. She didn't need her mom to affirm those traits. Technically, she didn't need anyone's affirmation, but that didn't mean she didn't appreciate having it.

Chapter Four

"I wish I had more to tell you. The brain is a complex organ. There are more factors at play here than we can even begin to comprehend." The dark eyes regarding hers were kind and concerned. "I promise I'll look into a few things and get back to you if I find anything helpful."

"Thank you, Doctor Patel," Kelly said, shaking the hand of her former schoolmate. The act made her feel old and helpless. Kelsey Patel may have been a brilliant physician, but she was two years younger than her. When had their generation taken over things as weighty as life and death? Where were the older, wiser leaders to guide them?

She turned to her father, his limp form seeming smaller and more frail than ever amid the tubes and monitors. She had spent years wanting to be like him, wanting to be his equal. Wanting to inspire trust and confidence and a sense of security. She'd gone so far as to pretend to be all of those things her entire life in the hope that her steadfast adherence to the vision would bend reality. Standing here, looking down on the man who taught her everything she knew about what she wanted most to be, she understood the full magnitude of her fraud.

She didn't know what to do. She didn't know how to fix the problems facing them now. She couldn't will him to wake up. She couldn't work her way into his brain and make the connections for him. She couldn't find his words or his will to go on. She couldn't save him, not through wit or strength or stubbornness. She wasn't even sure she could save herself without him.

"Kelly, do you have someone to talk to?" Kelsey's voice was quiet, soothing, but she still startled at the sound of it. She'd forgotten Doctor Patel was still in the room.

"I'm fine."

"I'm sure," Kelsey said seriously. "It's just, strokes involve a long-term recovery process. There are people who specialize in the physical aspects and rehab, but there are also specialists for the emotional toll a stroke can take both on the patient and their caregivers."

She clenched her teeth and her fists, then tried to slowly release them. "I don't need a therapist."

"Right, but is there someone in your life? A friend, a partner?"

"I'm not married." Her face flushed. She didn't want to dodge these questions, not now. She didn't ever enjoy the task, but especially not here, not with her nerves so raw and her father so close. Some people believed patients could hear things or sense them even when they weren't conscious. She didn't believe them, but she didn't take chances. Not ever.

"A friend, then? I know you were close with Beth and Rory. What about Stevie and Jody?"

She winced. "I don't like what you're implying."

Kelsey's brow furrowed. "I'm not sure what you think I've implied."

"You listed a bunch of . . . a bunch of . . ." She couldn't even say the word in front of her father.

Kelsey had no such problem. "Lesbians? Oh no, I didn't mean to imply anything salacious. Honestly, I forget people find gay couples salacious."

Dr. Patel shook her head sadly, and Kelly felt a new kind of shame. This time it burned her chest instead of her face. She was assumed to be either a lesbian or a homophobe, and she honestly didn't know which felt worse. No, that wasn't true. She knew which one she'd chosen repeatedly, but she still didn't like the way the choice made her stomach roil.

"I only meant that I remember you being close with Beth after high school. I know she and Rory are close with Stevie and Jody," Kelsey continued. "They're a good group of women, smart and thoughtful. I see them for dinner every few months, and I always feel better afterwards. I have a stressful job with a lot of responsibility, and surrounding myself with good people goes a long way toward healing parts of myself that would never show up on an X-ray or CT-scan."

Her heart hurt, a dull ache in her chest, but she set her jaw against the pain. She exhaled through to a point where she could speak. "You're out of line, Dr. Patel. My personal life isn't the purview of anyone in this hospital. I'm not the patient here. I'd appreciate it if you'd focus on my father."

Kelsey nodded sadly. "If you change your mind, I'm in town every second and fourth Wednesday of the month, and I'm always open to consult."

Kelly didn't respond. She stayed facing her father until Kelsey left the room, then she sank into the chair beside the bed. She didn't need any help. She might need sleep or food or a few Advil, but she could get those things herself. She didn't need Kelsey Patel, or even worse, Rory and her cadre of lesbians to step into her family's business.

Her family business. The office. Elliot.

She eyed her dad's sleeping form. He seemed peaceful amid her turmoil. Why couldn't she just talk to him? He would tell her she was being hysterical, overly dramatic. He would remind her they had work to do, and tax season waited for no man. He would chastise her for leaving the office in the hands of someone else, someone they didn't even know.

Her heart beat faster as she felt herself being torn between the desire to stand guard over him and the knowledge that he'd rather she take care of the business he'd built. She shouldn't have to choose between the man she idolized and the legacy he cherished, but she knew if the choice were his, he'd send her back to work, and he'd expect her to do so with a lot more command than she had this morning.

She thought about kissing him on the forehead before going, but the act would likely embarrass them both, so she merely patted his hand and whispered, "I'll be back tonight," just in case those hippie subconscious believers were right.

The clock on the dash of the Buick she'd inherited from her father read 1:30. Between the nurses and waiting for the primary physician and the consult with Dr. Patel, she'd been away from the office for over three hours. She fought down the bile in her throat at the thought of all the things that could've gone wrong and tried not to imagine angry clients, IRS investigations, or the entire building going up in flames. God, she'd been so wracked with fear when she left. The full impact of what she'd done hadn't sunk in until this moment.

"Please, God," she prayed quietly, "I promise I won't do this again. Just please don't let anything have gone wrong. Please let Elliot just have gone home."

She turned the corner just before she reached the town square and pulled her land boat into the narrow alley behind her office. If only Elliot had bolted at her first chance of escape, everything would be okay. She wouldn't have had the chance to mess up. Kelly could call Beth immediately and tell her this arrangement wouldn't work. She could fire her or fail her or whatever she had to do to get her office, her sanctuary, the better part of her life under her control.

She strode quickly to the office door that only people in the know would ever use. "Please, just let her be gone," Kelly prayed one more time as she pushed into the office that felt so much like her home.

◆ ◆ ◆

"Hi," Elliot said with a polite smile as Kelly froze in the doorway. "Welcome back."

Kelly blinked her dark eyes a few times as if adjusting to the lights, or maybe to her presence. Her shoulders were tight and her expression void except for the thin, pressed line of her mouth. Kelly seemed almost startled to see her, despite the fact that she was still standing in exactly the same spot where she'd been when Kelly had left.

"You're still here."

"Yep."

"It's been hours."

Thanks, Captain Obvious. "A few."

"Have you been here the whole time?"

"All except for that twenty minutes when I went to knock off the liquor store." She regretted the comment immediately as the creases on Kelly's forehead grew deeper. "I'm kidding. I barely stopped scanning since you left. I got so deep into work mode, I barely noticed the time."

"Barely?"

"What?"

"You said you barely stopped scanning."

God, what was with this woman? Did she intend to pick her apart like a vulture with a carcass? "I stopped at one point to go to the bathroom. Thanks for leaving that door unlocked, by the way. And then I stopped because a lovely old lady came in to grill me about her taxes. 'Mrs. Anthony' I believe she instructed me to call her."

"Damn it." Kelly swore, and somehow the word sounded downright scandalous coming out of her mouth. "She's a very difficult client."

"I sort of got that from her. When she saw me instead of you, you would have thought she'd stepped into a leper colony. She even got a dig in about my suspenders being rather 'mannish.'"

Kelly used both hands to rub her temples. "Please tell me you told her to come back later."

"I mentioned that option."

"But?"

"But she said if I intended to work in a CPA office during tax season, I'd better learn to handle your forms."

Kelly might have actually swayed a little bit under the weight of the realization that Elliot had actually interacted with one of her clients. Elliot enjoyed her fear a little more than she probably should have. Served her right for her little comment about learning to use a scanner—not to mention her blatant distrust—but the woman had clearly had a bad day, so she cut her a little slack and picked up the folder currently beside the scanner. "Don't worry. I found your client organizers on the front desk and walked her though all the questions. She had her papers pretty well in order, so I assembled everything into her file and labeled it like the others I'd already scanned."

Kelly eyed her skeptically, one dark eyebrow arched as she tentatively reached for the folder in Elliot's outstretched hand.

"Go ahead, it won't bite. On the contrary, I'm sure you'll hurt it more than it hurts you."

"I'm not afraid of the file," she snapped.

That was about the third time she'd snapped at her in less than an hour in each other's presence. Elliot hadn't expected effusive praise, but a simple "thank you," might've been appropriate. Kelly's flushed skin and clenched jaw didn't quite mesh with her mother's meth theory, but something wasn't right. Kelly didn't act like a professional mentor. She didn't act like a professional anything, expect for perhaps a professional asshole. Maybe interns ranked slightly above grubs around here, but if Kelly resented her presence so damn bad, maybe she should've kept her job at the college.

"You weren't authorized to talk to my clients," Kelly said as she flipped open the folder. "Financial records are confidential."

"Really? I'm only four months from a master's degree in public accounting, and no one ever mentioned confidentiality before." This time she didn't feel guilty when Kelly winced. "You think that would've come up in the two separate courses I had to take in business law and business ethics."

"Excuse me?"

"No, excuse *me*. My presence here seems to be a massive inconvenience for you, and I'm not sure why," Elliot said. "You agreed to have an intern, you're a CPA, and it's tax season. You're the only other person here, so I assume you've got work for me to do. I haven't broken any rules I know of or spit on your doorknobs—hell, you haven't even been around enough today for me to do anything to offend you."

"You spoke to one of my clients."

"Something I wouldn't have done if anyone else had been here, but you weren't, and then when you come back you don't even wait to hear what happened before you cut into me? You busted through the door like you expected to find the place ransacked. What did you think I was going to do?"

"I don't know," Kelly admitted. "I don't even know you."

"Exactly. You don't know me, and already you've made up your mind that you don't trust me. You don't like me, and that's fine. You don't have to like me, but don't I at least deserve to know why?"

"No." Kelly threw up her hands. "You don't deserve anything.

You're not entitled to anything. You're not guaranteed anything, and you don't get any awards for not destroying my office."

"Seriously?" Elliot pushed. The logic didn't add up. Kelly clearly felt a good bit of disdain toward her, but she didn't want to admit why. "You're going to make this about me being entitled? That's really what's bothering you?"

Kelly opened her mouth then closed it and exhaled through her nose. "I don't have to explain myself to a . . . to a . . ."

Elliot's stomach clenched as she steeled herself for the slur. Her mother's warning about homophobia among the "children of the corn" rushed through her ears. She should've seen this coming. Deep down she'd known it would happen eventually. Everyone back home warned her about going to school in a rural area. She told them she could handle whatever the locals threw at her, but that didn't mean she didn't still get a little nauseated every time one of them let fly a rabid bout of homophobia. She refused to let the fear show, though. She lifted her chin. "Go ahead, say it."

Kelly stopped her stuttering. "Say what?"

"Dyke." She practically had to spit the word out. She'd said it plenty of times. Dyke march, dykes on bikes, dykes to watch out for. She knew the politics, but all efforts to reclaim the word be damned. It still sucked.

Kelly took a step back and her eyes went wide and white, but Elliot wouldn't let her off the hook. "That's what you meant, right? You don't have to explain yourself to a dyke?"

Kelly shook her head almost frantically, but her face flamed red. "Don't put words into my mouth. Especially not that one."

"What word did you intend to use then? Queer? Homo? It doesn't matter which one you choose. Your judging me based on my sexual orientation is discrimination, and it's illegal in the state of Illinois. It has been since 2006, even in the little hick towns."

"How dare you!"

"How dare I what? Stand up for my rights under the law?"

"How dare you talk to me like this in my father's business. You are so far out of line right now."

"So far out of line that what? You'll fire me? Try it," Elliot challenged, "but look over the work I did first, because it's flawless. If you fire me after one day of perfect work, I'll hit you with a lawsuit so fast you won't even have time to pick your jaw up off the floor."

"Did you just threaten to sue me?"

"Try me and find out."

"Get out," Kelly said, her voice full of steel. "Get out of my office."

"Fine," Elliot said, "but look over the work I did today and talk to your lawyer, because I'll be back tomorrow, and if I'm not judged on my merits you'll hear from mine."

She grabbed her coat, then brushed past Kelly and slammed the heavy back door on the way out. She loved the way the metal crashing into metal echoed through the frozen alleyway. She arched her head back and took deep, gulping breaths of sharp, icy air as she stared up at the high brick walls enclosing her. If she were in Chicago, she would worry about getting jumped in an alley like this, but after what had happened inside, she felt like she'd faced the worse and survived. Sure, her hands shook and she might vomit at any moment, but no one else had to know that. Especially not Kelly Rolen.

∽ ∽ ∽

Kelly stared at the door as her chest rose and fell rapidly and the sound of her own pulse pounded through her ears. Her fists trembled from the comedown of her adrenaline rush, or maybe from the anger still coursing through her. Both emotions combined with sheer exhaustion to blur her vision. Or maybe those were tears causing the haze over her eyes. She blinked them away. She would not cry, not now, not after everything else she'd been through. Not over that smug little shit's gross mischaracterization of her motives. And the worst part was, Elliot wasn't even the first person to level those accusations at her. More than a few people over the last few years had suggested she and Beth weren't as close as they used to be because she couldn't support Beth and Rory's relationship. Well, maybe that part happened to be true, but not for the reasons they suspected.

Why did everything come down to sexual orientation? First Kelsey Patel and now Elliot. In the space of one hour she'd had to defend herself against charges of being gay and of being a homophobe. How could she possibly be both? She shook her head to prevent the answer to that question from lodging there. Couldn't she just dislike someone because they annoyed her? Couldn't she be close with a woman without fear of being called a lesbian?

Or better yet, couldn't everyone just leave her alone?

People generally meant well, but they couldn't help, not really, and maybe that's what bothered her most. No one could help in the ways she needed. No one could heal her dad, and no one could fill the void his absence had left in her life. In the years since she and Beth broke up, he had been her only constant, the only person in her life who had never left her for something better, the only person she could count on to do right by her, no matter what the cost.

Not to mention, her dad always lived up to high standards. He'd taught her to do the same. To accept less than perfection in the business he'd built would be a disservice to his legacy. What would he think if the first time he missed a tax season she let the whole place fall apart? He'd think her unworthy. He wouldn't say so, but he'd think it, and more importantly, she would, too.

She couldn't let that happen.

Which brought her back around to Elliot.

She tapped her fingers on the outside of the file folder the intern had pushed on her before storming out. She didn't even want to see the forms inside, didn't want to face another mess, and yet she had to. It was her fault for putting herself in this situation. Well, hers and Beth's. Also, Elliot had to take some blame for barging in like she owned the place, with her long legs and her hot temper. Kelly shook the image of her, flushed and indignant, from her mind. Who cared who held the blame? She had to deal with the outcome.

She flipped open the file and carefully eyed the client organizer. At least Elliot had excellent penmanship. She'd neatly filled out all the information Kelly already knew about Mrs. Anthony, her name, address, place of employment at the local grocery store. Anyone with a third grade education could fill out the top part of the intake forms. She quickly moved down to the numbers, unclipping Mrs. Anthony's W-2s and receipts as she went down the lines for wages, investment income, social security, and Schedule A deductions. She spread the documents out in orderly fashion, finding they didn't take much rearranging as Elliot had already put everything in the appropriate order. Still, with all the scanning she'd done, she'd had ample opportunity to memorize the correct order. Paying attention to detail wasn't a plus in this business, it was essential.

She grabbed a pen and slid it down the side of each form, connecting numbers on original documents to their counterparts in Elliot's clear, concise strokes. She reached the bottom of the form and immediately flipped back to the beginning. She ran through the process twice more before putting everything back as neatly as she'd found it and closing the folder.

She clenched and unclenched her jaw before straightening her shoulders and lifting her chin. Then taking a deep breath, she picked up the phone and dialed a number she'd dialed so many times before she didn't even have to look at the keypad.

Chapter Five

A knock on her apartment door pulled Elliot off the couch. She'd been trying to cool down for an hour, but breathing exercises and meditation had done little to assuage her frayed nerves. After walking home in the frigid cold, she'd convinced herself that her trembling hands were merely a product of the bone-deep chill, but after running them under lukewarm water and chugging a cup of coffee, she felt thoroughly warmed through, and still she shook. She hated herself for getting so upset, but bravado went only so far when it came to covering real pain.

"Who is it?" she called through the door. She might be in Darlington, but today had reminded her that "small town" didn't always mean "safety."

"It's Kelly Rolen." Her voice was muffled through the door, but Elliot still heard the mix of hesitancy and annoyance.

"Shit," she muttered. She did not want to see her. She certainly didn't want Kelly in her personal space, alone, not without having time to get her guard up. But if she sent her away, wouldn't that reveal Kelly had gotten under her skin? If she couldn't hold her own with one bitchy bigot, how did she ever stand a chance with something bigger at stake? The risks of facing Kelly Rolen seemed slightly more bearable than the risk associated with not.

She cracked the door enough to get her face through, but not enough to expose her whole body. Kelly seemed equally conflicted. She had her arms folded across her chest and one hip cocked to the side almost defiantly, but her eyes remained firmly fixed on the toe of her slick black shoes as she mumbled. "Can I talk to you?"

"How did you get my address?"

"I called Beth."

She swallowed a wave of mixed emotions. Had Beth betrayed her by delivering her up to a homophobe twice in one day? Surely not. Nothing about that scenario rang true to what she knew of Beth. But Rory had told her to be careful. She'd seemed to leave something unspoken, too, and Rory didn't usually keep much to herself. How did she reconcile those two things? Especially with Kelly at her door.

"Look," Kelly said, still staring at her feet. "I know you don't trust me, and that's fine, but I didn't mean what you thought I meant."

She didn't know how to respond, so she simply didn't.

"You jumped to a very unfair conclusion. I felt attacked in my own place of business."

"So you mentioned. Loudly. Did you come over to repeat yourself, in case I missed you shouting the same thing at me an hour ago?"

Kelly blew out a frustrated breath. "No. I came over because of the files you worked on."

Her heart rate accelerated. What was Kelly accusing her of now? Had she messed something up? No, her work had been flawless. Maybe she was being framed. This was how they always got rid of you. They couldn't fire you for being gay, so they had to trump up some charges.

"After you left, I looked over the intake forms. Then I looked over the documents you scanned into the computer. I also noticed you'd begun to input several of the returns."

"I didn't have anything else do to," she sulked.

"You could've left," Kelly said, her voice tight, but not raised. "You could've played on your phone or rummaged through my stuff."

"That's not the kind of person I am."

"I'm glad to hear it," Kelly said. That thought hadn't crossed her mind. Had she really grown that used to being disappointed in the people around her? And how had Elliot, of all people, been the one to buck that trend? "Surprised maybe, but glad. You did everything right, by the way. All the work on Mrs. Anthony's form and the scanning and the inputting."

Elliot nodded, trying not to gloat or get too comfortable. "I know."

Kelly's jaw twitched a little bit, but to her credit she plowed on. "You can come back to work tomorrow."

"I planned to."

Kelly let her arms drop to her sides. "Okay then, fine."

"Is that really all you came to say?"

Kelly hesitated a few seconds. "I guess so."

Elliot stared at her, incredulous once again. So she admitted Elliot had done everything right at work, and she also asserted she wasn't anti-gay, and yet all Elliot got was, she could come back to work? Something she'd told Kelly she planned to do all along. That hardly seemed worth a trip to her apartment. No apology. No explanation. Nothing personal in any way.

"Look, I said you did fine today, and you can come back tomorrow. What more do you want from me?"

"How about you explain why you were in such a bad mood?"

"That's none of your business," Kelly snapped.

"Oh, are we back to that again?" She shook her head. "Forgive me for thinking that when someone screams at me unfairly, I have a right to know why."

Kelly clenched her jaw again, and Elliot wondered how the woman hadn't given herself TMJ yet, but when Kelly met her gaze, her eyes were no longer defiant. She blinked a few times, as if fighting back tears, but by the time she focused, Elliot saw no evidence of them. Whatever emotions she was concealing all seemed to lead back to anger. "I'm not going to stand in a hallway and explain myself to my intern."

Back on familiar footing, Elliot should've been able to respond in kind, the sharp tone, the angry retort. But she'd seen something human in the half-second between Kelly's tirades, something that pulled at her chest in an uncomfortable way. "You could come inside," she offered. "I mean, if you're afraid of being overheard."

"I just . . . I, um," she looked toward the ceiling and bit her lip. "I had a really bad day."

Now Elliot's heart thudded for a different reason, this one less to do with fear or anxiety and more to do with compassion she didn't really want to feel for Kelly right now. Whatever this woman's problem was, she'd made it clear it was *her* problem, not Elliot's. She didn't need her boss crying on her shoulder any more than she needed her to yell. She didn't need her to be anything other than a normal freaking boss. She needed intern hours to graduate. She needed a letter of reference. She needed practical experience that would allow her to get a job and move on to bigger and better things. She needed to get away from anything and everything that complicated her plans.

Instead, she took a step back and swung the door open wide.

ᔕ ᔕ ᔕ

Rented couch. College housing. Frat boys. Stains. Body fluids. Those were the things Kelly thought about as she took a seat as lightly as possible on Elliot's furniture. Those thoughts, horrifying as they were, kept her mind off less pleasant subjects like the ones that caused her to cave, in one of those increasingly common moments of weakness.

"So, here's the magic elixir," Elliot said, setting down a rainbow-shaded mug on a coffee table that had more dents and scratches than she had reasons to want to get out of there.

She picked up the mug and sipped the steaming liquid more for a distraction than out of any real desire to taste anything, but as soon as the coffee hit her taste buds, everything changed. The light seemed brighter, the air lighter, even Elliot's wary expression seemed bearable. "Wow."

"Wow?" Elliot asked, a little grin showing over the rim of her own mug.

"That's, oh—" She took another sip and closed her eyes to savor the flavor filling her mouth. "What brand is this?"

"Oh, it's not a brand. I buy it on the black market."

Kelly coughed and quickly wiped her mouth. "Does it have drugs in it or something?"

Elliot threw back her head and laughed, the first unguarded show of emotion Kelly had seen out of her all day. She had a great laugh, hearty, deep, and so wonderfully full it made Kelly forget she was the one getting laughed at.

"I know a guy," Elliot said, as her laughter trailed off. "He orders

45

the beans raw from all over the world and he roasts them himself to whatever specifications I need for any given situation."

"Any given situation?"

"Sure. Some days you need a dark roast to get you through. Some days you need a medium roast to keep you in your groove. And some days, you have a girl over who can't handle her java like a grown-up, and you need to ease her in with a blonde roast."

Her face flamed and she went back to counting nicks in the coffee table before she finally managed to squeak out. "What kind is this?"

"Dark," Elliot said coolly. "Seems warranted after the day we had."

She sighed, curling her fingers fully around the mug and taking another strong pull. "You have no idea."

"I really don't. I sort of hoped you'd fill me in though."

She set her mug down and folded her hands in her lap so Elliot couldn't see them shake, but she immediately missed the warmth and comfort offered by the coffee. How should she even start? What did she really want to give away? Nothing, actually, but she had to tell her something. Or not. She could just make an excuse and leave. She didn't have to reveal any more weakness than she already had.

"Sometimes it's easier to talk to a stranger," Elliot said softly. "I don't know you. I have no investment in who you've been before now, or even in who you'll be four months from now after I graduate and leave. That's one of the things I really liked about coming to college here. I got a clean slate with no strings attached."

Kelly nodded slowly. She hadn't considered the relative anonymity angle before. Everyone she knew, she'd known all her life. She didn't meet many new people around Darlington, and even if she did, they would likely be inserting themselves into town life soon enough and would no doubt hear the whole story eventually. The only place where local lines didn't usually cross was at the college. Bramble College existed largely as a separate entity on the edge of town, like some foreign outpost of people who barely spoke the local language. Students rarely ventured beyond a row of bars that catered to them, and even most of the professors kept to themselves in tight cliques. With the exception of sporting events, locals and college folks rarely interacted.

There was something freeing in the realization that Elliot wouldn't have anyone to tell about her boss's meltdown today. Well, except for Beth, but Beth already knew she was here. Beth knew more about her than anyone else ever would. Elliot couldn't possibly tell Beth anything new.

She met Elliott's sea-glass green eyes and said, "My dad had a stroke."

"Today?"

"No, a week ago, or maybe a week and a half. The days are all starting to blur together. He's still in the hospital."

"And that's where you went today?"

"Yes, they called because he had a seizure. They needed me to approve a new treatment option. He should be getting better, but he's not. He may actually be getting worse."

She'd thought admitting that might feel like a betrayal, as though she didn't believe in him enough to think he could beat everything that plagued him, but once the words fell out, she felt only relief. The weight pushing down on her chest and shoulders lessened significantly as she continued. "No one has answers. No one can tell me what he needs, or even why he's not responding to the treatments, not even the specialists from St. Louis. They keep giving me these vague platitudes about the brain being complex and time being a key element."

"Sounds terrifying," Elliot said sympathetically, "and exhausting and maddening."

"Yes. All of that."

"I see why you'd be on edge. And I guess the business was his business first?"

"He built it. He taught me from the time I was old enough to add and subtract. This is the first tax season without him." Funny—in all of this, she'd never said that out loud. Everyone she spoke to knew their past, knew their present, knew what his absence meant, and yet she hadn't gotten the time or the chance to fully comprehend those things herself. At thirty-two years old, she'd never done her job without her dad.

"Tax season is stressful enough, right? And now you have all of these changes, and forgive me if I'm off base here," Elliot said, her grin returning, "but you don't seem like the kind of person who really thrives on change."

She snorted softly. "Not really."

"And now, not only is your dad not there, I came into the office and reminded you about everything you can't control. I bet every time you looked at me, you remembered that he wasn't there."

"No. I mean, maybe. But I don't need any help. I didn't even want an intern."

Elliot blinked at her, startled. "Then, why did you . . . Beth?"

Kelly nodded, her chest tight again at the sound of her name leaving Elliot's lips so casually.

"So Beth convinced you to let me come help, but you didn't want any help because you're trying to go it alone and you're already stressed out enough . . ." She blew out a frustrated breath of air. "I was screwed before I even walked in. I could've been your fairy godmother, an Olympic level CPA, and straight as an arrow, and none of it would have mattered."

She didn't like that conclusion. She didn't like being painted as unreasonable. She didn't like being backed into a corner. She didn't like being pegged so perfectly, so quickly, especially since she'd yet to get a clear sense of Elliot's personality. On one hand she seemed arrogant and aggressive. Her temper flared easily, and she'd jumped to wild conclusions earlier in the day. And yet, now she appeared calm and perceptive, even in her criticism. Kelly wasn't sure she would've been quite so open to listening if their roles had been reversed, and while she wouldn't admit it to anyone else, she didn't like being out-graced by a hothead lesbian intern. Oh yeah, the lesbian thing had gotten her labeled a homophobe. Her stomach tightened again. She couldn't get so comfortable around Elliot that she made the big mistake. "I didn't even think about you being gay. It wasn't a factor."

Elliot arched an eyebrow.

"I mean it. I don't go around thinking about people's sex lives."

"Being gay is about so much more than sex."

"Fine." She waved her hand quickly. She couldn't go there, for so many reasons. "I don't care unless it affects business, and I don't see any reason why it needs to."

Elliot scowled, her lips pursed together, and Kelly fought the urge to say more, to soften her words, to seek some sort of understanding without actually communicating anything more, but she couldn't. This wasn't a new conflict, and she wouldn't make new mistakes.

"So where do we go from here?" Elliot finally asked.

"Back to work." She rose and took a couple more hard, hot swallows of coffee. "If you want to come back. You understand the situation now. It's up to you."

Elliot stood and walked with her to the door, her expression pensive. "I'll be there tomorrow."

Kelly respected her concise, uncomplicated, and unemotional answer, but she did wonder what Elliot left unsaid. What thoughts made her smooth brow wrinkle as she held open the door? What argument died on her lips? Nothing outside work really mattered, but just because it didn't matter didn't mean part of her didn't want to know more.

⌇ ⌇ ⌇

Elliot stood back from the ancient coffee machine as if it might explode at any moment. She was relatively certain she'd done everything right, but the gurgles and hisses emanating from the contraption sounded more like death throes than the happy bubbling she got from her Cuisinart DC-122 at home.

"Shhh," she warned the machine. Kelly was in her private office with a client, and she wanted to surprise her. At least that's what she told herself. If she were being completely honest, she also didn't want to set her off before she managed to get her fully caffeinated, and since she hadn't been granted explicit permission to touch the coffeemaker, she worried she might have crossed another invisible line.

The peace had been tentative so far, as her arrival was met with polite disinterest and her instructions largely mirrored the day before. She'd spent the first twenty minutes snuggled up next to her friend, the document scanner. Kelly had said, "Good morning," and "you can scan those files," both without a hint of disdain or even annoyance, but she could hardly consider those few words a large enough sample size to make any decisions about her mood.

Should she mention their talk the night before, or maybe ask about her dad? It seemed rude not to bring him up after what she'd learned about his condition. And yet, knowing how the subject affected Kelly, maybe it would be more merciful to stick to neutral topics. She had been pondering this since the moment she walked in the door, but before she had made up her mind on a course of action, a young man in jeans and a heavy flannel jacket had come in, and the two of them had been in a meeting in Kelly's private office ever since.

She'd finished scanning the stack of documents Kelly had given her, and she certainly wasn't about to interrupt her meeting with a client, so she was at a loss. Hence, the coffee-making. The fact that she'd stashed a few of her own freshly ground beans in her work bag before coming in that morning may have been a tip that she'd spent some time thinking of Kelly outside work hours, but only in an attempt to avoid a repeat of yesterday. Her motives were born from a mixture of self-preservation and caffeine addiction, nothing more.

Suddenly with a sputter and a spit, the coffee streamed through the ancient office relic and ran happily into the pot below. She lifted her fist in silent victory. Now whatever else the day brought, at least they would both get to face it with coffee. The thought bolstered her so much she wandered back over to the computer next to the scanner. She clicked through a few screens of the things she'd scanned, checking for the third time to make sure everything was in order. She understood this process. She understood the next step, too. She could input the information from the documents she'd scanned into the Pro Series DMS. The payroll service she worked for in Chicago had a tax prep department that used the same programs, and all the files she'd worked with so far were straightforward and well-organized.

She opened the tax software, waiting patiently for it to load. She found a client's name and clicked to open the file. Elliot verified that the name, address, and phone number hadn't changed over the last year, then clicked on the W-2 screen and started inputting information from the documents she'd already scanned. Kelly had admitted the inputting work she'd toyed around with yesterday was spot-on.

Why not push a little further down the same line? She plugged in a few more numbers—medical expenses, real estate taxes, and charitable contributions. Her fingers took over the keyboard, and before she knew it, she'd filled out two full returns.

She stretched and looked at her watch, then blinked. Crap, she'd lost track of time. The door to Kelly's office swung open, and she walked out with the young man close behind her.

"Thanks Kelly," he said. "I know I'm kind of a mess. I didn't think I'd be able to get this all put together without Mary's help."

"We'll get it all worked out, John. Don't worry."

"I appreciate it. I know you have enough going on right now."

Elliot glanced up to see Kelly's tight smile. "Working keeps my mind off of things."

"Yeah, I know," he said, his own smile grim. "About that, um if you ever need anything, a hand around the house, or a meal or someone to talk to, I'd be happy to buy you dinner sometime. I mean to thank you for everything you're doing."

Elliot quickly turned back toward her computer screen. *Thank you dinner, my ass. This guy just asked Kelly out.* So much for sexuality not interfering with work. She and farmer dude spend over an hour quietly ensconced in her office and leave with plans for a date.

"I'd like that," Kelly said, "but probably won't have time until after tax season."

"Of course," he said seriously, than laughed a little. "I'm sure we'll see each other again before that."

"Probably," Kelly said kindly. "Stay warm out there."

Well, she hadn't accepted the date exactly, but she hadn't turned him down either. What did that mean? Why did she care? She typed quickly, trying to act natural, as though she hadn't eavesdropped.

"What are you doing?" Kelly asked.

"Working." Elliot said, keeping her head down.

"Scanning?"

Her shoulders tensed, but she tried to continue in a normal tone. "I finished the scanning. Now I'm inputting the data."

She heard Kelly shifting around close behind her, and then felt her body heat as she leaned over her shoulder. The warmth of her there was disconcerting on multiple levels, some she didn't care to examine too closely.

"Scroll up," Kelly said in a firm but even voice.

She complied wordlessly, feeling every bit like a cadet under inspection. Would Kelly launch a grenade if she found her work lacking? No, her work was flawless. She had too much at stake.

Finally Kelly stood and backed away. "All right. You can take over the inputting on the simple returns, just make sure you flag the ones you do for my review before we finalize and process them."

She raised her eyebrows at the computer screen. It wasn't exactly a compliment, but the increased responsibility surely implied approval, right? She tried not to turn around until she'd gotten her grin back to neutral. "I also made coffee."

"Is that what I smell?" Kelly asked, and took an audible inhale. "I thought maybe you just brought some with you, for yourself."

"No. I mean I did bring the beans from home, but to share. I thought we might need to stay fully caffeinated this tax season. Plus, it's a good smell for the office, right?"

"Are you implying my office smelled bad before?"

"No," she answered quickly. "It smelled like an office, like paper and copy toner. Totally normal."

"But coffee is better?"

"Well . . . yeah."

Kelly nodded thoughtfully. "Okay, you're in charge of coffee every day, too."

She didn't know if she should be thrilled to have done something else correctly, or to be offended that being designated the office coffee monkey felt like such a reward. "So I scan, I input, I make coffee. Got it. Anything else?"

Kelly looked around the office, slowly turning in a circle before lifting her arms and letting them fall back to her sides. "I've never had to make these decisions before."

The plaintive note in her voice made all of Elliot's frustration dissipate. "I guess we can just figure it out as we go along."

"That's not how I usually operate. The wait and see approach isn't generally my style."

"No, I wouldn't have guessed it is."

Kelly regarded her more seriously now, her intensely dark eyes traveling deliberately up the length of her; this time the inspection felt less formal, but no less nerve-wracking. Elliot squared her shoulders and lifted her chin, refusing to turn away from the implicit challenge.

Suddenly Kelly shook her head and sidestepped to the coffeemaker. "We never officially discussed your hours. I should've paid better attention, but Beth blindsided me. I'm not sure she ever said how much you should work."

The abrupt change of subjects, or more importantly, tone, caught Elliot by surprise. One minute Kelly had felt so close, her eyes intense and clear, then in an instant the distance between them felt so much more than the few feet of physical divide. Everything from her body language to her tone shifted drastically into a detached business mode.

"Well, I've already filled my hours of professional service for licensure with my previous work in the field." That wasn't exactly what Kelly asked, but she wanted to make sure she made it clear she wasn't the average intern. "So, for my course credit, I need twenty hours a week for sixteen weeks, but I talked to my advisor, and she said it doesn't matter how we spread out the workload, so long as I get 320 hours."

"So if we crunch that down to the nine weeks left in tax season, you'd be here thirty-five and a half hours a week."

Elliot tapped her temple. "You did the math in your head. Have you ever considered a career working with numbers?"

Kelly didn't laugh or even smile as she poured coffee into a mug with the local high school's initials on the side in red, white, and blue. Okay, maybe the joke hadn't been a side-splitter, but not even a grin or a good-natured eye-roll? Tough crowd. She transitioned back into business. "We could overlap hours all the time if you want to keep an eye on me, or since I know you've got other stuff on your plate, I could stagger my hours with yours to make sure we have coverage."

Kelly nodded thoughtfully. "I'm not sure what my schedule will be. I generally work even on nights and weekends. I'm not sure that's allowed for you."

"Everything's allowed for me. I mean, barring any law-breaking. I can work nights and Saturdays. I can open for you when you're at the hospital. I can man the front desk, the phone, or the scanner." She didn't know why she was volunteering so damn much, but the words kept pouring out of her mouth before she thought them through. She felt like she had to prove her worth to Kelly, though she didn't care to examine why her opinion mattered quite so much. "If I go over my 35.5 hours a week, I won't tell on you. No one would have to know."

"I would know," Kelly snapped for the first time that morning, a hint of fire returning to her eyes. "Just because you can get away with something doesn't make it right."

"Fair enough," Elliot responded evenly, "but I'm just as new as you are to this whole intern thing. I've been an employee and I've been a volunteer, but I've always heard interns sort of get abused in the name of experience."

"There are laws against that now."

She smiled broadly in spite of the tension still radiating from Kelly. "There are, but most people don't know that."

"Ignorance of the law is no excuse for breaking the law," she said in a clipped tone that made it clear the subject matter was closed. "Just keep a log of your hours, and I'll sign it at the end of each week."

"Okay."

"And tell me if you don't understand something, or if you don't feel comfortable with something. You're in my family business. The buck stops with me."

"I will."

"Good," Kelly said curtly. "And your school work comes first, so if you have any commitments at the college, let me know. You shouldn't miss school for work."

Well that sounded awfully motherly, though nothing like her actual mother. "I can let you know at least a week in advance when I'm available."

"Then think about scheduling and get back to me. In the meantime, keep doing what you've been doing." Without waiting for a response, she turned, coffee in hand, and strode purposefully back to her office and closed the door.

Elliot flopped into the chair at the reception desk. Who was this woman? What kind of person in the middle of a personal crisis and a professional overload refused to accept extra hours from an intern who volunteered? And who in the middle of tax season took time to lecture the intern about the importance of putting school ahead of work? She'd always heard that during this time of year, chaos reigned and all hands were required on deck at all times. Honestly, part of her had looked forward to the thrill of the fight. Instead, she felt as though she'd been patted on the head and told to just keep doing her house chores. She would've been disappointed or even angry at the patrician tone Kelly kept using with her, if not for the intensity behind even her most coddling comments.

Like it or not, and she wasn't at all sure which side she fell on yet, there was something compelling in Kelly's drive, in her focus, in her unflinching dedication to doing everything right, and with full command. Hell, there was always something intriguing about a woman in charge, and a beautiful woman at that.

Nope. No. Bad thoughts.

She'd just begun to make progress here. She'd only in the last few minutes righted the ship after the whole homophobia throwdown yesterday and gotten them both back in straight-up business mode. Thinking of Kelly as some sort of beautiful accounting dominatrix would only lead to disaster. She needed to follow Kelly's not-so-subtle cue and get back to work.

Chapter Six

"Is that another one of your attempts to change the smell of my office?" Kelly asked, hoping Elliot caught the disdain in her voice.

Elliot glanced up from the plate of whatever awful dish she was currently shoving into her mouth. "What?"

"Exactly. What in the world is that?"

"Thai-style curried vegetables," she said, as if the words should mean something to Kelly. Sometimes Kelly couldn't tell if it was her city roots, her queer sensibilities, or a quality unique to Elliot, but she got the sense that they had completely different expectations for the world. Their different assumptions in any situation tended to be maddening, and even more frustrating because neither one of them ever seemed wrong so much as plain different.

For instance, they had completely different understandings of business attire. Kelly owned a series of slacks ranging from gray, to black, to navy, and any of them could be paired with almost any of her lightly colored blouses or oxford shirts. On casual days she could sub in khakis, and on formal occasions she had a couple of skirts and two suit coats. Everything could be matched with a low-heeled shoe or flats, or if absolutely necessary, high heels. Endless options, all classic, all solid, all business standards.

Elliot, on the other hand, wore everything from brightly colored button-ups to polos layered under long sleeves. She wore suit vests with jeans and sweaters over slacks. And patterns, Kelly never knew so many patterns existed, herringbone, paisley, pinstripe, nothing ever seemed quite static on Elliot. She never left anything un-accessorized either. Ties and wristwatches, suspenders, infinity scarves, and belts that all matched her loafers or boots or wingtips.

Today she wore skinny jeans that accentuated her long legs and an electric blue dress shirt under a gray chevron-striped vest. She bottomed the ensemble off with Doc Marten oxfords. And damned if she didn't look good. Not as feminine as one would think appropriate for Darlington, and certainly over-styled, but good. She projected an air of confidence, capability, and magnetism. Kelly couldn't make a single complaint about the appropriateness of the ensemble, but the contrast with her own attire left her unsettled. If Elliot's outfit seemed so perfect, and yet was completely different from her own business wardrobe, what did that say about her own clothes? She didn't know, and she wasn't sure she wanted to, so she redirected and picked on an easier target.

Kelly took another sniff. "Do you have to eat that at the front desk?"

"I could go back to the break room." Elliot stood up and made a show of looking around. "Just show me where that is?"

She rolled her eyes. In the last week she'd gotten more used to Elliot's dry sense of humor, but her reaction generally depended more on her mood than Elliot's comments. Sometimes she even enjoyed the banter and the caustic outlet it gave her, though she'd never admit that. "Maybe you can co-opt one like you took over my reception desk."

"Oh, did you mean for me to work standing up? What happened to not breaking rules for treating interns fairly? I'm pretty sure OSHA would have something to say about me having to be on my feet without a break all day."

"I'm not sure tax interns are covered by OSHA."

"You've got an answer for everything," Elliot said with a little grin.

"It's one of the side effects of being right all the time."

"I know," Elliot said with a smile. "I meant it as a compliment."

"I took it that way." And she had, surprisingly. She didn't feel nearly as defensive around Elliot as she had a week ago. In fact, she felt less defensive around Elliot than she did around anyone else these days. Maybe the difference stemmed from having no past or future. As Elliot pointed out, she didn't know who Kelly'd been before her dad's stroke, and she wouldn't be around long enough to hold any grudges.

Or maybe the power dynamic helped her feel safer. Elliot wasn't trying to horn in on her business. Kelly didn't have anything to prove to her. Elliot was short-term help on Kelly's terms—nothing threatening there.

Then again, maybe she just needed someone to talk to.

The last option scared her more than the others.

She hated to admit to being lonely. She was introverted by nature, but not a recluse. Tax season always meant letting go of things like church groups and the Rotary Club for a few months, but she'd never minded because she'd always worked with her dad. They talked more and shared meals, often debating new deductions or laughing about scattered clients. It might not have been a rollicking good time to most people, but this time of year generally brought an increased sense of purpose and connectivity. Maybe she just missed him and had turned to Elliot to fill the void. The thought made her uneasy.

"You can keep your stinky food at your desk unless a client comes in, then try to put it away."

"Wouldn't want to let them see the hired help eating anything, or they might think of me as human—wait, did you just call it, 'my desk'?"

Damn, she had. "Fine, it's your desk, but . . ." She didn't know what she intended to say after the "but," but there had to be a caveat, didn't there? She couldn't just give her a semi-permanent post without setting some limitations.

"But?" Elliot asked.

"Keep it neat, and don't leave confidential information out for people to see, and, and . . ." Elliot's green eyes danced with mirth as Kelly struggled to remain authoritative.

"Put my stinky food away when clients come in?" Elliot offered, her expression of amusement only amplifying her playful tone.

"Yes," Kelly said, struggling to remain frustrated.

"Hey, have you had lunch yet?"

She shook her head and didn't add that she hadn't had breakfast, either.

"I have more of this stinky food to share."

"Thanks, but no thanks."

Elliot laughed. "Let me guess. You're not big on trying new things?"

"I have an intern, don't I?"

"Fair enough," Elliot said, "but you have to admit the intern thing is really growing on you."

"I suppose you're doing pretty well," she admitted grudgingly. "Other than the food."

"Wow, that was almost a compliment."

"Don't let it go to your head," she grumbled, trying not to notice the little flutter in her chest at Elliot's broad smile.

"Why? Because you're afraid I'll realize you like me?"

Her chest tightened. "I don't like you or dislike you."

"You're completely neutral?"

"Absolutely. I don't even really know you." The last thing she needed was for Elliot to get cockier.

"I'm an open book. What do you want to know?"

"Nothing. I didn't mean I wanted to know you. Or that I didn't want to know you. I just—" How did Elliot always manage to take such a little thing and turn it into something more? "You're an intern. You do decent work. The end."

"And what about you? You're a CPA, you do decent work, the end?"

"Yes," Kelly said.

"But I'm also a student."

"Sure."

"And a woman."

"Obviously." She felt a little twinge in her stomach. She wished she could forget that particular fact, but no matter what clothes Elliot wore, they always showcased her physical form, and despite her androgynous style, her body had more than a few curves to mark that form as female.

"I'm also a lesbian."

"Not relevant."

"To you?"

"Not relevant to your work, and therefore not relevant to me."

"I can see where you'd see the situation as cut and dried, but for

59

me, it's not. The fact that I'm a woman, a gay woman, very much affects my work and how I view my place in the larger community."

She should walk away right now. She didn't need to get any deeper with Elliot. It was bad enough that she was warming up to her as an intern. She didn't need to know what lay behind those sea-glass green eyes, or what sparked the confidence she brought to every situation.

"I want to change the world. I want to make life better for the people who the current system either ignores or abuses."

"The system is neutral. The rules are the same for everyone."

"Are they?" Elliot asked what she clearly meant to be a rhetorical question.

"Of course."

"So you don't get extra deductions for being married? Or for having kids?"

"Of course you do."

"Then the system favors people who are married with kids. And guess who is more likely to be married with kids?" Elliot didn't wait for her to guess. "Straight people."

"Gay people can get married now," Kelly said, trying not to think about the ring on Beth's finger. "And have kids."

"They can now, but what about the people who lost spouses before the Supreme Court ruling for marriage equality, or those who don't believe in marriage? What about military benefits and pensions? What about single parents, or single people in general? You're single. Do you work any less than a man who has a wife and kids?"

"No, but—"

"And what about loopholes for large companies? Why does a woman who divorces an abusive husband now have to pay a higher tax rate while some multinational corporations pay nothing? And don't even get me started on the penal code. If a multimillionaire robs his employees and drives the company into the ground, he gets a golden parachute while the people he laid off get stuck paying more taxes than the people who caused the whole mess in the first place. Why should wrecking an entire company be less punishable than wrecking someone's car?"

Kelly waved off the barrage of comments. "None of that has anything to do with being a CPA. It's all politics."

"Politics and finance are inseparable. Just think about any issue on the modern political landscape, and you can easily follow the money trail right back to a straight white guy."

"My dad is a straight white guy," she snapped. "Blaming him for single mothers on financial aid is an insult to him and his life's work."

"It's not. It's not about any one individual. It's merely acknowledging that some types of people are more likely to know how to work the system to their advantage. Your dad was clearly successful. He got an education, he learned the tax system, and he used it to build a business. He didn't do anything wrong. Still you have to admit he could only do those things because he could afford to go to college in the first place, and because he had someone teach him how the system works, and because he had the support of a family or peers who helped him along the way. He didn't do anything alone."

"You don't know my dad." She practically spat, fully engaged now. "You know nothing about what kind of support he had or what he had to do to work within the system."

"Then tell me," Elliot said softly, the challenge in her voice replaced by genuine interest. "Help me understand."

Kelly clenched her jaw, fuming that she'd let Elliot get to this point. The whole conversation had gone way too far. She should've walked away as soon as things turned personal, but now she had to either defend her dad by revealing things she didn't want Elliot to know, or refuse and let her believe she'd won. She should choose the latter. What did it matter if Elliot thought less of her? She'd admitted she didn't know him. Elliot barely even knew her. And yet, loyalty demanded something, didn't it? "My dad was a single dad. His parents died before I was born. He raised me completely on his own while working full time, and he never once complained or asked for a handout."

"So do you think he should be denied a tax break given to married people? Was he any less valuable to society, or to you, without a wife by his side?"

Kelly folded her arms across her chest.

"And the business he built, does it matter any less to the people who depend on it than Proctor and Gamble or Chrysler do to the people who depend on them?"

"No."

"See what I mean?" Elliot asked triumphantly. "There are people working hard and raising families and building businesses all over the country, but the only people getting rewarded by our tax codes are the ones who fit the mold of what certain people value."

She couldn't disagree with the concepts, but something about the tone irked her. It reminded her of someone or something, and even if she couldn't think of who at the moment, the association wasn't a pleasant one. "So you just want to be a CPA so you can go around Robin Hooding? You're here to bend and break rules?"

"No, I want to be a CPA so I can learn the system, learn how to use it like the rich guys do. I want to learn every loophole, every unfair law, every trick of the trade the old boys use to keep their network in power. Then when I'm so far into their pyramid of wealth, I want to start tearing it down from the inside."

Rory.

Elliot sounded just like Rory. She even looked a little like her, too—tall and athletic with a swagger to match. No wonder she got on Kelly's nerves so badly. Elliot reminded her of everything she couldn't stand, of everything she'd lost . . . no.

She wouldn't go there.

Rory wasn't the problem, or at least not all of it, and Elliot wasn't Rory.

It was just their shared rhetoric that scared her. Talk of inequality and toppling the system threatened her last black-and-white refuge, the last place in her life where things felt fair and controlled. Elliot had no such issue as she forged on.

"As long as the same few people control all the wealth and hold all the positions of power, nothing will ever change. But if we get women and minorities and people raised in poverty into positions in Congress and tax policy centers and the IRS, we can begin rebuilding the system in our image instead of theirs."

"Don't include me in your, 'we.' I've no desire to be the king or queen of anything." She wouldn't get caught up in an impassioned speech, especially not one from one of Rory's student disciples. "I like the rules. I like order. I like helping my friends and neighbors make sense of their businesses, their finances, their responsibilities as American citizens, and while you're working in my office, I expect you to do the same."

"Fine. I understand," Elliot said, the passion in her voice replaced with disappointment.

"Good." Kelly turned back toward her office. Back to business, both literally and figuratively.

"One more thing though," Elliot called just before Kelly reached her office door.

"What's that?" she asked, determined to remain cool and distant.

"I was raised by a single parent, too," Elliot said, her smile smaller and more reflective than earlier, but no less sincere. "We have more in common than you think."

She shook her head. She wouldn't get caught up in the unsettling emotions the little connection inspired. She had nothing in common with Elliot, at least not anything that mattered.

ဆ ဆ ဆ

"Good morning, Mrs. Anthony," Elliot greeted the old woman as soon as she waddled through the door. She stood squat and hunched under the weight of a heavy down coat and multiple scarves.

"Good? It's negative fourteen windchill out there."

The weather conversation again. "Going to be like this for a few more days, I hear," she said, in her best impression of the farmers who came and went all day long. They all, every one of them, told her they hadn't seen a winter like this in decades. Too cold to snow, they all proclaimed. All the hassle of freezing temperatures with none of the water needed to hydrate the fields or raise the natural water table. She had learned to echo their clipped sentiments without ever mentioning global climate change. "Dryest February on record."

"Indeed," Mrs. Anthony agreed as she set about unbundling herself. First the zipper, then the sleeves of the fluffy blue coat, then the buttons on a heavy wool sweater she let hang open before starting on the scarf. Elliot watched in amusement as she held the end of the scarf still and turned her entire body in a circle. She fought the urge to offer help, because she didn't think she could prevent herself from giving one quick tug and sending Mrs. Anthony spinning around the waiting room like a dreidel. Instead, she folded her hands in her lap and waited until the pile of winter apparel was safely hung on the coatrack and out of reach before asking, "How can I help you today?"

Mrs. Anthony turned slowly as if really seeing her for the first time, and she didn't seem to like what she saw. The woman hooked one bony finger over the rim of her glasses and pulled them lower on her nose to give her a more thorough once-over. "You cannot help me with anything, except to get Miss Rolen for me."

"I would love to, trust me," Elliot said with exaggerated sweetness. "But Ms. Rolen is not in yet this morning."

She made a show of looking at her rose-gold wristwatch. "It's nine o'clock on a weekday. She's supposed to open at eight."

"The office does open at eight, which is why I'm here, but Ms. Rolen had some other business to attend to."

"When will she return?"

"I expect her in this morning, but I don't know what time." She never knew what time to expect Kelly's arrival or departure, and if she had to guess, Kelly didn't know, either. Sometimes Elliot would come to work and find Kelly had already been there for hours. Other times she'd arrive to an empty office only to find the coffee already brewed. The same went for evenings as well. Sometimes Kelly would run out for no apparent reason. Other times she'd still be there at eight o'clock at night. She never offered any information about her whereabouts, and Elliot had stopped asking. She suspected Kelly's father wasn't improving, only because Kelly had finally relented and given her a key so she could open the office without her. She got the sense that handing over even that little bit of control wounded Kelly, so she reasoned she wouldn't have done so unless she felt like their situation would continue for at least a while.

"I'll wait then," Mrs. Anthony said with a heavy sigh to make certain Elliot understood the extent to which she felt put upon.

"Really, Mrs. Anthony, I'll gladly help you with anything I can. I'm familiar with your tax file and—"

She bristled. "I don't want you in my financial information, young . . . lady."

The last word twisted the old woman's mouth the same way it twisted Elliot's chest. She knew "lady" was still a term of respect in some situations, but this clearly wasn't one of them. "Well, you had me fill out your forms when you came in last time."

"I thought you were a receptionist. Had I known Miss Rolen intended to leave you in charge of her business on a regular basis, I would've taken my taxes elsewhere."

"I assure you, I'm more than qualified to input simple returns, and Ms. Rolen personally checks all the work I do." As in checks and double-checks and sometimes triple-checks. She couldn't turn around without finding Kelly looking over her shoulder. Some days it felt as though she was still looking for an excuse to fire Elliot on the spot. She liked the challenge though, or she liked the experience it gave her toward bigger challenges. Even the absence of complaint had come to feel like a compliment of sorts, but earning Kelly's grudging respect obviously meant nothing to Mrs. Anthony, who still looked at her like something she might have to wipe off her shoe. "In fact, I think all you need now is to sign a few forms, and we'll file your return."

"Yes, I know. I received a call to that effect."

"Then, why don't I pull the file for you so you can be on your way? I wouldn't want to inconvenience you by making you wait in my presence."

"See, there's the kind of sass I expect from you people."

Her face flamed. "You people?"

"I know what you are. You people always flaunt your lifestyle in defiance of God's will. I am *shocked* a Christian woman like Kelly Rolen would allow homosexuality to defile her father's business."

"Excuse me?" Kelly stepped out of the back hallway, causing both of them to jump. How had she gotten in without either of them hearing? And how long had she been there?

Elliot straightened her shoulders and lifted her chin. "Good morning, Kelly. Mrs. Anthony was just asking for you."

"I heard," Kelly said, her eyes darker than usual. "I also heard her make some assertions about your lifestyle and my father's business."

"It's unpleasant," Mrs. Anthony sniffed, "but women like us have a Christian duty to point out Satan wherever he may hide."

Elliot stifled a gasp as the comment hit her in the face. Then she thought about shouting, "Boo," like the devil popping out from behind her desk. She didn't think the other two women would find the image amusing, but if she didn't laugh she would no doubt cry.

"Miss Garza is my intern. She works in my office, and I have been charged with teaching her this business. She is in my care and under my supervision. I personally approve any return she processes. She wouldn't be here if she hadn't proven herself capable of doing the work," Kelly said evenly.

Whoa, that was a real compliment with no "but" behind it. Kelly found her capable. She would've felt almost gleeful if not for the hint of danger still hovering over the situation. Kelly had yet to raise her voice, but her tone held an edge she'd never heard before, not even in their most tense moments with one another.

"It's not her work I find issue with," Mrs. Anthony said.

"Then you find no issue in anything having to do with my office. What Elliot does in her private time is her business."

"It's not her private time if she shows up to work dressed like *that*." She flicked one hand in Elliot's general direction as if to make her point.

Elliot looked down at her gray slacks and sweater over a deep turquoise button-up shirt and a silver tie tucked in just below a perfectly executed Windsor knot. Aside from the tie it was a pretty dressed-down look for her. And yet Mrs. Anthony wouldn't look past the tie, or maybe she would peg her for gay even in a light pink silk skirt like the one Kelly wore today.

She could never pull off the business-shark-with-a-subtle-hint-of-femininity look. Kelly, on the other hand, rocked the buttoned-up businesswoman attire. Today she wore low pumps with a navy skirt that hugged her hips and gave just a little flare at her knees. The look was totally inappropriate for minus fourteen degrees, but she guessed Kelly had her reasons for choosing it. She seemed to always have a reason for everything.

"In my office, Elliot is expected to be professional. She's expected to be proficient. She's expected to do her work right and treat people with respect. Her job description doesn't come with a fashion clause," Kelly said, and Elliot stifled the desire to cheer for her and for feminism in general.

Mrs. Anthony was far from cheering though. "It's a very slippery slope, my dear. You've seen yourself what happens when people of her persuasion are allowed to thrive around normal women. You know what happened to poor Beth Deveroux when Rory St. James returned to town."

Elliot sprung from her chair ready to fight, but even in her knee-jerk reaction she wasn't fast enough to get past Kelly, who simultaneously stiff-armed her and leaned close to Mrs. Anthony. "We're done here."

Mrs. Anthony blinked in shock. "Excuse me?"

"Elliot, get Mrs. Anthony's file. All of it." Her voice was so low and cold Elliot shook off a shiver as she quickly shuffled through a stack of processed returns. Her fingers fumbled through a few tabs before she caught hold of the one she wanted, but she willed her hand not to tremble as she placed the entire folder in Kelly's outstretched hand.

"Take this with you and don't come back."

Mrs. Anthony's gray eyes were wide and she stuttered. "You cannot be, I am a longtime client, and your father, your father would never—"

"My father is not here," Kelly said, her voice gravelly with the emotions she always kept in check. "I am, and I don't want to see you in my business ever again."

Elliot noticed that for the first time Kelly referred to Rolen and Rolen as her business, not the family business or her father's business. This anger and the action it inspired were hers and hers alone. She had come to Elliot's defense, and to Beth's with even greater fervor. And damn if she didn't inspire something powerful in the process.

Kelly's dark eyes burned with a passion she'd never seen there before, and her normally fair skin flushed pink. Her strong, graceful hands didn't shake, but her knuckles went white where she gripped the thick file that held a lifetime's worth of shared work. This was no easy break, and yet Kelly made it swiftly and soundly. Elliot felt a shiver of something powerful race up her spine.

Mrs. Anthony finally snatched up the file and gathered her winter coats without bothering to put them on before storming out of the door.

Elliot flopped back into her chair with a heavy sigh, but Kelly remained standing, her gaze fixed on the exit Mrs. Anthony had fled through. The silence stretched between them, and she wondered if Kelly's pulse pounded through her ears the way hers did. She didn't move, she didn't speak, she just stood and stared.

"Holy shit," Elliot finally said.

"Watch your mouth. This is still a place of business."

"Okay, but you just threw her out."

She nodded. "I did."

"Hasn't she come here like, forever?"

"She has. Now she'll go elsewhere."

"She'll probably go all over town."

Kelly covered her face with her hands. "Oh God."

"Are you okay?"

"Yes," she said, dropping her hands and taking a deep breath. "Are you?"

"Yes. I'm fine." She bent the truth a little for Kelly's sake. "I'm sorry I cost you a client."

"You didn't. You handled that as well as anyone could."

Another compliment she would examine later, but right now her main concern was how pale Kelly looked as her adrenaline faded. "Why don't you sit down while I get you some coffee?"

Kelly set her jaw like she might argue, but she either didn't have the strength or the inclination. "Thank you."

"No, thank you," Elliot said, pouring a mug of steaming coffee, black. As black as Kelly's hair, as black as her mood. "You didn't have to do that for me."

"I didn't," Kelly said as she took the mug and inhaled the steam. "Don't get a big head."

"You didn't do it for me?" Elliot replayed the incident. Kelly had clearly been annoyed from the moment she entered the conversation.

Elliot had watched the anger tighten her muscles and color her complexion with each passing exchange, but she hadn't snapped until Mrs. Anthony had insulted Beth and Rory. Elliot had seen nothing but red in that moment, so she'd assumed Kelly had put herself between them in order to protect her, but maybe she'd had her own reasons.

Beth. That unexpected and unexplained connection again. She rolled the idea over in her mind again, and said almost to herself, "You were protecting Beth."

"Stop it," Kelly ordered, her voice once again low and dangerous. "Don't you go telling her about this. What happens here is confidential. Do you understand?"

She didn't really think tax law extended to homophobic comments by rude clients, but she wouldn't argue with her, not now. "I understand, but won't word get out?"

Kelly hung her head. "I can't control what other people say. I cannot control the rumor mill. I cannot control much of anything about other people."

The comment revealed a lot about her mental state, and the ache returned to Elliot's chest. She went from being awed by her power and fortitude to feeling an overwhelming urge to protect her fragility. "It's okay. You handled the situation well. You did the right thing."

"I did what I had to do. No one can treat my staff or talk about my business like she did." Kelly stood. "If she wants to yell at a gay intern, she needs to get one of her own."

"Um, thank you?" Elliot asked, not sure what to make of the comment.

"Don't thank me any more. Just get back to work."

She didn't wait for a response before heading back to her office, leaving Elliot to wonder once again what in the hell had just happened.

Chapter Seven

Kelly rounded the now familiar corners of the Darlington hospital hall-ways. Her dad had been in the same room for over two weeks now. Every time she visited, they hinted at the possibility of moving him to a rehab floor if only he could do one more thing, but that one thing always seemed to change. He'd be awake more but unable to speak, or he'd speak well for a day only to have another seizure. Then once he went three days without any complications he had a sudden and dangerous drop in blood pressure. There seemed to be some new and not easily explained complication every few days. It wasn't that he was getting better or worse so much as a mixture of both at the same time, so while she entered the same room twice a day every day, she had no idea what version of her father she might find in the bed before her.

Taking a deep breath outside his cracked-open door, she gently peeked in. She'd expected to find him asleep since he slept a lot these days, but this evening he was sitting up, or at least his bed had been propped up to hold him in a seated position. He wore a new set of blue pajamas she'd dropped off earlier, and his hair had been combed. Most surprising was the half smile on his face. While it wasn't a full, toothy grin, the left side of his mouth had visibly quirked up as he looked at someone opposite him. Kelly pushed the door open all the way to see Beth sitting in a chair near the end of his bed.

Her heart couldn't seem to decide if it should sink or soar. The joy she felt at seeing her father better than he had been in days was tempered by the realization that Beth had been the one to spark his smile. She couldn't stop the pang of pain or the rush of regret washing through her. Her father had always liked Beth. What would he have said if—

"Hey, Kel." Beth turned to face her. "I was just telling your dad how handsome he looks in blue. I may have even suggested that all the nurses would fight over which one of them got to comb his hair next time. I've always been so jealous of the dark hair that runs in your gene pool."

"And I've always been envious of your curls," Kelly said. Maybe envious wasn't the right word, but she had always admired them on her.

"Isn't that the way it always goes? Girls with straight hair want curls, and the girls with curls want silky-smooth locks." Beth laughed.

God, how she missed that sound. She'd come in bracing herself for her father's condition, but she hadn't been prepared for the wave of loneliness that accompanied the sound of Beth's voice. It always surprised her how she felt so much more alone in Beth's presence than she ever let herself feel while actually alone.

"How you feeling today?" she asked her father in an attempt to focus on something, anything other than the emotions Beth sparked.

He nodded and held up his left thumb.

"Good." She noted he hadn't produced the word but had found the motor skills to control his hand. She picked up the chart from the end of his bed and scanned the notes there. She'd come to understand every notation, every abbreviation, and every number recorded. What she didn't know was what they told her about the future, or if they even could. She wanted answers so desperately, something to cling to, something conclusive to at least say they were going in the right direction. At least her father's progress got regularly tested and charted. The same couldn't be said for her own life.

It had been almost three years since Beth had sat on her couch and asked her how she saw their future. Three years since she'd lashed out instead of stepping up. Three years since Beth had walked out of her door, but not quite out of her life. What did she have to show for those three years? She had the same job, the same fears, the same closeted existence, only now she faced them alone. No one to hold at night, no one to call in the middle of the day, no stolen touches, no gentle words whispered, no one's eyes to meet over shared meals. Three years of nothing and nobody.

No.

Not nothing.

She looked away from the chart and at her dad. Was he nothing? Had he built nothing? He made his own choices, and he made a good life for them. She could do a lot worse in life than follow his example.

He yawned lopsidedly out of the left side of his mouth.

"Oh no, I've worn you out with all my gabbing," Beth said. "Or bored you to sleep more like it."

He shook his head slowly and managed to squeak out the word, "No."

Kelly smiled in spite of her inner musings, but it was Beth who leaned forward and patted his hand. "You're such a charmer, but you should get some rest and store up that energy for the pretty night nurse who comes on shift in an hour."

He smiled again, and Kelly watched his fingers tighten around Beth's hand. Did he feel the cold metal of her ring? Did he understand what it meant for Beth? Could he possibly understand what it meant for his own daughter?

"Dad, I'm going to walk Beth out," she said. "I'll be back in a minute, okay?"

He nodded and gave a little wave.

"He seems to be improving," Beth said as they stepped out into the hallway.

Kelly closed the door behind her. "It's a lot of ups and downs. We'd hoped to transfer him to a rehab facility by now, but yes, he seems to be having a good day."

"And what about you?" Beth asked. "How was your day?"

The muscles in her shoulders tightened to hard knots. "Don't ask questions you already know the answers to."

Beth smiled. "I don't know the answers. I've heard rumors, but I don't know what happened for sure, and I definitely don't know how you feel."

"An old woman behaved inappropriately in my business. She insinuated some unflattering things about an employee and my faith."

"And?"

"And you," Kelly said the word on a quick rush of breath, like ripping off a Band-Aid. "So I informed her she could take her business elsewhere from now on."

"You know she's an awful human being, right?"

She did know. She'd known it forever and should've said so years ago. Another regret.

"I have to ask though," Beth said hesitantly, "was this Elliot's fault?"

"No," Kelly said emphatically, unless Elliot could be blamed for merely existing in the world, and even she wouldn't go that far.

"She can be a bit . . ." Beth seemed to struggle for the right word.

"Defiant?" Kelly suggested. "Stubborn? Cocky? Assertive?"

Beth laughed. "So you noticed that, huh?"

"Yeah." Kelly smiled despite her best efforts not to.

"But she's also smart, right?"

"Yes."

"And helpful?"

"Yes."

"And you're glad to have her there?" Beth asked hopefully.

Kelly rolled her eyes. "Most days."

"Fair enough," Beth said. Brushing her hand down Kelly's arm, she added, "I only want what's best for you."

She shook off the touch. "I'm fine."

"I know you are. I just worried after the first day when you called and asked for her address that you intended to fire her, and then when you didn't I thought maybe things were going okay. Until today."

"You started having second thoughts about Elliot because I told Mrs. Anthony she could have someone else do her taxes from now on?"

"It's more than that, Kel," Beth said softly. "I know how . . . private you are. Elliot's smart and honorable, and she's got a good heart. I know she'd never hurt you on purpose, but she doesn't always think before she speaks. If she accidentally put you in danger, I'd never forgive myself."

"She doesn't know," Kelly said softly, then looked over her shoulder around the empty sterile hallway.

"She's astute." Beth pushed. "She's intuitive."

"She thinks I'm a homophobe." Kelly almost laughed. "Or she did, until today, and maybe she still does on some level. I don't know. I didn't exactly raise a rainbow flag over the office."

"But what did you tell her? I mean about Mrs. Anthony?"

"I told her that if Mrs. Anthony wanted to yell at a gay intern, she should get one of her own."

This time Beth's shot of laugher bounced loudly off the cold tile and echoed down the hallway. "You've got a way with words, Kelly. Sometimes you and Rory are more alike than either of you would care to admit in that area."

Kelly stiffened. "I need to get back to my dad."

Beth sighed. "I'm sorry."

"There's nothing to apologize for."

"It was an insensitive comment."

"No." She shook her head. "You're never insensitive."

"Not on purpose, but I never have been able to keep myself from saying the thing that hurts you."

"You didn't hurt me," she lied, even though Beth knew the truth. The lie had never been for Beth's sake.

"Okay." Beth played along. "But since you're already starting to shut me out again, could you at least answer a question I've been afraid to ask for a while now?"

"Beth . . ." she warned, to no avail.

"I worry about you being so alone right now."

"Please don't," she whispered.

"Is there, has there been anyone else?"

She clenched her jaw and shook her head.

Beth's blue eyes shimmered. "Not at all?"

"I can't do this," she snapped. "I have to go check on my dad." Beth reached for her, but she stepped away. "Goodnight, Beth." This time she didn't wait for her to walk away. She wouldn't watch her go again. She pushed through the door to her father's room and quickly closed it behind her. She fastened a fake smile on her face, but the effort was in vain. Her father had already fallen asleep.

She sank into the chair beside him and blinked back her tears.

Anger, frustration, helplessness, and loneliness bubbled up like bile. She couldn't go on like this. She knew she was headed for a breakdown or a breaking point, but she couldn't stop herself. She didn't know how. She didn't have the strength. She didn't have anyone or anything left to turn to. Every part of her life had turned and twisted in the tumult. Darkness closed in around her again. She could lie down, like her father, say she couldn't go on and submit to defeat. She eyed him, his normally strong features hollow but serene. What would he say to her now?

He'd tell her to buck up. He'd tell her not to be dramatic. He'd tell her to take care of business and let the rest of it go. The emotions, the what-ifs, the petty concerns of other people never meant anything to him. He was as steady as a rock, as unfailing as her North Star. She never saw him falter, and while she'd always taken comfort in his example before, now she found it daunting.

She didn't have his fortitude. She never had, no matter how hard she'd tried, although she'd never lacked his drive. Surrender might feel good for a moment, but how could she ever live with his disappointment, or her own? She couldn't give up. She couldn't give in. She might not be calm, she might not even be capable, but she wouldn't quit. She rose and rubbed her eyes. Frayed nerves and exhaustion be damned, she had to go on.

She had to get back to work.

သာ သာ သာ

Elliot glanced at her watch again. Nine o'clock was kind of early on Friday night to be at the bars. The college PRIDE students were all going to St. Louis, and the general student population didn't venture out until closer to ten. She probably should've waited, but she'd promised to pick up some hours Saturday morning. She had a hard enough time waking up at the ass-crack of dawn without adding a late night and a hangover to the mix. She could've gotten some Fireball Whisky from the liquor store and taken it back to her apartment. At least then she wouldn't have to brave the cold, but despite her contrary nature, she actually sort of believed the social edicts about not drinking alone.

75

Then again, she probably should've given more credence to the gay community edicts about not going to local bars alone, too.

She tried not to make eye contact with anyone except the bartender as she signaled for a second glass of Coke laced with a heavy dose of Fireball. One more and then she'd go. It wasn't like there was anything going on here anyway. Aside from a few rednecks playing pool, the place was dead. No one talked to her or even seemed to notice her existence, and as much as she'd never been a wilting wallflower, sometimes being in a place where nobody knew your name offered a little safety.

She should've gone over to Rory and Beth's house. They never turned her away, which was way more than most professors would offer, but they weren't peers. She wasn't really close with many of the undergraduates, either. Since she came to school a year late, she'd always been older than most of her classmates to begin with, and now, in the latter half of her fifth year, even most of the other gays she'd started with had graduated and gone. She was left behind, limboing in the middle. Too old to be a college kid, too young to be a professor. Still, third-wheeling with Rory and Beth beat sadly looking over her shoulder in a dimly lit bar.

"Here you go." The bartender slid a glass down the bar and she caught it, gently enough to keep the whisky from sloshing out.

"Thanks." She stared at the TV overhead as college basketball flashed brightly on the screen. She didn't care about either of the teams playing, and she would've rather watched a women's matchup, but at least the game gave her a semblance of distraction while she thought more about Beth and Rory. More accurately, she wondered about their connection to Kelly—which meant she thought mostly about Kelly.

She tried not to. She acted like she didn't care, and if anyone had actually asked her what happened at work today, she would've shrugged and said she didn't know. She would've said this town was crazy and her boss was odd. All true statements. And yet none of them scratched the surface of what she really thought. She couldn't even begin to sort through her emotions, much less verbalize them.

She swung wildly from anger and the desire for vindication to confusion. She'd been attacked for being gay. Kelly had defended her as a good worker. Then she'd gone a step further and kicked the hateful biddy out into the cold, but not quite on her account, and not quite because of the old woman's homophobia. It didn't add up. Maybe if you rounded out the pieces the sum total looked the same, but she didn't round numbers. She didn't make estimations. She suspected multiple unknown variables had come into play, but she couldn't solve them if she didn't know the full equation. Beth factored in. Mrs. Anthony had made the connection between Beth and Kelly, and Beth and Rory, but it'd all happened so fast she wasn't sure she remembered exactly what the woman had said, much less understood what she'd implied.

"Hey, I paid for next game," one of the rednecks in the corner called out.

"You paid for the game, not me," a woman answered sharply, and Elliot's shoulders tensed.

She looked to the bartender, who shook his head and found something to clean at the other end of the bar. She listened more closely now, but couldn't make out any more of the conversation over the low din of the basketball game on TV and some country music party song on the jukebox.

She didn't need to turn around. She didn't need to get involved. There was no problem. Or at least that's what she told herself. She'd had a bad enough day without getting sucked into some hetero townie mating ritual.

Not that her day really should've been that bad. She swallowed another big swig of her drink. The burn of the cinnamon and whisky warmed her face, and masked the mix of shame and anger that welled up every time she tried to replay the confrontation. Everything had happened so fast, and she had gone from being a key player to a bystander. They'd practically talked about her as if she wasn't in the room, but then all of a sudden it didn't feel like they were talking about her at all anymore.

If only Kelly would ever just fucking talk to her like a person. She always snapped or ran, or snapped then ran. Occasionally she ran, then came back and snapped some more. Elliot should've hated her.

She should've been angry about her unrealistic standards and her unwillingness to give a freaking compliment or have a normal, civil, casual conversation. Why did everything have to feel like a cryptic inquisition or a stupid macho pissing contest?

A woman pushed up to the bar next to her. She purposefully didn't look up, but she could tell it was a woman. Women smelled different, they took up space differently, they gave off a different vibe. She'd taken enough women's studies classes to understand the power of socialization, but she'd also been through enough tense situations to recognize someone who wanted to be left alone. She was generally pretty good at reading people. Why the hell couldn't she make sense of Kelly?

Why couldn't Kelly just say, "Mrs. Anthony was out of line to judge you and Beth and Rory that way"? Why couldn't she just say what made her mad enough to throw the woman out? She hadn't had any trouble talking to Mrs. Anthony. And why the shitty, gay intern comment? She downed the last of the drink quickly, hoping to lie to herself about the heat spreading through her now. Liquor and shame both burned the same way in a dark bar.

Get her own gay intern. What the fuck? She didn't even try to hide her anger from herself anymore. What she worked to conceal now was her hurt. She'd done a good enough job of that at the office, not that Kelly had stuck around long enough to notice how much her comment stung. She probably wouldn't have cared even if she did notice. Apparently all her comments about Elliot being competent and good at her job weren't actually personal at all. Elliot was just a thing to claim ownership of. A gay intern was akin to a good computer program, not something—someone—with feelings. She hadn't come to the defense of her friend or her colleague or even a valued employee. She wouldn't have cared if Mrs. Anthony had attacked someone somewhere else for being gay. She probably wouldn't have minded if she'd attacked Elliot anywhere other than the office. She had merely defended what was hers.

"Hey," a man's voice close by startled her. "I asked you nicely."

"And I told you 'no' nicely," the woman next to her replied coolly.

"Why? You got a boyfriend?"

"No, I just—"

"You're just a dyke?"

"Are you fucking kidding me?" Elliot asked.

"What?" the man asked, stepping closer to her now.

Uh-oh, had she made that last comment in her out-loud voice? "I wasn't talking to you."

"And I wasn't talking to you."

"Good." Elliot nodded emphatically, and the room tilted just a little bit before everything righted itself again. Except for the little whisper that called her a coward.

Mr. Redneck pushed closer to the bar, right between her and the woman he'd returned his focus to. He smelled of chewing tobacco, a scent she'd never recognized until moving to Darlington and still couldn't stomach even after years here.

"Why do you come into a bar alone on a Friday night if you aren't looking to get hit on?" he asked. It took Elliot a second to remember he wasn't talking to her.

"I'm just waiting for some friends."

Neither Elliot nor Mr. Redneck bought that excuse, but Elliot didn't think he deserved an explanation in the first place. He apparently disagreed.

"I offered to buy you drink," he said, the frustration boiling behind his patronizing tone.

"And I said, 'no thank you.'"

"Then you came over to the bar to prove you do want a drink, just not from me?"

"Why can't you leave me alone?"

"Why do you have to be such a bitch?"

"All right," Elliot said, apparently out loud, but she didn't care this time. She'd had enough of bullies for one day. "She asked you nicely to leave."

"I'm not talking to you," the guy said sharply.

"Yeah, but you're not listening to her either."

He turned slowly so he towered over her on her stool. "This is none of your business."

If one more person tells me something isn't my business . . .

She pushed back the stool and rose. Her height wasn't as high as his but it was enough to make him lean back and look her over for the first time. His mean little eyes were set close enough together to make her wonder how far up his family tree the first cousins had married, but he wasn't dumb enough not to peg her dark jeans and white men's oxford shirt under a chocolate brown sweater as out of place.

"Who the fuck are you?"

"I'm Elliot," she extended a hand, which he sneered at until she withdrew it. "Okay, great to meet you, Captain Caveman. Now would you mind leaving us alone?"

"Us?" He turned back to the young woman he'd initially been harassing. This time he pressed hard into her personal space, and while Elliot couldn't see his expression, she saw the woman shrink away in fear. "Now you're here with this dyke? I knew it. You are a carpet muncher."

"Hey," Elliot shouted. "Back off."

He didn't turn around. He wouldn't even acknowledge her. Well, fuck that. She wouldn't be ignored. She'd had enough of being cut out and written off and talked about like she didn't really exist. She wouldn't give into the cowardice this time. She'd prove herself to everyone, and by everyone she mostly meant herself. She was here, and she was pissed, and she was damn well going to be heard.

"I'm talking to you, you worthless, brain-dead, cocknozzle."

Everyone looked up at her now. The woman, the caveman, even the bartender turned around.

"I get it. I really do. You smell like horseshit. Your jeans are so tight they're giving you a moose knuckle and showing off your pencil dick." She couldn't have stopped the tide of pent-up anger even if she'd wanted to. "You're about as attractive as the farm animals you're probably used to fucking, so I get how calling women 'dykes' makes you feel better than being faced with that insurmountable list of your shortcomings."

His face turned so red she half expected to see fire shoot out of his ears.

"But if you want to call someone a name, you can point all your paramecium-brained reasoning over here because I'm the dyke. She's just out of your fucking league."

He clenched his fists and literally seethed through his tightly clenched teeth, but instead of lashing out at her, he hauled off and grabbed the other woman by her upper arm.

Oh hell no, laying hands on a woman wasn't just a no-no. It made Elliot's vision flash red. She was on his back before she'd thought anything through. Thankfully the bartender had finally heard enough as well, and he came over the bar in a hurry. For a second, all four people in the bar were locked together in a mass of bodies and tight fists before the bartender managed to pry the caveman off of the woman. Elliot, however, was on her own as the guy shook his shoulder violently and threw up his arm. His elbow caught Elliot right above her eye and sent her sprawling. She grasped fruitlessly first for the bar then for her stool before hitting the ground so hard all the air left her lungs in one guttural oomph.

"Get outta here," the bartender shouted at the caveman, "before I call the cops."

The big oaf screwed up his face and stomped his foot like a child about to throw a tantrum before he shouted, "Fuck you" and stormed out of the bar, slamming the door as he went.

"God, what's wrong with you?" the woman asked with a heavy sigh.

"Me?" Elliot asked when she could breathe again. "You're welcome."

"You could've got us both killed," she said, shaking her head so that her blond hair fell over her shoulders.

Elliot pushed up onto her knees and grabbed onto the stool before the throbbing over her eyes and the spinning of the room caused her to reevaluate her life choices.

"I didn't need your help," the woman continued.

"Yeah, that's totally the sense I got." She pulled herself upright. "What with him calling you a dyke and shaking the shit out of you."

"He didn't do any of that until you got involved."

Was that true? Everything felt so fuzzy now. She wasn't the first person to suggest Elliot's temper caused situations to escalate quickly. "I just don't like bullies picking on people."

"Yeah, well, it wasn't really any of your business."

She threw her head back and almost fell over again. She had to get out of there. As soon as she stopped spinning she intended to bolt.

"Hey, are you okay?" the bartender asked.

"Yeah. Just give me a minute."

"You're bleeding," the woman said.

"Don't worry. You can't catch my gay that way."

The bartender and the woman exchanged an awkward glance but said nothing. They couldn't even look at her. They didn't want her there. No one wanted her there, but no one had the balls to say so. At least the big hairy caveman had been honest about his feelings. She almost preferred his venom to these people's false politeness. At least people like him and Mrs. Anthony gave her something to rail against, some sort of legitimate outlet for her anger, but if she started screaming at people in bars who ignored her existence, they'd all think her crazy. Hell, maybe she was crazy. She certainly felt unstable right then in more ways than one.

Slapping a ten-dollar bill on the bar, she realized she'd way over-paid for her drink, but she didn't want to wait for change. Change didn't come nearly fast enough in places like this, and the only way to save herself was to get the hell out of there.

∽ ∽ ∽

Kelly had finished only two tax returns in the last two hours. Not a terrible rate, for a rookie, or someone with time to kill, but she wasn't new to the job, and she wasn't anywhere near on schedule. She should've flown through returns at this stage in tax season, but she couldn't get any momentum going. Between trips to the hospital and checking Elliot's returns, she worked fourteen hours a day to do less than she should've accomplished in ten.

Yeah, blame Elliot, she thought. Blame her dad. Blame anyone and anything other than Beth. Beth with her impromptu visits and her soft touch and questions she had no right to ask. No, she couldn't go there. She couldn't let the anger well up again. Anger felt safe, and maybe it offered a relief when she was strong, but she couldn't trust herself to stop there anymore. Anger was a gateway emotion. It opened the door to sadness and fear and regret. She had more than enough to contend with this tax season. She didn't need to reexamine choices she couldn't unmake. She couldn't give in to distractions, not emotional ones. Once she wandered down that dark path, she might not find her way back.

She scanned the brokerage statement in front of her. Black and white. Clear lines. Neat rows and columns. The tangible, the concrete, the formulaic. She had to hold on to the only thing helping her maintain control, but a sound pulled her attention away once again.

She listened carefully. Something or someone shuffled the gravel near the back door. Please be a raccoon, she thought, but a key in the lock blew a pretty big hole in that hope. She looked at the clock. 10:15. Her chest ached.

Beth.

She took a deep breath and tried to compose herself as the heavy metal door swung open. It took a few seconds for the cloud of frozen air to snake its tendrils into the open door of her office. How long before they reached her heart?

Clearing her throat and trying to sound more perturbed than anxious, she called out, "It's awfully late for you to be out in the weather, Beth."

"Shit." The startled voice definitely didn't belong to Beth. "Kelly?"

"Elliot?"

"What are you still doing here?"

"What are *you* doing here?" she asked, perhaps a bit more sharply than she intended, but the emotional whiplash knocked her off guard and undercut her determination to stay calm. Turned out the only thing more unsettling than an unexpected visit from Beth was preparing for Beth, only to actually find someone else. Oh God, she'd said Beth's name, acted like she expected her. What kind of tone had she used? Had Elliot noticed, or had she been equally startled by the unexpected exchange?

"I was out," Elliot muttered, still standing outside the cone of light from her office. "And I needed to, um, use the bathroom."

"Oh, okay." Except the explanation didn't make sense. "Out where?"

"Out. Just out getting a drink."

One of the bars near the square, no doubt. She sighed. She didn't have it in her to care about Elliot's social drinking habits, but why not use the bathroom at the bar instead of walking all the way over here, interrupting her work, and startling her into feeling things she didn't have to feel? Annoyance reigned at the forefront of her emotions once more. "Elliot, I don't think it's appropriate for you to come here late at night, especially if you've been drinking."

"Yeah, you're right. I'm sorry. I'll go," she said from outside the doorway.

Kelly's suspicions piqued. She'd never known Elliot to agree with her so easily. She'd been contrary since the moment they met and argued over much less. Had she come around to being more compliant? Or was she looking for an easy out? And did it matter? She should let her go and get back to work, and yet, from the sound of her soft breathing, she hadn't left yet. "Elliot?"

"I didn't mean to interrupt. I'll go."

"Wait a second." She closed the folder on her desk with an exaggerated exhale. "Come here."

"What do you need?" Elliot asked from the hallway.

"Nothing, just stop lurking in the shadows."

"Why?" Elliot's voice sounded almost strangled.

"What do you mean 'why'? It's creepy. Are you high?"

Elliot laughed, a more normal sound from her, and Kelly's shoulders relaxed. "I'm not high. Are you?"

"Me? Why would I be high?"

"I don't know. You're working at ten on a Friday night when any normal person would be exhausted after the day we had."

"So what, you think I'm on speed?"

"No one does speed anymore," she snorted, then added, "I thought you might be on meth, though."

"Oh for goodness sake, do I look like I'm on meth?"

Elliot peeked her head into the open doorway, but before she could offer an assessment, Kelly gasped. A dark rivulet of blood ran down from her eyebrow around her almost incandescent green eye. The contrast of such bright color only made her pale skin and lips appear even more pallid under the florescent light. "You're bleeding."

Elliot shrugged. "I thought so."

"You thought so?" Kelly asked incredulously. "That's all you have to say?"

Elliot shrugged again.

Sure, now she had no comeback. The one time Kelly actually wanted to hear one of her flip explanations, Elliot offered no smart response. The silence made Kelly wonder how much blood she'd lost, and that thought made her stomach lurch. She couldn't take more loss tonight.

Springing into action, she practically vaulted from behind her desk and crossed the hallway in two quick strides, grabbing Elliot's hand as she went. She pulled her into the bathroom and flipped on the lights. Both of them winced at the onslaught from the overhead bulb, but Kelly recovered and rummaged through a small cabinet for the first aid kit.

"Sit," she ordered, nodding to the toilet seat, and Elliot, for the first time ever, obeyed without so much as an eye-roll. She must feel bad. Maybe she had a concussion. Damn it, if she had to go back to that hospital tonight, she would have a nervous breakdown. "No," she mumbled to herself as she found the metal box holding her first aid supplies. "No, you won't. Everything's fine. You have this under control."

"What?" Elliot asked.

"Nothing. Just relax." She opened the box and pulled out a wash-cloth before soaking it in hot water. "Look up."

Elliot complied, shedding her dark chocolate coat before closing her eyes and angling her face toward the ceiling. God, she was beautiful. Kelly shook her head. That was not the kind of distraction she needed. She didn't need to think about her flawless skin or the thick shock of auburn hair across her forehead.

Focus.

Kelly cupped Elliot's chin firmly in one hand to hold her in place and then dabbed the warm washcloth against her bloodstained skin. She started down along the collar of her blue oxford shirt, her fingers brushing back the fabric from her neck. Working slowly, she inched up along the square line of her jaw and over the smooth plane of her cheek. Stopping to rinse the rag, she tried not to think about the amount of red-tinged water spinning down the drain or the sight of Elliot's blood on her own hands.

"Thank you," Elliot whispered, her voice startling in the previously quiet confines of the small space.

Kelly jumped, then internally chastised herself. She had to pull it together. Her nerves were too frayed. She needed to stay busy and not overthink anything. "Do you want to tell me what happened?"

"It was stupid."

"Things that leave you bleeding from the head usually are."

The corners of Elliot's mouth quirked up. "I got into an argument."

Her stomach clenched, but she kept her tone deliberately cool. "With whom?"

"Cowboy Caveman," Elliot muttered, then flinched as Kelly dabbed the washcloth nearer to the cut.

She pressed the rag gently directly to the wound now. It wasn't very wide. She'd expected worse, given how much blood she'd wiped away, but she couldn't tell how deep it went. She focused more on the gash than the story Elliot wove beneath her. "And Cowboy Caveman is what? A cartoon?"

"More like a caricature of the Midwestern American male."

"You got punched by a stereotype?"

"He didn't punch me. He elbowed me in the face."

She sucked in a sharp breath. "A man, an actual man, struck you?"

"Yeah. Did you think I got bloodied up while shadow boxing?"

"I thought you were drunk. I thought you were speaking metaphorically, or I don't know, but I didn't think a man would just hit a woman. I mean, I know it happens, but not out in the open, not in a bar fight, I am . . . I am . . ." She fought a wave of nausea at the thought of someone striking Elliot.

She reached for a large Band-Aid and tried to steady her hand as she unwrapped the paper casing. The idea of someone purposely hurting Elliot caused something fierce and frightening to fill her chest, and she worked hard to force it down. She took Elliot's chin in her hand once more, tilting it up so she could patch the wound.

Only this time, she'd lost her ability to remain clinical. She saw the blood, saw the residual fear and uncertainty in those green eyes, felt the blow as surely as if it had been delivered to her. Her vision narrowed as the darkness rose up to meet her.

"Kel."

The name hurt to hear, so soft and dreamy with a hint of concern. "What?"

"You're kind of hurting me."

Trying to blink away the haze, she glanced down at her own hand as it clutched Elliot's face, her knuckles as white as the pale skin beneath them.

Pain on top of pain.

She released her grip and looked away, but the tiny room tilted in her field of vision. Wringing her hands, she stood in limbo, the two-foot gap between Elliot and the sink seemed an endless chasm. Her thoughts spun. Pain, fear, helplessness—she'd held them at bay for so long, but suddenly there, with blood in the sink to one side, and that perfect, beautiful face sliced open to her other, she couldn't take any more. She barely had time to wonder why this, of all things, sent her over the edge. She felt herself falling before it even happened.

Then Elliot caught her, swift and sure, as if she'd seen her more clearly than she saw herself. The whole thing happened so fast she didn't understand how it had happened at all. One second she didn't know which way to turn, the next Elliot cradled her in her arms. Kelly felt the rise and fall of Elliot's chest against her back and the warmth of her breath against the side of her face.

"What happened?" she whispered hoarsely, as she tried to pull away, but Elliot's arms clasped tightly around her waist, pinning her close.

"You wobbled."

"I didn't." Had she?

"Your face went white," Elliot said softly, leaning down so her lips brushed close to her temple. "And then you closed your eyes and swayed."

"I don't think I did. That doesn't make sense." Nothing made sense anymore. Nothing had made sense for weeks. "I was fine. I just needed, you needed—"

"Just stop."

"Stop what?"

"Kelly," Elliot said as if it were the most obvious answer in the world. "Look at me."

She tried to do the opposite. She tried to turn more fully away, but doing so left her staring straight into the mirror, the mirror that reflected the most intense green eyes she'd ever seen. Those eyes held her every bit as tightly as the arms around her waist.

"Stop fighting."

"Says the woman who's here because she got into a bar fight."

Elliot smiled at her in the mirror. "I told you we had more in common than you thought."

Kelly shook her head. "You're a mess."

Elliot laughed. "So are you."

She wanted to protest, but her shaking muscles gave her away. She could barely stand anymore, literally or figuratively.

"It sucks to feel helpless," Elliot said softly.

She nodded, unintentionally relaxing against the steadiness Elliot provided.

"I get it," Elliot continued. "When Mrs. Anthony lashed out at me today, I wanted to cry, and I hated that. I hate that people still have the power to make me feel vulnerable. I hate myself for giving her the power. And then tonight, when I saw some douchebag do the same thing to some other woman, I just snapped. It felt good. I felt strong. The anger felt so much better than the pain or shame, but it doesn't last."

She didn't reply. She couldn't. Her heart seemed to have crawled into her throat only to pound painfully there. Elliot had given voice to everything she'd tried so hard to deny, even to herself. She couldn't hold the emotions back any longer. Giving them a name gave them all the power she feared.

"It's okay," Elliot whispered again, her lips so soft and close. They brushed her ear. "I mean it. We really are more alike than you want to admit."

She lifted her eyes, once again meeting Elliot's in the mirror. The light green she'd grown accustomed to had turned darker, almost as dark as her own expanding pupils. She saw herself, her fear, her need in their shared reflection, physical proof they were more alike than even Elliot knew.

She could deny it. She could lie. She could look away from what she saw. She could fight herself and everyone else the same way she had for years. She could still walk away. She turned slowly in Elliot's embrace and placed her hands flat on her chest. She could push her away. She had to.

Instead she clutched her shirt and pulled her closer until their mouths collided.

᷍ ᷍ ᷍

Holy shit, Kelly was kissing her . . . hard.

And amazingly.

Elliot's shock quickly gave way to surrender, which burned into abandon. Wrapping her arms tighter around Kelly's waist, she held them together even though she didn't need to. Kelly wasn't going anywhere. She still held Elliot's shirt in two tight fists as she arched up to keep Elliot tightly against her in as many ways as possible. One kiss blurred into hundreds. Opening their mouths, tongues sought and found more fully, more completely. Stealing air in tiny breaths, they refused to break the connection.

God, her mouth felt fantastic. And skilled.

It had been too long since she'd held a woman like this. Maybe she'd never held a woman quite like this. Whatever they conveyed to each other with this clash of bodies and emotions, it was bigger than attraction. It amounted to more than lust. Kelly exuded a need that made her dizzy from the mix of power and raw vulnerability. Passion verged on desperation that hinted not at exploration, but at something well known or something long lost, having been found just in time. Kelly kissed her like Elliot's lips held the key to survival.

Perhaps they did. Maybe the pain and the fear and the futility could only be endured if met with equal doses of pleasure. What if their mutual combustion wasn't just the result of a breakdown? What if it offered their only salvation?

She slid her hands down, cupping Kelly's ass through her skirt. If drinking from this cup provided her with the life needed to endure whatever came next, she wouldn't sip; she would guzzle. She would take every drop until Kelly cut her off or until they both grew drunk on each other.

Kelly released one hand from her shirt long enough to snake it up into Elliot's hair. She raked her fingernails across her scalp, pulling her head down farther. Elliot willingly bowed to the exquisite pressure, tearing her lips away only as far as Kelly's neck before renewing the feast. Her skin tasted of sweat and the sharp winter wind.

She licked along the curve of her throat to the tight muscle of her shoulder and then across the defined ridge of her slender collarbone. She inhaled the scent of shampoo and perfume, something clean and crisp, like fresh air after being locked inside for too long. Every inch of her flesh begged to be united with every ounce of Kelly. She intended to take her, *right here. Right now.*

Thoughts flowed, fast and loose. Passion, lust, need, greed, control, boss, straight, sex.

Oh God, what were they doing? Where could they go from here? Could there be anything but oblivion after this moment? The question filtered through the haze only to disappear quickly in the murky dark of moral ambiguity as Kelly began to unbutton Elliot's shirt. She wouldn't think. She couldn't. She had to have her the way she had to have air. Maybe she'd lost her grip on sanity, or maybe this was her only way not to.

Cupping Kelly's ass tightly once more, she lifted her off the ground and leaned forward the inches necessary to prop her on the edge of the vanity. She ran one hand up a firm thigh, pausing only a second as she reached the navy fabric that had ridden up Kelly's beautifully toned leg. Part of her couldn't believe she'd been granted access, and yet she might die if she weren't.

She continued to kiss along Kelly's neck, her throat, her chest, as her hand worked higher. There were no words. Nothing to break the spell they incanted through heavy breaths and wet kisses. If Kelly were going to be the one to stop this, she surely would have done so by now, and as Elliot's fingers brushed against the warmth of her center, she found all the evidence she needed to prove she wouldn't finish this downward spiral alone.

At the touch of Elliot's hand, Kelly's hips rocked up, her body saying what neither of them dared. Elliot pressed closer now, bunching Kelly's skirt up as she settled between her legs. Something primal, instinctual took over. She hadn't felt so sure of herself for weeks, months. This is where she belonged. The heady sense of control filled her chest as she lifted her free hand. She cupped the back of Kelly's head and urged her closer. Then taking her mouth once more, she pushed her whole body forward.

The friction grew painfully perfect as they ground against one another, breaths heavy, urgency overcoming finesse. She gloried in the press of her weight against the thrust of Kelly's need. She wanted to stay here forever, never letting go of the physical sensations overriding all emotion, if only Kelly would let her.

Then as abruptly as the whole thing began, Kelly's back went rigid and her hands clenched in fists. She hung, suspended in that arc of ecstasy until with one sharp cry she went limp. Resting her forehead against Elliot's chest, she breathed slowly in through her nose and out through her mouth.

Elliot wasn't sure she was really breathing yet at all, but if she were, the oxygen didn't seem to be reaching her brain enough to let her make sense of the drastic change of pace. She hadn't been with tons of women, but enough to know orgasms usually came with more build-up, and generally a little bit of afterglow.

"Would you mind extracting your hand from my skirt?" Kelly said, her voice low, but without a hint of softness.

Okay, so no afterglow. She leaned back slowly, afraid to make any sudden movements, but when her entire body was free of any connection, Kelly hopped gracefully off the vanity and brushed her skirt back into place.

"I think you've stopped bleeding," Kelly said, matter-of-factly.

It took a second for Elliot to realize she meant the comment literally, and she lifted her hand absently to the Band-Aid over her eye.

Kelly stepped out of the bathroom into the hall, but the physical distance didn't feel nearly as far as the emotional separation, as she casually added, "I don't think you need stitches."

No, stitches wouldn't do anything to make sense of the dysphoria that plagued Elliot now. Maybe she did have a concussion after all. If not for Kelly's bruised lips and her unwillingness to make eye contact, Elliott might have believed nothing that transpired over the last twenty minutes had actually happened.

Certainly nothing made sense. Her very straight, very uptight boss had kissed her like a woman who knew what she was doing and driven her into such a frenzy that she'd fucked her on the office sink. Things like that didn't just happen, and yet it had. She knew it had, even if she didn't understand how. Had one of them had a nervous breakdown? If so, which one? And what the hell should she do about it?

"I think it's probably time for you to get home," Kelly suggested calmly, but in a way that left little room for argument. Besides, listening to her seemed easier than trying to figure out what the hell was happening.

"Yeah," she said, finally speaking for the first time since everything spun out of control. "I probably better."

"Do you, um, need a ride?" The little waiver was the first hint from Kelly that she felt anything other than complete control.

"No." She buttoned the part of her shirt Kelly had popped open and picked her coat up off the floor before joining her in the hallway.

"So . . ." She waited. For what, she didn't know. An explanation? Some emotional cue? The camera crew to reveal themselves and unveil the most elaborately inappropriate prank in the history of all humanity?

Nothing happened.

Nothing other than Kelly standing stoically still with her hand on the steel door to the alley and her eyes anywhere but on Elliot.

Okay. Fine.

Nothing to say.

Nothing more to see here.

92

Elliot slipped on her coat and braced herself for the cold. Kelly pushed open the door, then stood back to give her room to pass without any part of their bodies so much as brushing against each other. It didn't matter though. No amount of distance, avoidance, or pretending could ever erase the imprint of them pressed together in the most intimate way. She knew she'd feel Kelly against her for hours, days, weeks to come. The only thing she didn't know was what the hell she should do about it now.

Other than leave.

Kelly clearly wanted her to go, and she didn't know what she wanted well enough to argue, so she stepped into the alley before turning back to seek Kelly's dark eyes one more time. Kelly refused to offer her even that as she looked past her, above her, or anywhere else.

"Thanks for the . . ." Elliot paused, unsure of herself but unwilling to fall apart in the face of Kelly's indifference, "the Band-Aid?"

Kelly's skilled mouth twisted in something akin to a grimace. "You're welcome."

Elliot shrugged. She'd tried. Perhaps not eloquently or smoothly, but she'd tried. She'd stood in the awkwardness long enough. She wouldn't beg for an explanation or an invitation. Kelly had kissed her. Elliot had practically jumped Kelly, and while she hadn't exactly said she wanted to go as far as they had, she hadn't stopped her, either. She'd had as much chance to control the situation as Elliot did. More control actually, if she could summon this icy resolve in the immediate aftermath of their meltdown. Kelly was apparently the queen of control, and for once, Elliot could only follow her lead.

"Goodnight, Kelly."

"Goodnight, Elliot," Kelly said. Then, without even waiting for her to go, Kelly closed the door behind her.

The metal clang echoed through the alleyway with a finality that made Elliot's knees buckle. Reaching for the wall, she steadied herself, first with her hands, then by resting her forehead against the rough wall. She relished the sharp points of gravel poking at the soles of her boots, the bite of frost at her fingertips, the coarse texture of the brick against her skin. The tactile sensations grounded her to reality, to this moment. She needed things she could touch, feel, and know, but no matter how much she attempted to anchor herself to the tangible, she couldn't prevent the blaring retort ringing through her mind. She finally gave it voice by whispering it into the frozen night. "What the fuck did we just do?"

Chapter Eight

Kelly slammed the lock into place and stumbled back to the bathroom. Bracing herself against the sink with one hand, she turned on the cold water with the other. She tried not to notice how badly her fingers shook as she ran them under the faucet. She cupped both hands and brought the water to her face. She splashed it across her cheek and rinsed her mouth as if she could somehow wash away the kiss and its multitude of implications. And yet the regret didn't come. At least not in the crippling way she expected.

Why hadn't the remorse overtaken her yet? She'd felt a veritable catalogue's worth of emotions over the last hour. Anger, fear, need, lust, abandon, ecstasy, relief, embarrassment, and shock. Why hadn't she fallen apart yet? She'd behaved totally out of character. She'd come unglued and surrendered to her baser instincts. And worst of all, she'd liked it. She'd relished every debauched second.

Not the aftermath. Not the awkwardness or the confusion as she tried to pull herself together. Certainly not the bewilderment in Elliot's eyes. No, least of all that. And yet even remembering the concern that had crossed her beautiful, youthful features as she'd broken away, Kelly couldn't summon any meaningful desire to undo what they did.

Slowly she lifted her gaze to the mirror, afraid of what she'd find, scared that somehow her reflection would reveal the woman she'd shown herself to be, and it did. In a myriad of little ways, her body betrayed her. From the flush of pink in her cheeks, to her still-enlarged pupils, to the deep maroon of her lips, she no longer appeared wan and pallid under the lights. She looked like a woman come to life, a shot of color in a previously sepia scene.

Her heart rate accelerated as the thoughts spun through her brain, causing her pulse to rush through her ears and her head to throb. She might regret how things ended, she might regret the awkwardness she'd have to face, but in no way did she regret what they had done.

What she had done.

Elliot had come along for the ride, eager and able, but never fully in control. It would be easy to blame her, but Kelly didn't have it in her to be so unfair, not even to save herself. Elliot's only sin came in the form of her skill.

God, she could kiss, and touch, and caress, and move. Her cockiness in every social situation wasn't merely false bravado or over-inflated ego. She not only possessed the wit and charisma to back them up, apparently she also had the sexual prowess. Her breath shortened at the thought, though she couldn't tell if the reaction stemmed from the worry that she'd be faced with similar temptation in the future or the fear that she wouldn't.

Surely Elliot wouldn't return.

Why would she?

Maybe if Kelly had offered her some explanation . . . but she hadn't, she couldn't, and Elliot had walked away willingly. She couldn't deny a twinge of disappointment in her lack of fight. She would've expected someone who threw punches for strangers to at least ask questions of someone she'd been intimate with. And yet, Kelly had kept the intimacy at a minimum. She accepted only what her body demanded and returned nothing. She didn't blame Elliot for taking the first available exit, and she wouldn't fault her for refusing to return. A woman with her skills, both on the job and in the bedroom, had many options that didn't include continuing to work with Kelly on any level. Maybe part of her would even appreciate a clean break. Elliot deserved better than Kelly could or would give her. She hoped Elliot would find everything she needed in her next placement.

Surely she could still find another placement. She didn't have to miss graduating. The university undoubtedly had policies in place for leaving internships. Would she tell her supervisor why? Would she tell Beth?

Her stomach turned and the bile rose in her throat. She splashed her face with another handful of water. There was the panic she'd expected. The dark cloud had merely been biding its time, giving her false hope of sunny skies. She might not feel any remorse for losing control of her body, but she would be made to feel plenty for losing control of her life. Her business. Her reputation.

Then again, didn't those things always go together? Sex and guilt. Relationships and fear. Love and disappointment. Wasn't that what she'd preached to herself for years? She'd never had the same options other people did. Everything she'd worked for and everyone she'd ever cared for came with a choice.

Tonight, in a moment of weakness, she'd made the wrong one.

෩ ෩ ෩

A knock sounded softly on Elliot's door, followed by whispered voices.

She rolled over and peeked one eye open just enough to see the clock: 8:02. She didn't have to be at work for another hour, and she didn't want to be awake or thinking any earlier than she had to.

She pulled the pillow over her head and tried to slip back out of awareness, but whoever stood on the other side of the door knocked again, this time louder.

"Elliot," Rory called. "If you're in there, you need to say so, or I'm going to call the police."

Police? What the hell?

She threw off the comforter and padded quickly through the apartment, picking up a shirt as she went. She'd never actually managed to strip off her jeans the night before. She hadn't had the energy or desire to take any more steps than those necessary to fall into the oblivion of sleep.

Rory knocked again, but Elliot swung open the door. "What in all the fucks are you—" Then she saw Beth standing beside her and stopped short. "Sorry."

Beth smiled. "I've heard the word before."

"Jesus," Rory said, ignoring the exchange and catching Elliot's chin in her hand. "You really did it."

97

"What?"

"We heard about what happened last night," Beth said softly.

"You what?" Elliot exploded, causing her head to throb and Rory and Beth to both wince.

"Can we come in?" Beth asked.

She glanced down the hallway, realizing her neighbors could probably hear everything through the thin walls. "Sure."

Beth did an admirable job of appearing calm and collected as she took a seat on the couch, but Rory paced across the living room like a caged lion. Elliot couldn't blame her. She felt as though she might crawl out of her own skin as she frantically tried to process their reason for being there. How had they found out? Had Kelly called them? She shook her head. Kelly had barely said two words to her afterward, and she couldn't imagine her spilling to anyone else. Then again, less than twelve hours ago, she wouldn't have imagined Kelly allowing herself to be taken in the office bathroom. Part of her still couldn't believe it, but Beth and Rory wouldn't be in her living room at the butt-crack of dawn on a Saturday morning otherwise.

"Okay," Beth said, seeming to collect herself. "Why don't you tell us what happened?"

"Um, okay. Well . . ." She ran a hand through her bed head and tried to figure out where to start, but only came up empty. She couldn't make any sense of what happened between them, not what started things, or what made them spin out of control, and she certainly didn't understand what caused Kelly's abrupt withdrawal. Least of all she didn't understand what Kelly would have told someone else between then and now. Hell, if anyone had answers to those questions, it was as likely to be Beth as anyone else. "Why don't you tell me what you heard?"

"Elliot," Rory warned, "this is serious. If word of this gets out around town, it could make you a target."

"A target for what?"

"Violence."

"Violence?" Why? Did they think she forced herself on Kelly? Oh God, did Kelly think that? She looked from Rory to Beth, who gave them both a little shake of her head. Nothing made sense.

Rory lowered her voice. "Probably not violence, but paybacks. Or just bad will. What if the dean finds out?"

Her internship. She hadn't even gotten that far in her worries. She'd been so focused on the emotional side of the equation she hadn't thought about work or school or the implications for her career. She needed to graduate. She needed experience and references. "Shit, this is going to wreck my internship. Am I fired?"

"Fired?" Beth asked. "Why would you be fired?"

"What did Kelly say?"

"Kelly?" Rory asked, shooting Beth one of their indecipherable looks. "Was Kelly with you?"

"Well, yeah."

"I told you," Rory said, shaking her head. "I told you we shouldn't have put them together. I knew something like this was going to happen."

"What? You knew something like this was an option?" Elliot asked, her head spinning. "'Cause I didn't know until like, well, when it was already happening."

"Wait a second." Beth hopped to her feet and came between them. "Both of you need to sit down and take a few deep breaths."

Rory and Elliot complied immediately.

"I need you to back up." Beth continued. "Obviously, we heard part of the story, the part that came through the public rumor mill, which is notoriously unreliable, but you've got a Band-Aid coated in dried blood over your eye, so something happened."

Elliot lifted her hand to her eyebrow and ran her fingertips to the crusted blood around the edges as the proverbial lightbulb went off in her mind. The police, violence, the blood, and no mention of Kelly. "You're talking about the bar fight."

"Yes, we have lots of questions about that," Beth said calmly, then raised an eyebrow. "But now I also have questions about what you thought we were talking about."

Elliot hung her head. Kelly hadn't thrown her under the bus. She hadn't told anyone. Confusion and disillusionment gave way to fear once again. Kelly hadn't betrayed her, but Elliot might have inadvertently hurt her. How could she back out of this situation without causing any more damage?

"I got so confused there," she said honestly. "You woke me up, and you know how well I function so early in the morning."

Rory snorted and made a show of looking at her watch.

"You woke me up," Elliot repeated with greater emphasis. "And you said something about police, and I had to find a shirt."

"All right," Beth said with one of her most soothing smiles. "We did sort of barge in, but we were worried. We got a call this morning saying one of the lesbian students from Bramble got into a bar fight where homophobic things were said, punches were thrown, and someone left bleeding."

"And you got scared," Elliot finished. Made sense.

"I started calling PRIDE students only to find out most of our undergraduates spent the night down in St. Louis. You were the only one unaccounted for, and you wouldn't answer your phone."

She felt her pants pockets, then grabbed her coat off the floor only to find its pockets empty as well. Her face flamed as she realized it must have fallen out while she and Kelly were doing whatever it was they'd done. She still didn't know what word to use. "I must've left it at the office last night."

"Right, the office," Beth sighed, "which leads me back to the question of Kelly's involvement in the altercation."

"Kelly wasn't involved," Elliot said quickly, and immediately regretted the defensiveness in her tone.

"Nice try," Rory said. "Was she at the bar?"

Elliot laughed. "Kelly Rolen? At a local dive bar?"

"Yeah, I guess that seems a little out of character."

"Stranger things have happened," Elliot said, staring at her bare feet in the hopes of hiding the blush coloring her face.

"But you believed I'd talked to Kelly, or she'd talked to me about something." Beth pulled them back to the original questions. "Something that might get you fired from your internship?"

She pursed her lips and tried to walk the fine line between not lying to Rory and Beth without revealing the truth about Kelly. "After I left the bar, I felt blood on my face where the guy hit me with his elbow, not a punch by the way. I didn't want to walk all the way home without cleaning up. I stopped by the office to use the bathroom, and Kelly was there working."

"Wasn't it late at night?" Rory asked.

"About ten, I'd guess."

Beth sighed again and pinched the bridge of her nose. "One thing at a time. Was Kelly angry?"

She cocked her head to the side and considered the question. "I don't think so. Anger? I mean I've seen her pretty angry, and last night she didn't seem . . . No. Not angry."

Both of them stared at her as if they expected more, but she couldn't give them anything without jeopardizing way too many things. She searched her brain for something benign to say. "Oh, she gave me the Band-Aid."

"Well that was generous of her," Rory said scornfully.

"Rory," Beth warned, "she's going through a lot."

"What about Elliot? She went through a lot last night, too."

You have no idea, she thought, but said, "I'm okay."

"You show up to her office at ten o'clock after getting jumped by a bigot in a bar, and all she does is hand you a Band-Aid?"

"She did more than that." Elliot defended her automatically. Given the way she'd been dismissed the night before, it was surprising how swift the urge to protect Kelly overtook her need to be cautious. "She was great, really. I mean she was tired, and I surprised her after a really frustrating day. I snuck in the back door and bled all over her office. I probably scared the crap out of her." Saying the words aloud forced her to think about those facts for the first time. She'd surely caught Kelly off guard. After the day they'd had and the altercation with Mrs. Anthony, Elliot showed up bleeding because she got into a physical fight with a bigot. God, what must Kelly have thought?

"You know her dad isn't doing well?" Beth finally asked.

"Yeah, she doesn't talk about him to me, but she goes to the hospital a lot."

"I saw her there early in the evening. I'm not sure I helped the situation. She seemed . . . I don't know, worn a little thin maybe."

"She is." Memories came back in waves. The pallor of Kelly's features, the turmoil in her eyes, the way her hands shook. Hell, she hadn't jumped into Elliot's arms, she'd fallen. The woman was so damn stubborn, so strong and capable. She wouldn't admit needing help, but she shouldn't have had to. She would never say she was scared or exhausted or overwhelmed. Women like Kelly didn't just lose control. They cracked, and Elliot had let her fall apart. Her stomach roiled. She hadn't just let her fall apart. She'd taken advantage of the situation.

She rose and ran her hand through her hair again, then looked down at the shirt she wore backwards. She looked like shit, she felt like shit, and maybe she deserved it, but if she was in this much turmoil this morning, how must Kelly feel?

"Hey," Rory said kindly, "are you all right?"

She nodded. "I am. Really, the bar thing, it wasn't as big a deal as I made it out to be. Just some frustration got out of hand and I made a mistake, or I might have. I don't know. But it won't happen again."

"Okay." Rory rose and placed a hand on her shoulder. "We trust you. You just worried us."

"Thanks, I appreciate it," she said seriously. She understood what worry could do to a person, which was why she had to cut this meeting short. "But right now I think I need to get to work."

ဟ ဟ ဟ

Kelly awoke to the sound of someone coming through the back door. Sitting bolt upright at her desk, she looked around frantically until she realized she'd fallen asleep on a pile of client files. Horrified, she took her only solace in finding she didn't appear to have drooled on any of them.

"Hey," Elliot whispered from the doorway, but even the gentle sound sliced through the silence and caused her to jump. "Sorry. I'm sorry," Elliot said. "I didn't mean to scare you."

Kelly blinked at her, trying to process her presence, so unexpectedly close, so vibrant and commanding in dark jeans and a hunter green sweater that made her eyes seem even deeper and more expressive than usual. She had to take a moment to decide if she could trust herself to speak. She finally said the one thought that seemed to dominate all the others: "What are you doing here?"

"I work here," Elliot said, with a smile that showed more nervousness than she probably intended.

Kelly nodded slowly, letting the implications of the statement sink in. Elliot had shown up for work, or at least she wanted to work. She hadn't quit. She hadn't run to the dean to report her for sexual harassment. She hadn't even called in sick to prolong the torture. Despite everything that had happened last night, she'd come back.

"I do still work here, right?" Elliot finally asked.

"Yes," Kelly answered quickly, her relief rushing out completely on that single word.

"Okay," Elliot said in a similar tone. "I really need internship hours, and I would hate to think that anything I did would have jeopardized—"

"No." Kelly cut her off. She didn't want to have this conversation. She didn't want to rehash anything or unearth any emotions. "You're a good intern. There's no reason for anything to change."

Elliot's lips quirked up as the hint of something cocky returned to the set of her shoulders. "You think I'm a good intern?"

Kelly rolled her eyes, unsure whether or not she liked giving Elliot something to brag about, but if they could focus on her accounting skills instead of her talents in other areas, a little well-directed bravado might be a fair trade. "You're a very good intern. Or at least you have been so far, and I wouldn't want anything to change. We've still got two months left of tax season."

"Point taken," Elliot said seriously, "but if everything's business as usual, why are you here so early? You didn't sleep here, did you?"

"I did," Kelly said with as much dignity as she could muster. "But I keep a spare change of clothes here. I'll be fine to work this morning."

"I didn't doubt your ability to get work done. I just . . . I know you have a lot going on, business-wise, and with your father being sick . . . and then I interrupted you last night and . . . caught you off guard."

She didn't like where this was going, but she felt powerless to stop the replay of events she didn't want to remember.

"You were really, um . . . wonderful. With my face." Elliot hung her head. "That's not what I meant to say. I just wanted to say thank you for cleaning me up and bandaging the cut, and not freaking out about all of that."

"You're welcome," she said, her voice tense.

"I appreciate that you're in a tough spot, and I didn't mean to make things harder for you."

Oh, for the love of everything holy, why is she still talking? Kelly'd said they could both go back to work. Why did they have to drag out the awkwardness? Were they destined to eight more weeks of dancing around each other and what they'd done? If so, maybe she needed to put them both out of their misery. A few moments ago she'd thought the most awful outcome involved having to explain what happened to someone else, but now she wondered if having to face the living reminder of her weakness every day might constitute a worse punishment.

"You were good to stick up for me yesterday, for whatever reason, and to not throw me out last night. Maybe you only did it because of other things going on in your life. Or maybe you weren't thinking clearly."

Her head spun as she tried to follow Elliot's logic or read between the lines. Everything about her tone and her body language had changed from proud to guilty or shamed. She recognized those emotions. She'd wrestled them all night, and yet at no moment had they stripped her bare the way seeing them on Elliot did.

"If you felt like I took advantage of the situation," Elliot said softly, her voice more tentative than ever. "Or if I pressured you into something when you were not in a position to say no, I would go away. Quietly."

"What?"

"I know you probably don't believe this, but I'm not that way. I mean I never have been before, but if I forced, or pushed too hard, or coerced you—"

Something in her broke as she finally understood what Elliot was saying. "Elliot, no."

She rose from her desk without thinking. The urge to comfort that particular torment overrode every instinct for self-protection. "You did nothing wrong."

"Really?" Elliot lifted her worried eyes. "Because consent is a really big deal for me. And not just 'no means no,' but that only 'yes means yes.' I don't want you to think I'm some sort of lesbian predator."

"You did *not* force yourself on me." It hurt to assume responsibility for something so damaging to her sense of self, but it would hurt even worse to let Elliot take the blame. No matter how much she wanted to avoid this conversation, she wouldn't do so at the cost of letting Elliot consider herself a rapist. She touched her arm gently, tentatively, afraid of where these feelings might lead. "I kissed you."

"I know, but you're dealing with so much, and you're exhausted and probably not thinking clearly. I mean, obviously you're straight."

"I'm straight." Kelly repeated the phrase, hating the way it grated across her lips. How many times had she let that assumption stand? Had it ever hurt anyone the way it tormented Elliot now?

"I know," Elliot pushed on. "And I've never done anything like that before. I mean even if you were gay, or questioning, not that I'm saying you are, or trying to recruit you or something, but if you were, I wouldn't want your first time with a woman to happen like that."

"My first time with a woman?" Kelly felt like a parrot, but she couldn't think of anything else to say. Elliot thought she'd taken her lesbian virginity in a bathroom, then left her to deal with the implications of those events alone. God, she'd been so afraid of what Elliot might tell someone she hadn't stopped to think about Elliot's own fears, or even that she might have any. She'd simply assumed someone like Elliot had women throw themselves at her on a regular basis. How much had it taken for her to face those fears and to come check on her this morning?

"Kelly?" Elliot asked softly, "do you want me to go?"

"No." She didn't. Maybe she should have. A clean break would be easier, but they'd passed that point hours ago. She had made this mess. She couldn't let Elliot carry the weight of it forever.

Her whole life had been a string of putting her own desires last in order to save other people. Doing so now wouldn't be anything new, except this time she wouldn't be able to protect Elliot with silence. For the first time in years, not saying the words would cause more damage than saying them would.

She took a deep breath and steeled herself for what had to be done, then in one swift exhale, she said, "Elliot, I'm gay."

Chapter Nine

"Yeah, I'm gay," Elliot said, then replayed the phrase. "'I'm gay.' That's what you just said, right?"

Kelly sighed. "I said, 'I'm gay.'"

"And by 'I'm ... you mean 'you'?"

She rolled her eyes. "People generally use the pronoun 'I' to refer to themselves."

"Okay, then," Elliot said, nodding like a bobblehead. "I'm ... well, I think ... do you mind if I sit down?"

"Mind if I join you?"

"Please," Elliot said as she flopped down into one of the client chairs opposite Kelly's desk. Kelly took the seat next to her in much more graceful fashion, crossing one elegant leg over the other and folding her hands in her skirt-clad lap. She still wore her clothes from last night, which suddenly struck Elliot as intimate. Oh crap, would she find everything about her sexy now? Had she only maintained her professionalism on the tenuous premise of Kelly's heterosexuality? Maybe she *was* a predatory lesbian. Would someone revoke her women's studies degree? No. She needed to back up a bit, or a lot, all the way to the point where Kelly came out to her.

"You're gay?"

"Yes," Kelly said emphatically.

"So many things don't make sense anymore," Elliot said, "and yet some things that didn't make sense before suddenly seem a whole lot clearer."

"Like last night?"

"Well yes, a lot of things that happened last night are much less confusing now, and yet not all of them. I mean the middle part. I get where that came from, at least hypothetically, but other than the main event, there are still so many questions."

Kelly sighed. "I don't really want there to be any more questions."

"Right. I sort of got that from you, and yet I still have questions."

"I might not be willing to answer them."

"And you have that right," Elliot affirmed. "Your body, your life. I'm a feminist, but the thing is, those things also kind of spilled over into my body and my life. I'm not complaining about anything, but I don't really know how I could've missed something so major."

Kelly stiffened. "It's not major."

"Feels kind of major."

"It's nothing more than a coincidence of nature. You didn't miss anything because there wasn't anything to miss."

"Until last night," Elliot added. She'd always prided herself on her gaydar, and yet she'd been so far in the opposite direction on this one. "I thought you were a homophobe."

"You mentioned that once or twice."

"And you could've told me then."

"I didn't want to tell you. I don't even like you knowing now."

"Then why do it?"

Kelly held her head in her hands, her thick, dark hair falling down like a shroud around her face. "I couldn't let you think you'd hurt me when in reality I hold all the blame."

Her chest constricted at the anguish in Kelly's voice. "Hey, there's no blame here."

"You thought you'd raped me, when in reality I abused my position of power and blindsided you, then kicked you out into an alley."

"Okay." Elliot sucked in a deep breath and summoned her best impression of Beth's calm voice. "I think we're both afraid of things the other person isn't feeling. I did not feel abused, and maybe you surprised me, but I'm a big girl. I had complete control of my decision-making facilities. I didn't stop because I didn't want to." She paused. "Did you want to?"

Kelly shook her head. "I should have."

"But you didn't?" Elliot's heart pounded in her chest. So much hinged on the next thing Kelly said.

She finally lifted her dark eyes. "I didn't want to stop. Not in the moment, but it's a moment we'll never get back. It changes everything."

"Not really." She tried hard to focus her relief amid a subtle twinge of arousal. Kelly enjoyed what they'd done while they had been doing it, but they had bigger issues now. "Not everything changed, and the things that did aren't all bad."

"I see no silver linings here."

"No, you probably don't, but ..." Elliot spoke slowly, trying to give them both time to let things sink in. They'd only skimmed the surface of sex and attraction and sexual orientation, and they'd found plenty of complications, but at least they'd started a real conversation. "I respect you a lot more now."

Kelly snorted and started to push up out of her seat. "I don't know what kind of woman you think I am, but—"

"Wait, please." Elliot placed a hand over Kelly's and she froze but didn't pull away, allowing Elliot to continue. "You're juggling more responsibility than I realized, but you're doing amazingly. You're finding ways to get through and get work done, and I haven't made things any easier on you. You got overwhelmed and acted in a completely human way. You're human, so am I, and for the record I acted in exactly the same way you did, so I couldn't condemn you even if I wanted to."

Kelly shrugged as if maybe she agreed with the logic or at least didn't know how to argue against it. "But afterward ..."

"Afterward, you needed space. I didn't really want any space, but it probably turned out for the best because I had time to think before we saw each other again, and when we did you could've thrown me out. You could have let me take the blame. I came here prepared to accept full responsibility."

"I couldn't let you do that."

"Exactly, and that's why I respect you," Elliot said. "I get the sense that you'd rather have a root canal than come out to me, but you did, and I'm not going to make you regret doing so."

"I appreciate the sentiment, but you can't really control my regrets."

Elliot almost laughed, the comment wasn't exactly what she hoped for, but at least it sounded more like the old Kelly. "You're right. I can't control them, but I want to alleviate them or at least understand them."

"What's to understand? We have to work together for almost two more months."

"We do, but it doesn't have to be awkward."

"Oh, awkward doesn't even begin to cover how I feel."

Elliot did laugh outright. "I take it you're not a big proponent of the sex positive movement."

Kelly stared at her as if she'd spoken another language.

"I've got a women's studies degree," Elliot said, going in to faux teacher mode. "Slut shaming is not my thing."

"Sl-sl-slut?" Kelly's face turned beet red as she stammered the word.

"No, no, no, not you." Elliot rushed to recover. "Men use that word to describe women who want sex, who admit to liking sex, but it's just a way of keeping women in their place. We can't internalize their misogyny."

"I can't even begin to respond to that."

"You don't have to. You just need to realize I'm not ashamed of who I am. I'm not ashamed of what I like, of what I need. I think last night both of us needed the same thing, and we took it. We owned it, at least in the moment. If we'd taken care of something we needed to do in the business world, we'd be proud of ourselves. If we'd taken care of something in our financial life or with our health, that would be considered smart or responsible. Why should our emotional or sexual needs be any different?"

Kelly listened, dark eyes brooding, but she didn't interrupt. She didn't even answer right away, and when she did, she started cautiously. "I'm not sure I agree with that." She cleared her throat. "That sex can actually be compared to work or treating the common cold, but I suppose I should be glad you think the way you do. I'm mildly relieved to know any misgivings I have are mine alone."

Elliot wouldn't go that far. She still had her share of concerns and questions, but voicing them now seemed secondary to soothing Kelly. "It happened. We share responsibility equally, but there's no need for shame or guilt. We're both professionals, and we have work to do. What we need in our personal lives doesn't have anything to do with getting through tax season."

"Work. Right. I guess we agree there. There's always work to do."

"Great," Elliot said, "then I'm going to go make a double batch of coffee."

Kelly seemed to almost smile as she offered a sincere, "Thank you."

Under other circumstances Elliot would've hoped for a better resolution. Some emotional touchstones or a hint as to where their relationship might head. Most women would've wanted some sort of closure, but if she'd learned anything over the last twenty-four hours it was that Kelly Rolen was nothing like any woman she'd ever met before.

ဢ ဢ ဢ

Kelly listened from her desk as Elliot answered a client's questions over the phone. Her voice was light and efficient, her answers concise and easy to understand. She blended professionalism and approachability in ways Kelly wasn't sure she'd mastered, even after more than a decade of doing the same job. She didn't need to check up on Elliot nearly as much as she did, but she couldn't seem to break the habit. At first she'd eavesdropped on everything Elliot said out of fear she'd mess up, or maybe in the hope that she'd falter and give her the chance to assert her own expertise. Somewhere along the way, though, she'd stopped wanting or expecting her to fail. Now she listened in because she found her presence comforting, maybe even enjoyable.

A week had passed since what she'd come to think of as "that night." Not that she thought of what'd happened any more than she had to. She refused to dwell on her actions or any implications her mind might try to draw from them, but late at night, or in times of deep exhaustion, her thoughts occasionally wandered to various explanations. She'd been tired. Overwhelmed. She had gone too long without an outlet for her feelings. She'd been caught off guard. She'd been upset about the prospect of something hurting Elliot. She'd experienced some weird transference of emotions or even a mental break. None of the theories were absurd, but none felt quite satisfactory either, and she chose to avoid looking for anything deeper. Avoidance was the most compelling option, or at least the most convenient one.

Elliot, for her part, had lived up to her promise not to make Kelly regret the confidence she'd shared. She'd never mentioned anything outright, and barely even hinted at anything that had transpired, other than occasionally asking how she felt, or if she wanted to talk. Kelly didn't want to talk about anything other than work, a fact she reiterated every time Elliot asked. She'd done nothing but work, visit her father, and sleep, though she never seemed to have quite enough time to do any of those tasks to the level she would have liked. Still, she stayed afloat, largely due to Elliot's shared dedication.

"Knock, knock," Elliot said from just outside the door.

"Come in," Kelly answered, straightening up automatically.

Elliot stepped into view and smiled. Today she wore a chocolate brown sweater vest over a starched white oxford with camel-colored khakis and a pair of men's loafers. She had brushed her auburn hair back with an almost debonair flair. Kelly didn't even try to pretend she wasn't insanely attractive. She simply tried to focus through the distracting way her breath grew noticeably shallow.

"We don't have any more appointments today," Elliot said, dropping into one of the chairs opposite her desk. Kelly tried not to stiffen at the move. If she had to pin down one thing different since "that night," it would be that she noticed Elliot's easy informality, even closeness, much more acutely. She couldn't tell if Elliot had gotten more familiar over the last week, or if she'd simply become more aware of her since then.

"You're free to go," Kelly said, then hearing the abruptness of her tone added, "if you want to."

"No. I'm going to stay and cuddle with my friend, the scanner, a little longer. We haven't gotten to spend as much quality time together since our client meetings and walk-ins picked up."

"Well, I wouldn't want to come between you two."

"No. You wouldn't," Elliot said cheekily, "but I was going to pick her up some food first, maybe some champagne and strawberries, and

I thought since I was running out anyway, I could pick you up something, too."

"Are you offering to buy me dinner?" Kelly asked, leaning back in her chair. She wasn't sure she should agree to that, but she was hungry, and she did prefer this playful side of Elliot to her concerned side.

"Sure, but you have to eat it in your office with the door closed so you don't interrupt me and the scanner."

Kelly smothered a grin. "What were you thinking? About the food, not the scanner."

"Well, it's Darlington, so we have so many options to choose from. We could have Thai, or sushi, falafel, or maybe saganaki."

Kelly rolled her eyes.

"Or baba ganoush, or tapas, or crepes, or poutine."

"Are you done yet?"

"Paella," Elliot said with gusto. "Okay, now I'm done."

"So Dairy Queen or chili?"

"Can one get chili from the DQ?"

"You could, but then I'd have to kill you."

"What?" Elliot feigned shock. "Really? Chili from DQ? That's where you draw the line?"

"We have the best chili parlor in the whole world right across the square. If you drove all the way across town to get some sad approximation, then yes, I'd have to kill you. It'd be a mercy killing, but you'd still be dead."

"Wow, a mercy killing. Aside from the fact that I could walk 'all the way across town' in about ten minutes, I feel as though it's not the distance or the effort that bothers you so much as the bad judgment associated with inferior chili."

"Obviously." Kelly shook her head. "How long have you lived here?"

"Um, well I transferred in the middle of my sophomore year, and it's a five-year program, minus going home for the summers, so, boots on the ground, I've probably spent around three here in Mayberry."

Kelly chose to ignore the slur against her hometown. One step at a time. She picked up her desk phone and dialed a number from memory. While it rang, she turned back to Elliot. "Three years is too long to go without this chili."

"Wow. Shouldn't I look at a menu or something?"

Kelly shook her head and spoke into the phone. "I need two large chilies delivered to Rolen and Rolen please. Put it on my tab. Thank you."

"You have a running chili tab?" Elliot asked as Kelly hung up the phone.

"Don't judge me until you've tried it."

"I wouldn't dare." Elliot's smile was playful, and instead of feeling annoyed, Kelly found herself amused. They shouldn't have been able to joke so soon, or even ever again after what had happened, but they could and they did, even if only about things as benign as chili. She couldn't remember the last time she'd joked about anything.

She tried not to overthink any of those facts as silence settled between them again. She was tired, and maybe more lonely than she cared to admit. Maybe she would've welcomed any good-natured company at this point. Only she didn't actually enjoy anyone else's company. Clients meant more work. Doctors and nurses brought too many questions and not enough answers, and on the rare occasion anyone made a social call, their pity only reminded her of everything she couldn't control.

Control.

She wouldn't have thought Elliot, of all people, could help her feel in control. Elliot, the person who had seen her fall, the woman who knew better than anyone else what a tenuous grip she held on restraint. How could she look Elliot in the eye after what she'd seen? How could she ever respect herself again, much less inspire respect in Elliot? And yet, there they sat bantering back and forth until their dinner arrived.

"How's your dad doing?" Elliot asked casually.

She sighed. She should've been grateful Elliot cared enough to ask, but she missed the more comfortable topics. "He's progressing."

"Progressing," Elliot repeated. She didn't push for more, but the silence between them didn't seem nearly as comfortable as before. Kelly had fielded these types of questions numerous times over the past four weeks. She'd learned to dodge or extract herself from them altogether, but she couldn't refuse to answer what Elliot didn't ask. She had a hard time summoning her standard defensiveness when Elliot refused to pry. She'd simply opened the topic and then waited for Kelly to return whatever she chose.

"They moved him to a rehab floor, but as far as I can tell, he's not actually experiencing much rehabilitation," Kelly said, much to her own surprise. "He speaks with a little more consistency, which I suppose counts for something, but his vocabulary is still limited. And he doesn't seem to have enough energy to care."

Elliot nodded, her eyes speaking the concern she didn't actually voice.

"They say it can take a year to understand the full effects of a stroke, but the doctors have hinted that his current condition might be the best we can hope for."

Elliot opened her mouth, but the bell above the front door rang, saving them both from whatever statement she'd intended to make.

"Hello?" someone called from the front office. "Chili delivery."

Elliot smiled weakly and rose to greet the delivery person. Kelly followed more slowly. She shouldn't long for more casual interactions with Elliot, and they certainly didn't need to have any deep emotional conversations. Business offered the safest retreat and also the most pressing distraction from everything that plagued her, so she needed to make this a business dinner, then get back to work in earnest.

❧ ❧ ❧

"Holy, shit!"

"Language," Kelly said, her normal stern voice undercut with amusement.

"It's hot," Elliot whined as her tongue took the brunt of the chemical burn.

"Blow on it."

"It's spicy hot."

"It's chili." Kelly laughed. "And you're a wuss."

"I'm not." Elliot wiped the beads of sweat dotting her forehead

114

and tried not to employ Lamaze-style breathing. "I just didn't expect something so spicy from Ms. I-don't-eat-ethnic-food."

"If you can't take it . . ." Judgment dripped from Kelly's voice.

Elliot took a swig of ice water. "I can take it. Really. I'm not a spice wimp. You just caught me off guard."

Kelly ate calmly and neatly, her cheeks barely pink, and probably more from enjoyment rather than the food. Add a high tolerance for Tabasco-style heat to the growing list of surprises she kept hidden from the casual observer.

She dabbed the corner of her mouth with a paper napkin. "So what do you think?"

"I think you're full of surprises, and every time I think I've gotten used to you springing them on me, you find another way to make me question my assumptions about you."

Kelly blinked a few times, the color rising drastically in her cheeks. "I meant, what do you think about the chili?"

"Oh." Elliot grimaced. "Sorry. I like the chili. Once you get over the shock, it sort of grows on you, ya know?"

"Not really. I don't recall needing a learning curve. I don't even remember the first time I ate the stuff. It made up a staple of our family diet from the time I could eat solid food."

"They feed this stuff to children around here?" Elliot asked. "No wonder you're all so hearty."

"Hearty?" Kelly asked. "I'm not sure that's a compliment."

"Oh, it is," Elliot assured her, taking another bite. "You Midwestern farm stock are a different breed with your up-with-the-sun mentality and drinking coffee black and wearing skirts in February."

Kelly glanced down at her classic black pencil skirt but didn't reply.

"Maybe you all have that no-nonsense mentality because parents inoculate you to pain at such a young age. You know, like how some parents give their kids shots for smallpox, or when Scandinavians have their infants nap out in the sub-freezing temperatures to boost their immune systems?"

"I'm not sure—"

"Oh, I know—this explains how they teach you to eat all the other bland meat and potato dishes everyone loves around here. After eating the chili, you can't taste anything else, so it doesn't really matter what random carb you put in your mouth."

"Are you finished?"

Elliot pretended to think hard for a few more seconds before smiling. "For now."

"Good," Kelly said in a dramatic show of exasperation, "and I'm not sure if all local families start their children on chili as young as my dad did. We've had some of the same tax season routines ever since I can remember. I always got chili and chocolate milk when he had to work late, which was a lot during tax season."

Elliot smiled, thinking of a miniature Kelly in her tiny business suits sitting at her huge desk poring over tax forms and drinking chocolate milk through a straw. The image might not be totally accurate, but she couldn't actually envision kid Kelly as anything other than a smaller version of her current self. Surely she'd been born with at least her drive, seriousness, and professional acumen fully intact.

"What are you grinning at?"

"Nothing," she answered quickly. "I used to have similar traditions with my mom. She's a lawyer. When she got absorbed in prepping a case we would have takeout picnics. We'd spread a blanket on the living room floor and line it with those little paper cartons, then just graze while I did homework and she reviewed documents."

"Single parents, making do," Kelly said wistfully. It was the first reference to their shared style of upbringing since the day Elliot had first made the connection. She'd wondered if Kelly had even cared enough to remember the detail. Finding out she had made the conversation feel more intimate. Her stomach tightened in a little churning way that had become entirely too common over the last week. She'd tried, really tried, to live up to her promise of complete professionalism and pretending not to think of Kelly as her sexy gay boss. Most of the time she succeeded, but occasionally when she least expected it, Kelly said or did something to make herself seem real, human, vulnerable. In those moments the memories overwhelmed Elliot before she had time to rein them back in.

"So your mom's a lawyer?" Kelly asked nonchalantly as she scraped the bottom of her Styrofoam container with a plastic spoon. "Is she the one who taught you to argue all the time?"

"Pretty much," Elliot admitted. "She's kind of a big feminist."

"No." Sarcasm filled Kelly's voice. "Your mom's a feminist?"

"Yeah, your dad's a CPA, my mom's a rabid feminist. Insert joke about apples and the trees they fell from. I'm part of the first wave of sisters doing it for themselves in the baby-making department."

Kelly seemed to have a hard time swallowing her last bite of chili. "Excuse me?"

"It was the early '90s. Fertility advancement met consumer culture, and a thirty-five-year-old single businesswoman suddenly had a lot more options than she used to. And what's more feminist than having a kid without a man? Just going down to the sperm bank and plunking down her own hard-earned cash, then walking out with one half of an Elliot in a vial."

"Wow." Kelly's complexion had gone a little pale. "I'm not sure anyone has ever used the word 'sperm' in my office before."

"I'd be fine if we never used it again."

"Me too," Kelly agreed. "But, having a baby on her own by choice? Your mom sounds . . . brave?"

"Or insane. Actually she's both. I think she'd admit now that she would've liked to have had someone to share the experience and the responsibilities with, but she'd never settle for someone less than a full partner, and she had a lot of herself invested in the idea that she didn't need a man to fulfill her. The great tragedy of her life is not being a lesbian."

"Wow," Kelly said again. "I think the similarity of our parents ends at the single part."

"Probably," Elliot said. "I've never met anyone else quite like Sydney."

"Sydney?"

"My mother. She doesn't like to go by 'Mom.' Says it limits her identity and puts an unnecessary sense of hierarchy on our relationship. In preschool, I didn't think I had a mom or a dad, just a Syd."

"I was always fully aware that I only had a dad," Kelly said, almost wistfully.

"Yeah? How come? What happened to your mom?"

Kelly stiffened immediately. "That's none of your business."

"Whoa."

Kelly rose quickly. "I'm sorry. I didn't mean to snap. I just . . . it's not something I talk about."

Elliot raised her hands and spoke in her most placating voice. "No problem. I understand."

"Well . . . good," Kelly said, her smile fake. "Because we need to get back to work."

"Sure," Elliot said carefully, unsure of what trigger she'd managed to trip, but she certainly didn't want to do anything else to set off another conversational landmine. "Thanks for the chili."

"You're welcome." Kelly gave a curt nod and quickly strode back to her office, shutting the door behind her.

Elliot dropped her forehead to the desk, feeling the cool wood beneath her skin. Why did conversations with Kelly always leave her confused and barely propped up? They weren't friends. They weren't lovers. They were barely even colleagues. Despite what had happened a week ago, Kelly was her boss, and Elliot had promised to respect her boundaries. But this back and forth between approachable and off limits made her head hurt.

Chapter Ten

Friday morning the bell above the front door jingled, causing Kelly to look up from the tax form of the local grocery store owner. His taxes took longer than any other business in town, and she'd already spent more than half her day poring over his receipts. She welcomed the chance to interact with another client for a while.

"Hey, strangers," Kelly heard Elliot call out a warm greeting. "Back from the Big Apple?"

"I only went for Presidents' Day weekend, but Stevie was there all month. She just got back yesterday."

"I'm surprised you two found the time or energy to be out running errands today," Elliot said, with a hint of suggestiveness that set Kelly's teeth on edge. She couldn't tell what bothered her more, that Elliot got familiar with one of her clients in the office, or that she seemed to know them well enough to feel comfortable doing so.

Stevie Geller and Jody Hadland made up fifty percent of Darlington's out-lesbian couple population, or at least they did during the school year. The rest of the time they spent jet-setting between New York and wherever else Stevie's plays were performed or her books were sold. Kelly knew them both in passing and suspected they knew about her sexual orientation, but she kept a polite distance for fear of being associated with too many lesbians.

Most people could overlook her friendship with Beth—everyone liked Beth. But for a single woman of her age to suddenly become close with a newly out teacher and her artist girlfriend would raise more than a few eyebrows. And really, what did she care? She didn't need some sort of lesbian cohort. Why base entire friendships on the gender she happened to feel attraction toward? If shared attraction mattered so much, she could just as easily become best friends with any random straight man who crossed her path. At least making friends with men could alleviate people's suspicions rather than arouse them.

Elliot didn't have to worry about other people's suspicions though. She had no problem chatting amicably with Jody and Stevie, even if she did sound a little awed as she said, "I can't imagine coming back to Darlington after a stint on Broadway."

"Off Broadway," Stevie corrected.

"Still, you have everything you need to be comfortable and successful in the center of the free universe. I don't know why you two keep coming back here."

"Of course you do," Jody said gently. "You understand better than just about any young person I've ever met."

Kelly wished she could see Elliot's face. Did she smile? Did her green eyes sparkle with a hint of mischief or mirth? She hadn't seen as much of those things from her over the last week. She hadn't seen as much of her, period. Not because they didn't work the same long hours. She'd heard of employees inflating their hours on a timecard, but she'd recently started to suspect Elliot deflated hers. She always seemed to be there, and yet when she turned in her log, the total always came to exactly what her internship director said it should.

Kelly kept meaning to mention her suspicions, but she never seemed to find the right time, what with trying to completely avoid casual conversation and open-ended questions. She wasn't proud of the way she held Elliot at arm's length. She didn't like the way she'd snapped at her last weekend. She hated the concern and confusion she saw every time she dared to meet her eyes.

For some reason it had never bothered her to avoid people like Jody and Stevie, but dodging Elliot brought her cowardice into sharp focus. Elliot wasn't a member of the larger Darlington community. She didn't contribute to the rumor mill, and Kelly had already given her plenty of fuel to throw on a fire if she wanted to. Elliot could've made her feel weak and vulnerable. Instead she'd behaved honorably, considerately, and with a great deal of grace.

"So, what do you guys have in the way of W-2 forms?" Elliot

continued in the other room. So easy, so comfortable, so confident. She knew her place, she knew what she wanted, and she knew how to get it. A twinge of something unfamiliar twisted in Kelly's chest. Admiration? Longing? Envy?

"Well . . ." Stevie drew out the word, "Jody has a W-2. I have royalties and honorariums and a few stipends and a grant and—"

Jody cut in. "We're complicated."

Kelly's chest ached, but Elliot only laughed and said, "The best things in life usually are."

഻ ഻ ഻

"You work all the time," Rory whined from the top of the bleachers.

"Oh, like you're one to talk!" Elliot shouted as her feet hit the shellacked wood floor and she broke into a sprint across midcourt.

"I think you're working harder on this internship than you did during any semester for me."

"Aw, are you jealous?"

"Maybe I'm wishing I could lower your grade retroactively," Rory grunted as they passed each other on opposite sides of the stairs.

"Good luck." Elliot shook a sweat-soaked strand of hair out of her eyes. She refused to quit running stairs first, but Rory seemed to have extra stores of energy tonight. "Besides, it's not like you've had time to hang out either, between classes and the gender symposium and wedding planning."

"Oh my God, longest engagement ever!" Rory panted, as she sprinted back to the other side of the gym.

Elliot tapped the top rung of the guardrail and pivoted back toward the court. "You should've eloped when you had the chance."

"Me and my political statements," Rory called over her shoulder. "Beth would've been happy to go down to the courthouse and then have a little picnic last summer, but I had to have a big gay wedding in Darlington, Illinois."

"Well, now you're paying for it in more ways than one."

"No kidding. Do you have any idea how much a caterer costs?"

"At least you get a faculty discount on the campus chapel."

121

"Nope. We're having the reception on campus, but Beth decided she wants to have the service at her church."

Elliot's foot faltered and her heel slipped off the stairs, sending her onto her ass with a painful thud.

Rory turned halfway up her flight of stairs. "Shit, are you okay?"

"Yeah." Elliot waved her off as she stood and rubbed a spot on her right butt cheek, where she'd surely find a bruise later. "I'm fine. I just thought you said you and Beth intended to get married at the little church off the town square."

Rory shook her head as she started back up the stairs. "We're gay, we pray, I guess they got used to us."

"Are you sure? Can you do that?"

"Apparently. Beth talked to the pastor, and he said he'd love to perform the ceremony."

"And what about you?" Elliot asked, turning toward the bench rather than trying to catch Rory. "How do you feel about this development?"

"It's the church her parents got married in," Rory said as she slowed her jog back down the stairs. "I think she thinks it'll help her feel close to them, and Lord knows my parents have been all over the wedding planning process, so who am I to deny her a small connection to her family?"

Elliot nodded as she grabbed her water bottle. "Makes sense. Families, they build us up, break us down, and rearrange the pieces."

"Yeah?" Rory asked. "Sounds about right for me, but I thought you and Syd were like the Gilmore Girls."

"We are. I mean, I wasn't really thinking about me specifically."

Rory sat on the floor and folded in half over her extended legs. "Who then?"

She didn't like lying. She and Rory had always talked openly about everything—sex, class, race, women, their hopes, their fears, their insecurities. Over the last three years, she'd told Rory everything that'd ever weighed on her mind for more than a few hours, and Rory had never failed to help her make sense of the world and her place in it. Part book-smart, part street-smart, part people-smart—at times Rory also felt like part God or at least part living legend—and she'd never withheld any of her observations. Surely if Rory could help her comprehend Judith Butler, she could offer some insight into Kelly Rolen. And yet, Elliot couldn't figure out how to broach the subject without betraying Kelly's trust.

"I didn't mean anyone specific, more of a general observation."

Rory glanced up at her as if she didn't quite buy the explanation.

"I've just noticed, working at the tax office, that a lot of people around here have family businesses. They do what their parents and even grandparents did."

"Beth's great-grandfather built the house we live in now."

"Exactly. On some level I wouldn't mind some roots. I guess I have them in my own ways, but what about when the mold no longer fits?"

"Then you have to break it, but around here, breaking molds and cutting ties—it's hard to explain and even harder to do."

"You did."

"I did, and I don't regret it. I am who I am because of the experiences I had, but I paid a price. I gave up a lot things, a lot of time, and the stakes were high for me. I had to get out in order to survive, at least for a while. Most people around here don't have the same motivation. They might not like everything about their lives, but they're safe, they're certain, and, like you said, family counts for a lot."

"What about family of choice?"

"They can count for a lot, too," Rory admitted, standing up and doing a few side bends. "But you and I, we understand that a family is something you make. I grew up hearing 'blood is thicker than water,' and maybe it's true, but in the gay community we've got more than water between us. We've got something stamped onto our DNA, something that marks us as belonging to each other every bit as much as we belong to our birth families. I'm not sure people outside the circle can ever fully understand a connection they've never experienced."

"But what about people who haven't gotten to experience either connection, not their birthright, and not their communal right, or maybe they've only seen parts of each?"

Rory froze, then stood up slowly, her green eyes searching Elliot's. "What's going on, Elliot? Did something happen at work or—"

"No," she said quickly. "No one specific, I mean nothing specific.

I've just come into contact with more people from the community the last few weeks, and I find myself wondering how you and Beth and Stevie and Jody all turned out the way you did when other people, random people, just keep doing the same things everyone who came before them did."

Rory shook her head and sighed before proceeding more carefully. "You're in a unique position at work. You can view things from an emotional distance that a lot of people are too close to see fully. But none of us ever really get the whole picture."

Did she know? Had something Elliot said given too much away, or had she already known? And if so, how much did she know? An echo of an earlier conversation filtered back through her mind. "*I knew something like this was going to happen.*"

"We all get called in our own ways and in our own time, and maybe some of us never answer," Rory said, "but it's got to be our choice. No one else can make it."

"Yeah," she said, grabbing her bag. "Thanks for the talk and the run."

"Let me guess. You have to get back to work?"

Elliot's smile felt less exuberant, so she could only assume it looked that way too. But she'd had to either pretend or fake so many interactions lately that one small smile hardly seemed to rank anymore.

ᔕ ᔕ ᔕ

"Hey," Elliot said as she pushed through the door on Monday afternoon. Kelly tried to remain neutral as she shed her jacket but noticed the warmer weather seemed to have an invigorating effect on Elliot. This morning she wore a gray suit coat over a white dress shirt open at the throat with dress slacks and turquoise Converse shoes. The style seemed the perfect cross between debonair and "who cares?," leaving Kelly to once again resolve to go shopping as soon as tax season ended. "How have things been today?"

"Busy," Kelly answered.

"Just the way we like it," Elliot said with a little grin. "Did you get the stack of completed returns I left in the hopper for you Saturday?"

124

"I saw them, but I didn't get to them yet. Was there something specific you wanted me to look over?"

Elliot shrugged. "Not particularly. They're mostly the ones you flagged for me to take over."

She wondered if Elliot had noticed that she'd started designating more returns for her and reading behind her less frequently. If pressed, she'd reason that as time went on and the workload got heavier, it made sense to give Elliot more responsibility. They both had to do their fair share, but while on the subject of fairness, she'd also have to admit to being impressed with Elliot's work so far. Thankfully, Elliot accepted the increased volume without question.

In fact, she hardly questioned anything anymore. Kelly tried not to let the professional distance disappoint her as she'd all but mandated it. She hadn't told Elliot to stop joking or arguing or asking too many questions, but she'd apparently shut her down enough times to send an equivalent message. And Elliot was nothing if not socially aware. She read people as well as anyone Kelly had ever met. The clients generally liked her immediately, and the ones who didn't at least ended up respecting her by the time they left. Kelly understood why. Despite her early prejudices, Elliot was just plain likable.

Maybe too likable. No. *Definitely* too likable, and not just in the business sense. Hence the need to throw up walls between them. She couldn't afford to like anyone as much as she could end up liking Elliot. For all her wonderful qualities, Elliot was still her intern, and only in town for a few more months. She was also flamingly gay. She'd initially wondered why Elliot didn't tone down her flamboyancy, but now she realized she simply couldn't. And that meant Kelly couldn't get too close, not emotionally, socially, or God forbid, physically.

Falling back on her old standby of having piles of work to do, she took Elliot's stack of completed returns and flipped through them. It didn't take long to scan the first few. They could both do a standard return in their sleep, and checking Elliot's work took even less effort, but something in the middle of the pile stopped her.

Her eyes flicked down the form, then back up to the heading. Stevie Gellar did not offer a simple return. She not only had a schedule C, she had to file in multiple states. A return like hers was so far out of the realm of Elliot's experience. Stevie's return should've never been in Elliot's to-do pile, much less in her completed files.

Kelly's temples pulsed a few times as she wandered back to her office and called up Stevie's tax file on her computer. Flipping through the forms, she scrolled simultaneously through the scanned documents in the DMS program. She double-checked all the identifying information, finding it correct. She'd likely have to redo whole sections, but at least Elliot had done the basic input work for her. And the expenses were correct, too, since everything that came out of Stevie's bank account worked for federal or Illinois statutes. She worried, though, that Elliot kept everything under the Illinois state income, so she clicked on the state allocation worksheet in the tax program and skimmed to the honorariums and stipends, and almost laughed. Pennsylvania, New York, California, Oregon—the list went on, but she'd done them all. At least seven different states. And so many of them figured at different rates depending on how the payment was earmarked. What's more, Elliot had itemized deductions for home office and utilities based on a percentage of time Stevie had worked both in Illinois and back at her apartment in New York City. She'd figured per diems for travel based on location as well.

Kelly sat back in her chair and pressed her index fingers to her temples. Perfect. Every single line. A return of this magnitude would've taken her hours, even after fifteen years of doing them, and she wasn't so fond of herself to believe she would've even taken on something of this level on her own, right out of school. She would've tried, but she would've had to check with her father several times. Why hadn't Elliot come to her? Did Elliot not need her help, or had she been too worried to ask for it? She didn't like the question, and she didn't care for either answer, though for very different reasons.

Her chest constricted at the realization of what an awful internship director she'd been for Elliot. She'd pushed her away, she hadn't asked her any real questions about her experience or her goals, and when Elliot had offered, she hadn't listened. She hadn't mentored, she hadn't taught, and apparently she hadn't even taken the time to get to know what Elliot was capable of. What else had she missed?

Curiosity piqued in her. Sure, she'd been able to overlook attraction, sexual orientation, and even sex itself, but a beautifully assembled Schedule C was too much to ignore. She wanted to know more about Elliot. Maybe work could offer her a safe way to have that conversation, or maybe it merely provided her a convenient excuse, but either way, she owed her more than a few curt compliments.

Heading to the front office, she cleared her throat, causing Elliot to look up from the scanner.

"Everything okay with those returns?"

"Yes, actually, it's great. You did a great job."

Elliot smiled broadly, then seemed to catch herself and nod less enthusiastically. "Thanks."

"No, thank you," Kelly said. "You've done a lot more around here than I've given you credit for."

"Just doing my job."

"Right, and it's my job to mentor you through the internship, but I realize I haven't even talked to you about your experience or your goals, other than smashing patriarchy of course."

"Well, that's the big one, but it's okay. You've got a lot going on. I don't even know when you eat or sleep."

"Well, I don't sleep much," Kelly admitted, "but I do have to eat, so I thought maybe we could do it together, tonight. Eat, I mean, not sleep."

Elliot's mouth quirked up and Kelly's face flamed, but she forged on through the awkwardness. "I usually get takeout and eat here. Nothing fancy, but if you wanted to stick around we could . . . talk?"

"Yeah," Elliot said, "sounds good."

"Good." Kelly said decisively. "All right then, go ahead and get back to work."

She turned and went back to her office, but she thought she might have heard Elliot chuckle softly. So the invitation wasn't her most graceful, but it wasn't a date. Oh God, did Elliot think she'd asked her out on a date? Surely not. Surely she'd made herself clear about the business, and the eating at the office, and the mentoring. Right? She shook her head. *Surely*, Elliot understood her intentions, because if she'd thought for one second that takeout in the office was the best date Kelly had to offer, she would've undoubtedly said no.

Chapter Eleven

"I didn't know for sure what you like, so I got turkey and pot roast with sides of mashed potatoes, green beans, and corn. And rolls, of course," Kelly said, pushing through the door with a leaning tower of to-go boxes.

Elliot sprang from her chair and relieved her of half the stack. The heavenly aromas made her stomach growl. "Wow, did you raid some grandma's dinner table? This smells amazing."

"It's just from the diner."

"What diner?"

"The Diner."

She stared at her, trying to figure out if she should simply know which diner Kelly referred to or if this conversation was the Darlington equivalent of "Who's on First." "Please tell me this diner has a name."

"It does," Kelly said spreading out the various containers across her desk. "It's called, 'The Diner.'"

"Classy. No wonder I've never ventured in there."

"Well now you can see what you've been missing."

Elliot didn't argue or offer any more comebacks. She didn't want to press her luck. This was the longest they'd talked about something other than work for two weeks, and she still had questions. So many questions, ranging from what had sparked the dinner invitation, to what Rory knew about Kelly and how, to what Kelly felt about what had happened between them. Still, the last time she'd actually asked a personal question, she'd about gotten her head bitten off.

"Go ahead," Kelly said. "Help yourself."

She didn't have to be told twice. None of her misgivings about the dinner had anything to do with food. "Wait, is any of this shockingly spicy?"

Kelly laughed. "No. I ordered off the spice-wuss menu."

"I'm not a spice wuss." Elliot defended herself while she filled her plate and sat back in her chair. "I just like to know ahead of time if someone intends to lace my gravy with napalm."

"Nothing to worry about here. It's all home-style cooking."

She took a bite of pot roast that fell apart in her mouth. "Nothing like this ever got cooked in my home."

"Really? Your mom didn't cook?"

"Syd?" Elliot laughed in spite of her worries about personal topics. "No. I mean, she can boil some pasta and put some sauce from a jar on top. She'll stack a mean deli-style sandwich, and she might arrange a fruit and cheese plate if she's feeling fancy, but I'm not sure I ever saw her use an oven for anything other than a frozen pizza. Mostly we ate out."

"I've heard of people in the city who eat out every night, but I've never met anyone who actually lived that way."

"Really? You cook every night?" Elliot asked without thinking, then braced herself for the reminder to mind her own business.

"Usually," Kelly said casually. "Tax season always requires me to eat out more than normal, but rarely as much as I have this year. I don't make anything as exotic as curried vegetables or whatnot, but given the time, I could easily prepare a meal to rival this one."

Elliot examined the food again. She had never seen anyone roast anything, but she assumed it didn't happen quickly or easily. "I would've never pegged you for the home and hearth type. You seem more like swashbuckling CEO material."

Kelly rolled her eyes. "You've had a skewed sample. I've been on edge lately."

"So you're not always so intense?"

She smiled. "I suppose it depends on who you ask. I guess a lot of people might call me intense. I may have also been called intimidating a time or two."

"No," Elliot said sarcastically, "not you."

"Yeah, well, I've always known what I wanted, and I've never been shy about doing what I needed to. That doesn't win any awards for congeniality in high school, but I like to think I earned some respect along the way."

"You did," Elliot said, both her confidence and comfort levels rising with every minute of casual conversation. "Your clients trust you, and they respect you. I see how easily they talk to you about their finances and the trials or triumphs behind them. These are private people. They'd talk about the weather for days before they'd admit to having trouble making ends meet, but they know you well enough to know you won't betray them."

"I have an abject hatred for the rumor mill," Kelly said stoically, then smiled. "But I didn't ask you here to fish for compliments or dish about Darlington."

"If you don't mind my asking, why did you ask me to stay for dinner? I'm not complaining, mind you, just surprised."

"I'm sorry." Kelly sighed. "I've never had an intern before. I know my short-comings, and I never thought I'd be a very good mentor, but circumstances necessitated your presence this year, and I've been so caught up about what that meant for me, I only just now realized I haven't been very fair to you."

"That's not true. You're one of the most fundamentally fair people I've ever met," Elliot said emphatically. "Even when I thought you might be on meth, and when I called you a homophobe and got angry at you for any number of other things, you always treated me fairly. You could've legitimately fired me at least three times now, and no one would've questioned you. Not even me."

Kelly pursed her lips. "I could have legitimately fired you on the first day, but the other times would've been iffy. Still, I'm glad I didn't. And I'm glad you're glad I didn't. But I feel like we've been through a lot without my really learning anything important about you."

"I got the sense you wanted to keep things that way," Elliot said carefully. She liked this sincere version of Kelly, but she worried about what lay just below the smooth surface.

"I guess I did, and part of me still does. But you did a very complicated schedule-C return today, and I found myself wondering who you are."

Elliot burst out laughing. "Really? After everything that happened, after the bigots and the bar fights and the coming out and—" She cut off the sentence quickly. "The everything else, the schedule-C tripped your trigger?"

Kelly's eye grew wide and her face flushed, causing Elliot to realize she might have crossed another invisible line. She tried to scuttle backwards as quickly as possible. "Okay, yeah, sure, 'cause we're having a business dinner and it's only natural to be here for business reasons. So, what do you want to know about my business?"

"Your business?"

"My business business, not my personal business."

"Right." Kelly recovered slowly. "How about you tell me where you learned about taxes?"

"Well, I've been in school for almost five years now, so I'm not a newbie or anything, but the type of stuff you're referring to came from working with the Volunteer Income Tax Assistance program. I'm not sure if you have much use for the VITA program in small towns, but it's a big deal in Chicago."

"I'm familiar with the process, but no, I haven't had more than a passing experience with it."

"Well, my mom's in finance law, so I knew a lot about the tax system from listening to her, and I always understood numbers, so when I saw that the Chicago Public Library system was training volunteers to help people with their taxes, I thought it would be a good way for me to get some service hours. You know, for college applications."

"You started doing taxes for underprivileged households when you were in high school?"

"Seemed like a better way to spend my time than walking dogs or babysitting," Elliot said between bites. "I already told you my mom is a major feminist, so I grew up knowing how privileged I am. I knew people with money could pay other people to find loopholes that help them keep or even make money off the tax system while people who didn't have the money or the education or connections usually got screwed. The rich get richer and the poor get the shaft. Shouldn't it be the other way around?"

"I'm not sure anyone should get the shaft."

"Right, because you believe in fairness," Elliot said with a grin. "But the more I worked within the system, the more I saw how subjective the system is, and it's even more so when talking about corporate taxes."

"And you decided all this by the time you finished high school?"

"Pretty much. I'd come out by then, too, so I'd started to feel a real drive to examine systems of power other people take for granted."

"Wait, you came out before you got to college?"

"Oh yeah." Elliot waived a hand. "I came out when I was fifteen." She laughed. "Honestly I could've come out sooner, but in my teenage angst I didn't want to give my mother the satisfaction of being right."

Kelly raised her eyebrows questioningly.

"Syd always thought I was gay. Some of it was wishful thinking, but she also saw the way I interacted with girls, and let's just say, I clearly didn't hang around them in the hopes of getting my hair or nails done."

"So she was happy when you told her?"

"Ecstatic. She rented the local LGBT center and threw a coming-out party."

Kelly shook her head slowly. "I can't even imagine."

"Yeah, I was horrified at the time. No fifteen-year-old wants to think they've fallen into their parent's plan from the beginning. I wanted to be my own person. I wanted to find my own way. I had to prove to myself and everyone else I had some fight in me."

"How could anyone doubt your ability to fight?"

"I'm one of the lucky ones, but that's all the more reason for me to want to help people who've been dealt a harsher hand. I don't want to waste my life doing something mundane, but I didn't want to just rebel in some clichéd way, either. I didn't want a blue Mohawk or a nose ring if I had a chance to make a real difference."

"I'm glad you didn't punch any holes in your face." Kelly's voice seemed somehow deeper, or more introspective. Her whole expression changed, as though her features were actually softening as the evening went on. "And I'm glad the hole left by a drunk's elbow seems to be healing nicely, too."

Elliot touched her eyebrow. The mark had all but faded over the last few weeks. "I don't know . . . it might have been cool to have a scar from a bar-fight story."

"You still have the story. There's no reason to tarnish your perfect face."

Elliot couldn't control her reaction to the compliment fast enough. She felt her eyes widen in surprise and her cheeks redden with pleasure.

"Don't act like that," Kelly said quickly. "You know you're good-looking. I'm sure you've been told a million times."

"Not nearly that many," Elliot said, then silently added, *and never by you.* "I don't fit a lot of people's ideals of traditional beauty."

"I just assumed that cocky little swagger you have came from being fawned over regularly."

She straightened her shoulders, her confidence soaring now. "I've got a swagger?"

Kelly scoffed. "Back to the topic at hand. So what's your master plan?"

Elliot needed a moment, after the unexpected compliment, to force herself back on track. "First I finish tax season here by helping you meet all our deadlines."

"Good answer," Kelly said. "What next?"

"I've still got some internship requirements, like a final paper, and I'm taking a CPA exam prep course online, but mostly I'll move on to the job search in earnest. Ideally I'd be at a non-profit organization that works for people who are typically disenfranchised by the financial system or who lobby for them. I'm also really interested in progressive policy think tanks."

"So you'll head back to Chicago?"

Elliot thought she heard a hint of disappointment in the question, but that could have been just her newly affirmed swagger talking. "Actually, I'd love to be in Washington, D.C. You know, take the fight right to the seat of power."

"Fight the power? Are you sure you're really twenty-five and not sixty-five?"

"What? You've never wanted to stick it to the man?"

"No," Kelly said dryly, "I've never wanted to get close enough to any man to stick anything anywhere."

Elliot laughed so hard she almost choked. "Wait a second, was that a gay pun? Did you just make an allusion to being a gay?"

"A gay?" Kelly whispered as she looked over her shoulder. "Is that what we call ourselves now?"

"As opposed to when?"

"I don't know," Kelly said, a hint of honesty edging back into her voice. "I believe Mrs. Anthony referred to something about the homosexual agenda once. Maybe we should ask her since she seems so well-versed on the subject."

"No way." Elliot shuddered. "There's no way someone that uptight has ever had sex with a woman."

Kelly stood and began to clean some of the food containers off the desk without further comment. She worked quietly, steadily, not rushed but clearly back to business. "Are you finished with your roll?"

"Uh, yeah," Elliot said, her bewilderment giving way to disappointment. She'd once again crossed one of those invisible lines. She felt helpless, and few things bothered her more than feeling helpless. She'd promised Kelly to respect her privacy. She'd promised to respect her position of authority. And more importantly, she'd promised to never make her feel shame or guilt or insecurity about what they'd done. And still, her disappointment gave way to frustration, tightening the muscles in her jaw and shoulders. Kelly had, once again, started this whole exchange. She had not only called this dinner, she moved the conversation into personal territory. She brought up the topic of being gay. Hell, she'd made the first joke. Why could she relax and speak her mind while Elliot had to tiptoe around trip wires she didn't even know existed?

"Not fair," she said aloud without thinking.

"What?" Kelly looked up.

"I think," Elliot started slowly, "I said 'it's not fair.'"

"Excuse me?"

"When you shut down on me in the middle of a conversation without telling me why. It's not fair."

"I have a right to—"

"Of course you do," she interrupted. "You don't have to tell me anything. You owe me nothing, and I haven't pushed you to give me anything, but you keep doing this little tap dance, two steps here then a quick kick back. One minute you're bringing up things I'm apparently not allowed to talk about, and you're joking like it's nothing, but then I say something in exactly the same vein and—poof, you're gone."

"Don't be dramatic," Kelly said, carrying their paper plates to the trashcan in the hallway. "I'm right here."

"You are, but you aren't. Not in the way you were here a minute ago. You're not laughing and talking. You can't even look me in the eye."

"I can look you in the eye. I'm just multitasking."

"Fine." Elliot got up and followed her down the hall. "Look me in the eye."

Kelly wheeled around. "I don't like being told what to do."

"And I don't like being told what I can't do."

"I didn't tell you what you can't do."

"No, you're right. You expect me to intuit what's going to set you off, and that's worse."

"I think this conversation is over."

"Of course it is." Elliot threw up her hands. "But can you look me in the eye and tell me why?" Kelly pushed open the door to her office, but Elliot caught her hand and gave it the gentlest of tugs. "Please, Kel. Tell me why."

Kelly froze and turned to examine her with those big, dark eyes. She didn't respond, but she didn't pull away either.

"I'm not demanding," Elliot whispered. "I'm asking. Please."

Kelly pursed her lips as though she might close up again, but instead she sighed. Her shoulders sagged and her fingers intertwined with Elliot's. "When you said no one as uptight as Mrs. Anthony has ever had sex with a woman, it occurred to me that other people would say the same if they ever heard rumors about me."

"Oh." Elliot didn't know what to say. She'd asked, but she hadn't been quite prepared for the answer.

"I don't like the idea of people talking about me."

"I don't think they are."

"Maybe not yet. But if anyone saw us together in any situation

135

other than work, they would talk. Half of them would jump right on the most salacious possibility and say I can't keep my hands off you, and half of them would say I'm too uptight to ever carry on an affair with you. And you know what bothers me the most?"

Elliot shook her head.

"They're both right."

"Kelly?" Elliot asked slowly, her chest full of emotions that pushed at her rib cage and expanded her lungs, but she didn't dare let any one of them take hold until she got some clarification. Only she didn't know which point she wanted to clarify first. "You can't keep your hands off me?"

Kelly glanced down to their intertwined fingers. "Apparently not. And I can't keep you at arm's length emotionally, either. I've tried. God—I've tried work, and distraction, and being outright rude to you, but then I go and suggest this dinner tonight—"

"Which was wonderful."

"Yes. But it shouldn't have been. It should've been business, taxes, case studies, and job searching tips, but all I can think about with you sitting across from me is what a great smile you have, and how your passion makes you even more magnetic, and how, no matter how hard I struggle against your pull, I only end up wanting to be closer to you."

Elliot's breath caught in her throat. She didn't know what she could possibly say in return to make Kelly understand how she'd just turned her insides to mush. Kelly liked her. Kelly wanted her. Kelly was holding her hand and looking up at her with those pleading brown eyes. And her lips—so full and red against her pale skin.

Suddenly the lack of words didn't matter. She didn't know what to say because she didn't have to say anything. A certainty she'd often hoped for but rarely experienced washed over her as she pulled Kelly close, wrapping her free arm around Kelly's slender waist and relishing the feel of their bodies pressed together for a few delicious seconds. Then, lowering her head, she took Kelly's mouth with hers.

෴ ෴ ෴

Kelly moaned, melting into the kiss. God, she needed this. She still had the awareness to realize she might regret the kiss later, but she simply didn't care. Right then, the only thing that mattered was the sensual press of Elliot's lips.

God, she could kiss. Kelly eagerly opened up to everything Elliot had to offer. Hot and wet, and so damn skilled, Elliot owned her. She backed her across the office until she bumped up against the desk. A cup full of pencils clattered to the floor, and Kelly felt as if the walls she'd put up to guard herself from this moment might make the same sound as they tumbled down.

Elliot's fingers splayed across the small of her back, holding her close and caressing her through the thin cotton of her oxford shirt. She wanted those hands everywhere. She had to touch Elliot all over. Needed to feel her smooth skin.

Cupping Elliot's face with her free hand, she caressed her cheek, then ran the tips of her finger up to the faint ridge above her eyebrow. She traced the thin line, remembering the wound that had split them both open the first time. This time she brought more composure to the encounter, but she didn't delude herself into thinking she had any more control. With Elliot, loss of control seemed to be just another one of her many draws.

She ran her fingers back down Elliot's jaw line, then followed the subtle cleft in her chin right under the lips that worked magic against her own. Elliot kissed her slowly, passionately, luxuriously, and still she craved more.

She slid her hand down Elliot's chest, circling each button before dipping lower until she hooked one finger through a belt loop and gave a little tug. Elliot pushed closer, spreading her legs just enough for Kelly to work one of hers into the empty space. She thrilled at the cool silk of Elliot's slacks against the heat of her own thigh.

Elliot pulled her lips away only far enough to skim them across the curve of her neck, first kissing, then nibbling as she went.

"God help me, I can't get enough of you." Kelly threw her head back in a primal show of surrender, but submission to whatever this thing between them might mean did not equate to passiveness. She worked her hand along the waistline of Elliot's trousers, caught hold of the zipper, and pulled. It made such a satisfying sound in the silent office, and she felt power surge through her. She could take, she could possess, she could have everything she wanted right now. Loosening her grip on restraint had finally given her the type of control she'd been missing for years.

Then the phone rang, harsh and shrill, an alarm waking them from the most wonderful dream. They both jumped, then stared at each other in surprise.

"Leave it," Elliot said, between heavy breaths.

Kelly nodded and grabbed Elliot's shirt, pulling her back in. "We're closed. They can call back tomorrow."

Elliot leaned close again, touching her forehead to Kelly's and waiting until the phone stopped sounding its warning before asking, "Are you okay?"

"Yes." Kelly kissed her cheek. "How about you?"

"Yes." The word fluttered against her skin, heating as it went.

"Good. Then where were we?"

Elliot sprang forward again, hips, legs, lips, and all of her body weight pinning Kelly to the desk in the most gloriously intrusive way, but before they even got back to the point where they'd left off, Kelly's cell phone rang and rattled its way across the desk.

"Kill it," Elliot said hoarsely into the arch of her neck.

She shared the initial impulse, and if only she'd had a hammer handy, she might have smashed it, but she didn't, and in reaching for it, she saw the number flash red across the screen. She stiffened, and Elliot immediately got the message.

"What? What's wrong?"

"It's the hospital."

Elliot sagged against her, then pushed back enough to let her straighten. "Okay. You have to take it."

Kelly bit her lip and tried to hold back a scream, but she used her free hand to retrieve the phone.

Elliott gave their still-connected hands a gentle squeeze. "It'll be okay. It's probably nothing."

She nodded, but she didn't believe it. Her life simply didn't work that way. "Hello."

"Miss Rolen?" an unfamiliar voice asked.

"Yes, this is she."

"I'm calling about your father. He seems to have had another stroke, a small one or a couple small ones. We call them TIA strokes or mini-strokes."

She knew the term. She'd read up on strokes enough to know they happened frequently enough to be a concern. She also knew they weren't a good sign, the opposite of the progress she'd hoped for. She couldn't think of what the opposite of progress was, and she didn't have the time or wherewithal to worry about semantics. "And my father had one of these TIA strokes?"

Elliot held her hand a little tighter.

"Yes, I'm afraid he's had at least one."

"At least one?" Why did she always end up reverting to just repeating things in these types of conversations?

"Yes, some of the side effects from his original stroke have returned. We've moved him back to critical care. He's stable, but the doctor wants us to be prepared to transport him to St. Louis if his condition worsens."

Kelly closed her eyes tightly. She couldn't handle this. She couldn't handle anything else right now.

"It's okay," Elliot whispered in her ear. "Tell them you'll be right there."

She took a deep breath and tried to draw strength from Elliot's soothing tone, then, finding her voice once more, managed to say, "I'm on my way."

She ended the call and looked up at Elliot, who managed to smile weakly.

"I'm sorry," Kelly said. "I can't believe I'm going to do this to you again, but—"

"I understand," Elliot said. "You have to go."

Kelly stood a little straighter. "Thank you."

Elliot opened her mouth as if to say more, then closed it again. She gave Kelly's hand one last squeeze, then released her. "I hope everything's okay."

"Me, too." Kelly blindly grabbed a few files off her desk and headed toward the door. "It's probably going to be a late night. I don't know if I'll be back."

"Of course. I'll take care of everything here," Elliot said, shifting back and forth, then looking down and noticing her zipper was still undone. Her cheeks turned pink as she pulled it back up.

She seemed so sweet and awkward and vulnerable. Kelly almost cried to have to leave her. Instead she stepped back and kissed her quickly on the mouth one more time. "I really am sorry." What else could she say? Whatever happened between them had to take a back seat to her real life. Her real commitments. The things that would really matter long-term. There shouldn't even be a conflict here. And still she felt torn enough to want to make them both understand.

Elliot forced a smile. "Just go."

And she did. She walked out the door without looking back because she had to. But for the first time in a long time, she really didn't want to.

Chapter Twelve

"Good morning," Beth said cheerfully. "I brought you some W-2s and homemade blueberry muffins. Which do you want first?"

"Muffins," Elliot said, then added an exaggerated, "duh."

Beth laughed, and a dark curl fell into her eyes. She was so damned adorable. No wonder Rory never could put her foot down about all the wedding business. "You want some coffee?"

"Some of Kelly's coffee? No, thank you."

"I took over the coffee-making responsibilities during my first week on the job. I even bring the good stuff from home."

"Well, in that case," Beth said sitting down in the chair opposite her desk, "fill me up."

Elliot poured them two piping hot mugs and added only slightly more sugar to Beth's than she did her own before she took her seat.

"So, you mentioned something about muffins?"

"You heard that, did you?" Beth opened up a reusable grocery bag and pulled out a tin full of yummy goodness. "These are for you *and* Kelly, so don't eat all of them."

Elliot took a big inhale of the fresh baked goodies. "Kelly who?"

Beth laughed again. "Is she in?"

"No." Elliot tried to hide her frown. "She got called to the hospital last night. I haven't talked to her since."

Beth's brow furrowed with concern. "I take it she didn't get good news."

She didn't want to betray anything, "It didn't sound like it. She left in a hurry."

She didn't take the departure personally. She understood why Kelly had to go. If it were Syd, she would've done the same thing, but she didn't have to like it. And she didn't have to like that Kelly didn't call or text. She really didn't like coming in the next morning to find the office dark and empty. But she couldn't very well tell Beth any of that. She couldn't tell Beth anything. Hell, she couldn't tell anyone anything.

"You seem worried."

She shook her head to clear her thoughts. "Maybe a little bit. Mostly I'm tired."

"You're not putting in too many hours, are you?"

"No," Elliot said quickly, then stuffed her mouth with muffin. At least she didn't mind lying about her work nearly as much as she minded lying about Kelly. Hour restrictions were silly. Or maybe they came from a good place, but Kelly didn't force her to put in the extra time. She chose to. She found the work challenging and wanted to help. Besides, she didn't exactly have anything else to do in Darlington.

"Okay, I just know Kelly can come across as . . . intense."

She loved the way everyone danced around those types of descriptors. Maybe rural Midwesterners saw intensity as a bad thing, but she admired Kelly's ferocity, even when she found it inconvenient. If she had to name qualities that drew her to Kelly, she would list things like competency and confidence and, yes, even intensity. Kelly might not always make the choices she would've made, but once she decided to do something, she damn well did it.

"Kelly's great."

Beth eyed her seriously. "Kelly's great?"

"What, you disagree?"

"No," she said quickly, "I don't. I think Kelly's a special person. She's very important to me."

Elliot raised her eyebrows as she once again got the sense of something unspoken beneath Beth's comments.

"She's loyal, fair, steadfast, and she's got a bigger heart than she likes to let on, but a lot of people don't take the time to see those qualities. I thought you might, but I worried the two of you would clash until you got to know her."

"We did at first," Elliot said, then realized they'd actually sort of clashed the night before, too, only in a different way. "We're in a better place now."

"Good," Beth said as though they'd just come to some agreement. "Then I feel good about leaving Rory's and my taxes in your very capable hands."

"Oh, I get to see what the great rebel warrior makes for a living?" she teased.

"Don't act too disappointed when you see the actual pay stubs. Telling people they're failing queer youth doesn't get her many big bonuses."

"Not the monetary kind, mind you, but I'm sure she's storing up treasures in heaven."

"You're too smooth for your own good, but I'm going to use that one next time she's depressed after balancing the checkbook," Beth said. "In the meantime, do you mind if I use your restroom?"

"Go right ahead," Elliot answered, flipping through the documents Beth left on her desk. She was already putting papers in order to be scanned when she heard a door open. It took her another couple of seconds to realize she'd heard the back door, not the bathroom door.

She sprang to her feet and met Kelly in the hallway.

"Morning," Kelly said. Her eyes were accentuated with dark circles, and she wore her hair down, which made her face seem even thinner than usual, but her smile at least appeared genuine.

"Morning," Elliot replied carefully, casting a purposeful glance toward the bathroom. "How's everything with your dad?"

"Not as bad as it could be," she said. "He's stable, and still at least somewhat verbal when he's awake, which isn't very often."

"Good."

Kelly sighed. "Thank you for being so understanding last night. I know I don't have a very good track record."

"No worries," Elliot said quickly, then nodded toward the bathroom door again, but the gesture seemed to be lost on Kelly, who stepped closer and took her hand. The contact was so unexpectedly sweet Elliot couldn't bring herself to pull away.

"Really, I didn't plan anything about how we ended things. Everything after dinner caught me off guard, but I didn't want a repeat of last time. You deserve better."

"Kelly—" She swallowed her emotions. She needed to hear those words from her. She'd been dying to have this conversation for weeks, but, they couldn't have it now.

Kelly pulled on her hand. "I'm not really good at talking about my feelings, and even less adept at admitting I have needs."

"Kel," Elliot pleaded, "listen to me."

The doorknob to the bathroom turned and Elliot jumped back just as Beth stepped into view. "So as I was saying, Beth stopped by to drop off her taxes." Elliot shifted awkwardly from one foot to the other. "And she brought muffins."

Kelly blinked a few times and then stiffened. Elliot watched the little muscles in her jaw twitch while she silently begged her to say something.

"Hi, Kel," Beth said airily.

The name sounded intimate, and she realized she'd just used the same one. Had Beth heard? Is that why she'd chosen to use it? Surely not. The connection had to be coincidental, and yet as she thought back, she couldn't recall ever hearing anyone else shorten Kelly's name.

"Hi, Beth," Kelly finally said.

"Did I interrupt something?" Beth asked.

"No," Elliot and Kelly both said quickly, perhaps a bit too quickly.

"Because I can leave if you two need to be alone."

Elliot laughed loudly. "What, to talk about our very clandestine tax filing plots? Don't be silly." Shit. The lie happened too fast, too easy.

To Beth.

She'd just lied to Beth about a woman.

And she'd done so quickly, easily, naturally.

"Elliot," Kelly said, "will you get Beth's files scanned for me? I'd like to look at them myself."

"Sure thing," she said, grateful for the cue to exit, but since her desk sat well within earshot of the hallway, she still heard everything they said.

"How are you doing?" Beth asked, slowly looking from Kelly to Elliot.

"Tired, but okay."

"And how's your dad?"

"He's stable, but not improving. In fact, he's relapsed a bit."

"I'm so sorry." The suspicion faded from Beth's voice as concern took over. "Is there anything I can do to help?"

"No," Kelly said, the exhaustion evident under a thick layer of tension. "I've got plenty of work to keep me busy, but I can handle everything."

"Of course you can," Beth said, "but if you want any help or company or . . . never mind." Beth must have realized she was speaking to the emotional equivalent of a brick wall or a locked door. Kelly might as well have not even been in the room. "You're in work mode. I'll let you get back to it."

"Thank you," Kelly said, her voice remote. "I'll let you know when your taxes are done."

"You can just have Elliot tell Rory next time they work out."

Kelly didn't respond, and Elliot didn't know if she'd just reached her breaking point or if something else had torqued her off even more.

"I'll see you later," Beth said to Elliot as she slipped on her jacket. "Why don't you come over for dinner later in the week?"

"I'll check my schedule, but I'm pretty busy."

Beth turned to look at Elliot closely once again, her blue eyes darker than usual, and her brow creased with concern or consternation. Elliot's chest constricted with the pressure to offer some explanation, but as Beth turned to glance down the hall, they both seemed to understand why she couldn't.

"Okay," Beth said, "but I hope you know, Rory and I are here for you any time. No matter what."

Emotion clogged Elliot's throat so thickly she could only manage a single word "Thanks."

It would have to be enough, for now.

෨ ෨ ෨

Kelly heard Beth leave, then she heard a great deal of paper shuffling followed by a couple of heavy sighs. A few minutes later, she heard the scuff of footsteps in the hallway accompanied by more sighs. She pressed her fingers to her temples, trying to hold off a headache. She should put Elliot out of her misery, but she didn't want to deal with her right now. She didn't want to deal with anything anymore, but quitting wasn't an option. Not for her. Normally she prided herself on never having been one to walk away from her responsibilities, but this morning she really did understand the urge, and that terrified her.

"Elliot, can I help you with something?"

"No. I mean, yes. Maybe."

"Well, those are all the options, aren't they?"

At least Elliot smiled as she poked her head into the doorway. "You're not too mad to be a smart aleck to me. Can I take that as a good sign?"

Why did she have to seem so damn hopeful all the time? If Kelly wasn't careful, some of Elliot's youthful optimism might wear off on her, and while that might not seem like such a bad thing, optimism made people take unreasonable risks. Risks with consequences Elliot wouldn't have to stick around to face.

"Come in," Kelly said. "Have a seat."

"Uh-oh, you sound very formal," Elliot said, but she complied with the request.

"We've got a rather serious situation here," Kelly started, then realized she did, in fact, sound overly formal. They weren't having a business meeting. She couldn't compartmentalize their relationship, no matter how much she wanted to, which, of course, was a big part of the problem. "I don't know what to say. Obviously, I've never been in a situation like this before. Nothing even remotely like this."

"You've never had a, um, fling?"

Somehow, hearing Elliot label what had happened between them made her feel worse. "No. And certainly not with an intern, and during tax season, and my father's sick, and—"

"Okay," Elliot said. "It's okay."

"It's not okay." A hint of panic rose in her voice. "We got caught."

"We didn't get caught. We had a near miss, but she didn't see anything."

"She doesn't have to. Beth is intuitive. She knows something's

146

going on." Beth didn't need to be told what Kelly looked like in the midst of a stolen moment. She'd lived them with her.

Beth.

Could there be a bigger betrayal? A bigger fall? If only it had been someone else, she could pretend. She could deny. She could even act like she didn't care, but the thought of Beth knowing how far she'd fallen would be too much to bear.

"She suspects something's off, but she doesn't know what. How could she, really? No one would peg you for gay."

Kelly bit her lip and stared down at her hands, suddenly riveted by the details of her own cuticles.

"Oh my God. Beth knows." Elliot's hands went to her face. "She's known all along. Rory, too. Shit, everything makes so much more sense now."

"What makes more sense?"

"Everything, the looks, the warnings, the checking on me. Even before I got the internship, they knew. Does everyone know? Am I the only one who didn't get the memo?"

"No, only a handful of people have ever known. I'm not out."

"You're out to them. This whole time I've been lying to them. I lied to people I love, people who have treated me like family, to protect you, and they knew."

"They don't know what happened between us."

"Does that matter?"

"Yes," she practically yelled, "of course it matters."

"Does it matter enough to make me a liar?"

The question caught in her chest. Had she asked Elliot to lie? She hung her head. Of course she had. Seeing the pain and betrayal in Elliot's beautiful eyes, she finally realized what a lie of that nature cost someone like her. And yet Elliot had made the sacrifice for her.

"I've been so selfish," she murmured.

"What?"

"We can't do this anymore," she said. Talk about unfair. She'd crossed so many lines with Elliot she didn't even know how to be fair to her anymore. Cutting her off now without a full explanation didn't seem right. And yet, weighing her down with any more burdens wouldn't do her any favors, either. Kelly had made her choices out of necessity, and she'd made her own peace with what she'd had to do, but Elliot deserved better. She could have better, if only Kelly would get out of the way. The closet might be the only reasonable option for her, but she couldn't wish that life on Elliot. Not even short-term.

"Elliot," she said, coming around to the front of her desk, "we can't do this anymore. It's too risky on too many levels."

"It's not. Beth wouldn't hurt either of us."

Just hearing those words hurt more than Elliot could ever understand. "Not on purpose, but it's not right to put her in that position. It's not right to put you there, either."

"I'm an adult. Don't I get to make that decision for myself?"

"No, you don't," Kelly said sadly, "not when I'm the one who has to live with the fallout."

"What fallout?" Elliot asked. "Why can't we face it together?"

"You can't understand," Kelly fired back. There would be no *together*. There was no *we*. Elliot would move on. She wanted to. She had to. Neither of them could risk their futures for something that wouldn't even exist in a few months.

"Help me understand."

Elliot didn't know what she was asking. She couldn't possibly, and she shouldn't have to. "This situation is so much bigger than you, so far beyond your comprehension you can't even see the edges, much less the big picture."

Elliot stood, putting their bodies entirely too close for Kelly to think logically. "Try me."

She took a step back and bumped the desk, a wave of visceral memories washing over her. God help her, she wanted Elliot's long, light form pressed against hers. She longed for the oblivion that came with surrendering to those baser instincts. Nothing would matter anymore if only Elliot's mouth would take hers again.

The bell on the front door chimed, signaling an unexpected arrival.

"Are you fucking kidding me?" Elliot grumbled.

Kelly certainly understood the sentiment, but she used the distraction to regain her composure. Straightening up, she slipped out from behind Elliot and headed for the front door.

She'd already plastered a fake smile on her face before she saw John Bale, but she had to fight to hold it. "John," she said, hoping he couldn't tell her teeth refused to unclench. "What brings you in today?"

"I got a call from your receptionist saying my taxes were ready to sign."

"My receptionist?"

"That would be me," Elliot said as she exited the office behind Kelly. "I'll get those for you, Mr. Bale."

"No need," Kelly said. "I'll take care of him."

John smiled almost bashfully. "Thanks, Kelly. I was actually hoping you'd be in when I stopped by. I know you've been out at the hospital a lot lately."

She tried not to grimace. She didn't like people following where she went or speculating as to why.

"I know this is your busiest time, and I thought maybe I could bring you by some dinner sometime."

"That's so nice of you to offer, but I can't really take time off."

"No." He shifted his weight to his other foot. "I don't suppose you can, but you have to eat, right?"

Kelly blew a stray strand of hair out of her eyes. Like she needed one more thing to deal with today. She glanced to Elliot, intending to signal for help, but when she saw those expressive green eyes watching her expectantly, she froze.

If John left, they'd be alone again, and she simply couldn't stand the turmoil anymore. Not with the temptation so strong. She had to put some distance between them, and not just in the physical sense. She had to let Elliot off the hook. She couldn't ask her to lie anymore, and she couldn't even leave her in a position where she felt obligated to do so. Kelly's chest constricted the way it always did when she did what she was about to do, but taking the steps necessary to protect herself had become second nature over the years. Surely she could take the same steps to protect Elliot. She owed her at least that much.

"You know what, John?" she said. "I can't plan anything too far out these days, but I do have some time for lunch today."

"Really?" His barrel chest puffed with pride. "I think I could make lunch work. What time?"

"Just give me an hour to wrap up a few projects here, and then I have a couple of errands to run, so I'll be out and about anyway. I could meet you somewhere by 11:30."

"The Diner?"

"Sounds perfect."

He smiled broadly. "Perfect, then. I'll see you soon."

Kelly nodded, her smile so tight it strained her cheeks until the door closed behind him.

"He didn't sign his taxes."

"Hmm?"

"He forgot what he came in here for," Elliot said dryly, "unless of course he came in here to ask a lesbian out on a date, in which case he got exactly what he wanted."

"Elliot . . ." This wouldn't be easy, but she'd gone too far to lose her fortitude now. "Please just accept the situation for what it is."

"Sure, if you will explain to me what the hell is happening here."

"This morning was a warning for both of us."

"Nothing happened!"

"But something could have."

"So what? Beth knows you're gay."

Something sharp twisted in her chest. "And the flippancy with which you just said that shows how little you understand."

"How can I understand when you won't explain it to me?"

Kelly sighed. "You're right. You can't understand. What I'm doing is beyond you and your life experiences, and I'm happy for you."

"What's that supposed to mean?"

"It means you don't get what it takes to stay in the closet. To live there for years, decades even."

Elliot's eyes widened. "Decades?"

"A lifetime," Kelly confirmed.

"Don't say that." Elliot's voice softened. "Things are hard right now, but they won't always be this way. You'll come out as soon as things settle down. You've already told Beth and Rory. They'll help."

Kelly's laugh was acidic. "And that right there is why I'm going on a date with John."

"What? Why? What did I say?"

150

"It's not what you said. It's what you assumed," she explained, no longer trying to hide the anger in her voice. "You just take it for granted that I want to come out someday. You think the right person can come along and liberate me. You think it's some foregone conclusion that everyone wants to be like you or Rory, but I don't want your life."

"You want to sneak around and hide and lie about who you are?"

"This is only a tiny part of who I am. I don't want to be defined by some small sliver of myself. I don't want to be some super-gay, crusading mascot." Elliot winced, but Kelly had her on the ropes now. She couldn't let up. She had to land the decisive blow, the one neither of them could ever recover from. "I don't want my entire identity to be defined by who I happen to sleep with occasionally, and quite frankly, I find it a little pathetic that you do."

Elliot gasped as though Kelly had punched her in the stomach. Her eyes watered and her face flamed.

Kelly had to get away fast, or she wouldn't be able to get away at all. She delivered a sharp dose of tough love in order to inoculate Elliot against a much greater pain, but in the face of the very raw emotions playing across her beautiful features, Kelly could no longer feel certain she'd chosen the right treatment.

Her heart thudded dully in her chest. What if she'd made a mistake? What if she'd just screwed up the only good thing left in her life? What if she'd hurt Elliot more than she could ever make up to her?

She shook her head. Even if she hadn't done the right thing, she'd done it for the right reasons, and she couldn't unsay what she'd said. The only thing she could do now was get back to work. "Now, if you'll hand me John's file, I'll take it to him at lunch."

Elliot snapped the folder up off her desk and thrust it into Kelly's outstretched hand. "Just tell him if he has any questions, he can call your receptionist."

Kelly literally bit her tongue to keep from responding. Nothing she could say now would help anything. She summoned all her remaining fortitude and did the best thing she could do for them now.

She walked away.

⁙ ⁙ ⁙

Syd answered the phone on the second ring. "Hey, Tiger." She'd always refused to call Elliot gendered pet names like "princess" or "baby doll," but she did favor some of the more traditionally fierce monikers that conveyed affection.

"Hey," Elliot said, not sure where to go from there. She hadn't really thought the phone call through before she'd dialed. She hadn't been able to make much sense out of anything since Kelly had walked out the door, but she'd desperately wanted to hear her mother's voice.

"Actually, I just set a reminder to call you tonight."

"Yeah? Does that mean you're too busy to talk to me now?"

"I've got a client coming in soon, but since I've got you on the line, I might as well spill the good news."

"Good news?" She could certainly use some.

"I spoke to one of the other partners here this morning, and she said her college roommate is dating a woman who works for the Tax Policy Institute."

Elliot tried to follow the train of loose connections, but her brain had a hard time putting things together while still trying to process everything that had fallen apart over the last half an hour.

"The Tax Policy Institute," Syd repeated for effect.

"In Washington, D.C.," Elliot said, to prove she had heard and knew of the organization.

"Exactly. Well, turns out they just got a big government grant to research ways to simplify the tax filing process."

Elliot couldn't manage to feel much excitement, and not just because the woman she'd most recently had sex with had just blown her off for a barrel-chested farmer John in a Rural King hat. Simplifying tax returns had long been a stated goal for both political parties, but the tax preparers' lobby spent millions of dollars every year fighting any bills that might put a damper on their business. The likes of H&R Block, TurboTax, and countless others benefitted from a complex system.

"Hello," Syd said, "are you okay? Do you have a fever?"

152

She smiled. Whenever something seemed off, Syd assumed she had a fever. It didn't matter that she couldn't remember the last time she'd actually had a fever. If she were in arm's reach, Syd would no doubt have a hand on each of their foreheads to try to gauge any temperature differences, mom-style. "No fever, just not sure where you're going with this."

"I'm not going anywhere. You, on the other hand, are going to Washington, D.C. for an interview. If you want one. I'm not telling you what to do, mind you."

"An interview for what?"

"Oh, did I not say they're hiring five research fellows?"

Elliot laughed. "No, you left that part out."

"Oh, well, they're hiring five research fellows. They're looking for people right out of school with CPA licenses and a few years' experience. How many people fit the bill better than you?"

"Probably hundreds," she said, but she got excited enough to stand and pace.

"But you're one of the best."

"You're biased, but yeah. I mean a lot of people don't get licensed right out of school, or they don't come out of school with more than one tax season under their belt." She felt her hopes rise. "I've also got work with small businesses and the university."

"And VITA," Syd added. "If they are studying low-income returns, you've got as much experience as anyone right out of college. Plus you're willing to relocate quickly, right?"

The question gave her more pause than it should have. Kelly had all but told her she didn't want her around. But still, Kelly's father was sick. She didn't have any other help. Sure, tax season would be over soon, but what about people who needed extensions? What about catching up on all the year-round work that got set aside during tax season? Could Kelly do everything on her own?

No, she couldn't think that way. She'd worked for years to have an opportunity at a job like the Tax Policy Institute. They were one of the premier think tanks in the entire field, and they had five open positions tailor-made for her. She'd be an idiot to pass up a shot at one of those fellowships for a woman who'd just called her pathetic.

"Yeah, of course I'd move quickly. I mean it's Washington, D.C. I'm sure I could arrange everything with the college. As long as the job starts after tax season, I will have completed my internship hours. I can submit my final papers long-distance, and my CPA exam course is online." She rattled off all the reasons she could go, choosing to focus on them instead of the one reason she shouldn't want to stay.

"Good, because you've got an interview next Friday."

Elliot felt a little dizzy. "How?"

"I told you. One of the partners' college roommates is dating a woman who works there," she said in the same tone of voice she used when Elliot left wet towels on her bedroom floor. "She knows all about you, and she'd like to talk to you."

"Do I need to send them anything?"

"I already emailed your résumé."

"Mom!"

"Don't 'Mom' me. This isn't like the times I let you dress yourself when you were three just to avoid a tantrum. If you'd sent your stuff, it would've gone into the slush pile with all the other applicants. This way it goes right to the committee members."

Her stomach tightened. "I don't want to get a job because my mom knows someone."

"You don't have the job. You have an interview. This is how business works. Connections get your foot in the door. You have to take it from there."

She wasn't sure she believed the logic completely. She was still getting an advantage many of the other applicants didn't have, but she would be the one to seal the deal or fall flat on her ass in the interview. Surely if she didn't belong in the same class as the top applicants, both she and the hiring committee would know soon enough. "Okay. So, a week from Friday. Ten days. I'll have to miss work."

"Surely your boss will be sympathetic."

Elliot snorted. The word sympathetic didn't seem an apt descriptor for Kelly, but Elliot didn't think she'd stop her. "I'll make it work."

"Good. We'll talk more later about how to prepare, but right now I have to run. My client's here."

"Oh, okay." Elliot wished Syd wouldn't hang up just yet, but she couldn't think of a logical reason to say so. "I'll talk to you later. And thank you. For everything."

"I love you, Champ."

"I love you, too, Syd."

She hung up the phone and flopped back into her desk chair. An interview. At a think tank. Doing research that could lead to actual policy changes. And in Washington, D.C. She couldn't ask for a better opportunity. Why wasn't she happier?

Did she really care about leaving Kelly in a lurch after everything she'd said and done over the last twenty-four hours? She owed her nothing. They weren't dating. They weren't lovers. They weren't even fuck-buddies. Kelly clearly didn't care about her at all.

Her stomach flip-flopped again. It didn't make sense. Not after last night. Not even after the way Kelly had come through the door this morning. She'd been sweet and affectionate. Hell, that's why Elliot hadn't been able to warn her about Beth sooner. Kelly had been too eager to talk to her, too emotional. Nothing like she'd been only moments later. Had the stress gotten to her? She'd made a legitimate point about Elliot not understanding the pressures associated with life in the closet.

"Fuck," she said aloud. Why was she sitting here making excuses for Kelly? Who let a woman she barely knew and had sex with only once treat her like crap? And who would then look for ways to absolve the woman? A doormat, a coward, someone with no backbone. Kelly's actions were unacceptable. A sick dad and a chosen life of closetude didn't give her the right to treat other people like shit.

More importantly, even if Kelly hadn't snapped at her today, Elliot couldn't give up her dreams.

Not for a woman who lived in Darlington.

Not for a woman who lived in the closet.

Not for a woman who didn't even want her around half the time.

"No, damn it." She couldn't let this decision be about Kelly. She couldn't give up on her dreams. Period.

Chapter Thirteen

Tensions ran high at the office for the next few days. She and Elliot had barely spoken about anything other than the basic needs to keep the office running. Kelly had to hand it to her though. Elliot remained professional at all times. She hadn't cut back her hours or slowed her pace. She hadn't sulked or acted out. If anything, she'd been more efficient while Kelly had grown less so.

Ever since her "date" with John she hadn't been able to focus, though she couldn't quite put her finger on why. The date itself was like so many she'd had over the years. She doubted she'd even remember the details six months from now. They'd had a nice, no-frills meal. She'd remained polite enough to be considered approachable, but distant enough to ward off any physical overtures. She'd perfected the tightrope act over a decade of practice. She'd left John with a vague comment about hoping they could get together again sometime when things settled down. More importantly, though, she'd seen and been seen by the people of Darlington. By the end of the day, her friends and neighbors would all know she'd gone on a date with John Bale. While the idea of giving people something to gossip about still set her teeth on edge, at least she'd controlled the story. She had to hold onto any ounce of control she could grasp these days.

Control.

She couldn't remember the last time she'd felt truly in control. No, that wasn't true. She'd felt in control with Elliot pressed against her, but clearly that type of control was an illusion. If she'd had a little more actual control before they'd gotten to the point of making out on her desk, maybe she'd be able to focus on her job instead of trying to figure out why she couldn't get anything done.

A gentle knock sounded on her open door, but Elliot stayed out of view. She'd given Kelly an extra-wide berth lately, a gesture she should have appreciated, but the distance only served as a reminder of why they couldn't be closer.

"Come in."

"I don't want to interrupt," Elliot started. She wore a white shirt with a red tie under a navy suit vest. Her hair was brushed back, away from her angular face, giving her a prep-boy-meets-boardroom appeal.

"You're fine. What do you need?"

"I wanted to let you know I'm going to have to leave early next Thursday and I'll be out of town all day on Friday, but I'll work this weekend to make up the hours."

Kelly nodded. "I don't doubt you'll get the work done, and I'll be able to cover everything here."

"Okay, well." Elliot stood in the doorway as if she had something else to say but wasn't sure if she should. Had she expected more of a fight? Did she want Kelly to ask why she'd be gone? She shouldn't. She didn't owe Kelly any explanation. She'd already worked overtime, and Kelly had made it abundantly clear she didn't want them to have any part in each other's personal lives. "I'll be back on Sunday. I could come in then."

"It's up to you. I won't lie and say I couldn't use the extra help. You know we've only got about a month left to do two months' worth of work, but you've already done more than your share. If you want to take a whole weekend off, you're certainly entitled."

"It's not that I want to take the time off. I have something I need to do, out of town, and I'm going to do it as quickly as I can."

Cryptic.

"Is everything okay?" The question sort of spilled out before she processed the personal implications of something so open-ended.

"Yeah," Elliot answered quickly. "I uh, I just have a job interview. In Washington, D.C."

"Wow." She didn't know what else to say.

"It just sort of happened. A friend of a friend. I'm sorry I'm going to miss work."

"Don't apologize. Washington, D.C. is your dream, right?"

"Pretty much."

Why didn't she sound more excited? "When does the job start?"

"Probably right after tax season."

"Wow." She had to find a new word.

"All my hours will be fulfilled, and you'll be through the bulk of the work."

"Of course. I understand," Kelly said quickly. "You have to take this opportunity."

"I've only got an interview. It's a fellowship at a really important think tank. I probably won't get an offer."

Kelly smiled sadly, wondering if Elliot really believed that or if she'd only said so for her benefit. She didn't know which option bothered her more.

"Well, they'd be lucky to have you," she said resolutely.

"Really?" The single word held both a hint of disbelief and defiance.

She finally let herself make eye contact, but only briefly. She couldn't handle the questions she saw there. She didn't have answers.

She picked up a stack of papers and rearranged them blindly. "If you need me to serve as a reference, I'd be happy to do so."

"Thank you," Elliot said. "I appreciate that."

Kelly nodded, ready to be done with this conversation. Elliot took the hint and backed out of the office. Kelly waited until she heard her desk chair squeak before she allowed her shoulders to slump.

A month. Elliot would be gone in a month, and they'd likely never see each other again. An early departure would make things easier, or at the very least, less complicated. She should've felt overjoyed that the end of their current awkwardness was in sight, because Elliot would surely get the fellowship. When Beth had first spoken of her, she'd said she was special. At the time she'd thought Beth might have chosen a bit of hyperbole to try to sell her on having an intern. Now she knew "special" was an understatement. Only six weeks ago, she couldn't imagine having Elliot underfoot for an entire tax season. Now her head hurt at the thought of no longer having her there.

The office phone rang, and she heard Elliot answer. She would miss hearing her voice. She'd never had the whole place to herself before. There had always been someone working just on the other side of her office wall. She'd always known Elliot's presence would be a temporary fix for her father's absence, but she didn't expect her to move on quite so soon, and she hadn't expected to find that prospect quite so lonely.

"Kelly," Elliot called, "it's for you."

She didn't feel like talking to anyone in her current mood. "Can you take a message?"

"I can," Elliot hesitated, the pause giving Kelly just enough time to realize something wasn't right. "But it's the hospital."

"I'll take it." She snatched up the receiver. "Kelly Rolen speaking."

"Kelly."

She recognized Kelsey Patel's voice immediately. "Dr. Patel, are you with my father?"

"I just left his room, and I'm afraid the news is not good."

She clutched the arm of her chair until her knuckles turned white. "Your father has a cerebral hematoma, which basically means blood has collected in a spot on his brain."

Her stomach roiled, and her throat went dry.

"It's a very small one, but it wasn't there when I ordered an MRI for him a month ago. I fear it's what's caused his most recent relapse. I have already started him on a new regimen of corticosteroids to try to reduce swelling and a different blood pressure medicine to try to slow the flow of blood to the area so I can get a better look at the site. Right now it's unclear if he's had a minor hemorrhagic stroke or if the swelling stems from an undiagnosed trauma, perhaps a holdover from when he fell, though this far in I consider that unlikely."

She heard Dr. Patel talking and fought her rising wave of panic to try to focus, but she had no more energy left.

"I've also sent the images to a colleague who specializes in brain trauma to get her opinion as to whether or not surgery is our best option."

"Brain surgery?" she asked breathlessly.

"Yes, but that's not a foregone conclusion. It's a very small amount of blood, and with your father's weakened condition, it's risky to move him, and even more to operate."

"So we have to wait?"

"I'm afraid so, and it's still unclear as to whether time is our ally or our enemy here."

"What should I do?" *Please someone just tell me what to do.*

"His condition is in flux. I don't want to alarm you any more than I already have, but I hope you respect my honesty when I say that if you have something to say to him, the window for doing so might be shrinking."

Her breath caught painfully in her chest. She didn't even have the will to process what sort of underlying assumptions the comment implied. "I'll be there shortly."

"I'll be here for the rest of the day, and I'll check in before I head back to St. Louis."

"Thank you." She hung up and rested her head on her desk. She had to get up. She had to go, but her limbs felt coated in cement. The lethargy overtook her at a frightening pace, as if her own body had begun to shut down like her father's.

She was running out of time. The imperative should've made her act faster. Instead it paralyzed her. Every second ticked by, a dire countdown to some silent internal bomb. She was helpless to stop time. She couldn't outrun the clock on any of their lives. She couldn't do anything for anyone, anymore.

"Kelly?" Elliot whispered from the doorway.

When she failed to respond, Elliot moved closer and laid a hand gently on her shoulder. "Come on, Kelly."

"I can't," she said, barely recognizing her own voice.

"Yes, you can," Elliot said. "I'll help."

"You can't help me."

"Sure I can. I'm a very helpful person."

"Why would you even want to?"

Elliot chuckled. "That's the same question I'm asking myself."

"And?"

"I have no idea, but I'm going to drive you to the hospital, okay?"

She took a deep breath and summoned the strength needed to lift her head off the desk. She had to pull herself together because somehow having Elliot beside her made her think she could.

"Where are your keys?"

"Jacket pocket."

Elliot fished them out, then held out the jacket for Kelly to slip into. The gesture was so sweet she almost buckled under another wave of emotion but she forced herself to take one step toward the door and then another. Elliot stayed right at her elbow through the alley to a gravel parking lot. "The silver Buick LaCrosse is mine."

"Of course it is," Elliot said, a hint of amusement back in her voice. "Buick, the choice of accountants everywhere."

She opened the passenger door and made sure Kelly was situated before jogging around and climbing in.

She put the key in and turned the ignition before staring at the dashboard for a few seconds.

"What's wrong?"

"Nothing, just acclimating myself. I don't want to wreck your fancy car."

"The hospital is only two miles away. I think you'll be fine."

"Sure. Right. Fine." Elliot put the car into gear and gingerly pulled out of the parking lot.

"Turn left," Kelly directed. "This road will take you out of town and past the plant. The hospital's just about a quarter-mile on the left."

Kelly closed her eyes while Elliot mumbled the directions over and over to herself. She tried to focus on what would happen once she got to the hospital. She tried to think of all the things she needed to do back at work. She even tried to be annoyed with how slow Elliot was driving or how often she tapped the brakes, but the only thought she could pull forward with any sort of clarity was, *What am I going to do without her?*

∿ ∿ ∿

Over the last three hours in the waiting room, Elliot had sat in uncomfortable chairs, paced brightly lit hallways, and seen snippets of more soap operas than she even knew existed. Kelly had given her the keys and told her to go, saying she'd get a ride back to the office later, but Elliot couldn't bring herself to drive away for any number of reasons. Not the least of which was the panic she continued to feel every time she thought of Kelly slumped over and unresponsive on her desk. The sight of her exhausted and broken had cut through the anger she'd carried with her for days. Kelly's words still hurt, but Elliot clearly wasn't the only one in pain. If Kelly was in as bad shape as she'd seemed today, the breakdown must've been a long time coming. And while nothing excused her behavior, this kind of upheaval could certainly offer an explanation.

She rolled her head back until it bumped against the wall. Then again, maybe she only told herself Kelly's actions could be logically explained because she didn't want to believe Kelly had meant all the shitty things she'd said and done. What if the stress hadn't over-powered her true nature? What if it had revealed it? God, what if Kelly really did find her pathetic? She hadn't seemed upset by the prospect of Elliot taking the job in D.C. What if she couldn't wait for Elliot to leave? Maybe she should just go. Maybe she should have never come to the hospital in the first place.

No, damn it, she hadn't offered to help Kelly because she expected something in return, or even because she hoped to make her feel a certain way. She'd helped because Kelly needed her, and because, like it or not, she still cared about her. Which, incidentally, was also the primary reason she couldn't just abandon her now.

"Are you, by chance, Elliot Garza?"

Startled, she shot to her feet and found herself looking down at a small woman of Indian descent. "Yes. I'm Elliot."

"It's nice to meet you. I'm Dr. Patel. I'm one of the specialists working with Mr. Rolen."

"Is everything okay?"

"I'm afraid I cannot talk to you about his condition."

"Right." She rubbed her face. "HIPAA violation."

"Exactly, but I'm not Ms. Rolen's physician."

Elliot arched an eyebrow, not sure where to go with that.

"So, if I were to make a suggestion about her welfare, it wouldn't be a formal medical assessment or suggested treatment."

"Oh, just some friendly advice, person to person."

162

"Exactly."

"Got it," Elliot said conspiratorially. "What's the completely non-medical suggestion, doc?"

"She needs some rest."

Elliot snorted. "You want to tell her that?"

Dr. Patel smiled. "I've tried, and from the look on your face I think you can imagine how the conversation went over."

"I'll give you points for bravery, but forgive me if I don't want to fall on the same sword."

"The brain and body are complex enough on their own, and the relationship between the two only magnifies the complexities. Emotional responses and physical are sometimes inexplicably linked."

"Okay," Elliot said, unsure where the doctor was headed.

"Stress cycles in one person can trigger physical responses in people who share strong emotional connections."

"What kind of doctor are you?"

She laughed. "I'm a neuropsychologist."

"A what?"

"Don't worry about the title, my completely non-professional opinion is that there's a vicious cycle occurring that's likely affecting everyone's physical and emotional well-being, and someone has to stop it."

"Look, I'm just Kelly's intern, and I don't even know Mr. Rolen. I'm barely involved in my own well-being. I can't believe I have any possible relationship to his."

"And yet, you've been sitting outside his hospital room all night."

She had a point. Not a clear one, or a pleasant one, but a point nonetheless. "Fine. What do I need to do?"

"Sorry, I can't tell you that."

"HIPAA again?"

"No." She patted Elliot on the arm. "I simply don't know. I'm a doctor, not a mind reader. I just know the mind and the body both have ways of protecting themselves when someone's hurt or scared or stressed. Sometimes those forms of protection involve shutting down systems vital to healing, or even survival, as we understand it."

"Wow, Doc. No pressure, right?"

"The body never gives us a flight instinct without offering a little something in the fight category, too. Or vice versa. Just think about it, okay?"

"I'm sure I'll think of nothing else."

The doctor smiled once again. She seemed young and competent, comfortable in her own skin. She supposed some people were just born knowing who they were and what they needed to do. She envied Dr. Patel. Elliot worked hard to project confidence, but more and more she felt everyone around her could see through the act.

"You're Rory's protégée, yes?"

At the name, she straightened her shoulders and lifted her chin like a soldier called to muster. "She's my mentor."

"Very interesting."

"What is?"

"The human psyche." Dr. Patel patted her arm one more time. "It rarely reveals what we want, but it always finds a way to let us know what we need."

And with that, she strolled away. Elliot waited until she'd turned the corner, completely out of view, before crashing back into the chair. She bumped her head against the wall and wondered if the universe really did send signs. If so, why couldn't it send them in an easier-to-read format?

The body shuts down in order to protect itself? That seemed counter-intuitive. Shouldn't the body fight to protect itself? What had she said about fight or flight? They work together? No, they were opposites, right?

She didn't have any answers. No one did, apparently. Maybe answers didn't even exist. Maybe they were all just grasping at straws trying to find something to make them feel a little less helpless. The thought rattled around in her chest and made her jumpy. She stood, shook out her limbs. Then she paced, but nothing helped soothe the restlessness building inside her. Maybe she needed fresh air.

Walking as calmly as possible to the doors, she fought the urge to sprint when she saw them slide open before her. She had the keys in her pocket. Why had she thought she couldn't leave? She could. She could go anywhere. Back to work, back to her apartment, back to

164

Chicago even. She jogged through the parking lot and skidded to a stop next to the Buick.

A Buick. She didn't know why she found the car so damn funny. Because it was such a stereotype? Because it was so expected? Because it was so Kelly.

Resting her head on the cool glass of the driver's side window, she smiled. "Damn it."

She always needed something solid to steady herself through the roiling waves of emotions Kelly inspired. What had the doctor said about fight or flight? What if she didn't run? What if she stopped leaving when the ground shook under her feet?

Pressing up off the car, she turned to face the hospital, now illuminated against the dusk falling along the plains, and her heart caught painfully in her chest. There, in the doorway, stood the answer she didn't think existed.

ᔕ ᔕ ᔕ

"Elliot." Kelly breathed the name more than spoke it as she took the first tenuous step toward her. The sight of Elliot standing there in the parking lot sent all the emotions roaring back. Joy, fear, disbelief. She couldn't process them all. She could only move toward her.

"Kelly." Elliot met her halfway amid cars, trucks, and fading light.

"I thought you left."

"I couldn't. I thought you wanted me to, though."

"I didn't." Her voice caught. "I said I did. I said so many things I didn't mean, and I haven't been able to say any of the things I do."

"Come on." Elliot wrapped her arm around Kelly's shoulder and nudged her toward the car. The embrace felt heavenly.

Once inside, Elliot turned on the heat and then turned to face her. "What do you need?"

"I don't know." She shook her head. "I think I do. I mean, I *thought* I knew. I was wrong. God, what are you still doing here? After everything I did, after everything I said to you?"

"I don't know." Elliot shrugged. "I've asked myself that question a hundred times. I even tried to leave, but I just can't."

"You just can't?" The logic seemed so flawed and yet so familiar.

Kelly searched her eyes looking for the turmoil, for the pain she'd caused. She needed a reminder of all the reasons she'd tried to push her away in the first place. She found nothing but clarity. Elliot's mouth curved up in the subtle way that always made her heart beat faster, and in an instant they were on each other.

Mouths collided, tongues tangled, hands grasped and clasped. The raw animal instinct took hold and then took control. They kissed so fiercely, breath came hot and rapid. The windows fogged around them, the heat of their bodies blocking the cold of their outside lives. She reached across the car, tugging at the hem of Elliot's shirt and pulling her over the console. Elliot practically growled in her ear as she wound her fingers tightly into Kelly's hair. Elliot clung to her, then, with a sharp jerk, broke free.

"No," she panted. "We can't do this again."

"What?"

"Kelly," she pleaded, "please, we can't let it happen again, not like this."

Kelly stared at her, mouth open, eyes wide.

"Please don't look at me like that."

She pressed her lips together and nodded. "Fine. You're right. I understand."

"I don't think you do."

Her chest felt cracked open, her nerve endings so raw tears stung her eyes, but she fought desperately to keep her reaction controlled for Elliot's sake. "Too much has happened. There's too much against us, and that's my fault, not yours. I don't blame you for not wanting me—"

"No." Elliot kissed her quickly on the mouth to quiet that line of reasoning. "I still want you very much. More than you can probably understand."

She could understand a great deal about want right now, with Elliot's lithe form pressed hot and close to her own. "But?"

"Not like this," Elliot said. "Not in a car, not in a parking lot, not fully clothed. I want you in my bed."

All the air left her lungs in a rush. She couldn't speak. She could only nod.

"Yes?" Elliot asked.

"Yes." She finally managed. "But Elliot?"

"Yes?"

"Drive faster than you did on the way here."

"Actually," Elliot said, climbing all the way over her, "you better drive. I don't have a license."

"You don't have a license? And you—"

Elliot stopped her with another searing kiss. "Drive first, yell later."

The ride through town was a blur of heat, stolen touches, and one painfully long red light.

At long last, Elliot wrapped one arm around Kelly's waist and pulled her into the apartment, kicking the door closed behind them as she went. "Do you have any idea how many times I've thought about having you naked in my bed?"

"How many?" Kelly asked between kisses.

"More than I should have," Elliot admitted, pushing Kelly's jacket off her shoulders and onto the floor. "I want to do all the things to you."

All the things? How many things were there? She'd only done two or three of them, and it had been awhile. What if she couldn't keep up?

Elliot snaked a hand up under her shirt, raking her fingers along Kelly's ribs, then cupped her breasts. Kelly's head lolled back and the doubts disappeared. Elliot kissed and sucked along her neck as she reached around and unclasped her bra. Her hands, hot and skilled, found newly exposed skin, causing Kelly to suck a breath between clenched teeth.

"Bedroom. Now." She commanded, or maybe she begged. The difference didn't matter anymore.

Elliot urged her backward across the small living room until her back bumped against a door that swung open with only minimal pressure. She opened her eyes long enough to see a lavish pile of pillows and blankets atop a mattress and box springs on the floor. There might have been more furniture, but in her lust-induced tunnel vision, she saw only the bed.

They eased across the room, kissing deeply until the back of her knees hit the mattress and she fell, taking Elliot with her. The weight of Elliot's body pinning her down triggered another level of arousal as her hips pressed firmly against Elliot's leg. She relished the friction of their clothes rubbing on sensitive skin, but now that they had the time and space, she craved a more complete connection. Elliot must've shared the desire because she unbuttoned two buttons on Kelly's blouse, then urged her up so she could just pull it the rest of the way off, taking her already unclasped bra with it.

Kelly reached down and flipped open the button on her own slacks, but Elliot shook her head. "Oh no, that's my job."

She arched an eyebrow, but didn't argue as Elliot kissed her way down her neck and shoulders to her collarbones. She lay back and enjoyed the path of Elliot's hot mouth over her breasts, down her stomach. Elliot took her time lowering the zipper and slipping the slacks over her hips, or maybe the process only seemed slow compared to the reckless abandon they'd used in the past. Elliot certainly moved with a purpose as she discarded Kelly's slacks and socks then kissed the arch of her foot before starting her progression back up. She kissed and massaged her way up Kelly's calf. Kelly held her breath as Elliot slid up her inner thigh, her mouth hot and so amazingly close to the center of her desire.

She'd never been overly demonstrative in bed, but she'd never experienced the all-controlling need she felt for Elliot. Call it primal, or even animalistic, but she couldn't fight against her instincts anymore. She didn't even want to. Elliot was so damn sexy. Her green eyes flashed with intensity, her intent completely clear as she lifted her gaze. Kelly answered the unspoken question by arching her hips off the bed to meet Elliot.

Years of stowed desires and hidden craving crumbled as Elliot took her into her mouth. The breath she'd held poured out in a cry of satisfaction. She hadn't been touched in any truly intimate fashion for years, and she found Elliot's talent almost too much to bear. Her breath came in jagged gasps as her back arched and her hips rolled in ways she didn't think herself capable of. She clutched the pillow behind her head to keep herself from holding Elliot right there forever. The emotions surging through tangled with the physical sensations and drove her into a near-frenzied state.

Elliot spread her open in every sense, and then gently, slowly worked her way inside. They moved in such a perfect rhythm, hands, mouths, the press of their now-joined bodies. She hooked one leg over Elliot's shoulder using her heel against her back to urge her on. Perfect pressure built at her core and spread through her body, coiling every muscle until, with one deliberate moan, she let go and willingly lost control.

ဢ ဢ ဢ

"God, you're so beautiful." Elliot pulled herself up over Kelly's body. She looked like some fair sex-goddess, her normally pale skin flushed and her dark hair fanned strikingly against the white pillowcase. Elliot kissed her cheek, then her forehead, before trying to lie down gently beside her, but Kelly caught her with a hand on each hip and held her in place.

"Where do you think you're going with all those clothes on?"

"Something about your tone tells me the answer to that question is, 'nowhere.'"

"Has anyone told you, you're very smart?"

"I've been told I'm a smart-*ass*."

Kelly slid her hands down until she cupped her ass. "Both statements are equally true."

"Has anyone ever told you you're insanely sexy?"

Kelly pursed her lips. "Never."

"You hang out with blind morons."

Kelly laughed and rolled Elliot onto her back until they'd swapped places. "I don't think anyone has ever seen me quite like you have."

"Lucky me," she said, her eyes fixed on the remarkable body above her. "If you showed everyone this side of you, someone would've snatched you up years ago."

Kelly's brow furrowed.

"What?"

"Nothing." She flashed a quick smile. "Except too many clothes in my way."

"That can be remedied."

Kelly straddled her waist and sat back, showcasing the fullness of her glorious form. All the blood in Elliot's body rushed to the point where they connected.

"I've always secretly been a fan of this layered look you favor," Kelly said trailing her fingers across the front of Elliot's vest, flicking open buttons as she went.

"Really?" Elliot asked, her eyelids heavy with lust as Kelly yanked the hem of her dress shirt from her jeans.

"Really, but now that I'm faced with removing them all, the idea of one person wearing so many articles of clothing seems a bit excessive."

"Agreed." Elliot swallowed hard. "The tie seems particularly restricting at the moment."

Kelly threaded the silk through her fingers as she ran them back up Elliot's chest. "I've never taken one of these off anyone before."

"Want me to?"

She gave the tie a little tug. "Maybe I should leave it on. It's kind of handy."

"It's always the quiet ones," Elliot quipped, but she honestly couldn't believe this was Kelly in her bed right now. She knew from previous experience that she would be passionate and commanding, but she hadn't expected her to be quite so open.

"No, I want you completely naked." Kelly leaned down and kissed her while she undid the knot and set to work on the buttons of her shirt. Once she'd completed the task, she spread everything completely open and smoothed her hands over Elliot's chest. Her touch felt so amazing. Elliot arched up, trying to pull her closer, but Kelly pushed her back with one hand firmly between her breasts.

"My turn," she whispered.

"But I—"

"Shh." She placed one finger on her lips. "Don't argue. In case you haven't noticed, I have control issues."

Elliot laughed. She couldn't argue even if she'd been inclined to. She hardly considered herself a pillow queen, but she liked a woman who knew what she wanted, especially when what she wanted was her.

Kelly pulled her attention back to the moment as she unclasped Elliot's belt and worked the zipper down. Elliot arched her hips off the bed so Kelly could pull her jeans and briefs all the way off.

"I want you," Kelly said, her eyes raking over Elliot's body.

"Take me."

"I want so much though, and it's been a long time. Years."

"Years?" Elliot hoped Kelly couldn't hear the shock in her voice.

"Years," Kelly confirmed.

Elliot couldn't imagine. Not just the celibacy, but that a woman of Kelly's beauty and ferocity could go without for so long. No wonder she had so many pent-up emotions and desires.

"I want so many things, and I don't think I know—"

Elliot surged up, capturing Kelly's mouth with her own, then placing one hand on either of Kelly's hips, pulled her back down so the length of their bodies melted together, skin on skin for the first time.

When Kelly relaxed into her, the subtle weight of her body pressed against all the right places. She broke the kiss and dragged her lips across her neck. Giving her earlobe a playful bite, she whispered, "Don't think. Take what you need."

The simple instruction made of her own desire seemed to give them both the freedom they needed. Within seconds they melted fluidly together once more. Kelly's body moved in ways no one would possibly expect when they saw her all buttoned up in her business suits. Her hips rolled, her back arched, her fingers worked magic along Elliot's skin. Slipping a hand between them, she explored every inch of flesh. Kelly kissed and touched every spot on her torso before going lower. Elliot bit her lip to keep from begging. In her more altruistic moments, she wanted Kelly to take the time she needed to feel safe and satisfied, but in flashes of honest self-awareness, she admitted she liked being made to wait.

She'd always found Kelly's emphasis on control a turn-on, and the more that trait took hold in bed, the more she realized its multitude of uses outside of the business world. As her confidence grew, so did her skill level. She played along the most sensitive areas of Elliot's body. Teasing and taking in equal measure, she circled just around the space Elliot most wanted her to claim. Was she testing her, torturing her, or seeking further permission?

"Kelly," she panted, "please."

"What do you want?" Kelly asked in a tone that made it clear she understood exactly what she was doing to her.

"I'm not going to last much longer."

"Hmm." She brushed her thumb over the spot that sent Elliot's hips surging off the bed. "Is that what you need?"

"More," Elliot gasped.

Kelly complied, causing her toes to curl.

"Yes, Kelly, yes." She clutched Kelly's back, short fingernails digging into amazingly smooth skin. "Inside me, please."

Kelly's breath grew hot and heavy against her skin as she worked her way in. The beat of their hearts raced in time to the thrust of their bodies. They crested up, then pulled back only for the chance to crash into each other again.

"Yes. Go. Don't stop," Elliot called until the babble of encouragement disintegrated into incoherency.

Kelly rode the wave of tremors through her body, kissing, pushing, pulling every ounce of pleasure she could out of her. Then when stillness reigned and they lay spent, she slipped into the crook of Elliot's arm and whispered. "Thank you."

Elliot kissed the top of her head, breathing deeply in an attempt to memorize the scent of her as she drifted off to sleep. The intimacy of the moment caused her chest to constrict as new emotions grew there, but she refused to acknowledge them. She wouldn't let the fear and doubt creep in yet. She wouldn't examine anything she shouldn't feel, nor would she judge the feelings she couldn't yet put into perspective. She wouldn't worry about tomorrow, or consequences. Not yet.

Chapter Fourteen

"So, you're very good at a number of things," Kelly said as Elliot pulled a frozen pizza out of her apartment-size oven. She'd started with the base of an off-brand pizza, then added chicken, spinach, and fresh parmesan cheese. "You never just accept what you're given. You always push for something better."

"I was groomed for excellence," Elliot said.

Kelly laughed. Of course Elliot had a quick comeback for everything, and Kelly actually preferred her that way. If all couldn't be right with her world, at least these stolen moments could help restore some sense of natural order.

"I'm not joking." Elliot slid the pizza onto the counter and fanned it with an oven mitt. "My mother has a lot of her worldview riding on me being well-adjusted and successful."

"How so?"

"I'm living proof that a woman needs a man like a fish needs a bicycle."

"You're kind of a big deal."

"I really am." Elliot gave her a cocky grin amplified by the fact that she wore only an apron. "I have to be. Or else I prove all the naysayers right."

"What naysayers?"

"The people who condemn single moms or lesbians or young women in general. The ones who believe a woman's place is behind her man. The men who think women don't belong in positions of power." She recited the words as if she'd either said or heard the speech before. "I have to show them I don't need a man to help me wield my power. I can do that on my own, but in order to show them that, I have to actually get into a position of power."

Elliot loaded a couple of mismatched plates with pizza and carried them back to the bedroom.

"We're eating in bed?" Kelly asked, following her.

"Why not? Let's live dangerously."

"I suppose it's the least scandalous thing we've done tonight."

Elliot took off the apron and tossed it to the floor with the rest of their clothing, then propped herself up on a pile of pillows, bare-chested like some Amazon warrior. Kelly had to summon all the manners ever drilled into her to keep from staring . . . or touching.

"Do you think I'm silly?"

"Hmm?"

"Do you think it's silly of me to believe I can make a difference amid all the small-minded men in Washington, D.C.?"

"Oh, well, not silly. No. You're a force to be reckoned with. I do worry the emphasis on gender is a bit misguided, though."

Elliot didn't seem the least bit defensive as she took a bite of pizza and chewed before asking. "Misguided, how?"

"I think you'll make a difference because you're smart and passionate and you care about something bigger than yourself. I don't think any of those things depend on your being a woman."

"You don't think women bring a unique perspective to conversations previously dominated by men?"

"Some women do, but I believe a thoughtful, reflective, feminist man could do the same. Not all women are necessarily more caring than all men, especially when given power they've been denied too long. Remember Margaret Thatcher?"

Elliot's forehead creased as though thinking took physical effort.

"Oh my God, you don't remember Margaret Thatcher!" Kelly pointed at her with the slice of pizza she'd yet to try. "What year were you born?"

"1991."

"I just had sex with a zygote."

Elliot laughed so heartily, Kelly's mortification faded. She couldn't regret what they'd done, no matter how old she might feel right then. Still, she marveled at the disconnect. "You weren't even alive in the '80s."

"Oh, come on. You're not that much older than I am."

"I'm old enough to remember at least half the '80s."

"So what, you're five years older?"

"Eight. I'm eight years older." She took a bite of her pizza and let the realization sink in. "At least you can cook. This pizza's pretty amazing, considering it was thrown together by a child."

"Eight years' difference is nothing in the grand scheme of a lifetime. Numerical age is what you make of it."

"Says the zygote."

"Oh come on. You're not even halfway through your thirties. I know plenty of lesbians your age who are clubbing every weekend and vacationing at Girl Splash or Dinah Shore Weekend."

"I don't even know what those things are."

"My point exactly," Elliot said with smug satisfaction. "Some people never grow up, but you give off the vibe of having been born as an adult. I bet you were a precocious child."

"I don't know about precocious, but I suppose I was more serious than my peers. I had more on my mind. I think I understood the gravity of the choices I had to make at a much younger age."

"Why?"

"I don't know." Her chest tightened at the lie. She knew why, but she didn't want to have this conversation. Not now, not in the safe haven they'd created to block out the outside world. Then again, carrying the secret around didn't seem to help much. Maybe if she'd just answered the question weeks ago instead of pushing Elliot away, she could've avoided the need to seek refuge in the first place, or maybe she would've found the refuge sooner.

"Did I cross one of those invisible tripwires?" Elliot asked softly.

"Excuse me?"

"You have topics, triggers, that upset you, and I'm never quite sure what they are until I trip over one of them. Sometimes I'm still not sure what I said, even after the explosion. But I think I inadvertently set something off again."

"No." Kelly sighed. "Maybe. Yes, you did, but it's not your fault."

"I don't want to hurt you. If I only knew how not to upset you, I'd try harder to avoid doing so."

175

"You don't have to try harder. Everyone else knows. I sort of liked that you didn't and that you wouldn't hang around long enough to find out."

"And now?"

"Now I'm not so sure." She wasn't sure she wanted to keep things from her and she felt even less certain about Elliot's waning time in Darlington.

"You don't have to tell me. We've all got our secrets."

"Except mine's not a secret," Kelly said, then bowed her head as the words poured out. "Everyone knows my mom left us just before I turned three."

"She left you?"

"Me and my dad. One day she just walked out. She took virtually nothing with her. She didn't say goodbye. She left no forwarding address. I think she left a note for my dad, but I never saw it."

"And you never asked him?"

"No. For years I didn't want to know what she'd said. I worried I'd done something wrong. I thought it was my fault."

"Oh, Kelly." Elliot took her hand and held on loosely.

"I know now I probably didn't have anything to do with it, at least not in any way I could have avoided as a toddler. People don't just run away from their husband and daughter because of normal kid behavior. She had to have been profoundly unhappy with our lives, but realizing that didn't exactly help me feel better."

"No, I guess it wouldn't."

"I know my dad isn't an exciting man. He doesn't like parties or dancing or cities or whatever she wanted, but he loved her. And he cared for us. He provided a good home and a steady income, and I find it hard to believe he would've denied her anything she truly desired."

"And you. You're amazing. She could've at least kept in contact."

"She didn't want to. She didn't see anything about our lives as worthy of salvaging, and I resented her for that." The anger still rose up in her so fast it rubbed raw against her throat. "I saw the good in us. Why couldn't she?"

Elliot seemed to understand the question was rhetorical, but her

176

eyes stayed on Kelly, not pushing, but never turning away from the grief pouring out of her now.

"We might not be adventurous, but we're loyal and trustworthy, and we made a good life together. I used to dream about her realizing what a terrible mistake she'd made. I had these elaborate revenge fantasies about her coming back to see us doing well. She would see the bond my dad and I shared and his successful business and our happy home. Then she'd learn that you can't run away from your problems. She'd understand we were right all along, and she was wrong. So stupid of me."

"I think that's a pretty natural impulse."

Elliot ran her thumb along the back of Kelly's palm in comforting patterns. How long had it been since she'd experienced the peace that came with casual touching? "I thought if I was just good enough and worked hard enough and stayed strong long enough, we would be vindicated. If only I could grow up to be just like my dad, everyone would see how superior we were, but that's hard to do when everyone keeps heaping pity on you."

"What do you mean?"

"It's a small town. People talk and talk and talk." She couldn't keep her jaw from tightening at the thought. "Whenever I went somewhere new or started a new activity, people would whisper about my sad situation. I could never just be Kelly. I was always, 'You know her, the one whose mom ran out on them.'"

"Didn't it get better with time?"

"No, it just got more deeply ingrained into the narrative." She could still hear the echo of their voices. "Everything I ever did made the rumor mill spin. And it didn't matter good or bad. When I wasn't perfect, I heard 'What do you expect? Her mother ran out on her.' It even tainted my accomplishments. Nothing I ever did was just impressive on its own. I was always, 'impressive' for a girl with no mother.' Worst of all, they couldn't ever just credit my dad with being a great parent. They always had to point out how much he did 'for a single dad, the poor man.'"

"I'm so sorry. I always thought people here lived these idyllic child-hoods. I guess I never really gave any thought to the downside of living someplace where people have known you your whole life. You never really get to change the story."

"I like to think we're past it now. I'm not a kid anymore, and I've worked hard to become known as Kelly Rolen, CPA or Kelly Rolen, Rotary member, or Kelly Rolen, all-around good citizen. I had to fight their whispers and their pity and their preconceived notions, but I guess the fight helped make me who I am today."

"I'm a little envious of you on that count," Elliot said wistfully.

"That I provided the whole town an eighteen-year pity party?"

"Not that count. The one where you had to fight for who you are so you came out the other side stronger. You know you've got fight in you and that you can sustain it. You're battle-tested and you stood firm." She lay back and stared at the ceiling. "I wish the same could be said for me."

"You?" Kelly scoffed. "You, who gets into bar fights to protect the honor of strangers? You don't know if you can stand your ground?"

"No. First of all, that was a worthless fight. I didn't think it through. It was a flash of anger, and then I felt terrible. I don't know if I can stay the course when it matters. Not over years, not over a lifetime."

"But you're so very . . . you."

Elliot smiled. "Am I? I don't know. I've never really been tested. I've never had to fight for my identity or my ideals. I've had everything handed to me. I'm the picture of ease and privilege."

Kelly shook her head. Elliot couldn't be serious.

"Think about my life. My mom's a lawyer—a damn good one. I had every opportunity, the best schools, travel, chances to interact with smart, influential people. Liberal, progressive minds all around. I only got to volunteer with VITA because I didn't have to have a job in high school. I worked with all these underprivileged families pretending to fight the power, but I wasn't one of them. I'm not a member of the working class. I'm a faux proletariat."

"You're a fauxletariot."

"Oh God, I am!" Elliot covered her face with her hands.

"So, you've got a good dose of privilege from your upbringing, but you acknowledge it, and you've dedicated your life to helping dismantle the system that gave you every advantage. That's pretty impressive. Most people would've taken the money and run."

"I may yet. Who knows until I'm really pushed? Deep down, I may be a fraud."

"But you're a gay fraud. You're out and proud. That takes fight."

"I was nowhere near the first out person in my high school. You're the most conservative person I've ever worked with, and you're gay." Elliot laughed. "You know I came to school down here looking for a fight?"

"I'm not surprised."

"Sydney was. I think picking Bramble University was probably the most rebellious thing I ever did. I had offers for scholarships from several other schools. I even started out at DePaul, but everyone was so damn liberal there, I knew I wouldn't catch any shit."

"Catching shit isn't something many colleges list in their brochures."

"It's not," Elliot admitted, "but when I met Rory I thought, 'she knows how to fight.'"

Kelly fought the urge to roll her eyes. "She always has."

"You're not a fan."

"Of Rory?" She shook her head. "We grew up together. We're on speaking terms."

"What a ringing endorsement."

She shrugged. She didn't want to talk about Rory in bed.

Elliot didn't seem to get the message. "It's odd that Beth comes by all the time, but Rory never stops in."

"I'm sure Beth visits a lot of people." She tried to keep the displeasure from her tone.

"Yeah, but Rory's usually close behind. Those two are a lesbian matched set. And Rory's all about building community. Does she know you're gay?"

"She does," Kelly admitted. "But we have differing opinions about what being gay means for our sense of self."

"No kidding. But still, you're so close with Beth."

"I'm not." Kelly snapped.

Elliot raised her eyebrows.

"I'm sorry. I'm just . . . weren't we talking about how you're not a fighter?"

"Yeah, I guess," Elliot said slowly, then stared back at the ceiling. "I thought if I studied with Rory, I'd learn what I was made of, and if I did turn out to be deficient, maybe she could teach me to be better."

"And?"

"And I watched her, I taught with her, I competed against her in every sport imaginable, but I still don't know if I'm just some sad imitation with a bad case of hero worship."

Kelly would have rolled her eyes again at the thought of anyone worshiping Rory St. James, especially someone as genuinely amazing as Elliot, but she heard the doubt in her voice. Emotions like that couldn't be laughed away. She'd done her share of pretending to be tougher than she felt, and she'd also lived under the threat of being exposed as less than everyone expected her to be. She lay down beside Elliot, and wrapped an arm around her.

Elliot snuggled closer until her head rested on Kelly's shoulder and one hand splayed across her stomach. "I froze in front of Mrs. Anthony."

"What?" Kelly asked.

"She was the first person in my whole life to actually make me feel subhuman for being gay, and I froze."

"She's a bitter old woman. Nothing you could've said would have made any difference."

"I didn't need to make a difference with her. I needed to make a difference with me. I needed to know if I could go toe-to-toe with someone who advocated everything I opposed."

Kelly's chest tightened. "You would have."

"I don't know. I was in the middle of appeasing her when you broke in. God Kelly, you were so magnificent. I felt so worthless."

"Hey, you weren't worthless. You did exactly the right thing." She hugged Elliot tightly. "That was my fight. I should've fought it almost three years ago."

"What was almost three years ago?"

"Doesn't matter now. The point is, we all make the decisions we have to make in the moment we have to make them."

"I hope so, but I'm not so sure. What if I'm nothing but swagger and hot air? If I can't handle a gray-haired old bigot, what chance do I stand of speaking truth to power in Washington, D.C.?"

"When it's really your moment, you'll do what you need to do."

"What makes you so sure?"

Kelly kissed the top of her head. "Because I'm older and wiser."

"And braver." Elliot chuckled.

Kelly didn't want to think about all the moments she wasn't as brave as she should've been. She didn't want to relive all the times she'd compromised or taken the cowardly way out. She didn't want to tell Elliot she knew for certain Elliot would do better because she knew what true cowardice looked like, felt like, cost to live with. Elliot would do better. She already had. She had more bravery in her little finger than Kelly had in her whole life.

Then again, Kelly realized if she had been brave in the moments she most regretted, they probably wouldn't be here together. Holding Elliot's beautiful body against hers, she couldn't help but wonder if her moment wasn't still to come.

୬ ୬ ୬

"I'll see you at the office later?" Elliot asked. She already knew the answer but continued to stall for fear that once they left the apartment the magic they'd captured over the last twelve hours would disappear.

"Yes. I need to change and check in at the hospital, but then I'll get to work."

"Okay. I have breakfast plans with Beth and Rory, then I'll head over."

Kelly frowned as she slipped into her jacket.

"Unless you need me to head right over."

"No," she said quickly. "We don't have appointments until ten o'clock. Go out and have a nice breakfast. We'll be swamped today. You'll need the fuel."

"Okay," Elliot said.

"It's just . . ." Kelly said almost apologetically, "I'd rather Beth and Rory not know I spent the night here."

"Oh no." Elliot took her hand. "I wouldn't tell them. You can trust me."

"I know I can. And thank you, by the way. But I also know you're close to them. I know you're used to being out and I'm . . . well, I'm not."

"Right," Elliot said, not quite sure where Kelly was going. "But it's not that you're gay, because Beth knows, and Rory knows too, then."

Kelly sighed. "Yes. Rory knows."

"And you're clearly thrilled."

"I just . . . it's complicated. And it's no one's business," Kelly snapped, then seemed to catch herself. Her dark eyes softened as the woman she'd been last night warred with the woman she'd always been before. "It's our business, so obviously I can't forbid you from telling Rory, or anyone else for that matter."

"And that's scary for you," Elliot said, the realization fully sinking in. "I have the power to set the rumor mill spinning again."

Kelly nodded gravely. "You do. I suppose it would be the price I'd have to accept for a night of weakness."

Elliot winced. "Is that what you think? Last night was some sort of weakness? Like sleeping with me is evidence of a character flaw?"

"No," Kelly said quickly, "not because of you."

"What then?"

"I lost control." She laughed sharply then shook her head. "You have that effect on me. Do you understand? No one else on earth has ever shaken my sense of self the way you do. You're not the only woman I've ever slept with, but you're the only one who has ever inspired such complete abandon in me."

The ache in Elliot's chest shifted to a more pleasurable kind of pressure. "I'm not sure it helps, but the feeling's mutual."

"It helps a little. But you and I have very different views on what that means for us as people. You're . . . what did you call it? Sex positive?"

"Yes. I don't think we should be ashamed of what happened between us."

"And maybe I don't either. Maybe that's part of the problem. I don't feel an ounce of shame about anything we've done. I know it doesn't sound like it, but I'm really not some self-hating gay. I know who I am, and I'm not ashamed."

"But?"

"But if other people knew, if they judged this, if they turned it into a scandal, something to be whispered about or passed around town, it would make it *feel* dirty and shameful. I can't take the thought of their condemnation of the only thing keeping me sane anymore."

Elliot exhaled slowly as the pieces fell together. Kelly couldn't stomach the thought of people talking about them the same way they'd talked about her family, the same way they'd talked about her father. Her father, who was quite possibly lying on his deathbed. She couldn't take one more thing she cared about being misconstrued and misrepresented.

"Okay." She sighed.

"Okay?"

"Yeah, what else is there to say?"

"Now I worry I've given you your own share of regrets."

"No." Her cheeks flushed as the memories of last night overtook her. "I have no regrets about anything we've done. It'll just be a new adventure to learn how we move forward."

"Right," Kelly said with a forced smile. "I don't know about you, but for me, getting back into our work routine would be a good place to start on that whole moving forward business."

"I agree," Elliot said enthusiastically, then kissed her quickly before opening the door. "I'll see you at work."

"See you there," Kelly said lightly, and then glanced quickly in each direction before walking away without looking back.

Elliot needed to go too, or she'd be late for breakfast, but she closed the door anyway. She took a few deep breaths, mentally trying to calculate how long it would take Kelly to get into her car and drive away. She didn't want to go through another awkward goodbye. Even more, she didn't want to see her and have to pretend they just bumped into each other, or worse, not acknowledge each other at all. She didn't want to think about all the things they'd have to ignore at the office.

Would they speak about anything other than taxes? Would they touch casually or steal kisses in between meetings? Would Kelly purposefully push her away in front of other people? Or would she act like nothing had changed at all? Hell, *had* anything actually changed at all?

She shook her head and swung open the door once more. She couldn't sit here all morning second-guessing and wondering about which version of Kelly she'd find once she got to the office. They had a lot of work to do, and she intended to do it, but she couldn't help feeling like the focus on work had less to do with moving forward and more to do with a convenient excuse to go backward.

∽ ∽ ∽

"So, when do you leave?" Kelly asked the following Thursday. Her voice sounded sharper than she'd intended, but the sight of Elliot's suitcase next to her desk made her stomach ache.

"My train leaves at one, so I'd probably better head out in a few minutes."

"And when do you get back?" She hoped she sounded business-like and not needy.

"On the three o'clock train Saturday afternoon, as long as my flight from D.C. to St. Louis is on time," Elliot said evenly. "I can come straight here when I get to town."

"I'm not sure you'd be much help that late in the day, after so much travel."

"Well, if you don't want me here . . ."

"Don't be silly." She waved off the hurt in Elliot's voice. "I'm only thinking of the workload. It's a bad time for you to take a weekend off. We've got less than a month to go."

"Which is why I offered to put in hours on Saturday night and Sunday."

"Right, I know you'll get your internship hours in."

A little muscle in Elliot's jaw twitched, but she refrained from making the obvious argument. Kelly knew Elliot had already filled her hours for the week. She'd likely worked overtime, though her time sheet would never reflect any extra hours. Elliot had arrived before her on Tuesday and stayed after she'd left on Wednesday. For all Kelly knew, Elliot might have put in more hours than she had. The implication was out of line, but Elliot wouldn't say so. She rarely called Kelly out anymore. She'd learned to clench her teeth or smile through the awkwardness, which of course only made Kelly feel worse.

She should've at least tried to start a personal conversation. She'd had her chance several times over the last few days. They'd worked side by side, or at least close enough to hear each other breathe, every day since the morning she'd woken up in Elliot's arms. They'd shared two meals, stolen a handful of tender touches, and even had a mini make-out session between appointments one evening, but she'd never given herself the emotional freedom to tell Elliot she would miss her. That she wished the best for her, but also wished she didn't have to go. She'd barely even admitted to herself how much she dreaded two days without seeing Elliot. How could she tell Elliot she would miss her so much more than she should?

Elliot had to go, and Kelly had to let her. She didn't have to be happy about it. She couldn't even think about the prospect of Elliot leaving forever. Her heart always gave a painfully dull thud at the prospect of saying goodbye, and she didn't want to dwell on all the reasons she shouldn't let herself feel that kind of emotional attachment. So she'd fallen back on the only recourse she had and buried them both in work.

"I better get going." Elliot sounded tired, or maybe resigned. She stood and pulled on a light-gray jacket, then turned to face Kelly. "Is there anything I can do to help you while I'm away?"

The question was open-ended enough to encompass the personal as well as the business end of their relationship, but the latter option seemed cleaner, clearer, easier to process. "No, you can't really scan or input data on the road. Just enjoy your time off."

Elliot's jaw tightened again, but she nodded.

She waited a few seconds more as if giving Kelly one last chance to connect, her eyes questioning, her facial expression expectant. Kelly could hardly stand the overwhelming feeling of futility, so she turned away and pretended to examine some forms on the corner of the desk.

"Okay, I'll see you in a couple days." With that Elliot grabbed her carry-on suitcase and whisked it out the door.

Kelly stood alone in the silence for several minutes, but the longer she did nothing, the tighter her chest felt. Regret, her old companion, had returned with a vengeance, only now it didn't linger around the periphery. This sense of loss welled up faster than she'd grown used to and even infiltrated her sanctuary.

She returned to her own office and pulled out a stack of papers. She didn't pace or wander. She didn't even want to glance around the space she'd always considered home. This was the one place she'd always felt safe, secure, content. Now she sighed and tried not to notice the quiet she'd craved not long ago. She had the office to herself with plenty to do and no one to interrupt her. She should've been happy, or at least productive. Instead, each deep breath brought the fading scent of Elliot's coffee and cologne. Instead of peaceful, the quiet felt empty.

The insidious cloud of remorse threatened to overtake her now. God, why hadn't she kissed Elliot goodbye? Why hadn't she told her good luck or asked her to call and let her know how the interview went? Such simple gestures. Why couldn't she admit she cared? Because she cared too much? It didn't much matter once Elliot had walked out the door. She'd missed her chance. She missed a lot of things already. What else would she miss by the time Elliot returned? More than the sex. Though, while alone, she could almost admit she had more need in that area than she'd previously thought. Still, she missed the intimacy more, and not just the physical kind. She missed Elliot's wit and her sharp retorts, even though there hadn't been as many of them lately. She missed the cups of coffee and the simple act of checking in with each other. She missed the comfort of having her right around the corner.

Pretending none of those things were true did nothing to actually make them untrue. For the first time in her life, she wasn't content with being alone.

Chapter Fifteen

"Thank you Ms. Garza. We know you traveled quite a way to be here during a busy time."

"It's been a pleasure speaking with you this morning." Elliot rose and nodded to the hiring committee. "I'm bolstered by knowing a place like this exists with dedicated people like all of you at the helm."

"Would you mind waiting in the lobby for a few minutes while we make sure we don't have any more questions for you?"

"I'd be happy to."

"Someone will check in with you shortly."

Elliot let herself out of the large glass doors enclosing the conference room, then strode purposefully down the hallway to the waiting area. She tried not to fidget or gawk at her surroundings. The space wasn't ornate, but the stone floors and walls accented with metal and glass elements spoke of power and efficiency. If the room was meant to inspire confidence, it achieved its goal. The three men and one woman she'd spoken with had functioned much the same way, not flashy or ostentatious, but carrying the kind of command that came from knowing themselves and their purpose. She hoped to be among them someday, but she couldn't shake the little whisper that called her a fraud.

The people who worked here knew everything about the American tax code. They had experience beyond small-town tax prep and simple volunteer work. These people held advanced degrees in economics and had been battle-tested in the halls of Congress. They wrote policy that changed the dialogue and represented the financial interests of the American people in the face of the most powerful multinational business corporations in the world. What made her think she belonged among them when she couldn't even find the courage to kiss Kelly goodbye?

She glanced at her watch. Almost two here in D.C., so not quite one in Darlington. What would Kelly be doing now? What would she say if Elliot called to check in? Would she ask about the interview? Would she admit to missing her, or would Elliot have to listen for the sighs of wistfulness or pauses hanging heavy with the unspoken? She'd come to crave those little signs of something more, but she feared they only promoted wishful thinking on her part. Did Kelly really hide her deeper feelings, or did she simply not have them?

She sank onto a rich-brown leather couch and stared up at the vaulted ceiling. Why was she thinking about Kelly? She'd just had the biggest interview of her life, and she'd done as well as anyone could've hoped for. She'd talked to the committee for well over the thirty minutes she'd been allotted, and they'd asked her to stay, which had to be a promising sign. If she hadn't at least sparked some interest, surely they would've been content to inform her via e-mail or phone at a later time. Kelly had been right. Syd got her in the door, but she'd kept herself in the conversation. Kelly, again. Why did everything come back to her, even here?

"Elliot?"

She jumped up to see one of the committee members approaching. Helen Hartwell. She quickly scanned her memories for any tidbit of information about her. Ivy league education, former CFO of an investment company, mid-forties, unattached, youngest woman on the board of the Institute, and a Chicago native.

"Hello, Ms. Hartwell."

"Please, call me Helen."

"Thank you, Helen. What can I do for you?"

"Nothing, officially. The interview is over."

Her heart sank a little. She didn't want this to be over.

"But I'm on lunch break and I wondered if you'd like a little tour of the area."

"I'd love one."

Helen's smile was bright and genuine. "Come on, then. We Midwesterners must stick together."

Elliot nodded and tried not to think of any of the Midwesterners she'd left behind. "How long have you been in D.C.?"

"Eight—no, ten years now. Time flies. I know people say that everywhere, but it honestly does feel as though life moves faster here."

"I'm sure the work keeps you busy."

"You have a gift for understatement."

Elliot laughed. "You may be the first person who's ever thought that about me. I generally get pegged as overly passionate."

"I'm sure you do in central Illinois, but as Dorothy said, you're not in Kansas anymore." Helen pointed them north, and they strode in a leisurely way along Massachusetts Avenue toward DuPont circle. "Here you'd be among a lot more like-minded individuals."

She didn't say she'd been around like-minded individuals her whole life. "Here I'd be around people with the power to put those shared ideas into actual public policy."

"Nicely played," Helen said, "and very true. The work we do isn't as flashy as the grandstanding on Capitol Hill, but I think you recognize that. We're not people who play on election cycles. We make long-term investments."

"That's what I'm interested in. The work of a lifetime."

Helen gave her a sideways glance. "I believe you."

"You sound surprised."

"When we got your résumé forwarded to us, I wasn't amused by someone going around the established channels. I'm sort of a stickler for procedure."

Elliot sighed. "That contact was made without my knowledge."

"And how do you feel about that?"

"Honestly, it embarrassed me pretty badly at first, but I also understand how business works. The old boys' network runs this town, and I'm a firm believer that women need to support each other as much as men do, if not more."

"Valid points."

"I only hoped my connections would cease to be material once I got into the interview. I believe women deserve equal opportunity, not special accommodations. If I get the job, and I understand that's

189

a big if, I'd need to know I'd earned the shot on my merits. If I felt otherwise, I'm not sure I'd be effective in the position."

"Did you just tell me that if I'd planned to offer you a job because of who you know, you'd rather I not offer you the job at all?"

"I guess I did." Elliot laughed away the sick feeling in the pit of her stomach. "I hope we didn't just take this little walk for nothing."

Helen's laugh sounded more natural. "No, we didn't. I wanted to show you this."

They stopped at a bustling intersection of cars spinning around a traffic circle. Stoplights switched from green to red, cars roared past in opposite directions, and she followed Helen across the crosswalk to a small park in the center of the roundabout.

"We're in DuPont circle," Helen said. "The Hill might be the center of the political world, but I believe this is where people like you and me can truly change that world."

Elliot turned around slowly. Helen didn't seem like a woman prone to dramatics. If she were making a point, Elliot wanted to make sure she took it in.

"Across the way is the Aspen Institute. The Vice President of the U.S. is currently working with them on solving issues of inequality as they relate to educational access." She pointed down another street. "The tall building down on the right is the Earth Policy Institute. A block over is the Women's Policy Institute. Behind us is the Embassy of Tribal Nations, and just out of view is the Progressive Policy Institute. Do you see a trend?"

"I do." She didn't just get the point. She felt all its implications stirring inside of her. Her heartbeat accelerated as she realized she stood at the crossroads of change. No—not just change. Progress. This was the kind of place where all her dreams could come true, dreams she hadn't felt connected to nearly enough lately. A sense of possibility spread through her chest, warming her and lightening her mood like a flame causes a hot air balloon to rise. Here, she could learn and grow, challenge and be challenged. Here, her life could have purpose. If only she could find the courage to face all this potential, she might actually leave behind the confusion that had clouded her vision for too long.

Her phone buzzed in her pocket.

"Do you need to get that?"

"No," she said confidently.

"Are you sure?" Helen asked. "I didn't mean to keep you so long. I just wanted to show you the world you'd be committing to if you accepted this position."

"Accepted?"

Helen smiled. "That wasn't an offer, far from it. We still have several more days' worth of interviews to conduct, and then there will likely be a week of discussion and at least another week of reference-checking, but you impressed some people in there today."

"Were you among them?" The question might've come across as bold, but she wanted to know, and Helen seemed like the type to respect people who spoke their minds.

"Let's just say you weren't what I expected. You left me wondering if I'd misjudged your initial application or misjudged the potential I saw in you during the interview," she said seriously. "Maybe I brought you out here as a test. I wanted to see you away from the shine and polish of a closed interview."

"The DuPont Circle test," Elliot said, making one more slow turn, trying to store up the sense of pride and purpose so she could carry it back to Darlington with her. Then looking back to Helen, she asked, "And, did I pass?"

"I think you may have," Helen said with another brilliant smile. "But that's no guarantee of a job offer. I'm only one vote."

"Of course," Elliot said, rocking back and forth on her heels in an attempt to keep from jumping up and down triumphantly. "I completely understand."

"I'd better get back to the office. Do you need directions back to your hotel?"

"No, I think I'll walk around here for a bit."

Helen extended her hand. "It was a pleasure to spend time with you today, Elliot. I hope to see you again very soon."

Elliot shook her hand. "The feeling is mutual."

She watched Helen walk back across the street before giving a little fist pump. She'd nailed the interview, and whatever Helen had seen in her had likely sealed the deal. She didn't want to count her chickens, or whatever, but standing there in the middle of Washington, D.C., she could almost sense her future being willed into existence. The shot of confidence was exactly what she needed to be able to see herself the way Helen saw her. For the first time in a long time, she truly believed she had what she needed to capitalize.

Her phone buzzed again. This time steadily, instead of the single pulse of a text message. Still gazing from one imposing building to the next, she absentmindedly fished the phone from her pocket. She glanced at the caller ID and smiled even more broadly as she read "Rory St. James." She couldn't think of anyone she'd rather share her exhilaration with. Then as quickly as the thought sparked, it faded, replaced with the image of dark eyes staring intensely into hers. Maybe there was one person she'd rather share the news with, but that wasn't an option.

She accepted the call. "Rory, you'll never believe the day I've had."

"Good or bad?"

"Well, they didn't give me the keys to the kingdom straight away, but I feel as though I'm destined to have them someday."

"Brava, Elliot, though I'm not a bit surprised. I feel as though I raised you myself."

"Is that why you're calling? So sure of your influence you wanted to gloat?"

"I wish it were, and I don't want to put a damper on your big day . . ."

"Uh-oh." She backed onto a park bench and lowered herself gently. "I'm sitting down now."

"I really am sorry. It's not like there's anything you can do from there, but Beth thought you needed to know before you got back."

"Are you okay?"

"Yes, it's not me, but Beth is at the hospital now."

"God, what's wrong with Beth?"

"No, it's not her. It's Kelly."

Her stomach flipped as all the breath left her lungs. "Kelly?"

"Her dad, he's had another stroke. A big one this time, and I'm afraid the prognosis isn't good. It could be a matter of hours."

"Hours."

Elliot looked around once more, but everything had gone so gray and dull. She probably should've taken a moment to consider how quickly Kelly's distress could make her dreams seem small and distant, but all she could think about was how she could get back to Darlington as quickly as possible.

"Elliot. Are you still there?"

"Yes," she said resolutely. "I'm on my way."

ဢ ဢ ဢ

"I'm so sorry," the young doctor said, unable to look her in the eye. "I've spoken with Doctor Patel, and she's shared your father's images with several of her colleagues. They're all in agreement that while other options might prolong his life, there's little hope of a significant recovery, and the likelihood of him surviving a transport, much less a surgery, is virtually non-existent."

Kelly pressed her index finger to her temple, trying to stem the headache point there, but to no avail. "So, you're telling me we're just out of options."

"I'm sorry, but in his weakened state—"

She waved him off. He couldn't tell her anything the parade of doctors hadn't told her all day long, and she'd lost the will to badger them. She couldn't bully medical facts any more than she could force time to stand still.

Time. She didn't have nearly enough left.

Suddenly, all the hours she'd spent at work trying to hide from her problems or feign control seemed small and wasted. She should've been here all along. She should've said more. She should've touched his hand, stared into his eyes, and memorized the contours of his lopsided smile. The regret pushed so hard against her ribs she feared they might crack.

"Kelly?" Beth asked softly. "What can I do?"

"Nothing." She turned back to the young doctor. "Can I see him now?"

"Of course, but he's in and out of lucidity. He doesn't know where he is, or even necessarily who he is. And his sight has suffered from

193

the pressure on his brain, as well. There's a good possibility he won't recognize you."

How much more could she bear? Even their final minutes might have already been stolen.

"Do you want me to go with you?" Beth asked.

She shook her head.

Beth squeezed her hand gently. "I'll be right here. You don't have to face anything alone."

She remained aware enough to realize she'd likely appreciate the gesture at some point, but right now no one else's presence mattered. Her life, so much of it, consisted of her father and her, side by side, the two of them against the world. It seemed only fitting for things to end the same way.

She pushed open the door to his room and stepped slowly inside, steeling herself for the worst. But as her eyes adjusted to the dim light, she breathed her first sigh of relief all day.

He looked the same. Whatever trauma had attacked his brain carried few outward signs. His dark hair was perfectly combed, streaks of gray lending a distinguished quality. His jaw and cheekbones beneath pale skin gave him a commanding profile, even with his diminished weight. For his age he'd remained rather handsome, and if not for the tubes and wires along his arms and under his nose, he would've appeared to be sleeping peacefully.

She pulled a chair close to the rail of his bed and sat down as quietly as she could against the faux leather finish. She took his large hand in both of hers, examining the wrinkles over knotted bones. How many times had she held that hand over the course of her lifetime? In crowded spaces, in tense moments, in joy and in fear, she'd always reached for him.

No, that wasn't true. There'd been times when she would've loved to hold this hand, times she'd almost reached out but didn't. Could she have? Should she have? She hadn't wanted him to worry, or think less of her, or God forbid, blame himself. Would he have seen a reason to cast blame?

She'd never know now. And wasn't that what she'd wanted? Hadn't she given up so many things in order to protect him, or more accurately to protect herself from the possibility of letting him down? In that, she'd triumphed. He would never be embarrassed of her. He'd never be disappointed. She'd never have to have the conversation she'd sacrificed so much to avoid. Why couldn't she take solace in that knowledge instead of sitting here wondering what might've been?

He stirred, slightly at first, just the twitch of his fingers, then the loll of his head toward the side closest to her. She stilled, her breath held painfully as his eyes slowly fluttered open. They were as dark as her own, but they didn't focus under the thin sheen of disorientation.

"Dad?"

He didn't move. He didn't blink. If not for the steady beep of machines, she might have thought he wasn't really there at all.

"Dad, I'm not sure if you can hear me or not."

He gave no response.

"I'm right here beside you."

Still he stared blankly as if looking past her or through her.

She remembered the doctor's comment about him not remembering where he was, or even who he was. "You're at the hospital."

His forehead wrinkled slightly as if he were trying to process, but nothing else about his expression changed. She bit her lip to keep from crying. He wasn't there. Not really. She was too late. Whatever she should've said would remain unspoken, or at the very least unheard. She was selfish to wish for more anyway. She couldn't make these moments about her. She had to try to offer what little comfort and peace she could.

"Dad, you're not alone. I'm right beside you."

His brow smoothed out again at the sound of her voice.

"It's me, Kelly."

His hand twitched, his fingers curling in as if he'd tried to squeeze her hand, and his pupils dilated.

"I'm right here with you. I'm not sure if you can hear what I'm saying."

His eyes focused and his mouth opened, first to a series of deep breaths that caused his chest to rise and fall dramatically as if each one took great effort.

"You can hear me," she said more for her own benefit. "It's Kelly, Dad."

195

"I know." He wheezed the words more than spoke them, but they were still intelligible.

"You do?" Tears filled her eyes.

"I know . . . who . . . you are."

She squeezed his hand tightly. "I love you, Dad."

"I know who . . ." He sucked in a heavy labored breath. "You are."

"Good." The word sounded every bit as jagged as his.

"I . . . know who . . . you are."

The beeps from his machine came more quickly, and a dull hum grew to a steady buzz. Something behind him seemed to be spinning or inflating.

"Okay, Dad." The panic rose in her. "Just relax."

He shook his head. "Need to know."

"You do," she said as a light in the corner of his monitor flashed red.

"I know . . . who . . . you . . . are . . . Kelly."

Tears ran down her face now as she leaned in and kissed his forehead. "I know you do. I love you."

"Love you," he whispered, his voice sounding faint against the roughness of his breath. "Know you . . . love you."

An alarm sounded as his eyes fell closed. She sagged against him, her forehead pressed to his as nurses rushed in.

She heard nothing. She saw nothing. Chaos reigned around them, but none of it mattered. None of it really existed. For as long as she could remember, it had been the two of them facing the world, and that is how they would face his exit from it.

She remained huddled against him, his hand in both of hers as slowly all the beeps and whirs, all the labored breath and rustling, all the shuffle of feet and whispered condolences faded back into silence.

Slowly she pulled away, straightening her back one resistant vertebra at a time. She stared down, the shock and horror filtering through the haze.

Her dad was gone.

The only constant she'd ever had, had just left the earth. She would never hold that hand again. She would never share another meal with him. She would never hear him working in the next office over.

Her breath grew shallow and raspy, the whoosh of it echoing through her own ears. Her thoughts raced at dizzying speeds. She couldn't go back. She couldn't fix this. No one could fix anything.

Done.

Over.

Never.

The words swirled at a frantic pace. The crushing sense of help-lessness caused her knees to buckle, but she couldn't stay here. She couldn't breathe here.

Turning blindly, she tried to flee only to find herself caught in Beth's arms. The familiar resting place almost broke through the frantic rush of fear and grief, but as Beth held her, stroking her hair and whispering soft shushing sounds, loneliness only compounded. She couldn't find solace in Beth's arms. It didn't exist there for her, not anymore. Another door closed for good.

She pushed Beth roughly away. She couldn't be near anyone, any-more. She had to face this alone. Alone was all she had. She could barely see to find the door, but once she did she ran, wildly.

Grief-stricken, she careened down the hall toward nothing and no one until suddenly the haze parted enough to reveal Elliot in her path. Could she really be there? After everything Kelly had said and done, everything she'd *not* said and *not* done, could Elliot really appear in this time of darkest need? Or had agony called up her image like a mirage rising out of the desert?

Elliot opened her arms wide, and the final piece of Kelly's stability crumbled. She fell into Elliot, having only the will to allow herself to be held as sobs wracked her body into oblivion.

〜 〜 〜

Elliot caught Kelly and braced them both against the tidal wave of grief slamming through her. Elliot wanted to wrap all the way around her, to absorb her pain completely, to take it on herself and lift the unbearable burden from Kelly's strong, proud body.

She didn't ask what had happened. She understood sorrow of this magnitude only came from an ending. She'd learned enough about

Kelly in the past two months to recognize that the bond she'd shared with her father made up more than a portion of her sense of self. She also knew, no matter how much she wanted to that she could not alleviate any of her anguish in the moment. She could, however, stand beside her, prop her up, hold her close, and make sure she understood that no matter what the immediate future might bring, she would not have to face it alone.

"I'm right here," she whispered, stroking Kelly's long, dark hair. "I've got you."

Kelly continued to sob, her face buried in Elliot's chest until her tears soaked through both their shirts.

"Let it all out," Elliot whispered, increasingly aware of eyes on them. She wouldn't shrink from their gaze. Surely they saw devastation of this sort in hospitals all the time, and yet she understood how much Kelly hated to be the subject of gossip. The thought of other people watching her moment of devastation might be too much to bear at a time like this. Elliot wanted to throw a cloak over them both and usher Kelly to safety like a mother covering her children from the rain, but she had no cloak and nowhere to take shelter. Instead, she held her tightly, her muscles absorbing the shakes rumbling through Kelly with each ragged breath. She would stand firm amid the swirling emotions, but with each passing moment she worried that holding Kelly this way might create another storm for them down the road.

She looked up and down the hallway, challenging anyone to question them, but no one would make eye contact. Every person turned away, either from the rawness of emotion or their unwillingness to let any of their own suspicions show through. No one could hold her gaze until down the hallway a single woman stepped into view, her eyes a piercing blue even at a distance.

They stood, staring at each other for several heart-wrenching moments as recognition played plainly across Beth Deveroux's features, followed by understanding. Her lips parted and her chest fell on a silent sigh, then her blue eyes flickered skyward as if lifting a prayer to the heavens. Which one of them was she praying for?

When their eyes met again Elliot could no longer separate all the emotions swirling there.

Kelly sucked in another body-shaking breath, pulling her attention back to where it was most needed.

"I'm right here," Elliot whispered again, burying her face in Kelly's hair and breathing the now-familiar scent of her. Her own chest felt as though it might be cracking open in the face of the heartache surrounding them all.

"Please," Kelly sobbed.

"What is it?" she murmured

"Take me home?" The words came out in a single sob.

She didn't look back to Beth or to the doctor or even to Kelly for further instruction. "Of course."

Then, still holding her as close as possible, she turned them both toward the door and simply walked away.

Whatever else needed to be said or done would wait until some of the suffering had subsided.

Chapter Sixteen

The next week flew by in a blur. She remembered so few of the details. So many decisions made in a haze. She had no recollection of meeting with funeral directors or picking out clothes, flowers, or a casket. She must have. Surely those decisions fell to her, and she had vague flashes of memories that always seemed to involve shaking hands or being handed Kleenex. Elliot seemed to have an unending supply of tissues. Come to think of it, Elliot had an unending supply of time and energy and compassion as well.

Had she left Kelly's side at all? Surely she had at some point. Others had come and gone. Beth, Rory, priests, funeral directors. There seemed to have been hordes of old ladies fussing and arranging things. Food magically appeared at odd times, and yet in the background of every cloudy remembrance, Elliot always hovered just out of view.

Kelly turned to her now. She knew exactly where she'd find her. When had she learned to expect her there, never close enough to crowd, but always near enough to catch Kelly if she fell? Even here at the cemetery, when most of the others had left, she remained, tall and steady like one of the large oaks in whose shadows they stood. "Did you go to the funeral home with me?"

"When?"

"When I took them his suit?"

"Yes."

A layer of fog burned away. "And last night after the wake, you stayed in the parlor?"

"Yes."

"And this morning before the service, you were in the chapel when they brought in the casket?"

"Yes, but don't worry. I told people I was your assistant."

She hadn't yet gotten to the point where she'd considered what anyone else would think about Elliot's constant presence. She wasn't even sure what to make of it herself. She didn't have the energy or the wherewithal for reflection.

"What about the office?"

"I went there with you, too."

More images flashed through her mind. She'd awoken on her office couch to the sight of Elliot in a cone of light, her shirt-sleeves rolled up and her hair tousled as she pored over a spread of papers on her desk.

"Did I sleep there?"

"Sometimes."

"Did I work?"

"Sometimes."

"Did you sleep?"

"At the office?"

"At all?"

Elliot's mouth curled up slightly. "Sometimes."

Kelly felt something foreign stir in her chest at Elliot's answers, or rather her dodging of them. Some spark of something warm, something almost alive. Then the guilt came quickly on its heels. "My dad is dead."

Elliot nodded slowly, stepping closer as Kelly turned to face the freshly dug grave that held his casket. She didn't remember watching it being lowered into the ground, and yet she must have. "I don't know what to do now."

"There's a dinner. At the church. I've hired a car to drive you."

"And you?"

"If you want. Beth is also here, if you'd rather."

Beth? Of course, Beth would be there. Beth was a natural in these sorts of situations. She would know what to do. She could manage everything if Kelly needed her to. Had she looked to Beth? She had no memory of doing so.

"Did Beth ride here with us?"

Elliot shook her head. "You asked me to."

201

A distant alarm sounded in her brain. Now that she was seeing more clearly, she examined Elliot more closely. Her eyes were sunken and accented by dark circles. Her skin had gone pale, and she might have even lost weight. What had Kelly put her through while she was going though hell? Reaching down, she took Elliot's hand, feeling the slide of their fingers against one another as they intertwined so easily. "Thank you."

"For what?"

She wasn't even sure she could answer the question, because she wasn't sure she would ever fully understand all the things Elliot had done for her any more than she'd understand why. "For everything."

Elliot gave her a tired smile. "Of course."

Of course. She said it so easily, so naturally, as if she'd never considered not being there for her. Didn't she realize no one would've condemned her for keeping her distance? No one would've questioned her stepping back. To the rest of the world, they'd barely worked together two months, and even Kelly, who'd been there for every intimate moment, wouldn't blame her for not wanting to risk their tenuous peace by getting involved to the level she had. They hadn't left things on the best of terms before Elliot's interview. Those memories were still as clear as the beautiful spring sky overhead. She'd behaved like a spoiled child who'd rather pout than admit she was feeling things she didn't want to. Denying those feelings hadn't made them go away, any more than her grief over losing her father had washed them away. In fact, she worried the emotions Elliot inspired in her may have been the only parts of herself left untouched by the sorrow that had consumed her.

"Are you ready to go to the dinner, or do you need a few more minutes? There's no rush."

"No rush," Kelly repeated. No, she supposed there wasn't any rush to make sense of things anymore. "Actually would you mind giving me a few minutes?"

"Not at all." Elliot squeezed her hand then backed away. "Take all the time you need."

She stepped up to the edge of the grave, smelling the loamy scent of damp earth. The sunlight streaming through the first translucent tree leaves overhead cast a lacy pattern over the mahogany casket below. She felt like she should say something, or pray something. Surely others had, but she couldn't remember any of their words. The only echo through her mind was a constant loop of Elliot saying, "Take all the time you need," and "There's no rush."

How much time did she need? Was there ever enough? Apparently, sometimes a lifetime wasn't long enough. More than three decades together hadn't been nearly enough for her to say the things she should've said. And now there was no more time. How strange to have no time, and yet no rush. She'd run herself ragged for as long as she could remember to please him, to prove herself worthy, to escape the unavoidable. Where had it gotten her? All was lost, and what did she have to show for her efforts?

Nothing.

She stared into the hole in the ground, feeling the void overtake her again. At least she preferred the numbness to the pain. She might survive if only she could stay in this emotional vacuum forever.

She turned back toward Elliot, and when their eyes met, her stomach gave an unsettling flip. The feeling was so foreign, so completely disconnected from every other aspect of her life right now, she couldn't help but catch her breath. Seconds ago she didn't think herself capable of feeling anything ever again, and yet with Elliot, nothingness didn't seem to be an option.

$$\backsim \quad \backsim \quad \backsim$$

"When did you eat last?" Beth asked as she collected used paper plates.

"I had some cheesy potatoes and some other white casserolish dish before the church ladies started to clean up." Elliot rubbed her eyes. The last week had been 90 percent church ladies and casseroles. They'd all run together days ago.

"And when did you sleep?"

"Last night."

Beth eyed her suspiciously. She'd noticed that happened a lot lately. But she could only deal with so many things at once, and as much as she hated it, Beth's suspicions weren't even in the top ten of her worries today.

"How long did you sleep last night?"

"Ah, you found the loophole inherent in that question. I slept for about an hour and a half."

Beth sighed. "I take it that's par for the course since you got back from D.C.?"

"Give or take." She extended her legs to their full length and looked over her shoulder under the guise of stretching her neck, but she was searching for Kelly. She found her at the end of the table with the same glazed-over stare she'd worn for days. A white-haired lady with turquoise glasses patted her arm and whispered condolences. Elliot scanned her body language for signs of excessive fatigue. In some ways it was easier to tell now. Without her natural defenses, she didn't hide her feelings as well. On the downside, she didn't seem to be able to process her feelings very well, either. She understood Kelly's need to close parts of herself off, but she wanted to make sure she didn't shut down completely.

At the moment, though, Kelly was sitting, she was nodding as if she heard what the woman beside her said, and she even had the strength and awareness to sip from the cup of coffee in front of her. She seemed a shell of the woman Elliot had grown used to, but the little hints that she was still functioning behind the protective veneer allowed Elliot to breathe a little easier.

She turned back to find Beth watching her, forehead wrinkled with worry. This wasn't the first time, either. Ever since their stare-down in the hospital hallway, she'd felt Beth watching her almost as closely as she watched Kelly. True to Beth's personality, she'd never pushed, and Elliot never sensed a hint of judgment, but the questions hung heavily unspoken between them. She hoped they would remain that way, mostly because she hated being put into a position where she felt the need to lie, but also because she wasn't sure she had the answers.

She'd been so sure of everything in Washington, D.C. Her dreams had felt so close, and for the first time she'd almost believed she could reach out and grab them. She'd felt alive and strong and purposeful in that world of endless possibilities. And then when Rory'd called, it had all faded away. In that moment and every moment since, she'd known to her very core she was meant to be with Kelly. She hadn't questioned or even doubted that call. Even now, the need to be near Kelly carried her though sleepless nights and thankless tasks. The desire to protect her, to shelter her, to carry whatever portion of the burden she could, felt as instinctual as breathing.

How could both impulses—the one to stay and the one to go—be true? If she couldn't tell which one offered the right path, how could she trust her instincts toward either? And if she couldn't trust her gut on this, how could she trust it on anything?

"Elliot?"

She jumped. "What?"

Both Kelly and Beth stared at her.

"Sorry." She rubbed her face, hoping they'd think she'd zoned out due to exhaustion and not a complete crisis of confidence.

"I think I'm ready to go," Kelly said.

"I'll drive you," Beth offered.

"Actually, I want to go by the office for a while."

Beth and Elliot exchanged a look as if to say, *Do you want to handle this or should I?*

"Are you sure?" they asked in unison, then smiled. Elliot wondered if this was how Rory felt when they did their mind-meld thing. Kelly didn't seem amused, though. She didn't seem much of anything other than tired.

"I have papers in my desk I want to go over tonight."

"I could go pick them up for you," Beth offered. "I planned on bringing the leftovers to your place later."

"No, I need to check in there, and I don't know how long I'll be."

"I'm not sure you need to be there at all after the day you've had."

"I actually have a few files to go over, too." Elliot cut in, sensing a showdown between two stubborn women. "Why don't I walk over there with her, and that way I can make sure she doesn't lose track of time."

"Thank you," Kelly said flatly. She didn't sound enthusiastic, but she'd accepted the offer of help without argument, and once again, she'd accepted Elliot's presence easily while discouraging Beth's. The trend had clearly not gone unnoticed by any of them.

"All right," Beth conceded. "But . . ." They all waited while she seemed to search fruitlessly for the right words. "Never mind." She waved them off. "Everything else will keep until later."

Elliot hoped the last comment referred to the assortment of casseroles and food trays still scattered about the church hall, but she suspected there was more below the surface. Either way, Beth had granted them a temporary reprieve.

"I'll make sure she gets some rest," Elliot offered, to help ease Beth's mind.

"Please see that she's not the only one. Neither one of you will be good for anything if you collapse."

"Thank you for taking care of things here. I'm not sure how you did it, but I am grateful," Kelly said, giving the first indication she was even aware of everything Beth had done to get the funeral together. Elliot took that as another small step in the right direction.

Beth seemed pleased, too, though she brushed off the compliment. "Don't mention it. Rory and I will bring the rest of the food by once we get cleaned up here. If you're not home, I'll leave everything in the fridge or the deep freeze."

"I can't remember if I left it open or not. Do you still have your key?"

Beth's smile held a hint of something wistful. "I do, actually."

Kelly nodded and swallowed visibly, then, looking to Elliot, straightened her shoulders. "Ready to go?"

"Yes," she answered. She didn't know why Beth had a key to Kelly's house, but she supposed that fact alone wasn't as odd as the exchange accompanying the news. As Kelly turned and headed for the door, Elliot realized she'd have to add it to the long list of things to ponder later.

"Elliot?" Beth caught her hand.

"Yes?"

"Be careful with her."

Her chest tightened as a thousand different implications flashed through her mind. She couldn't process any of them fully, but she felt relatively certain she'd long since left the chance for caution behind.

"Kel?"

Elliot leaned up against the door jamb. She'd shed her suit coat and rolled up the sleeves of her emerald dress shirt. The buttons at her throat were open, revealing just a hint of her collarbones. Her hair had lost most of its body, and little splays of auburn locks wisped over her ears and forehead. Dark circles underlined her bright green eyes. She looked totally exhausted and absolutely stunning. Kelly's breath caught painfully in her chest.

"I think it's time to call it a night."

"What time is it?"

"Almost eight."

Kelly blinked at the clock on her computer to confirm what seemed impossible. They'd been at the office for hours and she hadn't made it through the four tax returns she'd hoped to finish today. Had she fallen asleep sitting up? Certainly she hadn't been fully present, but apparently she'd done little other than sleepwalk for days. She'd been tired before. She'd zoned out or lost track of time, but this was something deeper. She felt almost as though she had ceased to exist in the world. What did she really have to prove that she'd even been here all afternoon? If not for the affection in Elliot's eyes, she might not even know she was here now. How could Elliot still look at her that way? Shouldn't she be done with her by now? Surely she could walk away any time. And what would Kelly do if she did?

"You want me to take you back to your place?"

"No," The answer held a frantic edge.

Elliot's eyes widened briefly, but her voice stayed level. "Okay. We'll stay."

She should let Elliot go. She should make her go. Kelly needed to go home, too, at some point. Keeping Elliot there wasn't fair, but she couldn't stand the thought of being alone. The emptiness inside was too much to bear without compounding it with an empty house. She just couldn't take it, but Elliot couldn't go on like this much longer, either.

Elliot did a poor job of stifling a yawn, then forced an apologetic smile. "Why don't I put on some more coffee, then I'll look over those returns for you, and you can double-check the ones I finished today."

God, she was too damn good. If Kelly had any piece of her heart left intact, Elliot's unwavering commitment to her would've broken it. She hung her head. "I'm sorry."

"What?" Elliot started forward as if to catch her, then stopped short when Kelly lifted her eyes again.

"I have to stop doing this to you, but I don't know how."

"Stop doing what?"

"Holding you here. Leaning on you. Making you carry my pain. I'm going to hate myself for this if I ever recover, but right now the prospect of a rebound seems so impossible that I can't feel any shame."

"There's nothing to be ashamed of." Elliot crouched down beside her desk, taking her hand and looking into her eyes. "I'm here because I want to be."

"I worry you're here because I can't stand to be left alone."

"Maybe the two are the same. If you can't stand to be alone, then I want to be with you."

"All night?"

Elliot's face flushed, but she didn't turn away. "Until you don't want me to be there anymore."

Why did she sound so certain of that inevitability? Because Kelly always made her so sure of the eventual rejection? Because Kelly pushed her away every time she got too close? Because she had more faith in Kelly's fortitude than she had in herself? "You deserve better than this."

Elliot lifted Kelly's hand to her lips and gently kissed her fingertips. "So do you. I wish I could do more."

"You've already done too much. If I ever come out on the other side of this, I might not be able to live with myself for taking advantage of you the way I have."

"Remember what I told you about consent? You haven't taken anything I haven't wanted to give."

Kelly's heart gave a hard thud against her ribs. The sign of life nearly shocked her. She couldn't remember the last time she'd felt her own heartbeat, and she didn't want to lose the feeling. "Please don't go."

"I promise I won't," Elliot whispered, "unless you go with me."

"Go with you?"

"Come home with me?"

Kelly closed her eyes and whispered her first conscious prayer in she didn't know how long. *God, give me strength.* She was aware enough to know she wanted to accept the offer and also aware enough to know she shouldn't. And yet, awareness did nothing to bolster any sort of resistance in her. She held tighter to Elliot's hand and nodded.

"Yeah?" Elliot asked.

"Yes."

Somehow saying the word made everything fall into place. She knew Elliot didn't magically transport her to the apartment, but it felt that way. Another disconcerting lapse in her time/memory continuum, only this time she didn't find the shift unsettling.

"Here's some pajama pants and one of my T-shirts," Elliot said, grabbing them out of a laundry basket. "They'll be a bit big on you, but they're pajamas, so big is good, right?"

"Thank you." She accepted the clothes and watched as Elliot rifled through a pile of stuff on the floor before picking up a sweatshirt, sniffing it, and then tossing it back. The move made her smile, and the expression felt pleasantly foreign—the first unguarded flash of something happy in she didn't know how long.

Elliot found something acceptable and turned toward the door. "I'll be right out here."

"No." The word escaped, raw and needy, and she hated herself immediately. "I mean, why?"

"I'm not leaving. I'll keep the door open. I just thought it might be better if I slept on the couch."

"You don't have to."

"I don't mind."

"You said I stayed here before, I mean, earlier this week. Where did you sleep then?"

"I . . . well, in the chair. Or on the couch. Sometimes the floor."

"So what you're saying is, you didn't sleep."

Elliot shrugged. "I slept as much as you did."

She reached for Elliot, one hand on the curve of her hip, the contact sending a rush of warmth through Kelly. She didn't realize until then how cold she'd been for so long. She craved the heat in a way that made her weak enough to ask for what she wanted. "Come to bed with me."

Elliot sucked in a deep breath. "I won't tell you no, but I don't want to take advantage of the situation."

"I do," Kelly said, pulling her closer. "I haven't felt anything but pain for over a week. For the last few days, I'm not sure I've felt anything at all. I've been a ghost. I barely even existed. Then you touched me. You're the only thing that makes me feel something other than suffocating nothingness. Even if it's just for tonight, especially if it's just for tonight, I want to take full advantage of this situation."

Elliot either sensed the urgency in her words, or shared it somewhere deep inside because she obviously needed no more convincing. Taking Kelly's face in her hands, she kissed her soulfully.

Kelly melted into her, the rigid set of her body going languid as it sagged against Elliot's. She had to fade into her until all their lines blurred. Falling, always falling now, Elliot caught her with a strong arm around her waist, only this time instead of using that strength to hold her up, she used it to hold them close.

Kelly ran her hands up Elliot's side, smoothing the folds of starched cotton against the curve of her ribs. She slid flat palms over her chest until, clutching her collar, she pulled them both down to the bed. Scooting backward on elbows and knees, they kissed and clutched their way up the mattress. Elliot kept one hand firmly pressed to the small of her back as she moved the other steadily up, massaging fatigued muscles until she reached the base of her neck. Sinking skilled fingers into Kelly's thick hair, she gently cradled her head all the way down to the pillow.

Never in her life had Kelly felt so cherished. The pieces of her shattered heart strained to contain the new feelings building there. Elliot continued to kiss her soundly, never breaking the contact between them, either intuiting Kelly's need for closeness or sharing it. The weight of her body proved a soothing anchor to the present. She would not drift away again with Elliot there to tether her. Kelly remained fully present, tasting her, sweet and hot, against the cold and stone that had encased her for too long.

Their mouths worked together seamlessly, with less urgency than before, but what they'd lost in ferocity, they'd gained in familiarity. She marveled at the sense of being known, of being seen in all her fullness or even weakness, and still being wanted. Her pulse ticked up another level as some pieces of her broken heart came back together. Pushing up, she rolled them both over without breaking the kiss. Popping open the top few buttons of Elliot's oxford as they kissed, she traced Elliot's collarbone with her fingers, then leaned down to kiss it. The scent of her, rich and clean, filled Kelly's head as she nestled into the hollow of her throat. Slowly Kelly's dormant senses reawakened. Elliot drew them back from the brink of nothingness. The world could not remain black and white, dull and dark, when something as beautiful as Elliot existed in it.

The intensity of her need startled her even now. She hadn't thought herself capable of something so all-consuming in her fragile state, but she didn't fear it, not with Elliot, not yet. Every time she reached, she found Elliot open and willing to meet her where she wanted to go in the moment. She unbuttoned the last of Elliot's buttons and spread the shirt wide, arching back only enough to look at her, to see her skin, to watch the rise and fall of her chest, to memorize the sight of her glorious form. Kelly's brokenness stirred, the pieces trembling before the whole of Elliot splayed out beneath her.

"Wow." She breathed the word more than said it. "I feel like I say that a lot around you, but I'm suddenly in a little over my head."

Elliot sat up as much as she could with Kelly still straddling her legs. "Is this too much?"

"Yes, but in a good way. You're stunning, Elliot. And you're open, and very good at everything you've done for me, at all the things you do, period."

"So are you," Elliot said, clasping her hands on Kelly's hips. She slid them up, taking the smooth material of her black dress with her as she caressed Kelly's waist, her ribs, her breasts before lifting it completely over her head. "You're also beautiful."

Kelly bit her lower lip and shook her head.

"You are," Elliot whispered, holding her close enough to kiss the top of her shoulder. "Beautiful and strong and whole. You just don't remember."

"I don't," Kelly admitted, "but I see those things in you. I see everything I lack when I look in your eyes."

"No." Elliot eased back, guiding Kelly down with her. "Anything in my eyes is a reflection of what I see in you."

Elliot rolled them over again in a tangle of legs, arms, and sheets. "Anything I do for you is only the expression of what you've made me feel."

She sank into the mattress as Elliot's words poured over her. She personified perfection. God, how Kelly needed her. Needed to feel her. Needed to believe in her. Needed all of her. Reaching up, she unclasped her belt and pushed her dark slacks over the curve of her hips, and Elliot kicked them away.

Lowering herself until each body part pressed flush and firm against its mirror, Elliot kissed her again. Kelly dug her fingernails into the rippling muscles of Elliot's back, pinning them together and still yearning for more. She wanted to pull her in so closely that they'd become a part of each other. She wanted to keep her there in her heart until she reassembled all the pieces of her brokenness.

With each caress and every kiss, her heartbeat grew a little stronger. She tasted Elliot's skin, felt her touch reignite numbed nerve endings, and breathed the scent of spring on every inhale. Reawakening, renewal, rebirth. Blood rushed through her veins. The sound of her own body coming back to life drummed through her ears.

The process almost hurt in the most beautiful way. To go from sleeping to waking in such brilliant fashion strained every muscle as it pushed through her. She reached out for life in the form of the vibrant woman above her. Pulling her down, she urged her forward until Elliot found the center of her need. Her head lolled back as a gasp escaped her lips. The pressure was almost too much to bear, and still she cried out for more. She had to feel Elliot move inside her in every way. They didn't have forever. She believed only in this moment because nothing else existed. She feared that outside this soaring release not even she existed. She had to learn to live here, or she might not ever live again.

Elliot pushed inside as light shattered the darkness. Slipping one leg between Elliot's, she sought and found the pulse of her own need. She pressed into the proof she wasn't alone, not in any way.

"Stay with me," she panted.

"Yes." Elliot's voice ran hoarse and hot against she skin. "I'm right here."

Their labored breath rasped between kisses until the pace grew frantic and Kelly buried her face in the crook of Elliot's neck. Her heart pulsed strong and rhythmic beneath Kelly's lips. The sign of life almost made her weep. So close, so real, so tangible. Her own heart raced to reach the rhythm of Elliot's. Matching pace, they raced together toward release, rocking and riding out the waves of completion cresting between them.

"Please," Kelly finally begged, "Elliot. With me."

"I'm right here," Elliot whispered. "I've got you. I promise I won't let go until you do."

The vow shot through Kelly like an electric current, the last drastic bolt needed to kick-start her heart back into its own cadence. She crashed back into the space in her life left hollow by the last week. A sense of something more than relief flooded in behind the release. Powerful, protective, and yet somehow laid bare. How much of herself had Elliot given? How much could Kelly give back? Surely nowhere near equal measure. No. Kelly held part of her now. And pieces of her heart would always be Elliot's.

Chapter Seventeen

Sunlight shone through the blinds and birds sang outside as Elliot snuggled closer to the warm body she'd curled around all night. Dreamless sleep accompanied only by the intuitive awareness of oneness held them cocooned through their rejuvenation.

They'd more than made it through the night. She didn't need to credit her own abilities to recognize the changes she'd witnessed in Kelly. She'd watched her come back to life. She wasn't naïve enough to think Kelly had miraculously healed every wound, but at least now they knew for sure the prospect of healing existed beyond the dark void she'd feared might consume them both.

Elliot fluttered her eyes open against the onslaught of light, Kelly slowly came into focus, lying on her back, one hand resting atop the sheet covering her chest and the other curled under Elliot's neck. Her dark hair spilled across the pillow, and her red lips parted only enough to admit the shallowest of breaths. The dark circles were gone from below her eyes, leaving her pale skin pristine as she rested peacefully. Elliot fought the urge to close her eyes to such a beautiful sight as an ache started in her chest. She didn't want to let that feeling take hold. She should turn away. She should pretend to sleep. She should do anything to keep from feeling the emotion stirring in her now. And yet, Kelly looked so much like a fairy tale, Elliot couldn't bring herself to spoil the scene. She'd played the role of prince so often over the last week, she couldn't resist the chance to wake sleeping Snow White, even if it meant the spell would finally be broken.

Hovering over her just long enough to imprint this perfection in her mind, she lowered her lips to Kelly's. She didn't startle awake so much as soften into it. The feather-light touch melted gradually into something more as her lips parted and her fingers twitched against Elliot's bicep before closing around her arm. What had been meant as a sweet hello, or even a type of goodbye, deepened until it stirred Elliot's blood. Easing over Kelly's body, she brushed lightly against her, breast to breast.

Kelly sighed dreamily against her mouth, then took hold of her ass and pulled her down fully against her. Elliot kissed her lips, the tip of her nose, her forehead, and then nipped at her ear before whispering, "Good morning."

"Yes," Kelly said slowly, "it feels like it might just be."

Elliot heard the wary hope in Kelly's voice and wished desperately she could protect her from the awareness bound to accompany her awakening.

"What day is it?"

Elliot had to think for a moment. "Saturday."

"The office," Kelly murmured through the kiss she placed over Elliot's heart.

"All your appointments are canceled until Monday. We can play catch-up until then . . . or we could stay here all day."

Kelly hummed contentedly. "Tempting."

"And yet? Tax season."

"Tax season," Kelly confirmed.

Elliot rolled softly onto her side and placed a kiss on Kelly's temple. "How about a compromise?"

"Not my strong suit," Kelly said, with a hint of humor that made Elliot's chest fill with hope.

"What about breakfast here in bed, then a nice long, hot shower together? Then tax season may resume."

"Can I make a counteroffer?"

"You may."

"Breakfast here in bed, then we each take nice, long, hot showers separately as a way of ensuring we actually make it back to the office by April 15."

"Less fun." Elliot pretended to pout. "But probably more responsible. I accept."

"You do?" Kelly's voice rose on a hint of surprise.

"Of course. I understand."

Kelly's dark eyes glistened. "I think you do. I think you've understood so much more than you should've had to. I wish I could've been better for you."

Elliot's heart constricted at the remorse she heard in the comment, and also the choice of past tense. "You've had a lot to deal with."

"But even before, before my dad . . ." She swallowed as if the word still hurt too much to say. "Before last week. I wasn't fair to you. I didn't want to admit how much I'd grown to depend on you, and when you left for Washington, I didn't tell you how much I would miss you because I couldn't acknowledge it, even to myself."

Elliot kissed her forehead. She didn't know what to say. Kelly had pushed her away because she feared wanting her to stay. The thought broke her heart.

"I know you have to go," Kelly whispered. "I want you to have everything you've dreamed of."

"Nothing's settled yet. I might not even get the job." Elliot thought of the look in Helen's eyes before they'd parted and wondered if she'd just lied.

"If not this fellowship, you'll get another one, and I need you to take it. But I also need you to know it's not because I don't care. It's because I do. I just might not be strong enough to say so at the time."

She searched Kelly's eyes and doubted her last statement. The sheen of disorientation had disappeared, revealing her darker depths once more. She wasn't her old self yet; she was still too open, too vulnerable, but she did not lack for strength. Grief had knocked her down, but nothing could actually take her out. She would survive the coming days. She would make the transition, no matter how hard it might prove. She was a fighter, and once back on her feet, Kelly would fight for the life she'd worked so hard to build.

Did the same hold true for Elliot?

The doubt crept in again, circling around her throat with icy fingers. She'd just witnessed a resurrection as she helped Kelly claw her way back from a cavernous void, but Elliot had lost part of her heart in the process. How many dark nights could they trudge through before they lost their way entirely? There had already been one painful goodbye in this season. Could she really bring herself to spark another?

"Hey," Kelly whispered, a pleading in her voice to call her back, "stay with me a little longer though, okay?"

Had she made the request for her own benefit or for Elliot's? Did the difference even matter if the answer remained the same? "I'm right here. I'm not going anywhere."

Kelly's smile held more relief than she should've had to feel. "Not going anywhere other than the kitchen, you mean?"

"Right. Because we settled on terms of agreement that included breakfast in bed."

"We did, and we sealed it with a kiss, which I'm pretty sure makes the contract binding."

"I won't argue. You're the CPA. I'm just the intern."

"And interns are also responsible for making the coffee," Kelly said, giving her a playful push. "I like my eggs over easy, so don't break the yolk."

"Oh, well, if there are special orders to follow, you'd better come supervise."

"You might regret that comment." Kelly sat up and kissed her quickly. "I'm going to go wash up, and then you're not likely to shake me for the rest of the day."

Elliot grinned as she pulled on her sweatpants and padded to the kitchen.

෴ ෴ ෴

If the week before had been a blur of devastation and sorrow, this week's haze consisted of sex and taxes. By the time April first dawned, they were only slightly more caught up on sleep or work than they had been the day of the funeral.

"Fifteen more days." Elliot groaned, rolling over to face her.

Kelly smiled, once again taken in by the sight of Elliot first thing in the morning. Her hair always stuck out at odd angles. Today's hairdo struck a balance between rakish pirate, and troll doll. She knew she shouldn't let herself get used to the view, but she'd yet to sleep in

217

her own bed, generally only returning to her home to change before work. Instead of pulling back as usual, they seemed to be pulling closer. Or maybe Elliot did the pulling and she was simply powerless to resist. Perhaps she'd lost so much lately that she wanted to make the most of their borrowed time. Did it really matter how she rationalized day six of waking up in Elliot's bed? She sighed and pushed herself to a sitting position. "Fifteen more days."

"It's April Fools' day, you know," Elliot said, pulling on the sweatpants Kelly had taken off her the night before.

"So?"

"So, consider yourself warned."

"I do not like to be made a fool of." Kelly reached for the closest article of clothing and found one of the Chicago Sky hoodies Elliot favored when at home. How had it ended up on her side of the bed? Had they resorted to throwing clothing in an attempt to get at each other?

"No jokes on April Fools' day, at all? You can't be serious. You can't ban April Fools' day. That's not in my contract."

"I can't control you, obviously, but I stand by my statement, and now you've been warned."

Elliot laughed in a way that suggested she didn't intend to heed the warning, and might, in fact, revel in the act of ignoring it.

Kelly braced herself for what had the potential to be a long day, but couldn't summon any of the frustration she would've normally felt at such a prospect. "Go make the coffee."

Elliot pulled on a threadbare red T-shirt before kissing her deeply. "Fine. That is in my job description, but when this internship is over, you're on coffee detail."

She shook her head as Elliot bounded through the living room in two steps. She refused to make plans for when the internship ended. She wouldn't even think about what would come next for them . . . or what wouldn't. She headed into the bathroom and splashed water on her face, then took a swig of Elliot's mouthwash since she hadn't brought a toothbrush with her. She could have. She could have brought a change of clothes, too. Elliot had offered on more than one occasion, but Kelly worried doing so would suggest a permanence that didn't really exist.

"Um, Kel."

"Yes?" she called as she rinsed the sink.

"Rory's here."

She froze, her heart instantly racing. Rory. Of all the people she didn't want discovering her here first thing in the morning, Rory had to top the list. Damn it, why would she come by so early in the morning? It wasn't even eight o'clock yet. And just stopping by, unannounced, first thing, on a day when Elliot had to work? Who did that?

She didn't hear any voices. She hadn't even heard anyone knock on the door. Suddenly she smiled at her own reflection. April Fools' day. Nice try. How long did Elliot intend to let her cower in the bathroom before she admitted to the gag? And what did she intend to do in the meantime? Relax on the couch and sip her coffee? Unacceptable.

Kelly had told her she didn't like to be fooled, and now she would show she wasn't easy to put one over on. She strode purposefully out of the bathroom and threw open the bedroom door.

"Nice try, but I'm not—" Whatever smart comeback she'd intended to employ died on her lips as her gaze fell on Rory St. James. Her mouth opened, but no words came out. Her only solace was that Rory wore the exact same expression.

"So, Kelly's here," Elliot finally said. "I guess I forgot to mention that."

"Yeah, you did," Rory said slowly. "Morning, Kelly."

"Rory." She nodded.

"I think maybe I dropped by at a bad time. Or, um . . . maybe I shouldn't drop by without calling. Ever."

"I can call you later," Elliot offered.

"No." Kelly lifted her chin. She would not hide from this. She would not let Rory see her sweat. She might not be able to undo what had been done, but she would set the tone from here on out. Sadly, this wasn't the first time she'd had to run damage control with Rory.

"Actually, you can stay. I'm on my way out."

Rory scanned her clothes, no doubt taking in the Chicago sweatshirt and the pajama bottoms that were several inches too long.

"Kel," Elliot pleaded quietly, "please."

219

She held up her hand. "I'll see you at the office. I'm sure you and Rory have plenty to talk about." She didn't want to think about that conversation, though she would likely think about nothing else for days.

"Kelly, really, I don't need an explanation," Rory said gently. "I'm glad to see you're both doing okay. I worried when I hadn't heard from Elliot for a while, but I see now I shouldn't have."

Shouldn't she have? Shouldn't they all have worried? Shouldn't someone have stopped this before they got to this point? She shook her head. She couldn't undo anything, even if she'd wanted to, though even through her wretched embarrassment she couldn't imagine making that choice. She could only extract herself as quickly and gracefully as possible. She couldn't stand to hear Rory's pacifying tone a moment longer.

She pulled on the brown loafers she'd kicked off as she'd walked through the door the night before. They didn't quite match her outfit, but fashion faux pas didn't rank high on her current list of priorities. She straightened up and rolled her shoulders back before facing Rory and Elliot. Any other time, she would've considered it a victory of sorts to render the likes of these commanding women speechless, but she took solace in the fact that their indecision gave her the chance to make her exit.

"Elliot, I may be a little late getting to the office. I'll be there as soon as I'm able."

Elliot nodded. "I'll handle everything until you're ready."

She would, too. Kelly didn't doubt her ability to soldier through this or any other situation. Elliot's resiliency far outmatched her own. Which, of course, was why she had to leave.

ဢ ဢ ဢ

Rory and Elliot stood staring down the hallway long after Kelly had left the building. Finally Rory turned toward Elliot, worry creasing her still youthful features. "Well, that just happened."

Elliot nodded. "Indeed."

"To be clear, she hadn't dropped by for some early morning tax prep lessons, correct?" Rory rubbed her head. "Sorry. That sounds like a bad euphemism. Did she sleep here? I mean, don't answer if you don't want to, but . . . it seemed like she slept here."

Elliot swung the door open wide. "You'd better come in."

Rory didn't hesitate, clearly both concerned and trying very hard not to freak out as she paced across the living room. "We can talk about this right? Because I know you're a student, but I also considered you a friend, and a mentee, and we've talked about personal stuff before. I mean, you've listened to all my wedding talk for months." She stopped and stared at Elliot as if waiting for her to jump in.

"Yeah," she finally managed to say. She couldn't process much else. She wanted to soothe Rory, but it felt like someone was squeezing her heart in a rusty metal vice. Kelly had walked out in a fit of shock, or embarrassment, or some mix of emotions Elliot couldn't decipher through the walls she'd immediately thrown up to protect herself. Elliot wanted to run after her, to hold her, and tell her everything would be all right, but she didn't know if she could make that promise. Clearly, she couldn't protect Kelly from everything. This time it was only Rory, and while Elliot trusted her completely, who would pose the next threat? Beth? Surely she would find out now. Then who? Would they keep running the risk of a John-Deere-driving farmer or a Mrs. Anthony walking in on them? How long could Kelly live that way?

How long could she?

"Yeah?" Rory asked.

"Yeah." Elliot crashed across the arm of the couch, her legs hooked over the side and her arm thrown over her eyes. "I think we'd better talk about this now."

"Okay." Rory settled more gently into the worn-out armchair. "Take a deep breath."

She did as instructed, in through the nose, out the mouth, stretching her lungs, her chest, and her back, as tense muscles strained. How long had it been since she breathed a true sigh of relief? "I don't even know where to begin. It's all too muddled to make sense of."

"Okay, well then, let's stick to the important points," Rory said, in her level-headed, making-sense-of-things tone. "You're sleeping with Kelly Rolen, right?"

"I am." Admitting was the first step.

"And this has been going on for how long?"

"Off and on for almost two months."

"Two months." Rory pushed her hand through her chestnut hair, which fell perfectly back into place.

"At first it just sort of happened, and then nothing for a while, but now it's been every night for a week."

She wouldn't have thought Rory's eyes could get any wider, but they did. "Every night? Wow. Give me a minute here. Normally I would offer my congratulations, but you know this isn't as simple as getting laid regularly, right?"

"Rory," she said in her most annoyed tone.

"Okay, just making sure. It's just that Kelly's not a bad person, but—"

"She's a great person. She just doesn't let people see her for who she truly is."

"I'm willing to take your word there, and you're not the first person to say so, so you're probably right. But I've known Kelly pretty much since we were born. I knew Kelly as a preschooler and a fifth-grader and a high school senior. Now I've gotten to know her a little as an adult, and she hasn't changed much in all those years."

Elliot wanted to argue. She wanted to say she'd seen major changes in Kelly lately, but had the changes all been circumstantial? When pushed, she reacted just like she always had. She squared her shoulders, lifted her nose in the air, and marched right out the door. Elliot didn't even want to think about what she'd do now to distance herself emotionally and socially. She grimaced at the thought of Kelly going on another date with some farmer.

"How did your job interview go?" Rory asked, the abrupt change of topic pulling her back fully into the conversation.

"Good."

"Good?"

"Great." She sat up and rubbed her eyes. "The place is amazing and the people are insanely smart. When you're there, you really feel like you're at the hub of the empire and anything could happen."

Rory grinned. "And you knocked their socks off, didn't you?"

"I won't go that far."

"But?"

"But one of the women on the committee took me for a walk around the DuPont Circle area, and I got the sense I'd won her over by the time she went back to work. But it's been two weeks and I haven't heard anything."

"Anyone who takes the time to get to know you would be wowed."

"You're biased."

"Maybe, but I'm also right. You're special, Elliot. You won Kelly over, and I don't say that to be crass. She's not a woman who opens up easily. Honestly, with everything I know about you and everything I knew about her, if you'd asked me two months ago what to expect, I would've said it'd be much more likely that you kill each other than sleep together."

"And still you sent me in there?"

"It wasn't my idea, and to be honest I wasn't thrilled. The whole internship sprang from Beth's brain, fully formed."

"Beth." Elliot sighed. "You have to tell her now, don't you?"

Rory managed to look mildly apologetic. "We don't keep things from each other."

"I understand. That's probably a good relationship policy."

"We think so. A lot goes into a relationship, but trust is a big one."

"Are you trying to make this a teachable moment?"

Rory laughed. "Maybe, but I'm not known for subtly, so here it is. I care about you. And while part of me would love to see you stay here, put down some roots, and continue to hang out with me on a regular basis, I don't want you to put your dreams on hold, or worse, let them go completely."

"She hasn't asked me to."

"Good. Maybe she's a better person than I used to think, but I notice you didn't say you wouldn't stay if she wanted you to."

She rolled her head back and stared at the ceiling, "What does it matter? She doesn't want me to."

"Actually, I think it matters a lot," Rory said. "*Please* tell me you haven't fallen in love with her?"

Elliot's chest tightened so much she thought her ribs might crack.

Is that what love felt like? If so, she didn't care for love at all. She'd expected fireworks and doves and little heart emoticons filling her eyes. The dull throb of her pulse pounding through her ears didn't make her want to write poetry or sappy songs. Surely all the emotions swirling around her today, or for the last week or . . . how long had she felt this way? It didn't matter because whatever she felt toward Kelly wasn't love, not the kind of love she wanted or hoped for.

"No." She stood up and wiped her clammy hands on her sweat pants. God, she was such a mess, how had she gotten this far without stopping to think about her future? "I know I have to go to D.C.—I mean, I want to. I can't stay here, and she doesn't want me to, so there's nothing to get in either of our ways."

"Good," Rory said, standing up and clapping a hand on her shoulder. "I just needed to hear you say so. I didn't want you to hold out hope for something that wouldn't ever work out for you. Trust me, I've seen how that ends."

Elliot searched her eyes. Another cryptic comment. Why did she always get the sense she never got to see the full picture? "Can you tell me what you mean by that?"

Rory frowned. "I just . . . like I said, I've known Kelly since we were toddlers, and she's had plenty of chances to change, but she's still basically the same person she was then, only taller. Even in preschool she liked rules and order and doing things her own damn way. I don't want you to think you can change her. Being stubborn to her own detriment is one thing. It's even a trait I admire at times, but she doesn't have a right to change you in the process."

"I don't know," Elliot said, a bit of the old fire returning at the prospect of being challenged by Rory. "I've got a stubborn streak, too, don't I?"

Rory laughed, deep and hearty. "That you have, my friend. All the earlier awkwardness aside, I'm impressed. And you're right about being as stubborn as she is. I don't envy either of you in a standoff, but I hope it doesn't come to that. I'd hate to see either of you get hurt."

"Yeah." She couldn't do anything but agree, even if she worried they couldn't possibly get out of this mess without one or both of them getting hurt.

Elliot was with a client by the time Kelly arrived at the office. Thankfully, they had an April 1 deadline for accepting new business to be completed before the fifteenth. Anyone just getting started this late in the season would have to file for an extension, a simple process Elliot could more than handle on her own. Still, Kelly listened to her voice for a few minutes. With a few notable exceptions, the customers had warmed to her quickly, despite her distinct style and outsider status in an insular community. Elliot's knowledge and amiability inspired trust. How would Kelly replace someone like her?

She couldn't. Not in the personal sense, but at least she could process the more logical aspects of Elliot's inevitable departure from her life. Which is to say, her work life, which needed more attention than she'd given it lately. Work had saved her before. Surely it could still do so, especially now that Rolen and Rolen was just Rolen. Tears stung her eyes, but she blinked them away. She would have time for grief after tax season. Until then, she had the very real responsibility of upholding her father's legacy. What would he think if he knew she failed to keep the business afloat even a few weeks on her own?

She shuddered and pushed open the door to her office. Dropping her keys on her desk, she stared across the hall to his office. She hadn't gone in there since his initial stroke. She hadn't needed to, and she couldn't think of any reason why she should do so now. The space had always been his inner sanctum, and she'd rarely even ventured inside when he was alive. Doing so now would feel like trespassing. Surely at some point there would have to be a will and deeds and other important papers, but he'd owned his house outright, and she was the only conceivable heir, so she added the task to the long list of things she could do after the fifteenth.

Still, as she sat down and powered on her computer, she didn't stop herself from wondering what she'd do next year at this time. Nine months of the year, she'd be fine. She could handle the local payroll contracts and audits on her own. In all honesty, Darlington didn't provide enough business in those areas for two people. It barely provided enough work for one, but she couldn't sustain her client base during tax season on her own. She would have to hire someone else, but in a town this size, the prospect of finding someone as capable as Elliot seemed one in a million. More likely, Elliot was one in a million no matter what town she happened to work in.

There she went again. She couldn't pine over Elliot. She couldn't conflate that loss with the loss of her father. They weren't the same, not even close, and she couldn't ask Elliot to fill the void he left. She couldn't even entertain temporary fantasies. She'd already done enough of that, and look where it had gotten her. Forget next tax season. What was she going to do about this morning's incident?

Why Rory, of all people? She put her head down on her desk and resisted the urge to bang it a few times.

Rory.

Rory, who broke all the rules and still got everything she wanted. Rory, who wore her sexuality like a crown. Rory, who despite every shortcoming, had proven herself more worthy of Beth's love and affection. Did she tell Elliot how little Kelly could be trusted to stand up for her? Had she explained that Kelly had been there before and failed? She hadn't appeared gleeful, but somehow her pity hurt even more than her usual smug superiority. Her pity, and the fact that she was right. Or at least, all the things she assumed Rory said after she left were accurate. She hadn't waited around long enough to hear any of them, which of course only proved the point Rory had most likely tried to make. She'd withdrawn to protect herself. It was all she knew how to do.

"Hey," Elliot said quietly, but the interruption still startled her enough to make her jump and crack her knee on the underside of her desk.

"Shit."

"Are you okay?" Elliot rushed toward her, but she held up a hand.

"I'm fine."

"Really?"

"Yes," she snapped.

"You don't sound fine, and I've learned 'fine' is a dangerous word, and tone kind of matters."

"Elliot, do you hear the warning in my tone right now?"

"I do."

"Good. Because we're running out of time to make the federal filing deadline. We are still considerably behind."

"We'll work around the clock, I promise. We aren't getting any more new returns, so the pile will only get smaller from here. I ordered an extra-large shipment of coffee to arrive on Monday, and I also took the liberty of stocking the mini-fridge with fruit and chocolate. Also booze," Elliot said, then smiled. "Just kidding. About the booze, not the chocolate."

Kelly smiled, then caught herself and tried to force a more stoic facial expression. She couldn't give in again. People who didn't learn from their mistakes repeated them, and she'd gone through this cycle too many times already. Taking a deep breath, she steadied herself, striving to set a new tone, the one that reminded them she was still the boss. "Thank you. I appreciate everything you've done, but you don't need to put in more than your internship hours."

"I don't mind."

"I do. I can't be any more indebted to you than I already am."

"You're not indebted to me. We're a team. I've only done what I wanted to do."

Understanding the truth of the statement didn't make it easier to bear. Everything Elliot had done for her had been genuine and heartfelt. She deserved the same in return, but Kelly couldn't give her that. At least not here, and not in a way she'd recognize. The only way to give her what she really needed was to push her away. "I won't be in and out during the day anymore. I'll take over your timesheet."

"Do you think I'm stupid?" Elliot asked, her voice low and laced with hurt.

"Of course not."

"Then why are you pretending you're upset about my internship hours?"

"It's not fair to burden you with my . . . workload." She sighed as she searched for the right words. "Your internship turned into something it shouldn't have. The situation led to things getting out of our control."

"Consent, Kelly," Elliot reminded her. "I never did anything I didn't choose. I hope you didn't, either."

"No," she answered quickly, "but, under other circumstances, I would've been a better mentor. And now that the situation has changed, I intend to reassert the original parameters of the internship."

"Reassert the original parameters?" Elliot stared at her as though she'd shape-shifted in front of her eyes. "You sound like an attorney. We aren't in court here. No one's on trial. Can't we please just talk about what happened this morning?"

"Actually, no." She couldn't, not if she wanted to keep her composure.

"Just no? Really? After everything that's happened, I get a plain old 'no'?"

That hurt, a little barb right to the heart. She grasped for the only anchor that had yet to fail her. "I have work to do."

Elliot's shoulders slumped. "Yeah, you do. But just not in the way you mean."

"Maybe," she admitted. She wouldn't deny Elliot that point. "But for the next two weeks, we need to focus on the type of work you can express on a timesheet."

Frustration radiated off of Elliot, from the hard set of her jaw to the fists jammed in the pockets of camel-colored slacks. For a second Kelly wondered if she'd had enough. Had Kelly pushed her far enough to make her snap? She wouldn't blame her if she did, but Elliot only seethed a moment or two before gritting her teeth and saying, "Fine. You're the boss."

She left in a hurry, as if afraid she might say something more. Kelly shared that particular fear. The urge to soften pulled at her chest like an emotional tug of war accented by the desire to hold Elliot. She could stroke her cheek, kiss her lips, and run her fingers through her hair until she quieted the storm in those beautiful eyes, but what could a temporary reprieve really offer? They'd only be right back here in a couple of weeks. She couldn't keep wavering back and forth, or someday she wouldn't have any strength left at all, and she desperately wanted to be strong for Elliot. She owed her the same kind of strength Elliot had shown her over the past few weeks. Anything less would be unfair on the most profound level.

With that thought in mind, she tightened her shoulders, clenched her jaw, and forced herself to focus on the inescapable certainty of death and taxes.

Chapter Eighteen

"Hey, Suffragette Sister."

"Hi, Syd," Elliot answered as she pinned the phone between her shoulder and chin.

"Uh-oh, what's wrong?"

"What? Nothing. I didn't say anything but 'hi.'"

"It's not what you said. It's how you said it."

"Oh." Elliot understood that lesson more and more these days. Shoveling her books into a backpack, she slung it over her shoulder and headed for the library door. It wasn't like she'd been working anyway. She'd pretended to study for her CPA exam, but all the work that really mattered now got left at the office at the end of her allotted hours, which Kelly now strictly enforced.

"There you go again," Syd said in a sing-song voice. "Don't make me pull out the tired mother clichés. I will not be happy if you make me say something like, 'A mother always knows when her daughter is hurting.'"

She snorted. "No, that would freak us both right out."

"Then what's wrong?"

Emerging into the great outdoors, she sighed. Spring had sprung. Buds lined every branch, flowers popped amid a sea of newly green grass, and birds sang overhead. She was young and had time on her hands. She should've felt as light and breezy as the gorgeous weather. Instead she couldn't shake the weight of the world from her shoulders. "Tax season, I guess. My boss. School ending. All of it."

"Senioritis? Doesn't sound like you."

"Maybe not in the traditional sense." Or not in any sense at all. She wasn't ready to cut out on her final year of school. She wasn't sure she wanted to leave at all sometimes, and yet other elements couldn't conclude fast enough for sanity's sake. At least if everything really came crashing down, she'd have her answers as to where she needed to be. Right now she felt stuck in a terrible limbo.

"You're almost done with it all," Syd said, "and I got a call today that might make the next few weeks a little easier to bear."

"Yeah?" she asked, eager for a distraction. "Some fun new client?"

"No, but a little bird told me a certain think tank from Washington, D.C. is checking your references."

Her heart hammered. "Really?"

"Really." Sydney's pride practically oozed through the phone. "I'm sure it's just a formality. They wouldn't have gotten this far if they didn't want to hire you."

"I don't know." She meant she didn't know what to say. The job interview had been in the back of her brain for the past few weeks, but the back of her brain had been foggy and unfocused amid the more pressing concerns of Kelly's crises. Sure it had come up, but always in the hypothetical sense. Checking references meant she had to at least be a contender, if not one of the final five candidates.

"What do you mean, you don't know? It's your destiny. You're headed to D.C. When should we go look for apartments?"

"Apartments?"

"You'll need a place to live, and a month isn't much time."

"A month." She eased gently onto a nearby bench, afraid any sudden movements might make the world tilt completely out of balance.

"Is there an echo on the line?"

"Sorry," Elliot mumbled, "I guess I just didn't let myself think about getting the job and what moving might entail."

"It's time to start thinking."

Something in her rebelled at the thought, as though her psyche dug in its heels at the idea of complete upheaval. "I haven't accepted the position yet."

"Right, but you know you . . ." Syd's voice trailed off.

She closed her eyes and breathed slow, steady, intentional breaths as she waited.

"Elliot Amelia Garza."

Uh-oh. The full government name meant the same thing, no matter how liberal or conservative a mother happened to be.

"You said you haven't accepted, not that you hadn't been offered."

"I haven't been offered anything yet, either."

"Right, but when you are offered, you will accept. Immediately. Right?"

"There's a lot going on right now," she offered weakly.

"What could possibly be going on that's more important than the dream you've worked so hard for finally coming true?"

"Well, the stuff I said earlier. You know, tax season."

"Which ends in two weeks."

"And school."

"Which is over enough to be wrapped up from D.C."

"And the move. It would all have to happen so fast."

"Which I've already offered to help with."

"And . . . my boss."

She braced herself for an outburst, but Syd's voice remained very low and quiet. "Your boss?"

"Her dad just died, and she's the only one left. I can't leave her when she's got a lot going on and—"

"Are you in love with this woman?"

"Yes." She shook her head as if Syd could see her. "I mean no. Not *in love* in love."

"What other kind of 'in love' is there?"

"I'm not in love, but we've been through a lot."

"Define 'a lot,'" Syd deadpanned.

She didn't want to go there. "It's complicated."

"I can't believe this." Incredulous didn't even begin to describe Syd's tone. "Of all the things I worried about happening to you—and trust me, I worried about quite a lot when you said you wanted to go to college in some Podunk, redneck country town—I never even considered this."

"There's nothing to consider."

"You found the only lesbian CPA in all of rural farmland there, became her intern, and in a matter of weeks fell so hard you're ready to throw away your entire future for her."

"Mom," she snapped. She didn't like Syd's summary of events. Not at all, especially the last part.

"Don't 'Mom' me."

"Then stop jumping to the worst case scenario."

"What other scenario is there?"

"The one where I'm a professional and a human being and I don't want to leave someone in a lurch. Not until I'm sure everything is settled. And yes, maybe that's because I care about her as a person."

The line was quiet for long enough that she felt the need to squirm a bit under the pressure.

"I love you," Syd finally said. "You know this, right?"

"I do." She tried to swallow the lump forming in her throat with only a modicum of success. "And I love you, too."

"Good, because I hope you understand what I'm about to say comes from a place of love."

Her stomach dropped.

"You're a good, kind, sweet soul. I'm proud to call you my daughter for all those reasons and more, but if this woman cares about you even a little bit, she wouldn't take advantage of you this way."

"Why do you assume she's taking advantage of me?"

"Because you're scared. I know you. You've gotten this close to having everything, and you're afraid you don't have what it takes to seize it. But if you stay there, you'll regret it. If she knew you at all, she'd understand that, and she wouldn't be able to live with herself for making you make that choice."

"She hasn't asked me to make the choice. She told me I had to go."

Relief flooded out of Syd in an audible rush of air. "I'll at least give her credit there. But then what are you still debating?"

"I'm not. I'm just . . . I know the job is what I always wanted, and I don't have a real future here, and Kelly doesn't even want me—"

"Wait, she doesn't want you?"

"No." Her voice cracked. "She doesn't. And I feel stupid because I should've realized the only one feeling conflicted here is me."

"She broke your heart." Syd's voice had gone soft again. "I'm so sorry. I'm going to come down there tonight. We'll file sexual harassment charges and also—"

"No!" Elliot said, horrified. A mother lion with a license to practice law—what a nightmare. "No charges, no visits. She never pushed me."

"She obviously led you on, and you were going to put your life on hold for her. God, Elliot, you're such a mess. I don't know whether I want to hug you or shake you."

"I know." And she did. She understood completely how crazy she kept acting. She rolled over every time Kelly so much as showed her a sign of affection, and she shut up every time Kelly cut off conversation. She gave and gave and gave, only to get pushed away repeatedly. God, who had she become? A pushover?

No. A coward.

Kelly had revealed her as everything she'd feared herself to be all along.

"You're not thinking like yourself right now." Syd confirmed the internal reprimand. "This woman has gotten in your head and under your skin, and I don't even want to think about where else, but you cannot give up your dreams for anyone, especially someone who doesn't feel the same way about you."

"I know," she repeated. Hearing everything laid out that way did nothing to calm her churning stomach or aching heart.

"You're not in the right state of mind right now. I need you to trust me. Your original plan is still the right one. Stay the course."

"Yeah." She couldn't disagree, not logically.

"Yeah? Are you ready to start looking at apartments in D.C.?"

"If I get the job offer—"

"When you get the job offer," Syd corrected.

"When I get the job offer, I will accept."

"And you'll call me? And we'll celebrate."

Elliot smiled faintly. "Sure."

"Really? I'm worried about you."

"Really. I know what I have to do." Or rather, the only thing she could do. Rory, Syd, Kelly, everyone had made the choice so clear. They'd all but made it for her.

"Okay. I'll talk to you soon. I love you."

"Love you, too."

"And Elliot?" Syd added.

"Yes?"

"I'm proud of you."

"Thanks," she said, then hung up the phone wishing she felt the same.

ᔐ ᔐ ᔐ

Kelly worked steadily in the quiet office. She didn't have to glance at the clock to know the time. Every minute had been marked with a silent kind of grief since Elliot had left at three. She'd made the rules, and she intended to stick to them, but she'd hoped each day would get a little easier. It hadn't, and time was running out.

Eight more days until the end of tax season.

Eight more days until Elliot was no longer her intern.

Eight more days to see her, to hear her voice, to feel her so close.

Maybe that's what made her absence so hard, the fact that she came and went. One minute, the office practically vibrated with possibility, and the next, it plunged into a void of nothingness. Perhaps without the transition, when Elliot finally left and stayed gone, the contrast wouldn't appear quite so bleak.

She nodded absently as she filed another completed return. Yes, Elliot's absence didn't cause the turmoil, her presence did. She'd tell herself that lie for a while to see if she could make it sink in. She doubted the merit of the plan, though. She'd lied to herself a lot over the last few years, but she rarely managed to believe herself for long. The regret always returned. Would the sadness associated with Elliot's departure merge with the remorse she'd grown so used to, or compound it in new and painful ways? Could she survive the addition of more grief to the already crushing pile?

On one hand, she'd already experienced so much loss. Surely her coping muscles were well-honed. She'd lifted heavy burdens in the past, even recently. She had no reason to doubt her ability to take on this new one, which by all accounts shouldn't compare to the ones she'd shouldered about Beth and her father. Then again, she couldn't set aside those other traumas simply because she'd picked up a new one. Could she add this one to the already substantial load? Or would Elliot be the brick to finally break her back?

Kelly could ask her to stay. The thought had crossed her mind. But at what cost? To live in the closet? To settle for a lifetime of small-town tax returns? To fence her in and block her out at the same time? Kelly would end up treating her the same way she treated Beth and inevitably come to the same end. And Elliot would have to give up a lifetime of dreams in the meantime. If she asked Elliot to stay, she would either say yes and they'd both regret it, or she would say no and then only Kelly would regret it.

Someone pushed open the back door. She quickly straightened, grabbed a few forms and pretended to work.

"Hi, Kel."

Beth.

Her shoulders relaxed dramatically. When had the prospect of having to explain herself to Beth become preferable to facing Elliot?

"Mind if I join you?" Beth asked, poking her head into the doorway.

"Not at all," Kelly said, then added, "maybe just a little bit, but I have a feeling you're here for a while anyway."

Beth smiled, and Kelly felt more wistful than aggrieved. There'd been a time when she would've said or done anything to get a smile out of her, now she was just glad not to see condemnation there. They hadn't talked since Rory'd caught her and Elliot together. She'd honestly expected a visit sooner. Now that the shock had worn off, she merely wanted to get it over with. Her embarrassment at them knowing she'd slept with Elliot still pulsed below the surface, but it no longer ranked very high among the other emotions battling for the right to cripple her these days. "I take it Rory told you we ran into each other at Elliot's last week."

"Wow." Beth seemed momentarily taken aback. "Jumping right in. Okay. She did mention seeing you there."

"I bet she did." Kelly's laugh sounded mirthless even to herself.

"She doesn't think what you think she does."

"Believe it or not, I don't really care what she thinks. I did in the moment, and maybe I will again, but right now I have much bigger concerns than your fiancée's opinion of me."

Beth nodded. "Okay. What about my opinion of you? Does that still matter at all?"

She paused to ponder the question. Did Beth's opinion still matter? It used to mean everything. No, maybe not quite everything. That had been part of their problem. Beth's opinion had mattered a lot, but never quite enough. But what did it mean now? With her father gone, Beth knew her better than anyone. They'd been closer longer than she had been with any other living human being. Surely their connection meant something. And yet, sitting there across from her, she realized it certainly didn't mean what it had three years ago. And as she searched her feelings, she had to admit Beth's presence didn't stir her in the way it had even two months ago. How could she explain those changes to herself, much less to Beth?

Thankfully, the phone rang, distracting them both.

"Go ahead and answer," Beth said. "I know you're on the clock."

"Rolen and Rolen, Kelly speaking."

"Hello, Ms. Rolen. This is Helen Hartwell, calling from the Tax Policy Institute."

All the air left her lungs in a rush.

"I'm calling to check Elliott Garza's references. Do you have a moment to talk?"

She nodded slowly, then caught herself. "Yes, a moment."

"Elliot is a finalist for a fellowship with my organization. Really she's the top finalist at the moment. She had an extremely impressive interview. She seemed smart, thoughtful and driven, as well as amicable and capable in relating to both people and the higher-order concepts needed to work successfully in the field."

"Yes." She squeaked out the word. She could've done without the total recap of what she'd lose in Elliot.

"I have a long list of questions I could ask, but I know you're in the final week of tax season, so I'll try to distill them down. Do you feel I've made an accurate assessment of Elliot's character and abilities?"

She pressed her pointer and index finger to her temple, trying to stem the pulse throbbing there. She couldn't believe this came down to her recommendation. She'd spent a week trying to push Elliot away, and yet the thought of being the one to provide Elliot the opportunity to leave felt like a knife to her brain. No. Not her brain, her heart.

A little insidious whisper curled through her mind saying she didn't have to. She could stop the whole nightmare right here. She could tell this Helen woman she'd gotten the wrong impression. She could say Elliot wasn't quite ready for D.C. She could do so politely, just drop little hints like, she would be a good CPA *someday*, or that she'd be a good fit *if* she had a little more time to mature. She could so easily plant a seed of doubt. She couldn't keep Elliot there forever, but she could buy, or rather steal, more time.

If only Beth weren't sitting right there.

Glancing up, she met those expectant blue eyes and felt nothing. Not regret, not disappointment, not even the usual flutter of something she didn't want to acknowledge. Years together, years apart, years of holding on to something she could never fully call her own—where had it gotten her?

Here, apparently.

In an office where she would soon work alone, across from a woman who would soon marry someone else, on the phone with someone who would soon work with the only woman who had offered her any real chance at something meaningful.

"Ms. Rolen?" Helen asked.

"Yes, sorry. I was thinking about what I should tell you."

"Uh-oh, that sounds ominous."

She shook her head. She wouldn't do this again. She couldn't hold on to something she had no right to own. She'd made her mistakes with Beth. She couldn't undo them. She didn't even want to anymore, but she didn't want to be sitting in the same position with Elliot three years from now. "No. I just want to make it perfectly clear that even your highest assessment of Elliot is likely an underestimation. She's everything she appeared to be and more."

"That's very high praise."

"And it's only the beginning. She's young, and she's just starting to learn her power and her poise. She's intuitive. She's brilliant. She's steady in a crisis. If given the right opportunities and the support she deserves, there are no limits to her potential."

"So you'd have no reservations about recommending her for this job?"

She smiled sadly. "I wouldn't go that far, but my biggest reservation is that I won't be around to see who she becomes."

"I've worked in this field for twenty years, and I'm not sure I've ever heard such a heartfelt endorsement of a job candidate before."

"When she came to work here, a friend told me Elliot was special," Kelly said, holding Beth's gaze. "I didn't believe her. Hopefully I can save you the trouble of finding out for yourself."

"Thank you, Ms. Rolen," Helen said sincerely. "I appreciate your time and your insights. I promise they won't go unheeded. Good luck with the end of the season."

"Thank you," Kelly managed around the lump in her throat, then quickly hung up the phone.

She and Beth sat in silence for a long, heavy moment while she collected herself and blinked away the mist from her eyes.

"Are you okay?" Beth finally asked.

"I will be," she said, then made a show of shuffling some papers. "Did you get the answers you came here for?"

"I guess I did."

"But?" Kelly asked, sensing a shared sadness.

"They were the answers I thought I needed to hear, but maybe not the ones I hoped for."

"There's nothing for her here, Beth."

"Okay then. If you believe that, then you did the right thing." Beth rose and smiled a smile that didn't crinkle the corners of her eyes. "I'll let you get back to your work."

She didn't much care for the insinuation in the comment or the way it made her stomach clench, but she understood Beth's summation. She had every right to make it. She, better than anyone, understood the odds, but she didn't understand what it took for Kelly to do what she'd done. Beth didn't know her anymore, not the way she used to. Kelly wasn't the same person who had fallen in love with her. She wasn't even the same person who had let her go. She would never be either of those people again. Maybe Beth didn't know her better than anyone else. Maybe no one would ever really know her. And wasn't that what she'd always wanted?

For the kid who grew up wishing no one knew her backstory, and the young woman who lived in fear of people finding out too much about her true identity—hadn't she just accomplished her life's goal? She'd molded and carved and rebuilt her public image in a lifetime of rebellion against the idea of being fully known. Or being known as anything other than the aspects of herself she carefully controlled. Once Elliot left, she would have succeeded. There'd be no more risk of being found out. No more risk of being talked about. No more risk of exposure or vulnerability. She would finally be safe, and secure, and respected.

She would also be completely alone.

∽ ∽ ∽

"Aren't you about done for today?" Kelly asked, picking up a stack of folders off the corner of Elliot's desk.

Elliot frowned as she glanced at the clock. Five o'clock would seem late on most Saturdays, but not the last Saturday before tax season ended. She would've expected to work around the clock right now. Kelly would, and she would've let a true partner do the same. Which only proved the point she was likely trying to make. She saw Elliot as nothing more than an intern. Thirty-five hours a week wouldn't get the work done, but Kelly would rather miss the filing deadline than have another breakdown in their professional hierarchy. Did she get some kind of kick out of pulling the strings on Elliot's contract, or did she merely want to prove she had the power to do so?

Maybe Elliot had misjudged her. She wouldn't have thought Kelly would let her ego get in the way of getting a job done. Then again, maybe her ego wasn't doing the talking. Maybe she only held so tightly to those internship regulations because she didn't trust herself to act on her own wishes—or not to act on them.

No. No more wishful thinking on her part. Consent mattered. She wouldn't take advantage of a stressful time. She wouldn't be a regret or a weakness for Kelly. Not again.

"As soon as I finish this file, I'll head out." She stood, stretching her arms in the air and arching her back until two compressed vertebrae each gave a satisfying pop. She had to let go of some of this tension or she'd be a hunchbacked mess before the fifteenth. How had Kelly carried so much stress for so long and still managed to stand so ramrod straight?

Elliot turned to her, intending to make a quip about her height, but the look in Kelly's dark eyes stopped her cold. Kelly's pupils had dilated as they raked over the length of her body, pausing where her shirt had ridden up, exposing her stomach and lower abs. Her cheeks flushed, but not nearly as bright as Kelly's when she realized she'd been caught staring.

"Good. Well then, have a good evening."

"Kel," Elliot whispered.

"Don't call me that." The words sounded more plaintive than commanding.

"Kelly, please."

She closed her eyes and sighed softly. "You should go now."

"Before you crack? Before you show me all those feelings you're doing a terrible job of hiding?"

Kelly's eyes flew open, a flash of anger doing nothing to hide the other emotions swirling behind it. "Don't tell me how I feel."

"Then why don't you tell me how you feel?"

"I need to get back to work."

"That's not a feeling statement." She stepped closer, and Kelly stepped back. "What are you so afraid of?"

"I'm not afraid." Kelly took another step back, but Elliot followed her. "I'm busy. I'm frustrated. I'm tired."

"You're scared."

She clenched her jaw. "Stop psychoanalyzing me. You can't read my mind."

"Then tell me yourself. Don't make me guess." She stepped forward again, and this time Kelly defiantly held her ground, lifting her chin proudly even as her chest rose and fell dramatically. "I don't have to explain myself to you."

"You don't have to do anything, but you want to."

"I don't want to talk about this anymore," Kelly said, then, looking away, she muttered, "You got the job in D.C."

"What?" Elliot shook her head at the abrupt transition.

"I spoke to Helen Hartwell yesterday. I gave her your reference, a good one. I expect you'll hear from her on Monday, but your offer and acceptance are merely formalities now."

"No." The word came out before she had a chance to think it through.

"No?" Kelly's voice rose, as she'd obviously regained the upper hand in the conversation.

"No," she repeated numbly. She wanted the job. She really did. Or at least she thought she did. But she couldn't process through that now. Not with Kelly so close. Not when she'd almost gotten her to open up again. She'd seen the emotions play so quickly across her features, but now they'd gone cold and hard once more. She couldn't take the interpersonal whiplash anymore. She couldn't stand to be shut out again, and she couldn't have her dreams used against her in the process.

Everything couldn't just change in this instant, not before she had closure.

Reaching out, she wrapped an arm around Kelly's waist and pulled her body tightly against hers. Kelly flattened both her palms on Elliot's chest, and she braced for a protest that never came. Instead of pushing her away, Kelly molded against her, hips to hips and forehead to shoulder.

"Elliot," she whispered, "I'm trying so hard to do the right thing."

Elliot's resolve melted at the anguish in her voice.

"I'm using every ounce of strength I have left to do right by you. God, haven't you seen how hard I've had to fight this? Don't you understand what it's taking out of me?"

"I do understand," she said, her voice thick with emotion, "because I've been here too, all along. It's never been just you struggling to do the right thing, but somehow you're the only one who gets a say in what the right thing is. What about me? What about what I want? When do I get my turn to say what I need to say?"

"You're right." Kelly nodded against her shoulder. "You have a right to say what you need to about your feelings."

"Me. My feelings. My needs. Why can't it be a conversation about us, our needs, what we are feeling?"

"I can't."

"You won't."

"Maybe."

"Why? Because I got too close? What happened between us felt too real?"

"Yes." The whisper made Kelly sound small.

"I understand it's scary for you. After everything you told me about your upbringing, I know having Rory see you at my place dredged up a lot of old memories and fears. I didn't blame you for wanting to run, but I didn't intend to abandon you. You don't have to face anything alone."

"Yes, I do."

"You don't. I got scared too, Kelly. When you walked out the door, the panic nearly swallowed me." Elliot's voice cracked, raw with the renewed terror of reliving the moment. "You're not the only one with something at stake here, but the major difference is, I can admit it."

"What does it matter what we admit? Nothing will change the fact that you're leaving. Am I supposed to ask you to give up the life you deserve for a lifetime of sneaking around and watching your back?" Kelly pulled gently away. "You'd come to hate me if you said 'yes.' I'd hate myself for letting you."

"It doesn't have to be that way," Elliot pleaded.

"It does. You say you understand, but you don't. You don't know what it's like here. I'm the one who's lived it. I know what this existence takes out of you and what it gives back. Only I can make that decision. I've made it my whole life."

"But you don't have to choose the same life now. Surely things are different with your dad gone." She felt Kelly tense and rushed to explain. "I know you're grieving, but you don't have to protect him anymore. You don't have to worry about soiling his image—not that your being who you are is a discredit to him, but you know what I mean."

"I don't. Or maybe I do, but you're wrong. I'm the only one left to protect his legacy now." Kelly held out her arm and gestured around the office. "There's even more pressure now. To carry on, to keep his work alive, to prove he raised me right. What will people think if I go under now?"

"You don't have to let the business go under. You can still be a CPA, only you can be out and happy at the same time."

"And let everyone think I had to wait for him to die before I could come out? Let them believe he held me back or held me down? I used to be closeted and sad until my dad died, but now I can finally be happy?" She let her hands drop heavily to her sides. "What kind of message would that send to people?"

Elliot couldn't win against that logic. "Why do you care so much what other people think?"

"What?"

"Who cares what other people think about you or your legacy or your relationship with your father? You know the truth. You know who you are, what you're capable of, and what he meant to you. Why does anyone else's opinion matter?"

"I can't go back to living like some small-town sideshow. Maybe you can, and that's all the more reason for you to move on to bigger and better things, but I can't take the whispers and the stares and the silent judgment." Kelly didn't sound angry or defiant so much as exhausted. "You think if I came out I'd be free, but I could never be myself here, not amid all the curiosity and condemnation. I would resent it. I'd suffocate."

"Then leave," Elliot said simply. There didn't seem to be any other option. Every other path she'd tried had led only to another dead end. "If you can't be yourself in the closet, and you can't be out here, then walk away. You say there's no future here for me, but it sounds like there's no future worth living for you either, so get out of here."

"I can't," Kelly practically sobbed.

"I don't believe you. I don't believe this is the future you really want."

"It doesn't matter what I want. It only matters what I can do. I couldn't make the leap the first time around. I won't be able to now. That's what I've been trying to show you. I don't want to fail you, too. You're too important."

Elliot let the last comments sink in. They didn't add up. "Wait. What did you try? Who did you fail?"

A veil came down over Kelly's features, her dark eyes once again void. "No one."

"Don't do that," Elliot shouted. She couldn't take any more blank canvases. "Who did you fail? Your mom? Your dad? I don't get it."

"Leave this alone," Kelly warned, with a fake calmness that struck her as familiar, too familiar when paired with the overly polite tone she'd heard from Beth and Rory when they both stopped short of saying something. Beth and Rory. They'd both hidden something, too. All along. "What's everyone trying to protect me from knowing?"

"Nothing. There's no 'everyone.' This is about me and my short-comings."

"You and someone else. Someone you failed. It's not just you. This is affecting my life too, now. Who did you fail?"

"It's not important who. Please just believe me. I've been here be-fore. This exact same conversation about futures and doing what's right." Kelly tried to return the blame securely to herself. "I've made a woman I supposedly cared about lie and hide. I hurt her every time, but I couldn't stop. I held her down for too long, and then I lost her. I won't do the same to you. I couldn't survive."

"Beth." Elliot said the name as soon as it flowed into her mind. The last piece of the puzzle pressed firmly into place. "You and Beth."

Kelly hung her head.

"All the times she stopped in. The way she takes care of you. And Rory keeps her distance." Elliot rambled now, verbalizing every thought as it occurred. "Why didn't I see sooner? You had Beth, and she left you for Rory."

"Not exactly," Kelly said, sounding resigned now. "Though it felt like it at the time. She left me because I was slowly choking her out. I made her feel ashamed of us. Or at least, I made her act ashamed."

"How long were you two together?"

"Years. Since college."

"Years? You had a woman like Beth for *years*, and you kept her in the closet?"

Kelly didn't respond. Her skin had gone so pale it appeared almost translucent. Did the truth hurt? Or just the fact that now Elliot knew?

Elliot rubbed her face with her hands and leaned back against the edge of her desk to steady herself. "I didn't believe you really wanted to live in hiding forever."

"I tried to tell you."

"You did," she admitted. Kelly never lied about what she wanted. "I'm sorry."

"No, I'm sorry. I didn't understand. I didn't listen . . . to anyone. God, I'm so stupid. I thought what we had was different. I thought we . . . I could... " She shook her head. "It doesn't matter what I thought. I was stupid."

"You're not stupid."

"I am, damn it. I didn't stand a chance, and everyone knew it but me. All this time. Everyone knew what was happening here but me. You and Rory and Beth, you'd all seen this play before."

"Elliot, please," Kelly pleaded. "What you and I had wasn't the same. You have to believe me. I opened up to you in ways I never did with her, and I felt things for you I never did for her."

"But it's still not enough." Elliot tried to do the addition in her head, but one and one had never made two when it came to her and Kelly. "Are you still in love with her?"

"No."

The answer came quickly enough. She might've been inclined to believe Kelly if she didn't feel as though her heart were being ripped out of her chest. Here she was falling hard for the first time, thinking she had something new and bold and brilliant, only to find out Kelly had been here before with someone beautiful in every sense of the word. She'd had the real thing, not just some sad facsimile, and yet even Beth couldn't make her care enough to risk the safe and secure life she'd built.

"Elliot," Kelly whispered, "this isn't about Beth. How can I make you see? It's not even about you."

Another knife to the chest. "Thanks."

"Listen to me." Kelly clutched her shoulders. "This isn't you coming up short. It's me. I've made my life. I've made my choices. These fights are mine alone."

"And there's no place for me."

"Not any place worthy of you," Kelly said sadly. "You're strong and beautiful and so much better than anything I can offer you. You're going to change the world, and you can't do that from inside my closet."

The words offered no comfort. The excuses felt too convenient, or maybe she felt too void to process them. It didn't matter anyway. Kelly didn't love her, not enough. Maybe she couldn't love anyone enough to lay down her shadow demons. And Elliot couldn't force her to.

"Yeah." She tried to take a deep breath, but her chest still hurt too much, so she settled for short and shallow. Maybe she'd been settling for too little, for too long. How was she going to move on from this?

"Elliot?" Kelly asked softly. "Are you okay?"

"I guess I have to be. I'm out of options."

"I'm sorry."

"Me too, but you've made your choice, which means I don't really have one."

"You've got bigger battles ahead. Someday I'm just going to be a sad memory for you, though maybe eventually not quite so sad as right now."

She didn't want to think about someday. She had no more fight left in her. "I'm going to go."

Kelly stepped back. "I never meant to hurt you."

She shrugged. One more thing she couldn't control. She could add it to the already too-long list, but it didn't change a thing. Every line item Kelly marked off, every emotional box she ticked equaled the same sum. She didn't have any say in the matter, and she had no choice left but to walk away.

Chapter Nineteen

Judging by the stack of file folders set to be sent out, she'd managed to complete several more returns. But since she had no memory of any of them, she'd probably better flag them for review before calling their owners in to sign. Hopefully she could regain some clarity in the coming days, though she had only a few more left.

At least now she'd had it out with Elliot. The worst had happened, everyone knew all of her darkest secrets, her weaknesses, her failures, and she'd survived. She had nothing and no one left to protect. Everyone saw her clearly, and they'd all walked away. She didn't blame them. She'd carried the weight of abandonment and anger too long. Anger first toward her mother, then toward the whole town, and later, even toward Beth. She had no anger for Elliot. She wanted her to go. She needed her to. As awful as she'd felt watching the sudden realizations batter her awareness, it would've been worse to have them unfold slowly over time, like a cancer eating away at something so vibrant. In cases where the treatment was likely to be as bad as the ailment, she'd rather dole it out in one brutal dose.

And the reality had been brutal. For both of them. At least Elliot would be free now. They'd bounced back and forth so many times in the last two months, but she'd finally seen the resignation in Elliot's eyes. Had Elliot been able to see the regret in hers?

She stood and shook out her limbs. She didn't actually regret what she'd done. She regretted having felt the need to do it. Or maybe she regretted not having the courage to make another option viable. Maybe she regretted that she didn't live in a perfect world, but given the constraints of her existence, she didn't regret letting Elliot go. At least she would have that to cling to amid all the other sadness bound to consume her going forward.

Stretching her legs, she circled around her desk and into the hallway. She noticed the lights of the bank clock across the square shining in the darkened windows. She'd worked past midnight, so technically it was tomorrow morning, which meant time for more coffee. She moved through the silence to the coffee machine to find it cold and empty. Of course. With Elliot gone, she would lose her connection to more than one addiction. Would she have to go back to making her own flat, bland brews? She sighed and let her eyes fall on Elliot's desk, now also empty. Without her there, Kelly would get the peace and quiet she'd craved not so long ago. And yet, as with the coffee, she couldn't help but worry things would forever feel flat and bland by comparison.

Deciding she could do without the coffee or any maudlin metaphors it inspired, she headed back down the hall. Even without the caffeine she wouldn't fall asleep any time soon, so she might as well get back to work. But as she reached her office, she stopped and stared at the closed door across from hers. Strange how she'd fixated on what the office would be like without Elliot's presence, the coffee machine, the desk, her voice, and yet she'd kept herself completely closed off to the prospect of considering what it would mean to have this door permanently closed.

Her father's office had never been an open space. Despite having spent her whole life in these rooms, his inner sanctum still remained sacrosanct. As a child, she'd had the run of almost the entire building. She'd read under the reception desk and napped in the waiting area. As a teen, she'd done homework in the office that would eventually become her own. He'd never kept her out of any part of the business, but his desk had always been off-limits. She'd never questioned the boundary and felt a sense of obligation to uphold his privacy even now. But what if he'd left work undone? And why hadn't she considered this before? What if, in her fixation on Elliot or her reverence for him, she'd missed something important? What if he'd made plans or appointments he couldn't keep now? For the first time, she let the realization seep in that his burdens, too, were now hers to carry.

Pushing softly on the door, she found it closed but not latched. The gentlest nudge from her swung it silently open. The space smelled musty, the air stale and every surface gray under a film of dust. For her, he'd only been gone a few weeks, but from the perspective of this office, he'd vanished months ago. She hadn't let herself remember that night, but now she recalled the days leading up to it. He'd been quiet, focused, steady as always. He'd worked late that last Friday, as had she. She'd never liked to leave before he did. Did he sense her eagerness to pull her own weight? Did he ever wonder where she went after work? Did he assume she spent her evenings alone? He'd never dated that she knew of. Why hadn't she found that odd?

She edged slowly into the room, one shuffling step after another, as she looked around from the diplomas on the wall to a few awards facing outward on his perfectly organized desk. She smiled. Of course he wouldn't have left anything out of order, not even after a late Friday night. She ran her finger along the edge of his richly colored wooden desk, collecting dust and revealing the natural cherry. Every detail spoke of him, and she luxuriated in noticing each one. She let her gaze drift and pause where it would in the cone of light from the hallway. Notebooks stacked neatly atop a large desk calendar still turned to January. Three pens to the right—one blue, one black, one red—would've left him ready for any writing occasion. A manual calculator beside the keyboard to a desktop spoke of his ties to the past even as his shiny new Mac showed his refusal to resist progress. He liked order and tradition but never stopped looking for ways to do things more efficiently.

Walking slowly around the desk, she noticed a brown cardigan she'd given him last Christmas. He'd hung it neatly across the back of his high, ergonomic chair. She caught the soft fabric lightly between her fingers and lifted it to her face. Inhaling deeply, she could still catch the subtle scent of him, or maybe memory filled the void and her imagination sent forth the spice of his aftershave over the fresh undertones of his soap. The visceral cue overwhelmed her, mist clouding her eyes as the ache in her chest spread rapidly to her limbs. She eased into his chair, still holding the sweater tightly against her.

With her eyes closed, she almost felt as though he were just around the corner. He would come back any minute and probably not be thrilled to see her sitting at his desk on the verge of tears.

"Kelly? What in God's name?" She could practically hear him. "Are you sick? Are you hurt?"

Those were the only reasons he ever expected her to cry. She wasn't sick, and heartache probably wouldn't have constituted hurt in his book, either. Not that he didn't understand the concept. He probably knew better than anyone what it meant to love and lose, but they'd never talked about it. She'd missed so many chances. She hadn't wanted to seem weak or needy. She hadn't wanted to disappoint him, or worse, make him think he'd let her down, but she'd never stopped to wonder if, in her attempt to protect him, she had missed the chance to really know him. She'd lived with remorse in so many areas of her life, but never with him. She'd always been so sure that, even when she came up short for everyone else, she'd at least done right by him. He had been the one person she'd never wondered "what if" about. Now, sitting in his empty office, clutching a sweater that offered her only reminders of a physical connection to him, she felt the finality of unanswered questions.

She tried to set her jaw against desperation. Opening her eyes, she blinked away the tears and saw a row of three small pictures. They didn't face outward like the awards. These three were clearly meant only for him. All encased in small, plain wooden frames, all snapshots, all candid and informal, none of them would've caught the eye of a stranger, but each one had a prominent place in his daily line of sight.

The one farthest right and most out in the open was of the two of them. She wore a graduation robe, its once-bright blue slightly faded from the years. He wore a suit, and his red tie was slightly askew because he'd pulled her close with an arm proudly around her shoulder. His smile was clearly for the camera, but the twinkle in his eye spoke volumes. They'd made this milestone together. He'd helped her study, packed her lunches, attended all the plays and parent-teacher conferences, and he'd graduated as much as she had. He had guided her to adulthood, and he seemed genuinely pleased with how she'd turned out. Her expression seemed more guarded, more quietly pleased. Had she truly let herself enjoy the moment, or was she already looking ahead to the next challenge? Probably the latter. Still, she could bask in his pride now, at least retrospectively.

The second photo didn't inspire the same kind of uninhibited joy. It was of her mother. She was heavily pregnant, but aside from Kelly's unborn presence, there was no one else in the picture. Still, she smiled brightly in a way that made Kelly suspect her father had held the camera. When had her mother stopped looking at him with so much love in her eyes? Why had he kept the photo? Didn't it serve as a reminder of how far they'd fallen, or did he want to remember what it felt like to have someone look at him that way? How had he faced the image every day? She couldn't take it a second longer, so she turned to the last photo, only to have her breath ripped from her lungs.

There, from inside a plain frame, she and Beth stared back at her. No, not back at the viewer, at each other. They were so young, or at least so much younger than she felt now. They sat in lawn chairs in her father's backyard, probably at a barbecue. She had no memory of the event or of the photo being taken. She felt almost certain she'd never seen it before, and yet amid all the unknowns, she had no doubt about how they felt in that moment. She would've recognized the look of pure love in her eyes even if she hadn't seen it seconds earlier on the face of her mother.

Glancing back and forth between the two photos, no one could mistake the resemblance. The shape of their faces, the subtle curve of their lips, the lift of their eyes. In that frozen moment, she'd looked at Beth the same way her mother had once looked at her father.

Her chest tightened so much she clutched the cardigan to her sternum. Why did he have the photo? Had he taken it? Why frame it and put it next to a picture of her mother?

She grabbed the frame and turned it over, looking for some clue. It didn't make sense. Digging, hoping for some explanation he could no longer give her, she unfastened the clasp with trembling fingers and pried the photo from the frame. Turning it over in her hands, she noticed his neat, concise handwriting across the back. The caption simply read, "Kelly and Beth, two years together."

She sank back into his chair as she fought to get a full breath of air into her lungs.

He'd known. He'd known all along. Why hadn't he said? Had he struggled with the idea? Was he grieving silently for her like he did for her mother? Was that why he'd put the pictures side by side? Did he feel betrayed? If so, why keep the constant reminder? Why frame and display something he disapproved of?

Why had she assumed he would disapprove?

Why had she never trusted him enough to ask?

Grief struck hard again, clawing at her from inside. Why? Why? Why? The endless refrain would echo into eternity. Dropping her head to the desk, she shivered from the cold seeping into her heart. Never. She would never have the answers, only the echoes of the past.

"I know who you are."

His last words hummed low through her ears. Lifting her eyes once more, she stared at the photo.

"I know who you are. I love you." She'd been glad he recognized her in the moment, that the stroke hadn't robbed her of a final goodbye, but had the words meant more?

"I know who you are."

He'd said it so many times. He'd repeated the phrase even though it clearly pained him to do so, even after she'd acknowledged its surface meaning.

"I know who you are. Love you."

Sitting up, she grabbed the photo and held it close. As her tears fell, she wiped them away with his sweater. He knew. He wanted her to know he knew. He wanted her to know he loved her. He wanted to remember the way her mother had looked at him, and he wanted to see his daughter look at someone the same way.

All the hiding, all the loss, all the guilt, all the fear, all the remorse—and he knew. He knew who she was, and loved her for who she was, and he used his last breath to make sure she knew it.

This time she didn't even try to stop the sobs as they wracked her body.

৩ ৩ ৩

"Hello?" she croaked hoarsely into the phone.

"Elliot Garza?"

The voice sounded only vaguely familiar through her pre-coffee haze. "Yes."

253

"This is Helen Hartwell."

"Helen." She sat upright and reached for her pants. She didn't want to be naked on the phone with a potential employer. "Hi. I mean, hello, how are you?"

"I'm well, and I'm sorry to bother you on a Sunday morning, but I didn't want to interrupt your work time in the lead-up to the filing deadline."

"It's fine. You're no bother," she said, not wanting to go into detail about how she wouldn't be going to work today, deadline or not. "What can I do for you?"

"You can accept a fellowship offer from the Tax Policy Institute."

She'd expected this phone call for days and had worked for it for years, but nothing had quite prepared her to actually hear the words.

"The pay is nonnegotiable because it's a grant-funded fellowship, but we can help you find housing, and you'll have plenty of support while you get acclimated. We'd really want you to start as soon as possible, ideally by the first of May."

The dull throb beneath her ribcage annoyed her. She should feel nothing but unadulterated joy right now. A quick departure was just one more blessing the job offered. She had no reason to stay. Not after what she knew. *Beth*. Kelly'd had a decade-long relationship with one of Elliot's friends, and neither one of them had told her. Shouldn't you mention that to the person you're sleeping with? Shouldn't Beth or Rory have brought that up in all their talks about being careful? Apparently none of them had trusted her enough to level with her.

"I'm sure you've had other offers," Helen continued, bringing her back to the questions at hand.

Elliot didn't correct her, but the assumption made her realize she probably should've sought other offers. Another missed opportunity. Had she gotten so wrapped up in Kelly that she'd sabotaged her other chances?

"But I think this could be a good fit for you. You'll be mentored, you'll be nurtured, you'll make connections that can take you any-where and allow you to do anything you want next."

"It sounds wonderful," she said wistfully.

"Good, because we've got important work ahead. We've got an

ambitious legislative agenda for the next congressional term. I want you to be a partner on that project. I want you to be a major part of our team going forward. It won't be easy. A lot of people won't like what you have to tell them, but everyone here firmly believes you're the person for the job."

She fought back a sob. This was everything she wanted. Everything she needed. Everything she'd ever hoped to hear, only it hadn't come from the person she'd hoped would say it.

Maybe that's all she'd get. The right time, the right situation, just from the wrong person. Two out of three. Most people in her situation would be thrilled. It wasn't like she had much choice. Kelly hadn't exactly made a counteroffer.

"Thank you," she finally managed to say.

"Well, you've said 'sounds wonderful' and 'thank you,'" Helen noted. "But you've yet to say 'I accept.'"

She hadn't. And she didn't quite know why, at least not in the logical sense. She had to accept. She didn't have any other choice. Why couldn't she bring herself to say the words?

"Look, Elliot." Helen's voice dropped into a more personal register. "I'm sure you've got a lot of people pulling you in a lot of directions, but you're an impressive young woman with a bright future. The choice is yours to make, and I'm sure you'll make the right one."

She let a tear fall silently, though this time the sadness and frustration blended with something else, something she hadn't felt in a long time. Confidence.

"If you need some time, go ahead and take a day or two."

"No," she said.

"No?"

"I don't need time. I know what I want. And I know what I need to do. I just needed to be reminded I could actually make that decision for myself."

"And?" Helen asked.

"I accept your offer. I'm looking forward to working with you."

Chapter Twenty

Kelly woke up with a headache and a crick in her neck from falling asleep in her father's desk chair, or rather, crying herself to sleep there, and yet moving did nothing to alleviate the pain. No amount of Advil or stretching would offer her the relief she craved. Still, she stretched and rolled her head from side to side. She'd done this to herself. Could she possibly undo the damage?

Straightening her father's sweater as best she could, she hung it neatly back across his chair, but she picked up the photograph of her and Beth. She carried it with her into the bathroom. Setting the frame on the sink, she splashed some water on her face before letting herself look in the mirror. She barely recognized her reflection. A casual observer would've found few similarities between the girl in the photo and the woman staring back at her now. Her face had grown pale and wan, her eyes darker and deep-set. Faint lines now creased her forehead, and her hair lay smooth and limp against her cheeks. Looking back, she could see what Beth had been drawn to in her then, but she couldn't imagine what would make anyone reach out to her now.

When had the transition occurred? Over the last few months, the last three years, or had it begun the day she decided to surrender parts of herself for the sake of preserving others? How long had she lived with the hurt, and how many others had she sucked into her cycle of increasing pain? She didn't know. She didn't even know if it mattered anymore. She couldn't go back. She didn't ever get those chances again. Not with her father, not with Beth, not with Elliot.

Hanging her head, she let the water drip from her chin and nose into the basin. She couldn't stand her ground anymore. The world was spinning, changing, always in flux. She could move forward or be pulled back into darkness, but she couldn't stay here. There were no do-overs, but maybe there could be a chance to do better.

She patted her face with a hand towel and crossed the hall into her office, but instead of sitting down, she reached for the phone and dialed a number now imprinted in her heart.

"Hi, it's Kelly."

"What's wrong?" the voice on the other end asked.

"I'm okay, physically at least. But I need you to come up here if you can." She sighed. This wouldn't be easy, but nothing had been easy for a long time. "I need to talk to you, and I . . . well, I need your help."

"I'm on my way."

She smiled faintly. Maybe some bridges hadn't been burnt completely, but if she intended to rebuild them, she had to do so better than before. So even as her stomach churned, she forced herself to add, "Rory can come, too."

౼ ౼ ౼

Elliot used her reflection in the plate-glass window in front of the office to straighten her tie and finger-comb her hair away from her face. She hadn't come there today to work, or even to try to impress. She merely wanted to see if the difference she felt showed. She couldn't tell. Between the gray clouds overhead and the nervousness coursing through her, she couldn't get any sort of accurate picture of herself right now. Or maybe there was no one, accurate version of her. She was in transition, and what she had to do now would likely say a great deal about who she would become.

Not that she actually knew what she had to do. She hadn't really thought through a plan, or a speech, or even a vague idea of what she wanted to say. Every time she tried, she got shaky and nauseated. Which was probably why she continued to stand outside the door. Once she went in, she'd have to say something. She'd have to face Kelly. She'd have to face herself. Maybe she should leave and come up with more of a plan. No. She had to go with the momentum of the morning before she lost it.

Maybe she couldn't think that far ahead. Once she made the choice to dramatically throw open the door, she'd have to say something. Maybe she couldn't make all the choices at once, but she could at least make the first one. With that thought in mind, she unlocked the door and pushed it open with gusto, the little bells up top clanking hard against the glass.

"We're not open," Kelly called, the abruptness of her voice startling Elliot. She braced herself for Kelly's anger, but she didn't emerge from her office.

We're not open? Did she intend to speak to a client that way and just leave them? The muscles in Elliot's shoulders knotted tightly. She forced herself to step as confidently as she could toward Kelly's open office door, but when she peeked in, she found it empty. Turning, she noticed another door standing ajar, one she'd never seen anyone use before, not even Kelly.

"Kelly?" she called.

"Elliot?" someone asked from inside the office.

"Rory?" She edged into the office as though she might be entering an alternate universe, and what she saw didn't alleviate any of those fears.

Kelly stood behind a beautiful cherrywood desk, her face grim and pale, her eyes unreadable as she looked at Beth and Rory, who sat in the client chairs opposite her. Beth, Elliot could understand, especially after what she'd learned, but why Rory? And why did everyone look so grim? Was it because she'd arrived? What kind of meeting had she interrupted?

"Elliot," Kelly finally said, "I didn't expect to see you today."

"Clearly," she said slowly, trying to remind herself why she'd come and what the new turn of events meant for her plan, or lack of plan. She'd made quite an entrance, and she had everyone's attention. What now?

"I'm here to tell you some things." She blew out a frustrated breath. Not quite the opening salvo she'd hoped for.

Beth rose to her feet. "Maybe we should give you two a minute to yourselves."

"No," both Elliot and Kelly said at once, then looked at each other with the same surprised expression.

"I've come to some big decisions," Kelly said, "ones I should've come to a long time ago. I haven't been fair to any of you, to varying degrees. I wish I had been better."

"Please stop with the wishes and would've beens," Elliot said. She'd already heard too many speeches about how Kelly would handle things differently if she could. "All the excuses you've made are just lies you tell yourself, and I'm not sure if you believe them or not, but I don't."

"That's a little harsh," Rory said.

"No. It's true," Kelly admitted. "I've made a lot of compromises at a very great cost. I know you think I'm strong, or stoic, but I'm not."

"No, you're not. You're more than that," Elliot said. "You're sharp and smart and beautiful. You excite me and you keep me on my toes. You frustrate me and challenge me. You make me believe I can hold my own with anyone after being with you. And I know your mind goes to dark places when left on its own, but not when we're together. You and I have moments when we're nothing short of electric. You can tell yourself whatever you need to, but you can't lie to me about how good we are together. I was there. I know it was real."

"Elliot," Kelly pleaded, "you have to stop."

"No, I don't. That's the problem. I let you make me think I had to shut up and wait and bite my tongue for fear of saying the thing that would push you over the edge or make you push me away completely. I let my fear of losing you turn me into the coward I always feared myself to be." Elliot laughed bitterly. "I was so afraid to lose you I turned into a silent shadow of myself, and then I went ahead and lost you anyway. So fuck it. Now it's my turn to talk."

Kelly, Beth, and Rory all wore the same wide-eyed look of astonishment, but none of them moved to physically restrain her, and that's what it would take to stop the runaway train of her mind from plowing forward.

"Everyone talks about the whole relationship crisis, decision-making process, whatever you want to call it, like it's a foregone conclusion. They act like there's no choice for me, or there's only one choice, and I'd damn well better make it or it'll be made for me, right?"

No one responded.

"Yes, that's right," she answered herself. "And I know they want what's best for me, but what if what's best for me is letting me make my own damn choice? All everyone's done is confirm for me that, when push comes to shove, none of you trust me to make my stand on my own."

"Elliot, we trust you," Beth said in her most placating voice, but Elliot wouldn't go for the soothing tones this time.

"No, you don't," she snapped back. "You've tried to protect me from the very beginning. From day one, you and Rory would share your silent looks of, 'Should we tell her? Should we step in? Should we worry?' And you must have been worried, or you wouldn't have come here to warn Kelly away from me."

"That's not exactly why they're here." Kelly cut in. "I actually called them."

"Okay, well they called you, you called them, let's not split hairs here."

"Actually the difference matters quite a bit this time," Rory added. "I think you should hear her out."

"Rory, I love you like the big sister I never had, but you basically told me I had to get out of here before I got in over my head and couldn't think clearly anymore."

"I did. You're right. I was overprotective. I'm sorry." She looked to Kelly. "To both of you."

Okay, no argument there. Surprising. She'd never known Rory to roll over, especially to protect Kelly. But, moving on. "And, Beth, did you or did you not talk to Kelly about me?"

"I did," Beth admitted. "I wanted to make sure she intended to do right by you. Knowing what I know now, I wish I'd handled things very differently."

Another easy surrender. When was someone going to try to stop her? She turned, ready to take on the only challenge that really mattered anymore. "And Kelly, you never really let me in. You never let me get as close as I let you get."

"I wouldn't go that far—"

"You always set the boundaries. You always called the shots. You

260

said you wanted to do right by me, and you let that desire rip you apart, but not one of you"—she looked around the room for full effect—"not one of you stopped to ask me what I thought was right. Or how I felt about the job offer. Or how I felt about the prospect of trying to make a life with Kelly or having to choose between the two."

She shook her head. "The only thing anyone asked was if I was in love, and every time, the question was couched in a way that made it clear the answer should be 'no.'"

"Was it no?" Kelly asked, a timidity in her voice that made Elliot's heart clench and her monologue roll to a halt.

"What?"

"You said they asked you if you were in love, but you didn't say what your answer was. You only said what they wanted it to be."

"Oh." Well that took the wind out of her sails. "It's just—all they talked about was how hard it would be, and they were right. They said I'd have to give up a lot, and they were right. They said you were closeted and stubborn and stuck in your ways, and they were right."

"And?"

"And I love you anyway. I mean, I love you totally. Not in spite of who you are, but because of who you are. I love that you're fair and witty and a smart-ass. I love the way you don't compromise your ideals. And I love the softer side you keep to yourself. I love how, when you do something, you do it all the way, whether it's a schedule C or making love."

Everything came out in a rush, but she didn't regret a word. She felt stronger and more confident than ever. "There, I said it. I'm not sorry. Saying that doesn't make me weaker or dumber or less likely to reach my full potential. I love you, Kelly. That doesn't mean I won't still chase my dreams. It doesn't mean I'm going to hide out in your closet with you, either. I won't walk on eggshells anymore, or tiptoe around some image you have of yourself or the image you want other people to see of you."

"Good," Kelly said, with a solemn nod, "I feel the same way."

"And I took the job in Washington, D.C. I got the offer and I accepted it and—" She stopped, her mouth still wide open. She stared at Kelly, watching the creases in her forehead fade as a smile stirred the corners of her beautiful mouth. "What?"

"I love you, too," Kelly said, then rolled her eyes playfully. "Maybe I should've led with that, but in case you've forgotten, you've got a bit of a stubborn streak yourself."

"I had forgotten, actually. You put me through a lot lately."

"I know. I've put a lot of people through a lot, and some of them I won't ever get back in my life. But I called these two in today to apologize, and to ask for their help in apologizing to you."

"Well . . . I'm sort of sorry I missed whatever grand gesture you were working on, but you could've just said you loved me. Like, right when I walked in."

"And missed your great speech?" Kelly laughed. "Not for anything. I don't want to miss anything with you, ever again."

Elliot felt a little dizzy, and not completely in a good way. "But I took the job. I'm supposed to move in two weeks. I can call Helen back."

"No," all three of them said in unison, then Beth and Rory managed to appear properly chagrined.

"I think it's time for us to make our exit," Rory said.

"Maybe you're right," Beth said. "They seem to have figured out the big stuff without us."

"Have we?" Elliot asked, still slightly woozy from the implications of what they'd said and where everything seemed to lead.

"Well, you haven't kissed her yet," Rory said under her breath.

"Rory," Beth scolded, pulling on her arm.

"Just saying," Rory mumbled as she headed out the door.

Beth shook her head and smiled, then followed her fiancée. "One of you call one of us later," she said, before they heard the bells above the front door jingle.

"Rory's got a point," Elliot said, stepping closer.

"She talks enough. It's to be expected she'd get something right occasionally," Kelly conceded, then grinned. "She might not be the worst person in town."

"Glad you approve, because I'm about to take her advice." In one fluid movement, Elliot caught her around the waist and drew her close, but this time instead of merely allowing herself to be swept up, Kelly grabbed the lapels of Elliot's jacket and pulled them fully together.

She luxuriated in the press of Kelly's lips, the familiar blend of taking and yielding. With one hand on the small of her back, she used the other to cup her face, sinking into the feeling of them melting so perfectly together. She took her time, for the first time, letting herself fully believe they had time, but when they finally broke apart enough to speak, the old doubt tried to take hold once more.

"I don't know how we're going to make this work."

"Me neither," Kelly admitted. "Not all of it, anyway, but I do want to make it work. I want it more than I want to hold on to a legacy or my reputation or some empty image I tried to project to everyone, including myself. And I want to figure out how to do everything with you by my side."

"Partners?"

"Partners, friends, lovers. I spent too long hiding and fighting. I had more chances than I deserve to get it right, but you're the first person to make me want to take those chances."

"And you made me want to fight for you. I know I can do it now. I can stand up for myself. I can stand up for us."

"It's not exactly a plan for the future," Kelly said, "but I think it might be a good time to start making one."

"After tax season?" Elliot asked with a grin.

"No." Kelly returned the smile. "Right after you kiss me again."

Epilogue

"Until death do us part."

The preacher turned to the congregation and proclaimed, "By the power vested in me, by the United Church of Christ, the State of Illinois, and now the federal government of the United States, I pronounce you married in both the eyes of the Lord and the eyes of the law. You may seal your covenant with a kiss."

Elliot leaned in and gave Kelly a light kiss on the cheek.

"He's not talking to you," Kelly whispered.

"I know," Elliot said with a smile, as she turned back to face the front of the church before adding, "just practicing for later."

Kelly's heart rate revved for the hundredth time that morning, but she managed to keep her hands to herself by applauding the happy couple as they turned to face the congregation.

Rory's normally cocky smile had been replaced by one of genuine happiness, and even Kelly had to admit she cut a dashing figure in her classic tuxedo, but Beth stole the show in a radiant, flowing white gown. She had little white flowers woven into her dark curls, and her cheeks naturally blushed the perfect shade of rose.

This scene had played in her nightmares for years. Beth had just married Rory in a beautiful and very public ceremony, and she'd had to sit there and watch the whole thing. She'd spent more than three years dreading this day, and yet, in the moment, Kelly felt nothing but happiness. Instead of breaking, her heart brimmed with joy. She wished them all the best, of course, but much of the emotion overwhelming her now stemmed not from the women in front of her, but from the woman beside her.

They both rose and applauded as Beth and Rory exited the church. Kelly and Elliot turned to one another.

"And now we make our getaway?" Elliot asked hopefully.

"I believe there's a reception with dinner and dancing, probably many toasts and speeches, too."

"There's got to be a back room or coat closet we can find somewhere."

"In a church?"

"Right, well I'm sure no one would notice if we went back to your place for a while."

"If we went back to my place now, we'd never make it back out tonight."

"Your point?"

She shook her head. "You're the one who had to plan your first trip back around this wedding, remember?"

Elliot groaned. "I know. I just never thought it would be so torturous to have to celebrate my friends' happiness."

Kelly laughed and got into the line of wedding guests slowly filing down the center aisle of the church. "I never thought I'd be the one to advocate for enjoying this particular occasion, so we're even."

"But, you are okay with it, right?" Elliot asked, a hint of concern in her voice. "I mean, I know there's a lot of water under that particular bridge, and . . ."

"And that's all that it is now. Water under the bridge. A bridge we've all crossed."

"I'm glad to hear it. I meant to ask sooner, but the time never seemed right. It's just been hard having conversations like that over the phone, and then we didn't really have time to talk when I got in this morning," Elliot said before amending the statement. "Well, we had some time, but we chose to spend it doing other things."

Kelly stared down at the high heels and dress loafers in line ahead of her as she tried not to remember the things they'd chosen to do with the few hours between Elliot's train arriving and the start of the wedding. She didn't regret those decisions, but church wasn't exactly the place to envision Elliot naked on top of her. "We'll have time to talk later."

"Later," Elliot repeated.

"Soon," Kelly added.

"Tonight," Elliot said, brushing her fingers discreetly across the curve of Kelly's hip.

She bit her lip, and fought another surge of arousal. Surely she'd be struck down by lightning any moment now.

Elliot had been gone only two months, but between wrapping up the end of tax season, selling her father's house, and putting all their business affairs in order, their time apart had been compounded both physically and emotionally. Elliot, too, had stayed exceedingly busy at her new job. They talked nightly on the phone or Skype, but they'd rarely had time or energy to do more than recount the events of their hectic days. Still, even across long-distance lines, it was clear Elliot loved the work. Kelly never tired of the excitement in her voice as she talked about the people she'd met or the things she'd seen along the way. After only a couple of months, she was already being invited to high-level meetings with Senate aides and Treasury officials. Kelly longed to share those moments with her up close, not at a distance.

At the feel of Elliot's palm on her other hip, she took a deliberate step forward and gave her a pointed look over her shoulder.

"Sorry," Elliot mumbled, looking properly chagrined. "I forget where we are. D.C. is a lot more liberal."

"It's not that," she said softly, and to her surprise, it wasn't. She'd barely given a second thought to who might see them together today. Most of the town likely knew that she was leaving to shack up with her young intern, or at least that's how they'd see it, but she no longer cared what anyone thought about them. She'd had her moments of doubt along the way, during the long days or lonely nights, but with Elliot here, she couldn't manage to feel any shame for what felt so undeniably right. "I'm not worried about other people. I'm worried about my own lack of restraint with you finally close enough to touch."

Elliot's smile shifted from shy to self-assured as she jammed her hands into the pockets of her pinstriped suit, her auburn hair catching a hint of summer sun streaming through the stained-glass windows.

Kelly lifted her gaze to the large cross at the front of the sanctuary and said a silent prayer, *Give me strength against this temptation, Lord.*

Either God listened or Elliot took the hint, because she softened her stance and said, "Did I mention our apartment is only a few metro stops from Chinatown?"

"Our apartment," Kelly said, "I like the sound of that."

"Yeah? You're not nervous about moving to the big city?"

"I probably should be, but I've only ever lived here, so I think the realities of a switch like that are still very vague for me. I've had so many tangible things to arrange and fuss over here I haven't had time to obsess over hypothetical crises. Maybe I'll freak out when I get there, but I have plenty of other things to worry about in the meantime."

Elliot laughed. "One meltdown at a time. You're so orderly."

"Every issue in its place. Today's survival challenge is to make it through this wedding and reception without succumbing to your charms."

"Again," Elliot said.

"Again?"

"Well, you already did give in to my charms twice since I've been here. So I think what you meant to say was, your goal was to get through the reception without giving in to them *again*."

Kelly was still trying to decide if she found the comment maddening or endearing when Jody and Stevie edged into line ahead of them.

"Welcome back to town, Senator Garza," Jody said with a playful smile.

"No, no," Stevie said, "she's going to be Secretary of the Treasury."

Elliot shook her head. "Sorry to disappoint you, but I'm a lowly post-graduate fellow at the moment. I mostly get coffee and proofread memos."

"She had a meeting at Senator Schumer's office last week," Kelly cut in, not even caring if the pride oozed out of her voice.

"The senator wasn't there," Elliot said.

"Still," Jody said, "it's a nice step toward your takeover of the nation's capital."

"What about you, Kelly?" Stevie asked. "Are you ready to take the political world by storm?"

"Hardly," Kelly said. "I'm going to stay as far away from the politics as possible. I'll mostly be taking on independent contracts for things like payroll audits."

"Well, you'll be missed here."

"She'll be back," Elliot said. "Every year, just like Santa Claus or the Easter Bunny, only with tax season."

"Yes, Beth mentioned something about keeping Rolen and Rolen open part-time," Jody said, "but I have to admit I don't know how that works."

"Basically, the business will transition from a full-service CPA firm to one that specializes in tax prep. I'll keep my client base as well as my father's for the purpose of filing returns, but I'm letting go of all the bookkeeping, payroll, and inventory audits we did in the past."

"So you'll only be in town from February to April?"

"With a few smaller stop-overs throughout the year," Kelly explained. "The rest of the time I'll be a free agent."

"Not completely free," Elliot cut back in. "She's kind of spoken for in a few areas, and some conditions apply no matter what state she happens to be in."

Jody smiled at them, then Stevie. "We certainly understand how that goes."

"How what goes?" Rory asked as she finished greeting the people ahead of them in line.

"Long-distance romances," Jody said.

"Not too long a distance these days though, right?" Beth said, wrapping Stevie in a hug. "Summer in New York suits you both."

"It does," Stevie said. "You two are the only people who could've pulled us back to the Midwest in June. Congratulations."

"We appreciate you all coming back for the big day," Rory said, throwing an arm around Elliot.

"Wouldn't have missed it for the world," Elliot said, causing Kelly to smile. Hadn't she been the one who only moments ago begged to skip out and find a room for just the two of them?

Rory turned and extended her hand to Kelly. "And thank you, too. I really am glad you're here."

Kelly accepted the gesture as just another surreal twist in her rapidly changing life. "Me, too."

"Can I second that?" Beth asked, reaching out for a hug.

Kelly smiled and wrapped her arms around her once more, or maybe for the first time, in this new way. She didn't feel any of the old guilt or regret, but rather an overwhelming press of gratitude.

Giving Beth a tight squeeze, she managed to say, "I'm happy for you."

"Thank you," Beth said, emotion thick in her voice as well.

Stepping back, Kelly turned to Rory once more. "I'd say be good to her, but I have a feeling you've already got that covered."

"I promise I'll always do my best," Rory said solemnly, then her green eyes flicked over to Elliot. "I trust you both to do the same."

Elliot rolled her eyes. "What, are you going to demand a dowry next?"

"I promise," Kelly said. "She does, too. She's just stubborn about doing things her own way."

"Hello, Pot," Beth said. "Meet Kettle."

All of them laughed before Jody said, "We're holding up the line. We'll see you all at the reception."

"Maybe they will, maybe they won't," Elliot muttered under her breath as they walked away.

"I heard that," Kelly said when they got to her car.

"You were meant to," Elliot replied cheerfully as she got in and closed the door behind her.

"You don't really want to skip out on them, do you?" Kelly asked, turning the key in the ignition.

Elliot sighed and then smiled. "No, I guess not. But I am really looking forward to getting you home, and not just tonight, but every night for the foreseeable future."

"Home," Kelly whispered, then glanced around the town square once more. The familiar streets and buildings filled her vision. Familiar faces lined the sidewalks. This was the only home she'd ever known, and yet in so many ways she'd never let herself be known in return here. At least not until Elliot had come along. Then the final piece had fallen into place. Maybe home wasn't a place so much as a feeling.

"You do want that, too, don't you?" Elliot asked, her voice once again soft with concern. "I know it'll be a big transition for you."

269

"It will be," she admitted. She turned to face Elliot once more, taking in the joy and wonder that filled her green eyes. "If Washington, D.C. is home for you, then it can be for me, too. Does it feel like home yet?"

"Not yet, but it's close," Elliot said with one of her broad smiles. She leaned in, and Kelly's heart rate spiked again. Just before their lips met, Elliot whispered, "All that's missing there is you."

Acknowledgments

I am in my hometown right now as I write this. For better or worse, this seems a fitting place to ponder how I've now managed to write three romances set in Darlington. I certainly didn't set out to write a series, and I don't think I have, but these books are connected by so much more than setting. Make no mistake: all of these of these newly dubbed "Darlington Romances" (*The Long Way Home, Timeless, and Close to Home*) are distinctly different and meant to be read as stand-alone novels. And yet, I think the questions that keep me coming back to my hometown are the same ones that keep me writing stories set in Darlington. How do the experiences, interactions, and decisions of our youth shape who we become as adults? How much do the circumstances of our upbringing define us, and how much can we change our core values? What sorts of responsibility do we owe ourselves, and what do we owe to the people we love?

As I wrote *Close To Home*, it felt like closure, a full circle, an ending to something I didn't fully see from the beginning. This could very well be the last of the Darlington Romances, but as I said, there's more connecting these stories than a shared plot. A thread runs between them, connecting me to something deep and driving. The major themes of these books are the themes of my life, and if there's one thing I've learned over the last eight years, it's that every time I think I'm done, something always manages to call me back. They say you can't go home again, and while there are times I've wished that were true, I haven't found it to be the case. For me, and seemingly for the characters who fill the world of Darlington, Illinois, home is something that sneaks up on you when you least expect it.

That being said, while this has been a long and unexpected journey for me, it has not been a solitary one. Thank you to the readers who have been with me the whole way. You have let me pull strings and push buttons I never anticipated. You have come along for the ride on three very different books, told in three very different ways, and you've showered me in your love and support at every stop along the way. I cannot tell you enough how much your feedback and encouragement has meant to me.

I'd also like to thank my Bywater team. Salem, Marianne, and Kelly have given me free rein to carry over characters and connections from my previous work, and while I think there may have been times they questioned their own sanity or mine in that process, they've never waivered in their support. I also owe a special debt of gratitude to Kelly on this one, because she actually gave me the idea many years ago, when after reading *The Long Way Home,* she said she didn't like that the Kelly in the book ended up how she did. Real-life Kelly requested that fictional Kelly have her own redemption story someday. I took my sweet time in getting her there, but I hope it was worth the wait. I'd also like to thank Ann McMan for another great cover design. I didn't give her much to work with, but she managed to capture the tone of the central conflict in the beautifully subtle way only she can.

Toni Whitaker and Barb Dallinger both acted as beta readers once again, making them the only two people to see early drafts of all three Darlington novels. I ran them both through the emotional wringer with this one, but they remained kind, understanding, and focused on helping me make the story as authentic as possible. I love them for it. I'm also thankful this time to Marcie Lukach, who did an early read on the manuscript as my CPA expert. She not only made it clear how very little I knew about taxes (who knew W-2 isn't the name of every form?), she also proved herself to be an awesome friend.

As usual, Lynda Sandoval was my substantive editor, my sounding board, and my middle-third therapist. She said nice things when I didn't think I could do anything right, she said irreverent things when I got too serious, and most of all she said really smart things that helped me bring Kelly into focus, both on the page and in my own mind. Nancy Squires, Caroline Curtis, and a slew of proofreaders including but not limited to Rebecca Cuthbert, Karen Davis, Cara Gould, Elaine Lynch, Ann Etter, and Carleen Spry rounded out the team with their eagle eyes, a true understanding of style, and an attention to detail I can only dream of.

And as always is the case, I am grateful to the daily support of friends and colleagues like Georgia Beers, Melissa Brayden, Nikki Smalls, Sarah Gerkensmeyer, Andrew Cullison, Will Banks, and the wonderful writers at Bywater Books, who all do their part to keep me focused, laughing, and sane. They all help to keep me writing on the days when I love my job, as well as on the days when I think I'm terrible at it.

Finally, my family is the best. I'm surrounded by so much love and support in a multitude of ways. Jackson makes my life so much fun. He's also what challenges me to look at the big picture of what really matters in life. Susan makes the life I love possible. Without her there to be my bedrock, I would have neither the financial nor emotional stability to do the work that I do. There's no way I can thank her enough, but I promise to keep trying every single day, come what may.

I know that every blessing I have comes not from my own hand or my own deserving, but from the God who is love incarnate. *Soli deo gloria.*

Rachel Spangler

Rachel Spangler is the author of ten lesbian romance novels and novellas. She has won both the Golden Crown Literary Society Award and the Rainbow Award for her work. She lives with her wife and son in Western New York.

You can find Rachel on Facebook, Twitter, Pinterest, Instagram, and at www.RachelSpangler.com.

Also by Rachel Spangler

Darlington Romances:
The Long Way Home
Timeless

Perfect Pairing
Heart of the Game
Does She Love You
Spanish Heart
Love Life
The Long Way Home
Trails Merge
Learning Curve

Perfect Pairing

"Spangler's complex and likable characters had me laughing out loud!"
—DIANE GAIDRY, film and theatre actress

"Spangler's novels are filled with endearing characters, interesting plot turns, and vivid descriptions. Her readers feel immersed in the worlds of her novels from start to finish." —THE OBSERVER

Perfect Pairing by Rachel Spangler
Print 978-1-61294-069-4
Ebook 978-1-61294-070-0

www.bywaterbooks.com

Bywater
BOOKS

At Bywater Books we love good books about lesbians just like you do, and we're committed to bringing the best of contemporary lesbian writing to our avid readers. Our editorial team is dedicated to finding and developing outstanding writers who create books you won't want to put down.

We sponsor the Bywater Prize for Fiction to help with this quest. Each prize winner receives $1,000 and publication of their novel. We have already discovered amazing writers like Jill Malone, Sally Bellerose, and Hilary Sloin through the Bywater Prize. Which exciting new writer will we find next?

For more information about Bywater Books and the annual Bywater Prize for Fiction, please visit our website.

www.bywaterbooks.com

CPSIA information can be obtained
at www.ICGtesting.com
Printed in the USA
LVOW11s1407180117

520980LV00005B/2/P